Also by

T0030888

KNOCKEMOUT SERIES
Things We Never Got Over
*Things We Hide From the
Light*

RILEY THORN SERIES
*Riley Thorn and the Dead
Guy Next Door*
*Riley Thorn and the Corpse
in the Closet*
*Riley Thorn and the Blast
from the Past*

**SINNER AND SAINT
SERIES**
Crossing the Line
Breaking the Rules

**BOOTLEG SPRINGS
SERIES**
Whiskey Chaser
Sidecar Crush
Moonshine Kiss
Bourbon Bliss
Gin Fling
Highball Rush

BENEVOLENCE SERIES
Finally Mine
Protecting What's Mine

BLUE MOON SERIES
No More Secrets
Fall into Temptation
The Last Second Chance
Not Part of the Plan
Holding on to Chaos
The Fine Art of Faking It
Where It All Began
The Mistletoe Kisser

WELCOME HOME SERIES
Mr. Fixer Upper
The Christmas Fix

STANDALONES
By a Thread
Forever Never
Rock Bottom Girl
The Worst Best Man
The Price of Scandal
Undercover Love
Heart of Hope

PRETEND
YOU'RE
Mine

LUCY SCORE

Bloom *books*

Published by Bloom Books, an imprint of Sourcebooks
P.O. Box 4410, Naperville, Illinois 60567-4410
(630) 961-3900
sourcebooks.com

Originally published in 2015 by That's What She Said Publishing

Printed and bound in the United States of America.
PAH 10 9 8 7 6

To my parents, who insisted the dinner table was for reading.

CHAPTER 1

This was officially the worst day of Harper's adult life.

What had she ever seen in that jackass? She yanked the sun visor down, squinting against the low spring sun. At least the setting sun meant this day from hell was almost over. Even if she still had no idea where she was going.

Which was just perfect.

She automatically reached for her bag before remembering that she had left it—and her wallet and phone—behind. Her phone with its GPS that could tell her if she was even heading in the right direction.

Hannah lived two hours southwest of the city. Harper wasn't sure how her college roommate would feel about a short-term couch crasher, but she was her only hope at this point.

The dashboard's orange low fuel light chose that moment to ding on. "Damn it." She had forgotten to stop for gas on the way home, and she certainly hadn't been thinking about it after storming out.

She spotted the next exit—a town called Benevolence, Maryland—and signaled. She was going to have to find a pay phone. Did they even have those anymore? Did she even have anyone's number memorized? Harper groaned.

Maybe she could borrow someone's phone, log on to Facebook, and beg nearby friends for a ride.

Just inside the town's limits, she coasted into the gravel parking lot of what appeared to be a bar gearing up for a hopping Friday night. It was a rustic-looking log cabin kind of place. No neon lights in the windows, just a simple hand-painted sign that hung from the eaves of the skinny front porch:

Remo's

There was a patio on the side strung with lights and sail shades. A few patrons were clustered around heaters and an open fire pit.

It felt friendly. And she could use a friend right now.

Harper climbed out of her aging Volkswagen Beetle, and the hinges squealed as she shut the door. Leaning against the faded fender, she let her gaze wander, looking for a friendly stranger with a smartphone. "How do I get myself into these situations?" she sighed, tucking a strand of blond hair behind her ear.

"I warned you!"

The guttural shout came from between a pair of pickups two rows back where a man towered over a tiny brunette. He had the woman by the shoulders and was shaking her hard enough to rattle teeth.

"I fucking told you, didn't I?" He shook her again, even harder this time.

Harper hustled forward. "Hey!"

The screaming giant barely spared her a glance over his shoulder. "Mind your own business, nosy whore." Harper could hear the slur in his words.

The brunette started to cry. "Glenn—"

2

"I'm sick of hearing it!" He closed a ham-sized fist around her neck and shoved her against the truck, lifting her off her feet. The woman clawed helplessly at the hand squeezing her throat.

Seeing red, Harper launched herself at his back.

At impact, she wrapped her arms around his neck. He shrieked, too high-pitched for a man of his size, and released the woman. Arms flailing, he slammed back against the pickup, trying to dislodge Harper.

She held on tighter as his weight crushed into her torso.

"Not so easy when we fight back is it, asshole?" she gritted out.

"You're fucking dead, you bitch!" he squealed.

She briefly thought about biting his ear but instead used her legs to shove them off the truck and squeezed her arms tighter around his neck. His face was turning bright red from the pressure.

Glenn gripped her arms and lurched forward, tossing Harper to the ground in front of the crying woman. She landed hard on her side and came up swinging. He glanced a blow off her shoulder, making it sing, and she caught him on the side of the head.

"Glenn!" A deep voice full of authority snapped out from behind them.

Harper used the distraction and fired a shot to his face, catching him off guard…but only for a moment. The drunken giant swung back at her, and the parking lot exploded into stars.

———

"Hey." There was that voice again, this time floating toward her through the haze. Deep and a little rough.

Harper was flat on her back in the gravel. The side of her

3

face felt like it was on fire. But what held her attention was the man hovering over her. Buzzed short dark hair and a five-o'clock shadow framed the deepest hazel eyes she had ever seen. A spectacular sunset was happening behind his head. It was a gorgeous picture.

"Wow," she whispered. "Am I dead?"

He grinned, and she saw a dimple appear next to his mouth. Holy hotness. She was definitely dead.

"You're not dead, but you could've been, taking on a big son of a bitch like that."

Harper groaned, remembering. "Where is the big son of a bitch? Is the girl okay?"

"He's facedown underneath a deputy, and Gloria's fine. Thanks to you." He touched her face gently, probing around the fist-sized ouch. "You take a hit like a champ."

She winced. "Thanks. Can I sit up?"

Wordlessly, he helped her into a seated position and held her by the shoulders. "How do you feel?" Concern colored those deep eyes.

She brought her fingertips to her cheek and felt the heat pumping off what had to be some serious nastiness. "I've felt worse." He had a scar through one dark eyebrow and the slightest crinkles around his eyes. His very fit right forearm was completely covered in a sleeve tattoo.

"That was a very brave, very stupid thing you did, taking on a guy that size." He smiled again.

"It's not the stupidest thing I've done today."

"You guys all right, Garrison?"

Harper stopped staring at him long enough to notice the crowd that surrounded them.

"We're fine." He turned back to Harper. "Think you can stand up?"

She nodded, moderately pleased when her head didn't snap off her neck with the motion. He slid his hands under her arms and gently lifted her to her feet. The crowd broke into spontaneous applause.

"About time someone put that asshole in his place," someone cackled, and the rest of the crowd laughed.

"Jesus, Luke, what did you do now?" A gorgeous raven-haired beauty in a denim skirt and a Remo's embroidered polo weaved her way through the spectators.

"Don't get all pissy with him, Soph." A deputy stepped forward. "He didn't start it, but one of them broke Glenn's nose."

Harper glanced down and noticed the split knuckles on her hero's right hand.

"There are enough witnesses for him to spend a few nights in jail even if Gloria doesn't press charges this time," he continued.

The woman hooted and grabbed Luke for a smacking kiss. "Mom is going to be so proud."

Luke rolled his eyes, hands still steadying Harper.

The brunette turned to Harper. "And what were you, collateral damage?"

"Are you kidding?" The deputy laughed. "I was pulling in when I saw her jump on his back with blood in her eyes. She went Xena, Warrior Princess, on his ass before he got in a lucky shot and Luke took him down," the deputy said.

"That settles it." She pointed at Luke and Harper. "You two are drinking for free tonight." The crowd erupted into cheers.

"Hey, what about me?" the deputy mock pouted. "I handcuffed him."

"Ty, you'll get your reward after your shift." She tugged him in for a hard kiss on the mouth and grinned up at him. "Don't forget to pick up eggs on your way home."

"Yeah, yeah," he sighed. "I'll hold you to that reward. Well, I'm gonna run this asshole by the ER on the way to jail." He winked and headed back to his squad car. Glenn was slumped over in the back seat. Ty slid behind the wheel. "See y'all later."

He flipped on the lights as he peeled out of the lot to the delight of the crowd.

The brunette tossed her dark curls and rolled her eyes heavenward. "That's my husband," she sighed. "So, Tough Girl. Got a name?"

"Harper."

"I'm Sophie. Welcome to Benevolence, Harper. How about some ice for that face?"

CHAPTER 2

Sophie set Harper up with some ibuprofen, ice, and an impromptu doctor's visit in the ladies' room.

"Okay, Harper, I'm thinking you may have escaped a concussion. You are very lucky," Trish Dunnigan said, leaning in to check Harper's pupils one more time. "I'd like to see you tomorrow morning though. I don't think your arm is broken, but it could be a hairline fracture. Same with the ribs. You need an X-ray."

"Oh, I won't be here tomorrow. I'm just passing through."

"All right, then make sure you see your primary care doctor ASAP."

Harper nodded, knowing that that wasn't going to happen.

"Thanks for the house call, Doc," Sophie said, leaning against the vanity.

"No problem. I was in the neighborhood getting some takeout. Happy to help." Trish waved on her way out the door.

"Sorry to be so much trouble," Harper said from under the ice pack.

"Are you kidding? You're a hero. Glenn has been wailing on that poor Gloria since high school."

Harper sighed. "What a dick."

"You got that right." Sophie leaned toward the mirror to apply a fresh coat of lip gloss. "So what's your story? I know you're not from around here."

Harper sighed. "It's a long story. Let's just say I caught my boyfriend-slash-boss in a compromising position with a delivery girl today and stormed off with nothing but my car keys."

"And then ended up getting punched out by a drunken jackass in a parking lot?"

"Yep."

"Wow. That is a bad day." Sophie studied her for a minute. "So no wallet, no phone, no cash?"

"Nothing. Also, I ran out of gas in your parking lot."

Sophie threw her head back and laughed. "Kid, it couldn't have happened in a better place. I'll take care of everything." She tucked her gloss into her front pocket. "My shift's starting, so meet me at the bar. I've got a beer and some nachos with your name on them."

Harper watched as Sophie breezed out through the barn-style door. What she wouldn't give for that kind of confidence in life.

She dropped the ice pack and looked in the mirror. The bruise was nasty all right. It flowed from temple to cheekbone in a mottled purple. What if Luke was still out there?

Harper yanked her hair out of her ponytail and brushed her bangs sideways across her forehead to cover some of the bruising. She let the rest of her hair fall, tousled around her face.

Not great. But it would have to do.

She pushed through the door and into a very lively Friday night. The log cabin theme continued in the main bar with timber beams and a huge stone fireplace off to the side. Twin pool tables drew a crowd in a raised alcove overlooking the outdoor patio.

And there was Luke Garrison, standing at the long, rustic bar with a beer, waiting. He nudged an empty stool toward her with his foot. The gesture walked the line between invitation and order.

He was smoking hot. Dressed in jeans and a plain gray T-shirt, he was seriously ripped. Like romance-novel-cover ripped. And those eyes. Green and gray and brown. No wonder all she could say was *wow*.

She slid gingerly onto the stool as her muscles whimpered. They stared at each other for a minute. The silence hung thickly, cutting off the volume of the rest of the bar noises.

"Hi," Harper said finally.

"Hi."

"I'm Harper." She extended her hand for the overdue introduction.

"Luke." He took her hand in a strong grip and held it. "Come here often?" He smiled, and the dimple appeared again.

Harper felt her heart stumble. Oh, good Lord. Not now. This was the worst possible time to develop a crush. She had sworn off men not two hours ago and promptly gotten her ass kicked by another one. She ordered herself to pull it together.

"First time. I hear the parking lot gets pretty rowdy on Friday nights."

He straightened and brought his fingers to her face, gently brushed her bangs back. "How's your face, Harper?"

"It'll be okay, Luke." She blushed saying his name. It felt strange to be so familiar with a stranger. "How's your hand?"

He was still cupping her face, running his thumb lightly over her bruised cheek.

Someone nearby cleared their throat. Sophie was behind the bar, grinning like an idiot at them. "Sorry to interrupt, kids, but this is for you," she said, tossing an ice pack at Luke. "And this is for you." She slid a beer bottle to Harper. "Nachos are on the way. On the house. Sit."

"Thanks, Sis," Luke said, barely sparing Sophie a glance while he sank down on the empty stool next to Harper's.

Harper blushed under his stare and grabbed the beer like a lifeline. "Thanks."

Sophie winked at her before hurrying away.

"Nice job out there, Luke." A beanpole of a man in a red baseball hat smacked him soundly on the back. "That was one hell of a shot you gave Glenn. They teach you that in the army?"

"Thanks, Carl."

"Down and out in one," Carl hooted, miming a right hook. "Remind me not to piss you off."

"Just remember that next time you don't give me a discount at the lumberyard," Luke said dryly.

Carl laughed again and turned to Harper. "It's nice to see Luke here in such pretty company. I didn't catch your name, Blondie."

Luke made the perfunctory introduction. "Carl, this is Harper. Harper, this is Carl."

"Well, Harper, if there is anything you need while you're in town, you don't hesitate to ask me. I'll be happy to do anything, anything at all for you."

"Yeah, I bet you would," Luke said. "How is your wife these days?"

"Big as a house. Baby Number Three is due next week." He puffed out his chest with pride. "This one's gotta be a boy. A man can't have three daughters."

"He can if he's getting paid back for raising hell in high school," Luke said. "Maybe you should go home and rub Carol Ann's feet to try and make up for it."

"Oh, I'm doing better than that. I'm picking up a cheesesteak for her."

Right on cue, Sophie reappeared with a large paper bag. "Three steaks, all the fixings." She slid it across the bar to Carl.

"Give Carol Ann my best," Luke told him.

"Will do. Will do. It was nice to meet you, Harper. If you get sick of hanging out with this soldier, just give me a call."

"Will do, Carl." Harper laughed.

"Don't encourage him," Luke said as Carl weaved his way past them.

"So, soldier?" Harper turned back to Luke.

"Captain in the Army National Guard," Sophie said, plopping down an overflowing plate of nachos and a pile of napkins.

Luke eyed his sister and said nothing.

Hmm. Military. That ranked right up there with firefighters and cowboys in the noble and sexy profession category. Was there anything that wasn't scorching hot about this man?

Harper glanced around the bar that was getting more crowded by the minute. It seemed like everyone was talking to everyone else at the same time. No one was alone, even if they arrived that way. Greetings and hands rose up from all corners of the room.

"I'm getting the feeling that this is a very small town and I'm the only stranger here," Harper ventured.

"Don't bother feeling like a stranger. It won't last," Luke warned. "See that woman over there in the Easter Bunny sweatshirt?"

Harper spotted her gabbing it up by the jukebox.

"That's Georgia Rae. She's probably already plotting on how to corner you and extract your life story."

Harper laughed and sampled a cheesy nacho.

"And that," Luke said, gesturing at a gray-mustached man by the pool table, "is my uncle Stu. I guarantee he already called my dad to tell him that I'm at the bar with the girl who took down Glenn Diller. And see how Sophie keeps checking her phone? That's my mom texting her to find out what you look like."

"Wow. I should probably get out of here before they invite me to Sunday dinner," Harper laughed.

Luke's phone on the bar buzzed. He glanced at the screen and grimaced. "Too late."

"Very funny." Harper rolled her eyes and took a sip of beer.

He held up his phone for her to see.

Mom: Ask your friend if she can bring a pie to dinner Sunday.

She choked, slapping a hand over her mouth. "This can't be real. I'm still in the parking lot unconscious, aren't I?"

Luke laughed and put a solid, warm hand on her back. "You wish."

Click.

Harper glanced up to see Sophie holding her phone extended toward them.

"Soph." Luke's voice held the sharp edge of a warning.

Sophie smiled innocently. "What? Oops, gotta go. Order's up."

"Did she just take a picture of us?"

Luke grabbed his beer. The spot on her back where he had touched her still felt tingly.

She put her head in her hands until she bumped her cheek and remembered the bruise. "I feel like I'm in some alternate reality. I'm not even supposed to be here."

"Where are you supposed to be?"

"Fremont."

"You're a long way from Fremont."

"Are you kidding me?"

"Harper, Fremont is four hours west of here."

"Son of a bitch. I was going the wrong way." She leaned forward and covered her eyes with her hands.

"Everything okay here?" Sophie reappeared. "What did you do now, Luke?"

"It's not him, it's me." Harper's voice was muffled by her hands.

"She was supposed to be in Fremont tonight," Luke supplied.

"Well, that's not going to happen, Harp. Fremont's four hours away."

"I know that *now*." Harper groaned into her hands. Sophie started to laugh, and Harper dropped her hands. "I'm glad you find my life so amusing."

It only made Sophie laugh harder. "This is ridiculous. Does stuff like this happen to you all the time?"

"Stuff like what?" Luke asked.

Harper dropped her head to the bar while Sophie gave Luke the brief details of her situation, mercifully leaving out any mention of the delivery girl.

"You left your house with nothing but car keys and then drove for hours in the wrong direction?" It was Luke's turn to swipe a hand over his face and sigh. "So where are you staying tonight?"

Harper sat up and took a mournful swallow of beer. "I don't know. The plan was to message Hannah on Facebook for a ride. But that's when I thought I was only ten minutes away from her."

"Maybe someone here tonight is heading in that direction and can get you part way there?" Sophie suggested.

Luke shook his head. "We're not putting her in a car with some half-lit stranger."

"What do you think cab fare would be to Fremont?"

"Soph, be realistic. Besides, why not just give her gas money?"

"I'll just sleep in my car," Harper decided. It wouldn't be the first time for that either.

"So you sleep in your car. Then what?" Luke asked.

"I'll message Hannah and beg her to pick me up in the morning."

"Here." Sophie slid her phone to Harper. "Log in and message her." She hurried away to grab a refill for a customer.

Sensing salvation, Harper pounced on the phone.

She keyed in her log-in and went to Hannah's page. "Crap! Hannah's husband surprised her with a weekend away at a cabin in freaking West Virginia."

"So giving you gas money to get there is a moot point. Hmm, if only you could stay overnight with someone. Hmm." Sophie arched an eyebrow at Luke.

Harper leaned back on the stool and tilted her head up. "I will figure this out. I will figure this out."

Sophie leaned over the bar. "Hey, what about Mickey?"

"For Christ's sake." Luke slammed his beer down.

"He's got an empty house now that his girlfriend moved out. I'm sure he wouldn't mind an overnight guest," Sophie chirped.

Harper narrowed her eyes.

"His girlfriend moved out because he got arrested for shoplifting at the liquor store," Luke growled.

"I thought it was because he's banging Sherri from the bank," Sophie interjected.

"Then why would you even suggest him?" Luke pressed his fingers to his temple.

"I'd let you stay at my place, Harp, but you'd have to sleep on a lumpy chair and probably wake up to a screaming, sticky-fingered three-year-old," Sophie said, pouring a pint from the tap.

"What happened to your couch?"

"Josh spilled a juice box on it, and then Bitsy decided to eat the whole cushion. She could sleep on *half* a couch. But no juice boxes allowed."

Harper hoped "Bitsy" was a dog.

Luke shook his head, and Harper could see his jaw tighten.

"So *your* plan is to sleep in your car, and *your* plan is to send her to sleep with a cheating alcoholic shoplifter?"

"Hey, at least we're brainstorming here. You're just shooting down ideas. I hate when you play devil's advocate," Sophie said and pouted.

Luke sighed again and looked down at the bar. "You can stay with me tonight, and tomorrow I'll drive you back to your place to get your stuff."

Sophie turned away but not before Harper saw the cat-that-ate-the-canary grin on her face. "Oh, no. I couldn't. I don't want to inconvenience anyone," Harper blurted, her eyes suddenly wide.

Luke looked at her. "I'll be more inconvenienced if you sleep in the damn parking lot. Besides, I promised the doc I'd bring you by in the morning so she can get a couple of quick X-rays if you were still in town."

"Well, why didn't you just say so?" Sophie asked in feigned exasperation.

Luke shot her a look, and she shut up.

"Thank you, Luke. You really don't have to. I should have to suffer the consequences of being an idiot. Then maybe I'd learn."

He smiled down at the bar, and she saw the dimple wink into existence.

"I think you've already had a rough enough day." He turned back to her. "Are you okay if we stay till closing?"

"Of course." She nodded.

What was it about those eyes? Maybe it was the shadow in them. Harper felt a pull every time she spotted it. He was quiet, clearly not at all inclined to talk about himself. Definitely not like Ted the Dick. But the way he observed what was happening around him made her think there wasn't much that he missed.

"So what's your story, Luke? I mean, I feel like I should know more about you if we're going to have a sleepover."

"No story." He scratched the back of his head.

"Uh-huh. Yeah. Sure." She raised her eyebrows and drank deeply from her beer.

He laughed again.

"My name is Luke. I've lived here my whole life. I'm in construction and the National Guard. And Sophie's my sister."

"That's all you've got?" Harper elbowed him.

"What else do you need?"

"How about arrest warrants? Bodies buried in the backyard? Unusual fetishes?"

He leaned in. Close. She could smell his soap. Something with a little spice.

She could feel his breath on her face. Harper parted her lips. Her breath caught.

"Define 'unusual.'"

CHAPTER 3

The evening passed in a blur of townsfolk greetings—Georgia Rae did make her appearance—beer, and bar food. Harper felt slightly buzzed and incredibly exhausted as she stood with Luke watching Sophie lock the front doors. She stifled a yawn. It was 2:00 a.m., way past her bedtime. And her face was starting to throb again.

"Thanks again for hanging out," Sophie said as they crossed the lot.

"Have a good night, Soph," Luke said, opening the car door for her.

"You too, big brother. Night, Harper! I hope I'll see you again."

Harper waved with her good arm and yawned her goodbye. "Thanks for everything, Sophie."

"Better get her home before she falls asleep standing up, Luke."

He tapped the roof of her car and waved as she pulled out. "Ready to go?" he asked Harper.

She nodded, crossing her arms against the spring night's chill. They were alone, and they would be for the next several hours. Harper wondered if she would lie awake all night on his couch thinking about him being so near…and presumably naked. Men like Luke didn't sleep in pajamas.

"We're over here," he said, pointing to a dark gray pickup at the back of the lot. "Need anything out of your car?"

"No, I'm good." The only thing in her car was her old coffee from the morning.

They started walking together, and Harper rubbed her arms.

"Cold?" he asked.

She nodded and felt a tingle exactly halfway between comfort and lust ignite as Luke draped his arm over her shoulder and pulled her in. The heat coming off his body instantly warmed her bare skin, and she didn't resist the urge to snuggle a little closer.

He opened the passenger door for her, and she levered herself up and onto the seat, trying not to wince as her aching body slid across the leather.

Luke slid into the driver's seat and started the truck. He pushed a button and Harper instantly felt heat under her ass. Seat warmers! He hung a left out of the parking lot, and in just a few minutes, they were pulling into the driveway of a tidy brick three-story with a sprawling front porch.

Harper blinked through tired eyes. "You live *here*?"

He glanced out the windshield at the house. "Yep."

"I expected something different. Like a bachelor pad apartment. Do you have roommates?" *A girlfriend? A wife and four kids?*

"Nope. Just me." He smiled, a quick, heart-tickling grin. "Come on."

The wide-planked porch was deep, wrapping around to the far side of the house. There was no furniture, but Harper could just imagine a porch swing and hanging baskets blooming with color.

Luke unlocked the front door and held it open for her.

She stepped over the threshold and waited while he flipped on the lights. The foyer opened directly to a wide-banister staircase. A pair of doorways mirrored each other from opposite walls leading into darkened rooms. Above the dark wainscoting, the walls were covered with ornate wallpaper with roses and hummingbirds.

"You don't really live here, do you?"

Luke tossed his keys on a skinny table just inside the door, the only piece of furniture visible to Harper. He raised an eyebrow. "What makes you say that?"

She trailed a finger over a paper rose. "No reason." Harper poked her head into the room on the right. From the streetlights outside, she could just make out an ornate sofa with wooden arms opposite a flat-screen TV on sawhorses. The rest of the room was empty.

"Did you just move in?"

"Not really." He looked sheepish. "I've been here a couple of years."

"Seriously?"

"I've been busy."

"Where did you get that couch?" She gestured at the carved wooden monstrosity with its lumpy red velour cushions.

"It was my grandmother's."

"Oh, thank God. I thought you went flea marketing one day and thought that looked like the perfect place to watch TV evangelists."

He cracked a smile. "This was my grandmother's house. I bought it when she passed away."

"Were you close?"

"As close as you can be to a crazy Italian grandmother who chases you with a wooden spoon. Most of the furniture that's here is hers."

"There doesn't seem to be a lot of it," Harper observed.

"I keep meaning to get more, but I've been—"

"Busy," she finished for him.

"Anyway, there's only one bed, so you can take that, and I'll take the couch."

Horrified, Harper stared at the unwelcoming lines of the couch. "Absolutely not. I'm not putting you out of your own bed."

"Well, you're not sleeping on the couch."

"Neither are you," Harper insisted.

"What do you suggest?"

She paused, weighing the options. "We are two exhausted adults who probably have a reasonable amount of self-control. Can we both sleep in the bed?"

"I don't think that's a good idea." His hands were out of his pockets now and cruising over the back of his head. He was nervous, and Harper thought it was adorable.

"Why not?"

"We don't know each other and…" He trailed off, and Harper scented victory.

"I think I can trust you can control your hormones and not jump me in the middle of the night," she teased.

"It's not *my* hormones that I'm worried about."

She smacked him in the chest. The very solid, warm chest. Maybe he had a point.

———

The only furniture on the second floor was in the master bedroom. A four-poster queen-size bed dominated one wall opposite an ornately carved dresser.

"Grandma's?" Harper lightly grasped one of the mahogany posts at the foot of the bed.

Luke nodded, hands back in his pockets.

"It's nice." Staring at his bed was suddenly making Harper feel a little shy.

"I can still sleep on the couch if you'd be more comfortable." He jerked a thumb toward the hallway.

"Don't be ridiculous. That thing looks like it would put your ass to sleep if you sat down long enough to tie your shoes. We're adults. This doesn't have to be awkward, right?"

Instead of answering, he turned and opened one of the dresser drawers.

"Here." Luke held out a plain white T-shirt. "You can sleep in this."

It was soft to the touch and obviously well worn. By him.

"Thanks." She took it, careful to only touch the shirt.

"You can change in there." He gestured toward the connecting bathroom. "I'm going to go lock up."

"Okay, thanks." They stared at each other for another minute. "This is awkward, isn't it?" Harper blurted out.

Luke smiled. "A little."

"It's just for one night." She wasn't sure if she was trying to reassure him or herself.

"Right."

"And we're adults."

"It would appear so."

"We're being silly," Harper reasoned. "It's just sleep." She could see his dimple again. At least he was amused. She nodded finally. "Okay, I'm going to go change."

In the bathroom, she splashed cold water on her face, careful to gently dry the bruised side. She didn't even look at the rest of her body. Judging from how sore everything was, it was probably just as purple as her face.

It was a good thing this wasn't some "first time" with

someone like Luke. She wasn't at her best—maybe even hovering near her worst. And if she was going to have a first time with someone like Luke, she'd want it to be perfect.

She rolled her eyes and tugged the T-shirt over her head and down her torso. It was ridiculous to be newly homeless and jobless and more concerned with the what-ifs of imaginary sex with the sculpted captain. She wondered what he looked like in uniform.

"Pull yourself together," she muttered. "It's one platonic night of sleep."

She ran a hand over the cotton and took a moment to be grateful for remembering to wear underwear today.

Harper tugged the neck of the shirt up to her nose and breathed deeply. It smelled like him. And she was about to crawl into a bed that smelled like him…with him. She hoped she could control herself in her sleep.

She was standing at the foot of the bed, fidgeting, when he came back upstairs.

"Everything okay?" he asked, opening a dresser drawer.

"Oh yeah. I just didn't know if you had a side," she said, playing with the hem of the shirt.

He suddenly seemed very interested in the contents of the drawer. "A side?"

"Of the bed. Do you sleep on a side?"

He glanced back up. "I usually sleep in the middle. So you can take your pick."

"Oh, thanks."

Luke grabbed a pair of pajama pants. "I'll be back."

As soon as the bathroom door closed, Harper gratefully flopped onto the bed and burrowed under the covers. She would just hug the edge, and he wouldn't even know she was there. No inconvenience at all.

She hoped she wouldn't snore.

The bathroom door opened. He stood in the doorway in nothing but untied flannel pants that rode low on his hips. Harper wet her lips and tried not to stare at his cut abs. Every visible inch of his torso was carved, muscled, and freaking hot. There was another tattoo, a phoenix, over his heart.

Oh my God. She was going to sleep with *that*.

No! She was not going to fall down the rabbit hole of crappy life choices again. She had promised herself that she was turning over a new leaf. Starting fresh, focusing on herself.

Harper was failing at not focusing on Luke's naked chest. Her fingers itched to trail over the tattoo, across his chest, and down those abs to the indecently low waistband. She fisted her naughty-minded hands in the quilt. There was no way she was going to sleep a wink. Not next to that perfect body.

He was staring at her too, but his eyes weren't bugging out of his head like hers. Harper thought she heard him sigh. But he moved toward the bedroom door and wordlessly flipped the light switch.

In the dark, Harper was relieved she had nothing to stare at. Until she felt his weight on the other side of the bed.

He seemed to have the same idea she did, hugging his side.

"Good night," she whispered into the darkness.

"Night."

"Luke?"

"Hmm?"

"Thanks for letting me stay here."

He sighed. "You're welcome."

"I really appreciate it."

"Harper?"

"Yeah?"

"Shut up and go to sleep."

CHAPTER 4

Luke woke suddenly in the middle of the night feeling warm. He didn't even remember falling asleep. He heard breathing and remembered he wasn't alone. Harper's head was resting on his shoulder, her hand splayed across his chest. Her thigh was drawn up and across his legs.

It had been a very long time since he woke up to a woman draped over him. He automatically squashed the memory. He was good at that. Staying focused on the present. That was how he got through every single day.

Harper made a little sound like a sigh and nuzzled closer.

The woman was a disaster. She had invaded his night and now his bed. It was taking an act of supreme willpower not to roll over and wake her up in the way his body was demanding.

Harper. It was an old-fashioned name for such a free spirit. He had already been heading in Glenn's direction when he saw the blond blur launch herself at him. It was incredibly stupid of her to get involved like that. Anyone with common sense would have just called for help.

But not Harper. She went in swinging. If tonight was any indication of how she lived her life, it was a miracle she was still alive.

There was no doubt that she was beautiful. Those wide gray eyes didn't miss a beat, and her full mouth always seemed to be smiling. And judging from the feel of her body plastered against him, she was built with the soft curves that commanded a man's hand to follow them. She had an energy that seemed to be trying to explode out of her at every second.

She was not a restful, careful person. He had known her for only a few hours and was already concerned for her safety.

No job. No home. No money. According to Sophie, Harper was screwed. She probably didn't even have a plan. Someone who stormed out of her own life with nothing but car keys didn't sound like much of a planner.

He would talk to her in the morning. Find out what she was going to do and then talk her out of whatever ridiculous scheme she came up with. He'd help her whether she wanted it or not.

Luke clenched his jaw in the dark as Harper slid her leg higher up his thighs and murmured something into his neck.

———

Harper woke up to sunlight streaming through the window onto her face. She tried to stretch but found her arms trapped.

Luke.

Hot and hard against her, he was spooning her. His breath was warm in her hair. An inked arm was thrown possessively over her, hand cupping her breast through the T-shirt that was now bunched up around her waist. Her ass was pressed against some impressive morning wood.

Now this was the way to wake up. Warm, safe, and wrapped in strong arms.

She pressed her lips together to stop the laughter that bubbled up inside. She had been the one worried about not controlling herself.

He twitched in his sleep, squeezing her breast.

Harper bit her lip. She didn't know Luke well, but she was fairly certain he wouldn't like waking up in such a…vulnerable position.

She was going to have to sneak out. After she enjoyed this for another thirty seconds.

She nuzzled in and breathed in his scent. His chest rose rhythmically against her back, his hard thighs cradling her.

She deserved a medal for leaving this bed. She held her breath and gently pried his hand off her chest. Holding up Luke's arm, she inched away from his perfect body and cursed herself as she did it.

Maneuvering to the edge of the bed, she eased into a sitting position.

Even in his sleep, Luke was sexy. Inky long lashes brushed his sculpted cheekbones. Except for those lashes, there was nothing delicate about him. He was built with power and strength. She let her gaze linger on the lines of his arm. The sinewy muscle of his biceps gave way to the sensual ink on his forearm.

She would have to ask him what it meant. A little conversation on their trip would help keep her mind off the memory of waking up with him pressed against her.

Feeling like she had been hit by a small car, Harper gingerly snuck down to the kitchen where she started a pot of coffee before opening the fridge. Considering the state of the rest of his house—there was nothing but a stack of boxes in the dining room—she didn't have high hopes for a bachelor's kitchen inventory but was happy to find eggs one day away from expiration, milk, cheese, and the remains of a loaf of bread. Scrambled egg sandwiches would start the day off.

The swelling in her face had gone down, thankfully, but the bruising had gotten uglier. Everything else ached. She had even discovered a baseball-sized bruise on her butt cheek. Hopefully that ham-fisted asshole was crying like a baby in a cell somewhere and Gloria had gotten her first good night's sleep in years.

Harper found Luke's laptop on the counter and, as the eggs cooked, checked Craigslist for job listings in Fremont. There were a few that would do, at least temporarily. It was almost a shame that she didn't know someone here in Benevolence. The sleepy town and its nosy residents gave off a good vibe. No one could be lonely here.

But the job market was probably nonexistent. Besides, Harper thought as she rummaged for sugar, if she stayed, she would make a fool of herself over Luke.

And who wouldn't? He was hot, protective…and those eyes. "Definitely a bad idea," she murmured to herself.

"Do you always talk to yourself when you cook?" The room got warmer and the air cracklier when Luke walked in.

She glanced up from the frying pan to where he stood near the refrigerator, studying her. He still wore the pajama pants but had added a T-shirt. Damn.

"Good morning," she said cheerfully, trying to shove the carnal thoughts out of her head.

"Morning. What's all this?" He nodded toward the stove.

He looked guarded. Harper handed him an empty mug.

"Breakfast. It's a thank-you for letting me stay here."

He took the mug and, after a second's hesitation, made his way to the coffee.

She watched him out of the corner of her eye while he poured and she plated. What would it be like to have this view every morning?

―――

"I really appreciate this," Harper said, sliding into Luke's truck.

He waited until she fastened her seat belt and then started the engine. "You already said that."

"Well, I didn't want you to think I'd gotten less grateful since breakfast." She looked out the window as they backed down the driveway and pulled onto the street. The town rolled by, neat and tidy. Well-maintained houses hugged the main street and historic brick buildings housed businesses with cute names like Common Grounds and the Sparkle Shop.

Growing up, she had dreamed of a town like this, a place to belong. They drove past the high school with its wide green lawn and football stadium. She wondered how different things would have been for her had life begun here.

"You're quiet," Luke observed, glancing at her.

"Just thinking. Did you play football? In high school, I mean."

Luke stopped for a red light. "Yeah. And ran track."

"Very athletic," Harper commented.

"You?"

"No, I never played football."

"Smart-ass." Luke said it mildly, and Harper caught a glimpse of dimple.

Harper smiled. "No other sports either."

"Why, because your school didn't have boxing?"

"Funny." She wrinkled her nose at him. "It was mostly circumstances. I moved around a lot."

"Skipping out on arrest warrants?"

"I'm starting to think you have a slightly skewed perception of me, Lucas."

"Can you blame me?"

"Hey, you're the one who picked me up at a bar."

"I picked you up off the parking lot."

"Details, details." Harper waved her hand.

Luke turned into a small parking lot next to a barn-red office. Dunnigan & Associates.

"Damn it, Luke. I told her I would see my doctor when I could."

"Suck it up, sweetheart. It's the price of a ride to the city."

Harper pouted. "I feel fine."

"Bullshit. You can barely move. Now be a big girl and get out."

She took her sweet time following him up the ramp.

"If you're in that much pain, I'd be happy to carry you in," he threatened.

Harper quickened her pace and slunk in the door behind him.

"They're not even open yet," she hissed at his back.

"Doc opened early just for your pretty little ribs."

Dr. Dunnigan hustled into the empty waiting room clutching a tall coffee. "Right on time, Luke. Ouch," she said, looking at Harper's face. "How ya feeling today?"

"Just great," she said. "In fact, I think we're wasting your time—"

Luke reached out and poked her right on the bruised butt cheek. Harper yelped. He either had spectacular bruise radar or had caught a glimpse of her ass when she had escaped bed this morning.

"Yeah, I think we still need to do an exam. Come on back. Luke, you might as well come too. While Harper changes, I'll show you where I'm thinking of doing the addition. Bra off, underwear on," she called over her shoulder to Harper.

Harper glumly pulled on the paper gown and tucked it under her for as much modesty as possible. She was not the biggest fan of doctors' offices. Time was what provided the best healing. She was just a little banged up. This didn't even make it into her top five injuries list. As far as she was concerned, everyone was overreacting.

A knock at the door was followed by Dr. Dunnigan's frizzy curls. "Decent? Are you okay if Luke comes in?"

Harper shrugged. "Sure, why not?"

She stared at her bare feet while they entered. Luke sat in the visitor's chair while Dr. Dunnigan wielded her penlight in Harper's eyes.

"I still don't have a concussion," Harper sighed.

"Speaking from experience?" the doctor asked, switching eyes.

"One or two. You don't forget what they feel like."

"So no nausea, vomiting?"

"Nope. And no blurred vision either."

Dr. Dunnigan laughed. "Well, in this case, I'm going to agree with your self-diagnosis. I think you're concussion clear. Which makes you very lucky or very skilled at taking a punch. Glenn has fists of concrete."

Harper remained silent and avoided Luke's gaze.

"Okay, let's take a peek at those ribs." The doctor tugged the paper gown open to check Harper's side. "Wow, that's a mess. We're definitely going to do an X-ray."

Harper winced at the gentle probing around the bruising. Dr. Dunnigan pulled the gown open a little wider, and Harper saw Luke's jaw clench. Wordlessly, he shoved out of his chair to pace.

Ignoring him, Dr. Dunnigan moved on to Harper's arm.

"Okay, Contusion Queen, let's get a couple of pictures for the police report and a few X-rays, and you can be on your way. I'm going to grab the camera."

Harper sighed and gingerly flopped back on the table. The

30

police report. A very loud part of her wanted to decline, but she thought of Gloria's terrified face as that ham-sized fist had closed around the slim column of throat. She'd do it. Besides, maybe if she got called to come back and testify, she could see Luke again.

Harper closed her eyes and tried to pretend she was on a beach somewhere wearing a floppy hat and bikini instead of crinkly paper.

"Harper." Luke was standing next to her. He spoke softly, but his expression was hard. "Can I see?" He held the edge of the gown between his fingers.

She nodded. Why the hell not? This was as close to getting naked with him as she was going to get.

He draped the material over her, careful to keep her front covered.

"Baby." He trailed his fingers over the side of her rib cage around to just under her breast.

Harper felt her heart rate kick up several notches. An awake Luke touching her was even hotter than being groped by the asleep one.

He gently splayed his warm palm over the bruising, the tips of his fingers just brushing the curve of her breast.

Harper looked into his eyes and wondered how she could see both simmering anger and tenderness in them.

"All right," Dr. Dunnigan said, pushing the door open. "Let's get this show on the road. Luke, can you help Harper up? We'll take these standing against the wall."

Luke's hands closed around her arms and eased her into a sitting position. Harper gritted her teeth as hard as she could to avoid wincing.

She held his forearms to steady herself as she stepped down onto the hardwood floor. When she craned her neck back to look at him, she saw a war of emotions tangling in his gaze. He brushed his knuckles gently across her cheek. "It won't happen again." The whispered promise was threaded with steel.

He stepped back and let the doctor take several shots of Harper's ribs, arm, and face.

"Okay, that should be plenty. Let's get a couple of X-rays down the hall," Dr. Dunnigan said, putting the camera on the desk.

Luke held the back of Harper's gown together for her as they made their way to the room. She tried to imagine a hundred different scenarios where his hand would be skimming the bare skin on her back that didn't involve treating her like an elderly invalid.

Sometimes life just sucked.

What if she had rolled into town in a cute sundress and her damn wallet? She could have bought him a drink instead of requiring saving and charity. If this wasn't a wake-up call about how it was time to start behaving like an adult, she didn't know what was.

Dr. Dunnigan led them to a small, windowless room and had Harper lie down on the table. She adjusted the position of the camera over Harper's ribs and draped a heavy lead cover over her.

"Just hold still right there, and this will be over in a minute." The doctor had Luke step back with her behind the protective curtain, and Harper heard the whir of the camera.

Dr. Dunnigan rearranged her and took a few more shots of the ribs and one of her arm before letting her sit up again.

She brought a laptop over to Harper. "Okay. Let's check these out."

Luke joined them, leaning against the table. His arm rested against Harper's.

Dr. Dunnigan zoomed in on an image. "Hmm."

"What does 'hmm' mean?" Luke demanded.

"This spot right here"—she tapped the screen—"is a healed fracture. So either you have superhuman healing powers, or you broke your ribs before."

"I think I had a fracture there years ago," Harper said, crossing her arms over her chest. It was embarrassing reliving her medical history with two virtual strangers.

Dr. Dunnigan looked at Harper over her reading glasses and waited. "Hmm."

Harper ignored her. She could feel Luke's gaze weigh heavily on her. She squinted at the screen. "No new fractures?" she asked cheerfully.

Dr. Dunnigan flipped through the series of images. "It looks like you're in the clear. This time."

"Told you," Harper smirked at Luke.

"You're awfully cocky for someone covered head to toe in bruises," he reminded her.

"Same story with your arm," Dr. Dunnigan said, tapping the screen. "Old break. This one looks like it healed better than your rib." She looked pointedly at Harper.

Harper shrugged and didn't respond. Time had healed those physical hurts a long time ago and, with them, the mental ones as well.

"Any new ones?"

"Nope." The doctor swiveled on her stool and put the laptop back on the counter. "A little swollen, a lot of bruising. But overall not nearly as bad as it could have been. I'll write you a scrip for some pain meds to help you sleep, and I'm telling you that rest is the best medicine."

CHAPTER 5

They rode in silence after leaving Dr. Dunnigan's, each lost in thought. Harper was the one to finally break the silence.

"So do your tattoos mean anything?"

Luke kept his eyes on the road. "Why?"

"Do you not want to tell me what they mean?"

"What makes you say that?"

"You're answering questions with questions. It's like a therapist trick."

"Is it?"

She sighed loudly. "I feel like I'm playing *Jeopardy* when I talk to you."

Luke grinned and said nothing.

Harper let it drop. She watched the road signs flash by, heading back to the city she had called home for the past two years. She had called a lot of places home, but it was for the lack of a better word. She had never really felt at home anywhere. Not since she was a little kid in a postage stamp–sized house with a mom and a dad who were now more ghosts than memories.

"So what's your plan once you get your stuff?"

Harper pursed her lips and sighed. "Gas up my car and head to Hannah's."

"You're putting a lot of hope on a friend's generosity."

She sensed judgment in his tone. "It's only temporary. I already checked out some jobs and apartments on Craigslist. I'll be off her couch in no time."

"What kind of jobs?"

"There's a couple of waitress/manager openings, an inventory clerk position, and, worst case scenario, one of those people who sit on stools in the middle of the mall and try to sell you a new bathtub."

"Dream job?"

"Any job that pays the bills is a dream job these days."

He changed the subject. "So do you want to talk about why you ran out of your place with nothing yesterday?"

"Not particularly," Harper said, looking out the window. She sighed. "Just a mistake on my part. Poor judgment followed by a nasty surprise when I came home early."

"Boyfriend?"

"Ex, as of yesterday."

"Cheating?"

"A bike messenger girl. She had great legs from what I could see."

"My God, Harper. You're a mess."

She puffed out a breath. "It would appear so."

An hour later, Luke pulled up in front of the beige town house that Harper pointed out. "Do you want me to come in with you? I don't want you moving anything heavy."

"No, he should be at work. And I don't have much to pack. It won't take me long." Harper opened the door and slid out.

"Just come out when you're packed, and I'll carry the stuff to the truck."

She hurried up the walk to the front door and let herself in. The beige carpet and off-white walls had never screamed "home" to her, and they certainly didn't make her feel homesick now.

It was time to go.

She grabbed her purse out of the hall closet, double-checking that her wallet and phone were there before hurrying upstairs to the bedroom. The sheets were still in disarray, and she could see two head indentations on the pillows. Messenger Girl must have spent the night. Or maybe he'd ordered pizza after he was finished with Messenger Girl.

She turned her back on the bed in disgust and grabbed her suitcase and duffel bag out of the closet. She emptied her dresser drawers into the bags and then moved to the closet. In less than ten minutes, she had both bags packed.

In the bathroom, she hastily applied some cover-up to her eye and dumped her cosmetics into a ziplock bag. She muscled her bags down the stairs one at a time to the front door.

Luke was waiting for her on the porch. "I told you I would carry everything." He took the bags from her and hauled them down the front steps.

Harper rolled her eyes. "I can handle a suitcase."

"How many more bags?" he called over his shoulder on his way down the walk.

"This is it for the clothes. I just want to do a walk-through and see if I'm missing anything important."

"All your clothes fit in two suitcases?" He stopped in his tracks and looked at her as if she had just grown an arm out of her forehead and asked for a high five.

"I lost a lot in the fire and haven't really had the chance to replace the bulk."

"The fire?" Luke blinked rapidly.

"Yeah, six months ago. My apartment building in South Side burned down. One of my neighbors was making a grilled cheese on a hot plate next to her drapes. Whoosh!" She jazz handed the air.

"Were you home?" He was covering his eyes with a hand now.

"Yep." She turned back toward the house.

"Is that how you broke your arm and your ribs?"

"Nope. I'm just going to grab some paperwork. I'll be right out."

"Uh, yeah. I'm coming with you. Knowing you, there might be a gas leak or an escaped circus bear in there."

"Aren't you cute when you're all protective?" Harper teased.

Luke shook his head and held the door open for her. "I can't believe you're still alive," he muttered.

Three already-packed banker boxes of documents and knickknacks later, Harper was ready to go.

"Are you sure this is it?" Luke asked, tucking the boxes in the back seat of his truck.

"That's everything," Harper said, working the key off her ring. "I'm just going to leave this inside. I'll be right back."

Luke got back in the truck and started the engine.

One minute turned into five before Harper came back out, stumbling under the weight of a giant stuffed and mounted fish.

Luke jumped out of the truck and yanked it out of her grasp. "Damn it! Stop carrying shit!"

"You can just throw it back there." She gestured at the bed of the truck.

He tossed it in the back before climbing into the driver's seat. "What's with the fish?" Luke asked casually.

Harper shrugged, securing her seat belt. "He bought it at a

yard sale and tells people he caught it himself. 'It took me four hours to reel in that swordfish,'" she mimicked in a deep voice.

"I'm pretty sure that's a marlin."

Harper stared at him for a beat. "A marlin?"

Luke nodded.

She burst out laughing, dropping her head against the headrest. "What an ass."

———

Harper insisted on buying Luke lunch halfway back to Benevolence. They stopped at a small family-run place that had excellent chicken pot pie and even better fresh-cut fries.

She paused chewing long enough to text Hannah.

Harper: Ted's dick not in pants. Moved out. Couch open?

Hannah responded within minutes.

Hannah: Always hated his stupid douchey goatee. Be back Monday night. Couch is yours.

"Excellent." Harper sighed with relief and jumped back into her pot pie.

"All set?" Luke asked, snagging a french fry.

"Yep. Hannah and Finn will be back Monday night, and I can stay with them then."

"What are you going to do between now and then?"

"I'll probably just get a motel room for the weekend. Oh! Maybe a hotel with an indoor pool! It'll be like a vacation."

After lunch, Harper had Luke pull the truck around to the dumpster behind the restaurant. He raised an eyebrow but didn't ask any questions.

He remained silent when she hopped into the bed of the truck and, after a brief struggle, hefted the marlin over her head and heaved it into the dumpster.

Neither of them said a word when she climbed back into the truck and belted in.

———

They returned to Luke's house where Luke unloaded the boxes and bags, stacking everything in the foyer. Harper watched uselessly from the couch where Luke ordered her to stay.

When he was done, he joined her on the lumpy antiquity. "Let's talk about what you're doing tonight—" Luke was cut off by Sophie yoo-hooing from the front door.

Harper was sure she heard Luke swear under his breath.

"Oh, there you are," Sophie said brightly. "How are you feeling today? Your face doesn't look too bad."

"Thanks, neither does yours," Harper said dryly.

"Smarty-pants. I'm going to get a drink. Anyone want one?" She headed back to the kitchen.

Harper shrugged at Luke, and they got up to follow.

"Soooo, how did the stuff collecting go?" Sophie helped herself to a soda from the fridge and joined Harper at the island while Luke got a beer.

Luke's eyes met Harper's.

"Uneventful, wouldn't you say, Luke?" Harper smiled innocently.

He leaned back against the counter and nodded. "Very uneventful. But I have a craving for fish sticks."

Sophie watched as they grinned at each other. "So, Harp, what's the plan? What are you going to do now?" she asked, toying with the can.

"For now, the plan is still to get to Hannah's and find a temp job there."

"I was thinking—"

"Soph." Luke crossed his arms.

"Now hear me out!"

"What? What's going on? What's happening?" Harper looked back and forth between the siblings.

"Well, I had an idea that I think could work to both your advantages."

"Our advantage or yours?" Luke snorted.

"If you'll shut your trap for all of ten seconds, Crabby Patty, I'll explain."

"Children. Don't make me turn this kitchen around," Harper sighed.

"Look. I'm just going to throw this out there, and you two can decide whether it would work. Harper, you have no money, no job, and no place of your own."

"When you put it like that, it doesn't sound good." Harper wrinkled her nose.

"Luke, you just had me draft an office manager job posting, and if you don't show up at Mom and Dad's with Harper tomorrow, Mom has June Tyler on standby."

Luke slammed down his beer. "The June Tyler who I took to a dance in seventh grade? The recently-divorced-with-four-kids June Tyler?"

Sophie nodded. "The very same. Mom figures if you dated her once, you'd date her again."

"Christ," Luke muttered and picked up the beer again.

"Hey, I told you if you didn't start at least pretending to date, Mom was going to take matters into her own hands. She just wants you to be happy."

Luke shook his head and stared out the window.

"Harper, help me out here," Sophie pleaded. "My idiot brother may not see the sense here, but you do, don't you?"

"Are you talking about me pretending to be Luke's girlfriend?"

"In exchange for a temporary job and a place to live."

"How temporary?" Harper mused.

Luke was watching her with an eyebrow raised. "Don't tell me you're even considering this."

"I'm starting to get offended by your reaction to me as a fake girlfriend."

He rolled his eyes. "It's not you, Harper. It's the idea of this act just because *my family* can't deal with the way I live my life."

"News for you, big brother. Last week, I had to stop Aunt Syl from posting an online dating profile for you. Your profile name was 'Handysome.'"

"Shit."

Harper tried to smother a laugh but only succeeded in coughing.

Sophie held up her hands. "Luke, I've held them off as long as I can. It's up to you now."

"How long exactly has it been since you dated, Luke?" Harper interjected.

Luke gave Sophie a long look. "A while," he said.

Harper kept quiet. There was something in that look that made her think this was more than just a meddling mom trying to marry off a holdout bachelor.

"I just thought that this situation might work out for both of you." Sophie walked to him. "What could it hurt, right? And it would just be for a month."

"What happens in a month?" Harper asked.

"Luke's unit ships out. They have a six-month deployment to Afghanistan."

41

Harper felt her stomach flip-flop. He was deploying?

"So what would Harper do at the end of the month?"

Sophie shrugged. "I don't know. You guys could stage an epic breakup fight or something." She turned back to Harper. "If you had a month to make plans, you'd be a lot better off than sleeping on your friend's couch, right?"

Harper shrugged noncommittally. "I suppose more time would mean a better plan." And more time with Luke. Pretending to be his girlfriend. Would that mean she would have the opportunity to kiss him? She bit her lip. A place to stay, a job, and an incredibly hot fake boyfriend for a month? What could go wrong?

Luke swiped a hand over his face and then his short hair. "Have any office management experience, Harper?"

CHAPTER 6

"Y ou don't have to do this, you know." Luke gripped the steering wheel of his truck like it was someone's neck. Five minutes earlier, they had pulled into his parents' driveway, a winding ribbon of asphalt that led to a charming two-story farmhouse with a porch that wrapped around both sides.

Harper bit her lip to keep from smiling. "Luke, they're your family. How bad could they be?"

"You'll see."

She patted his shoulder. "It'll be fine, boyfriend. Or should I start calling you something gross like Lukey Bear?"

He grimaced.

"Poor baby, it'll all be over soon. Let's get in there and get it over with. Unless you just want to hang out here and make out."

"You don't know what they're like."

"Are they mean?"

He shook his head. "More like well meaning. Obsessively so."

"There are worse problems than a family who loves you and wants you to be happy," she said, arching an eyebrow.

"I realize that. I'm just having trouble thinking of any right now."

She pinched him. "I thought you were this big, tough,

manly guy. And here you are cowering in the driveway because you're scared of a little family get-together."

"I'm not scared."

"My mistake." Harper glanced out the window and made a chicken noise.

He sighed and reached over to ruffle her hair. "Come on, *dear*. Let's get this party over with."

"Dear? Seriously? Is that the best you can do?"

They approached the house by way of a meandering walkway. He slung an arm around her shoulder and pulled her closer. He smelled like spices and sawdust. Harper tried to quell the pitter-patter of her pulse. It was just a fake relationship. Nothing to get physically excited about. They were doing each other a favor, not actually banging like red-blooded adults.

"Ready?" he whispered in her ear.

Harper was suddenly the nervous one. "What if they don't like me?" she whispered back.

"Now who's scared? Trust me, you could have two heads and a criminal record and they'd still want to like you."

"Because I'm awesome?"

"Because I'm fake dating you."

Harper snorted.

"Actually, that gives me an idea," he said. "Mind if we have a little fun with this?"

"Oh, way ahead of you. We met online two weeks ago in the Craigslist missed connections," she said.

"I just couldn't say no to your topless profile picture." He guided her up the walk.

"Don't be modest. That shot of you in just a tool belt was pretty spectacular."

They stepped up onto the wide front porch, and Harper saw the lace curtain twitch.

"I think they're watching us," she said without moving her lips.

"Uh-huh," he answered through a jaw-straining fake smile.

Luke pushed the bright red Craftsman-style door open without knocking and found the entire family—all eight of them—standing awkwardly in the airy foyer.

"Hi, guys."

"Hello, sweetheart." A woman with a pixie cut and a soft pink sweater stepped forward to kiss Luke on the cheek. "We were just checking out a squeak in the floor."

"The one that's been there for twenty years?"

The woman ignored him and held her hands out to Harper. "You must be Harper. Since my son's manners seem to have deserted him, I'm his mother, Claire. This is Luke's dad, Charlie," she said, gesturing to the tall, silver-haired man at the back of the pack.

Charlie raised a hand in a silent greeting.

"Our youngest son, James," Claire continued, pointing at a slightly younger, leaner version of Luke who was making short work of an apple. He winked at her. "Sophie you know," Claire put her hands on her daughter's shoulders, and Harper was struck by their resemblance, all dark hair and olive tones. "And this is her husband, Ty Adler, and their little one, Josh."

"Nice to see you again, Slugger," Ty, in a hooded sweatshirt and jeans instead of his deputy's uniform, said while tickling his mini-me toddler on his shoulders.

"This is Uncle Stu and Aunt Syl," Claire said, waving at the mustached man Luke had pointed out at Remo's last night and his smiling, lanky wife. "And I think that takes care of the introductions."

"Hi, um, everyone," Harper said, waving awkwardly. "I'm Harper."

"Hi, Harper," they answered in unison.

Luke sighed and took Harper's hand, leading her through the throng. The floor did, in fact, squeak under her foot.

"Smells good in here, Ma. What's for dinner?"

The crowd filed into the spacious kitchen behind them. Something bubbled away on the granite island's range. Claire slapped Luke's hand away from the glass candy dish.

"Pot roast with mashed potatoes and roasted root vegetables. We'll be ready in about half an hour, so why don't you give Harper the grand tour and get out of my way? Harper, can I get you a glass of wine?"

"I'm fine, Mrs. Garrison. But I really would like that tour."

"It's Claire, please. And you two go ahead. We'll call you when dinner is ready."

"You're finally going to let me have a girl in my room? It's about time." Luke put his hands on Harper's shoulders and pushed her back down the hallway.

"Sorry," he whispered in her ear.

She enjoyed the tickle of his breath against her skin. "That was only a little awkward."

"Awkward and suffocating." He guided her toward the stairs.

The farmhouse was laid out in a simple four-square formation on the first floor with the two rooms on the right opening into each other to create one large gathering room. Pictures plastered the walls and flat surfaces, and there was a mixture of antiques and modern amenities. It was homey.

His hands slid to her hips as she started to climb the stairs. She leaned back against his chest as they ascended.

"If this is too much, tell me," he said. "Soph said to sell it."

"I don't mind," she said, her pulse jumping.

The stairs opened into a wide hallway of sorts with a

46

window seat built over short bookcases. "What a great way to use this space!" Harper leaned down to get a closer look. The shelves were stuffed with paperbacks and photo albums, each neatly labeled with a year range or name.

Luke stuffed his hands in his pockets. "Dad and I built this years ago after Mom ran out of room in the den."

"Can I look at Luke One?" Harper fingered the spine of a navy-blue linen album.

"Uh, sure," he said unenthusiastically.

Harper didn't wait for him to change his mind. She plopped down on the thick cushion of the window seat and began to page through. "You were pretty adorable as a toddler." She peered at a picture of three-year-old Luke trying to put on his father's tool belt, grinning with pride.

He sat down next to her and grimaced. "Why don't we look at Soph's album—"

"Don't even think about it, Handysome."

"Repeat that name again and I'm going to have to murder you."

"Roger that, Lukey Bear," she said, unfazed by the threat. "Oh, look at your first day of kindergarten! That backpack is bigger than you are."

Luke sighed heavily and wiped his hands down his face.

Harper paged through Luke's childhood, pausing to admire his woodworking skills on a birdhouse in Boy Scouts. On the pages of the album, he transformed from a gawky preteen to a hunky teenager. He was captured triumphantly crossing the finish line at a track meet and grinning as he led his football team off the field.

"Wow. You must have broken a lot of teenage girl hearts."

"I'm sure you did your fair share of impressing the boys."

"I was flat-chested and gangly until I was seventeen. It wasn't impressing, it was depressing."

"I'd like to see photographic evidence of that," he teased.

"Thankfully, there is no photographic evidence of my awkward teen years."

"How is that even possible?"

His grin faded when she turned the page.

"Look at you at homecoming!" Harper pulled the album closer and studied Luke in a suit, stoically staring at the camera on a gray speckled backdrop, a gaudy crown perched on his head. He had his arm around a willowy brunette in a sparkling silver gown that perfectly matched the tiara. "Homecoming king and queen? You really had a fairy-tale life, didn't you?"

Luke pulled the album out of her hands and slammed it shut. "We're falling behind on the tour. Let me show you the upstairs, and then I'll introduce you to Mom's chickens."

"Um, okay." Harper was confused by the sudden change in him. He half dragged her away from the window seat and toward the first door.

The quick tour of the upstairs bedrooms revealed spacious rooms with very little clutter. The master was a sunny space with a claw-foot tub in the bathroom. Luke's bedroom had been converted into a sewing room for his mother, and the other two rooms were outfitted as guest bedrooms. It was a tidy home designed around a bustling family life.

The free-range chickens in the backyard were Claire's current pride and joy. The chicken coop that Charlie built was nicer than most of Harper's apartments.

Everything seemed like a fairy tale to Harper and left her wondering what had made Luke distance himself from it all.

———

Luke accepted the basket of rolls from Harper and passed it on to James at his right. He usually didn't mind his family's monthly Sunday meals—too much—but having Harper with him added another dimension.

He watched as she chatted with his father about gardening while making faces at his nephew, who was refusing to eat his turnips. She seemed relaxed, but he knew she couldn't help but notice the long looks from his relatives.

Under the microscope.

He was used to the intense study, having been under it himself for quite some time. But he imagined it was more awkward for someone unaccustomed to it.

Sophie winked at him from across the table and nodded subtly toward Harper. Luke got the message loud and clear. It was the first family meal in a long time that he hadn't had to suffer through poorly disguised fix-ups and casual attempts to discern his mental state.

He just might be getting as much out of this deal as Harper was or at least more than he bargained for.

———

The family adjourned to the deck for slices of the peach pie Harper brought from the grocery store and homemade vanilla ice cream.

"Go easy on that pie, Bro," James teased Luke. "I want you to put up some kind of fight in football before I destroy you."

"Ooooooh," Sophie and Ty cooed tauntingly.

Harper snickered.

"Don't you start, Harper. You're the ref," Luke warned, taking a sip of his beer.

"I want to play!"

"No." His tone left no room for argument. "Not in the shape you're in."

Harper sulked and took another bite of pie.

They picked teams with Sophie and James pitted against Ty and Luke. The game's action quickly escalated from casual fun to all-out war. Competition definitely ran in the Garrison blood, Harper noted, as Luke tripped James after his brother "accidentally" kicked him in the shin.

She stayed on the sidelines and enjoyed the chaos. The players tiptoed around Josh when the toddler chased a chicken across the field of play, and no one batted an eye when Sophie put Ty in a headlock so James could run down the field.

Distracted by Claire asking her if she'd like some coffee, Harper didn't see the freight train of Luke and James hurtling toward her after a long bomb thrown by Ty until it was too late.

Luke caught the ball out of midair, and she saw the exact second when it registered that he was about to crush her.

He twisted open in the air and wrapped one arm around her while cushioning their fall with the other. They landed halfway in one of Claire's flower beds. Surrounded by azaleas, Harper stopped moving under Luke's weight.

His hips pressed into hers, and she forgot all about bruises and the ground beneath her.

"I keep finding you like this," he teased, his breath warm on her face.

"It's nice to not be unconscious this time."

She saw the subtle change in his eyes and held her breath as he lowered his mouth closer to hers. Harper parted her lips.

"Touchdown, Unca Luke!" Josh threw himself on Luke's back.

———

That night, Harper stared into the mirror's reflection as she brushed her teeth. She had wondered if Luke would acknowledge their "moment," but he had simply pulled her to her feet and gone back to the game until it was called on account of darkness and they said their goodbyes.

Claire had wrapped Harper in a gentle hug and told her she was welcome any time. It had been a great day with his family.

Luke rapped on the door. "You decent?"

Harper spit and rinsed. "Yep." She reached for her hairbrush while Luke joined her at the sink.

"I really like your family," she said, tugging the elastic band out of her hair.

Luke shrugged, loading up toothpaste on his brush. "Yeah, they're not bad in small doses."

"Not bad?" She ran the brush through her hair. "Everyone gets along. Your mom's an awesome cook. There was no bloodshed at the table. I'm starting to think you conned me into this charade with a phony story about how crazy they are."

"There's nothing fake about their crazy. They just haven't shown it to you yet," he said, starting to brush.

"Maybe you're just overly sensitive and can't tell normal from crazy anymore," Harper offered.

Luke glared at her in the mirror, and she laughed.

"Anyway, I had a really nice time. It was fun hanging out with everyone talking and eating and picking on each other. I like them a lot."

Luke rinsed and put his toothbrush back in the holder. "They like you." He was quiet for a moment, watching her brush her long hair in the mirror before skirting around her to the doorway. He paused. "Thanks for doing this."

"Don't thank me yet. I might be a disaster at the office tomorrow." She winked, and he turned on a sigh and left the bathroom.

CHAPTER 7

Luke sipped the coffee Harper had brewed while he was out for his run and looked out the back window. He woke up feeling unsettled. He blamed it on the fact that it was the first time he had taken a girl home to meet his parents since... Since.

It was just a month, he reminded himself. Then everything would go back to normal. If another deployment counted as normal.

After that moment with Harper under him in the flowers, it had been a sleepless night. Looking down at her, seeing the surprise, the wonder, in her eyes, it felt like a vision of things to come. Things that couldn't be.

He thought about buying a blow-up mattress and sleeping in one of the spare rooms upstairs, but he liked waking up to Harper plastered against him. He liked knowing she was safe. And feeling those soft curves against him was bringing back to life feelings he thought were long dead. He was playing with fire, but somewhere inside, he didn't care.

He heard the creak of the back porch swing and spotted her, shoulders hunched, swinging in the silence of early dawn.

Luke let himself out onto the back porch. Harper heard his approach and straightened up, swiping a hand over her face.

"Morning," he said, testing the waters.

"Morning." She said it brightly, but she wouldn't look at him. "Just getting an early start for my first day on the job."

He didn't say anything. He knew a crying woman when he saw one, which, growing up with Sophie, had been often.

She jumped up from the swing and tried to step around him. He blocked her and set his coffee down on the railing.

Harper stepped to the other side, and he easily met her. "Harper." He put his hands on her shoulders, and when she still refused to look up, he nudged her chin with his fingers.

The tears in her gray eyes overflowed, coursing down her cheeks as soon as she met his gaze.

"Shit." He pulled her in and rested his chin on her head.

"I'm fine," she mumbled against his bare chest.

"Uh-huh." He held her a little tighter.

"It's nothing."

At least that was what he thought she said. Her voice was muffled. But she wrapped her arms around his waist.

"Okay."

He held her that way, rubbing gentle circles on her back until he felt her breath get deeper.

"You know, Harper, if you really don't want to work for me, you don't have to."

The teasing helped. She leaned back, looking up at him with a watery smile.

"It's not the job. At least not yet. Who knows what kind of work environment you'll provide? I was just having a moment, and now it's over."

"A moment?"

She nodded.

"And now it's over? Just like that?"

Harper nodded again.

"Don't you need to talk about something…or something?"

"Nope." She gave him another sad smile.

"As your fake boyfriend, I should probably know what you're upset about."

Harper laughed. "You're very sweet, and I'm fine. How about some breakfast?" She made a move to step past him, but he stopped her and grasped her wrists. She was clutching a picture in her hand.

"What's this?" He took the picture from her and studied it.

"My parents and me."

A miniature cherub, she was wearing a flowered dress and perched on a bench between a lean man whose smile was almost hidden behind his mustache and a stunning blond in a blue dress. They were all laughing.

"You were a pretty cute kid. Where are they now?"

"They died a long time ago." Harper took the photo from him.

"I'm sorry. How long ago?"

"Nineteen years."

"Jesus, Harper. I'm sorry. What happened?"

"Car accident. Sometimes I still miss them a lot. Especially after spending time with other people's families."

"I've had lots of people cry after spending time with my family."

She poked him. "Funny."

"So who raised you?"

"A lot of different people. I was in foster care until I aged out."

"Aged out?"

"Once you hit eighteen, if you haven't been adopted, you're officially on your own."

"You don't have any family?"

"I make my own family." Harper said it brightly and meant it. "Now, how about I make breakfast? It's a big day today." She laid a hand on his chest. "Thanks for being nice to me, Luke." Harper went up on tiptoe and planted a kiss on his cheek and headed into the kitchen.

———

Luke slapped the cover of his tablet shut and tossed it on the seat next to him. He should be focusing on the task at hand, but instead of reviewing the timeline for the Riggs' addition, he couldn't stop thinking about Harper.

He had given her a cursory tour of the office and left her to set up a workspace. He had a list of office tasks he planned to give her the next day once she'd settled in. After their talk that morning, he wanted to ease her into the job without overwhelming her.

Harper had bounced back, chattering cheerfully about her plans for a quick lunch at Common Grounds while she whipped up omelets and toast. He had let her talk, interjecting appropriate responses, but his mind raced.

She had no one. Hadn't had anyone since she was seven years old, which explained a lot. No wonder she was a walking disaster. She never had a family to keep her out of trouble.

She must have been in the car with her parents. That had to have been when the broken arm and ribs happened. Did she remember it?

How many foster homes had she been through? Who did she spend Christmas with?

Luke dropped his head against the headrest. His own family could drive him crazy, but there wasn't a day that went by that he wasn't grateful for them.

Maybe it was time he started acting like it again. He glanced at his watch. He had enough time before his afternoon meeting to make a few unscheduled stops.

———

Luke pushed open the screen door of his parents' home. "Ma?"

"Back in the kitchen." Her voice floated to him with the scent of fresh baked chocolate.

"I wasn't sure if you worked today," he called, following his nose down the hallway. Claire worked part-time for the florist in town and often got called in for extra shifts.

His mother turned from the oven, clutching a glass dish. "That damn Pinterest. I saw a recipe for mudslide brownies and couldn't help myself. Oh!" She looked at the flowers he was holding. "What are those?"

He held out the lilies to her. "Trade?"

"You brought me flowers?" She put the brownies on the counter and grabbed the bouquet. "What's the occasion?"

His mother's shock and joy were enough to make him feel a little guilty for not thinking to do this sooner.

"No occasion. Just saw them and thought of you."

Claire buried her face in them. "They're beautiful, Luke!"

He scratched the back of his head, embarrassed.

"Do you want to stay for lunch?" Claire offered.

"Can't." Luke checked his watch. "I'm picking Dad up in fifteen for lunch, but I'll take two brownies."

"As long as one of them is for Harper."

Luke smiled. "We'll see if she hasn't run screaming for the hills yet after getting a look at the last six months of unfiled paperwork."

"In that case, I'm packing four brownies, and Harper gets to decide if you get any. She's a lovely girl, Luke. I really like her."

"I do too."

And he meant it.

———

Charlie Garrison was a broad-shouldered man who had worn his silver hair in the same style since the '60s. In homage to the brisk spring temperatures, he had traded his heavy Carhartt for a lighter flannel jacket. He slid into the booth across from Luke and pushed the menu to the edge of the table. He always ordered the same thing. They both did.

Luke accepted the unordered cup of coffee from the waitress and smiled as she slid a Coke into his dad's hands. Claire had a strict no-soda rule for her prediabetic husband that was only broken at the diner.

"The usual, boys?" Sandra asked, not bothering to pull out her notepad.

"Yes, ma'am." Charlie handed her the menus, and she winked as she walked away. A retired elementary school music teacher, Sandra owned the diner and worked the lunch shift four days a week.

Luke leaned back, resting his arm on the back of the booth. "I wonder what she'd do if we ever ordered something different."

"Probably bring us the usual anyway." Charlie plucked the straw out of the glass and put it on the table before taking a deep drink. "So what's the occasion?"

"For lunch?"

"It's been a while."

Luke nodded, toying with his mug. "Yeah." It had been. What years ago had been a standing weekly tradition had slowly morphed into a sporadic occasion.

Sandra mercifully arrived with their food. A tuna melt and fries for Charlie and a bacon cheeseburger for Luke.

"Can I get you boys anything else?"

Charlie shook his head and reached for the ketchup. "No, ma'am."

"Thanks, Sandra," Luke said, hefting the burger.

"All right, try not to cause too much trouble," she said before bustling off to the next booth.

Luke took a big bite of burger and watched his father dig in to his sandwich. "How's the basement reno coming?" While technically retired, his father still liked to oversee a handful of projects every year. His neighbors, the Nicklebees, had hired them to finish their walkout basement.

Charlie took a swig of Coke and reached for a fry. "It's coming along. The wiring's finished, and the plumbing's almost done."

"I saw your note about them adding a wet bar," Luke said between bites.

"Yeah, I gave a copy to Harper this morning so she could update the work order and the estimate."

Luke nodded. He had wondered how long it would take his dad to bring up Harper.

"So what do you think?"

"A wet bar is always a good idea."

"Very funny. I mean of Harper." His father followed the old-school businessman's creed of keeping your opinions under lock and key so as not to offend customers. But he was a fair man, and Luke valued his opinion.

Luke snatched a fry from Charlie's plate.

"Nice kid."

"Yes, she is. Don't you think I moved her in awfully quick?"

"Son, you could have moved in Angry Frank, and I'd be happy. You have good timing. Your mom was getting ready to start calling cousins to set you up with."

Luke felt himself go pale. "Isn't that illegal?"

"They were mostly seconds and thirds," Charlie quipped. He grinned, showing a dimple just like Luke's.

"Christ." Luke grabbed for his coffee and leaned back.

"A mother's love is a blessing and a curse," Charlie said philosophically. "She was just worried."

Luke scrubbed a hand over his head. "I know, and I appreciate it. But there's nothing to worry about. I'm fine. Everything is fine."

"I'll relay that to your mother. She likes Harper. Thinks she's just what you need."

"What? Barely controlled chaos?" Luke's lips quirked.

"'A breath of fresh air,' I believe she said."

"She's more like a hurricane."

"She's definitely not Karen."

Luke felt the familiar stab at the mention of her name. It had dulled over the years, but the wound was still there. It would never be gone. "No, she's not."

"That's not a bad thing. Karen would never have taken on Glenn."

Luke smiled in spite of himself, remembering the surprise in those big gray eyes when they opened to find him over her. "No, she wouldn't have."

"Did you get the numbers together on the Broad Street reno proposal?"

Luke knew his dad was changing the subject on purpose and was grateful. "I put some preliminary figures together but nothing solid yet."

"Well, we have until Monday to turn in the bid. Maybe Harper can help you over the weekend."

It was weird to think that he now shared his weekends with someone, at least temporarily. He had grown to value his solitude, but there was something appealing about waking up to her in the mornings. It still gave him a little jolt to find her in the kitchen digging through the fridge or hunched over his laptop in the front room. She brought life to the house. He just wasn't sure if he was ready for that.

"She's got her hands full at the office. Have to see if she's ready for me to dump another project on her."

CHAPTER 8

Harper shoved her hands through her hair, hastily pulling it up in a messy knot. Luke's files were a disaster. Nothing had been updated in the system for the past eight weeks. There were piles of disorganized paperwork everywhere. And the database was a joke. But she loved a project.

The office was on the second floor of one of the brick buildings in downtown Benevolence. It had high ceilings and huge half-circle windows that filtered sunlight onto the scarred, wide-plank hardwood floors.

She huddled over an old drawing table she had repurposed as a desk. She set it up in a corner and angled it to have a line of sight into Luke's office. Not that he was in there now. And from the looks of the stacks of paperwork covering every flat surface including the floor, he probably didn't spend much time there.

Harper moved the now neatly organized stack of files to the edge of the desk and reached for a new pile. She liked being here. Liked being surrounded by Luke's work. When he said he was in construction, he left out that he ran a ridiculously successful contracting and building firm.

Digging through the files, she discovered that both the

bank on Second Street and the sprawling farmhouse on the outskirts of town that she had admired were Garrison projects.

Where some men couldn't shut up about every minor accomplishment of their day, Luke was a vault. He could thwart a bank robbery and deliver a baby on his lunch break and the only thing he'd volunteer was that he had a BLT.

It only made her want to pry information out of him.

Harper jumped as a brown paper bag landed on the keyboard in front of her.

"Mom sends her best," Luke said from behind her.

Harper pounced on the bag. "What. Are. These. Never mind, don't tell me." She unwrapped a brownie and took a bite. "Mmm. Heaven!"

"She said you could share if you want to," he hinted.

She eyed him over her brownie. "Let's see if you've earned it. Did you save any old ladies from harm's way?"

"No, but I didn't put any in harm's way either."

"Good enough for me." She handed him a brownie. She watched him unwrap it and take a manly bite. "How's your day so far, boss?"

"Not too bad. Just checking up on a new employee, making sure she's not painting her nails and napping on the company's dime."

Harper wrinkled her nose at him. "Speaking of work, you should meet my boss. What a whip-cracker."

Hmm, Luke with a whip. That was pretty hot. Hotter if he was shirtless.

Oblivious to her fantasy, Luke eyed her desk setup. "Have everything you need here?"

She kicked back in her chair and took another bite of brownie. "I think I can get by for the next month. And when I leave, you're going to miss me."

"We'll see." He said it with a smile.

A shrill jingle interrupted them. Harper snatched her cell phone off the desk and groaned.

She answered it with a vicious swipe. "Stop calling me," she shouted into the phone and hung up.

"Problem?"

Harper rolled her eyes. "It's Mr. Can't Keep His Dick in His Pants."

Luke frowned. "How many times has he called you?"

She scrolled to her call history. "Only twenty-three since Friday night."

"Is he leaving voicemails?"

Harper adopted a slightly slurred baritone. "Oh baby, I want you back. Tiffany means nothing to me. Do you know where my Batman shirt is?"

Her phone shrilled again, and Luke snatched it out of her hands. "Do you want him to stop calling you?"

"Uh, *yeah*! How are you going to make that happen?"

"I'm your fake boyfriend. I have many powers." Luke straightened away from the desk and answered the phone.

He walked a few paces away, and Harper strained to listen. He stood with a wide stance, hand on hip, staring out the window. There was always such an intensity about him. Power and control were the driving forces behind everything he did.

Luke rarely divided his attention, making it seem like he was always fully focused on the task at hand. It was that focus that Harper felt every time he looked at her. She felt important. Worthy. Interesting.

And now the man who made her feel important, worthy, and interesting was in a conversation with the man who treated her as replaceable.

Luke hung up and walked back to Harper. He tossed her the phone.

"Well?" she asked.

"He won't be calling you anymore, and he's sending your last paycheck here to the office."

Harper jumped out of her chair and whooped. She tossed her arms around his neck and planted a smacking kiss on his cheek, savoring the feel of his stubble under her lips. "I'm taking you out to dinner with that paycheck."

His hands settled on her waist and held. "Don't you think I should pay for our first date?"

"An unconventional relationship calls for unconventional etiquette. Besides, we've already slept together, and you brought me brownies. That your mother made for me. We're practically engaged."

He looked nervous again. She could tell he wanted to back up and get some space between them. Harper liked that she could make him a little uncomfortable. It partially made up for the pointy butterflies that went careening around her stomach when he looked at her with those soulful eyes.

"We'll see," he said, stepping back. "I'm going to get some paperwork done and head out again. Need anything?"

"Nope. I'm good." And she meant it. She watched Luke head into his office and smiled. This was her life now, at least for the next month. A good job in a great office with a boss and roommate so good-looking she couldn't stop staring at him.

She tried to focus on her work but felt her attention pulled to the office in the corner. She had a direct line of sight to Luke at his desk, frowning at his computer screen, kicking back in his chair to make a call. Every glance or two, she found him already looking at her. Maybe he was as disconcerted around

64

her as she was around him? Every time one of them caught the other looking, Luke's frown deepened.

After nearly half an hour of mutual sneaked peeks, Luke pushed back from his desk and grabbed a stack of paperwork and his tablet.

"I'm heading out to a meeting. I probably won't be back in after it."

"Okay, boss, have a good day." Harper smiled. She tried to keep her eyes on her monitor instead of his ass as he walked out. It wasn't easy.

Harper got in almost another hour of work before she was interrupted again.

A short, slim man in blue flannel sauntered in, suspenders holding up his carpenter pants. Weathered blue eyes stared at her above a frizzy beard that was more gray than red.

"So you're the girl who's got the whole town riled up," he said, crossing his arms.

Harper raised her eyebrows. "It's a small town. I have a feeling it doesn't take much to rile it."

He squinted at her. "The way I heard it, you're supposed to be six foot one. And a redhead."

"Sorry to disappoint."

"I do like redheads." He shook his head, clearly disappointed.

Harper didn't know how to respond to that.

"I can't decide if you're stupid or crazy," he said, leaning against the cabinets on the wall.

"Is there an HR department here that I should complain to about you?"

He snorted. "Don't be so sensitive."

"Wait a minute. Do you even work here?"

He snorted again. "Do *I* work here? I've been with this company since Luke started it, and before that, I worked for Charlie."

"Got a name?"

"Frank."

"Frank, I'm Harper."

"The boss moved you in awful fast, don't you think?"

"To his house or the office?" Crap. Three days with Luke, and he already had her answering questions with questions.

"What I'm saying is the boss had his reasons for taking you in, giving you a job. I'm not here to question his judgment—questionable though it may be. I'm here to warn you that if you mess with this company or that family, you'll answer to me. They've all been through enough these past years and don't need some crazy hothead coming in and messing things up for them."

"You think I'm a crazy hothead?"

"You tackled a man twice your size screaming like a banshee, didn't you? You've got that fist-sized black eye. Rolled into town homeless."

"Maybe I just had a bad day."

"Yeah, well, maybe so. Just don't go taking that bad day out on everyone else around here. This is a nice town, nice people. So if you're not in it for the long haul, move along."

"You must care about the Garrisons a lot to feel like you have to defend them from a potential threat like me."

"They're okay. Maybe you're okay too. But I don't know you. I do know Luke and the rest of them. So if you're good to them and stay out of my way on the job, we'll be just fine."

"Fair enough, Frank. I'll keep that in mind. And just so you know, if you're good at your job, not pissing off customers or coming in here and yelling at me every day, we'll be fine."

He nodded briskly. "Fair enough. Be seeing you." He threw a little salute and walked out the door.

This town was way too small.

CHAPTER 9

As promised, Harper's last paycheck arrived at the office. Whatever Luke said to Ted must have scared him bad enough to stop calling too, because her phone was blissfully silent.

And as promised, she took Luke to dinner.

She researched restaurants beyond the borders of Benevolence before settling on a cozy steak place fifteen miles east. There would be no quiet dinner in town with the attention she and Luke stirred up.

It wasn't a "real" date, she reminded herself, but that didn't mean she couldn't go to a little extra effort to be presentable.

Harper kept her outfit casual with capris and a ribbed V-neck in emerald green. She added a little more curl to her hair, letting it hang loosely past her shoulders. A hint of smoky eye and a slick of lip gloss, and she was ready to go.

She checked her reflection in the powder room downstairs and realized she had forgotten to put in earrings. She went back upstairs to the bedroom and was rummaging through the drawer when Luke came in from the bathroom.

Wearing only a towel.

Droplets of water clung to his chest. The ink on his arms,

as always, drew her eye. The towel hung indecently low on his hips, showing off the plains of his chiseled abs.

The silver hoop she was holding slipped through her fingers and clattered on the floor.

"I…uh…" She stooped and picked up the earring. "Um. Sorry."

Cheeks flaming, she hurried out of the room, leaving Luke grinning after her.

Harper dashed into the kitchen and stuck her face in the freezer to cool the blush until she heard him on the stairs. She made a show of filling and drinking a glass of water from the faucet and avoided eye contact when he came into the kitchen.

"Ready to go?" he asked, sliding his hands in the pockets of his jeans.

He was wearing jeans and a gray striped button-down with the sleeves rolled up. Harper wondered if he had just reached into his closet and grabbed or if he, like her, had gone through several options. Either way, he looked good enough to undress right here in the kitchen.

"Sure, let's go."

She led him outside to her car in the driveway. Luke paused next to the Beetle. "You want me to ride in this?"

"I asked you out. Therefore, I'm driving."

"Okay." He folded himself into the passenger seat with a wry smile. "Let's get this date started."

Harper felt a nervous flutter in her belly. When was her body going to remember that this wasn't a real relationship? It should stop overreacting to the stimulus that was Luke Garrison. She sighed and climbed in behind the wheel, trying to ignore how close they were and how good he smelled. She should have let him drive. The center console of Luke's truck provided a better barrier.

The Beetle started with a coughing tremor that had Luke's eyebrows raising. A belt squealed under the hood for a few seconds before Harper shifted into reverse.

"Jesus, what's wrong with this thing?"

"Don't listen to him." Harper patted the steering wheel. "You're perfect the way you are."

"Baby, this car is older than you are. Don't you think it's time to put it out to pasture? Maybe get something less like a tin can?"

"I love this car. She just needs a little maintenance, which I'm saving up for, and she'll be good as new."

"How many times has it let you sit on the side of the road?"

Harper cranked up the radio and grinned. "What? I can't hear you. Radio's too loud."

He shook his head and shifted in his seat. His knee grazed her hand as it rested on the gearshift. Neither made the effort to move.

Luke finally leaned forward and punched the button, turning the music off.

"So how are things going at the office?"

In just a few days, Harper had made a significant dent in the back work, but there was much more to be done. "Good so far."

"Any areas you see we need to improve on yet?"

Harper glanced at him to see if he was joking. "You want my opinion?"

"You sound surprised."

She tried to remember the last time a guy had asked her opinion. Ted certainly was never interested at work or at home. When she tried to talk to him about changing his bookkeeping software, he told her not to worry her pretty little head about it.

"I've only been there two days."

"You're a smart girl." Luke poked her leg, and Harper prayed he didn't see the goose bumps that cropped up everywhere from his touch. "Don't hold back. You won't hurt my feelings."

Harper eyed him suspiciously. "Okay." She cleared her throat. "There's a few areas that could stand some attention."

"Go on."

"Well, your software is pretty old-school. I think we could find some kind of integrated package that would replace your job costing and invoicing systems, plus your database, with one Swiss army knife tool that does it all. So you'd only have to enter changes once instead of two or three difference places. It shouldn't cost much more than you're spending now, and you could really develop a CRM."

"CRM?"

"Customer relationship management system. Say Frank is on the job site and a client mentions they're thinking about upgrading to granite in the bathrooms. Frank can grab his iPad or laptop and plug that into the system so it kicks a notice back to the office to price out the upgrade. The next day, the pricing and options are in the CRM and Frank can walk through it with the client."

Luke nodded. "It's not a bad idea."

"It's better than Frank forgetting all about it and the client changing his mind and sticking with whatever the regular countertop is."

"What else can a CRM do?"

Harper took a deep breath and launched into the basics. She could tell she was losing him when his frown deepened. "Just think of it as a robot assistant," she said.

Luke nodded. "I like robots."

"So tell me about Frank. What's his deal?" She adjusted the visor against the sun.

70

"You mean, why is he so pissed off all the time?" Luke grinned behind his sunglasses. "It's just part of his charm. He giving you trouble?"

"Not really. I kind of like him. I was just curious. He seems…"

"Insubordinate?" he supplied.

"Well, yeah."

Luke sighed. "Frank and I go way back. I've known him since I was a kid. He's a good worker. One of the best. He knows more about the ins and outs of this business than anyone. He's just a loudmouth pain in the ass."

Harper snorted.

"How is it working with your dad?"

Luke shrugged. "It's good." Harper looked at him pointedly, waiting for him to continue. "He ran a contracting business for years and I always knew I wanted to build. So about ten years ago, we decided to give it a go and started the company."

"You're awfully nonchalant about it."

Luke grinned. "About what?"

"I've only had a peek at your books and the incoming checks, but it looks like you're quite the thriving builder, buddy," she teased.

"We do okay." He smirked.

Harper rolled her eyes. Since when did she find smirking sexy? Since right now, apparently.

"With as busy as you are, how did you not already have a full-time office manager?"

Luke shrugged. "We really started growing about three years ago. And Beth—you'll meet her later—used to be full-time office help until she had the twins. Now she's part-time and just does the bookkeeping."

Harper slowed and pulled into a gravel lot. Luke took in

71

the renovated barn that backed up to grassy fields. The smell of steak hung thick in the air.

"Nice place. What made you pick it?"

It was Harper's turn to smirk. "I thought we'd draw less attention here than Benevolence."

"Good call."

"Are you some kind of famous bachelor or hometown hero? Everyone seems to be incredibly interested in you."

His gaze leveled with hers, but instead of the laugh she expected, she saw a coolness. "Have people been talking?"

Harper tilted her head. "Talking about what?"

"Nothing." His demeanor changed and he reached over to squeeze her leg. "Come on. I'll let you buy me dinner."

The hostess, a tiny pixie with dark-framed glasses and purple streaks in her hair, led them back to a cozy corner booth next to a window overlooking a pasture and a pond. The sun was just beginning to sink behind the trees.

Luke glanced around at the textured walls of stone and plaster and the thick ceiling beams. "Nice place."

"I thought you might like it," Harper said, grabbing the beer list. "Meat and a cool building seemed like the right way to say thank you for everything."

"Are you ever going to stop thanking me?"

"Are you ever going to stop doing things that deserve gratitude?" She batted her eyelashes.

"Smart-ass." Luke grinned.

They ordered draft beers and steaks as a small band set up in the adjoining room.

"So tell me about yourself, Harper," Luke said, stretching his arm across the back of the booth.

"You're taking this date thing pretty seriously. What do you want to know?"

The waitress returned with their beers, and Harper took a sip.

"Well, we are fake dating, so I should know some things about you. Like, when's your birthday? Where did you go to school? What was it like growing up without parents? Why are you the way you are?"

Harper laughed. "That's a lot of questions." She snagged his beer and sampled it before sliding it back across the table.

Luke spun the glass around before picking it up, tasting. Harper wondered if he purposely drank from the same spot she did. "I find you interesting."

"That sounds like it's not really a compliment."

"I also find you smart, beautiful, funny, and brave. But I can't figure you out. How does someone who goes through everything you've gone through walk around with a permanent smile on her face?"

"You mean because of my parents?"

"Your parents, the fire, your idiot of an ex. Your resiliency is impressive. How does that happen?"

"It's not really impressive when there isn't another option. What am I supposed to do, be all 'woe is me' for the rest of my life? I still get access to the same sunrises everyone else does, the same twenty-four hours in a day. And if I don't take advantage of those things, it's my own fault."

"So the world is too big and beautiful to be sad?" He was teasing her.

"I can still be sad. But I don't have to wallow or completely ignore the good that is still waiting for me. That's careless and wasteful."

Luke was silent for a moment, twisting his glass on the tabletop.

"Also, since you asked, my birthday is March third. I went

to the University of Maryland and got a bachelor's in business. I'm halfway through my MBA online. And growing up without parents was hard. Every holiday, every birthday, graduation, I'm always acutely aware that I'm missing something. Someone."

Luke nodded. "Favorite color?"

"Red. But not a maroon or pinky red. Blood red. Do I get to ask you questions?"

Luke shook his head. "Let's focus on you."

"Nice try. What was it like growing up with parents? And having a brother and sister?"

"Chaos. You've been to Sunday dinner."

Harper tossed her napkin at him. "I'm serious!"

"So am I." But he relented. "I don't know. Sometimes I wished that I could just be alone, and other times I was grateful to have them all over me. We're close. Sometimes too close. But I grew up with my dad at every football game. I sat through all Sophie's dance recitals. James and I spent every summer barefoot and playing in the creek from dawn to dusk. Mom forced us to sit down at the table every night. Sometimes it was four thirty, and sometimes we didn't eat until nine, but we were all there together."

Harper smiled. "That sounds how I always imagined it."

"Didn't you ever live with other kids?"

"Sure, but it's just different. I was only there temporarily. Some of the homes had a ton of kids, so there wasn't enough time to pay attention to us all. Others had biological or adopted kids who were in established routines and activities, and that took precedence. Most of the time, I was just lost in the shuffle."

"And you wanted more."

Harper nodded. She had desperately wanted more. Still did.

"Don't you?"

"Sometimes."

She laughed. "You like your nice, quiet life."

Luke cracked a smile. "It's not very quiet these days."

"Are you nervous about deploying?"

He sliced into a roll, buttered it. "No."

"Have you been to Afghanistan before?"

"Yes."

"Chatty Cathy over here."

"What did you see in this Ted guy?"

He changed the subject with no attempt at subtlety, and Harper decided to give him a break. But it necessitated a large gulp of beer. "Ugh. I've been asking myself that. My friend Hannah warned me. I was new on the job. I thought he was cute except for the goatee. He seemed like he was a good boss. And then he started bringing me coffee in the mornings. Sending me funny emails…"

"You're a hearts and flowers girl."

"If by 'hearts and flowers,' you mean a romantic, then yes. I still believe there's a guy out there who's going to sweep me off my feet and live happily ever after with me."

Luke smirked. "The knight in shining armor who rides in to save the day."

"I don't know about *that*. Sometimes you have to save yourself or someone else. But I wouldn't mind riding off into the sunset with someone."

"You women and your desire for grand romantic gestures."

Harper laughed. "Please, the only time a woman needs a grand romantic gesture is when she doesn't know she's loved."

"I'm not buying that. What about the girls who pick out their own fifteen-thousand-dollar engagement ring and demand a wedding for four hundred guests?"

"Apples to oranges. There's a difference between being on

75

the receiving end of a grand romantic gesture and demanding to be the very expensive center of attention. On one hand, you have someone who wants to make sure that you know beyond a shadow of a doubt how they feel about you. On the other hand, some poor schmuck is just buying a gimme girl off with sparkly presents and lots of attention."

"A gimme girl? Now that paints a picture." Luke laughed, and Harper warmed at the sight of his dimple.

The waitress returned with their food, and the subject was dropped while they dug in. They enjoyed their meal and made small talk about work, food, and Benevolence. She felt relaxed, remarkably, considering that most of her time with Luke was spent wavering between extremes of nervousness and lust.

It was a constant battle that she hoped would dull soon. It was embarrassing that every time she saw him shirtless, she had to stop herself from licking her lips.

The band in the other room switched to a slower tune. Harper gasped as the first few chords of the Jeff Healey Band's "Angel Eyes" echoed through the room. "I love this song, Luke! This is my all-time favorite romantic fantasy song. Dance with me?"

"Romantic fantasy?"

"There are all kinds of fantasies, Luke. Romantic, orgasmic…"

"No one else is dancing."

"Who cares? We don't know anyone here. What's the worst that could happen?"

"Is that how you make decisions? 'What's the worst that could happen?'" he mimicked, tossing imaginary long hair.

Harper ignored his question and tugged him out of the booth toward the floor in front of the band. He was right. No one else was dancing, but someone always had to be first.

Luke's grip stopped her where she was, and he pulled her back into his arms. Her breasts flattened against his warm, solid chest, their mouths an inch apart. Luke's hands splayed across her back, holding her to him.

"You're not dancing," he whispered.

She could almost taste his words.

Harper bit her lip to keep from biting his and wound her arms around his neck. She didn't have to pull him closer. He came willingly.

He led, and she followed. Her attention was on every sensation that touching him ignited. One hand slid higher to rest gently over her bruised ribs, his palm and thumb intimately hugging the curve of her breast.

She knew he could feel her heart pounding, knew he could hear her short breaths.

They swayed together, oblivious to anything but the music and each other. Luke pulled her closer. She could feel the length of him hardening against her.

"Stop looking at me like that," he growled.

"Like what?" Her voice was breathless.

"Like you want me to take your clothes off and taste every inch of your body."

She felt the dull ache at her core increase to a steady, hollow throb. He was a freaking mind reader.

"I wasn't thinking that," she lied. "I was thinking about… dessert."

"Liar." His hand skimmed the swell of her breast on its way up to gently brush her hair back from her face. He grinned when she gave a breathy gasp. His erection twitched against her, and she knew she wasn't the only one thinking about…dessert.

She didn't notice when the song ended, but Luke did.

Hands on her shoulders, he pushed her back a step,

breaking the spell. Harper's cheeks flushed. She had completely lost track of their surroundings. She hadn't even noticed that other couples had joined them on the floor.

Luke kept her hand and led her back to the table.

"Well, that was some fantasy," she sighed, sliding back into the booth, her face still red.

"We should probably head back. I have an early day tomorrow."

His tone was flat, but his voice was rough. There was something going on beneath the surface, but Harper couldn't tell what it was.

The check was waiting for them, and when Harper reached for it, Luke snatched it out of her grip. "Not gonna happen, sweetheart."

"I asked you to dinner. This is my treat," Harper said, reaching across the table.

"No." It was a refusal more solid than the stone walls surrounding them.

"Luke—" she tried again.

"Harper. No. Now finish your beer."

She frowned at him. One little physical reaction, and he turned into a statue.

———

Luke kept Harper's hand in his and half dragged her to the parking lot where the sound of crickets was carried on cool air. He pulled her toward the Beetle's passenger door. "I'll drive." He stopped her before she opened the door by putting his hand on it. "Look, I have to set something straight here." Harper leaned back against the car, and Luke shoved his hands in his pockets. "This can't happen."

"What exactly can't happen?" She looked amused.

He glared at her. She was going to make him say it. "We can't complicate things with sex."

"What's so complicated about sex?"

"Harper," he growled.

"Sorry. Please continue." She smiled, and he wanted to throttle her.

"I don't want you to get the wrong idea and think that we're going to start some romantic affair—"

Her eyes widened. "Who said anything about an affair or a relationship, which I'm sure is your bigger concern? You're leaving. I'm leaving. That doesn't mean I don't like how I feel when you touch me. Because I really do. It makes me wonder."

"Wonder what?" He knew he was stepping onto very unsteady ground. He was already standing too close to her. He couldn't ever seem to make himself put distance between them.

Harper put her arms around his neck, pulling him closer until her breasts rubbed against him. "I wonder what it would feel like if we kissed." Her voice was whisper soft, full lips parted, inviting him in.

He stopped breathing. He could have pushed her back, told her to knock it off. He should have. But he stood his ground and let her rise up on her toes to bring those soft lips to his, because there wasn't anything in that moment that he wanted more.

Her eyes fluttered closed, and she gave a sexy little sigh.

That was all it took for him to stop fighting it. He brought his hand to her hair and yanked it back to get better access to that sweet mouth. His tongue boldly stroked past her parted lips, finding hers eager for him. Tasting her did nothing to mellow the kiss. His mouth crushed down on hers, and he used his tongue to thrust in over and over again, mimicking the strokes with his hips.

Harper's arms tightened around his neck, and he growled. His hands streaked up her sides under her tight little sweater, and his fingertips felt lace.

He felt it before he saw it. The slight wince as his hand cruised over her sore ribs.

He pulled back immediately. Cursing himself and maybe her too, he yanked the passenger door open and manhandled her into the seat.

Ten minutes down the road, his cock was still painfully hard. He had almost mauled her in the parking lot. Had he not seen that wince of pain when he pressed too hard against her side, he would have found a way to fuck her right there in the parking lot. His lack of control was humiliating. He forgot that she was hurt. Forgot the rules that he had carefully laid out, the plan that he had been following for years. All of it out the window because he couldn't stop touching her.

He shouldn't be having this physical of a reaction to her. And yet here he was, walking around with a hard-on every time he saw her.

Leaning over the counter in the kitchen in her little shorts? Hard. Prancing around in his white T-shirt that she still slept in? The white T-shirt that did nothing to hide her perfect tits that begged for his hands? And every pair of sexy little underwear she wore underneath? Raging hard. He was afraid that she'd never start sleeping in something he couldn't see through or, worse, that she would.

If he was within three feet of her, he was fucking hard. How was he supposed to survive a month-long erection? Maybe he should see a doctor.

He was a ticking time bomb. If he did fuck her, there was a good chance he might kill her. He wanted to believe that his reaction to her was because it had been so long. But he knew that was a lie. There was something about Harper that drew him in and tied him up.

"Are you mad?" Harper, her lips still full and flushed from his assault, asked from the passenger seat.

He didn't answer her but gripped the gearshift a little harder.

"I'm sorry for coming on so strong, Luke. I didn't mean to upset you. I just wanted to see what it would be like to kiss you. I promise to be more respectful of your feelings."

She was promising to be more respectful of *his* feelings? He was the one who mauled her like a rabid teenager.

"Harper—"

"I'm really sorry." Those big gray eyes were staring at him contritely.

"What exactly are you sorry for?"

"For making you kiss me when you didn't want to. I thought that you were attracted to me like I am to you. It didn't occur to me that you weren't, and then I practically ate your face with my tongue. I don't usually try to devour men like that."

"You think I'm not attracted to you?"

"Isn't that why you gave me the whole 'no sex' talk?"

Luke pulled the clunking Beetle over abruptly and came to a stop on the side of the road. "Harper, it's not possible for me to be more physically attracted to you than I am. It's a constant battle of self-control to not rip your clothes off and slam my dick into you just to feel you come on me."

Harper's jaw fell open.

"See? Those are the kinds of thoughts that go through my head when I'm around you. You make me hard and stupid, and I don't like it."

"But if you want me, and I want you, then why —"

"Baby, I just can't. I'm not...ready. And if I were, you

would be the first to know it. But I just can't take my focus off work and deploying. I know that if I were inside you, I'd lose complete fucking control, and that can't happen. I just don't have room in my life for you."

Harper finally closed her mouth and looked down at her hands clasped in her lap.

Luke reached over and took one of her hands. "You are a beautiful, sweet, sexy girl, and someone is going to be very lucky to be devoured by you. It just can't be me. So I'd appreciate it if you'd start wearing parkas and shit around me so I don't keep fantasizing about your hot body."

"So you do want me, and I am offering myself to you with no strings attached, but you want your order and focus more?"

He squeezed her hand. "When you put it that way, it sounds really stupid."

"You're a complicated man, Luke."

CHAPTER 10

Luke kept his distance from her at work, and that was fine with Harper. She felt guilty for pushing him and disappointed that Luke wasn't willing to explore the attraction that they both felt.

She was surprised to see his truck in the driveway when she got home. She felt like she was unintentionally chasing him out of his own house, so maybe this was a good sign.

Harper let herself in and took the grocery bags back the hall to the kitchen. There was no sign of Luke in the house, but she heard voices coming from somewhere.

She let herself out the back door onto the porch and spotted Luke at the far end of the yard. He was standing in a loose triangle with two boys. They all had baseball gloves.

"You've got to tighten up on that grip when you throw it, Robbie," Luke instructed the taller boy with sandy, shaggy hair. "Here, let me show you."

She watched him demonstrate the grip and hand the ball over.

"Give it a shot." Luke jogged back to his spot. "Let 'er rip."

The boy wound up and released a perfect curving pitch that smacked into Luke's glove.

"Yeah, baby! Did you see that?" The boy hooted and sprinted to Luke.

"Now that's a curve," Luke laughed. They fist-bumped, and Luke tossed the ball back to him. "Try it again. Make sure it's not a fluke."

Robbie hustled back to his spot and adjusted his hold on the ball. He fired another pitch into Luke's glove.

"Me next! Me next!" The smaller boy threw his glove in the air. "Mr. Luke, I want to throw."

Luke repeated the process with the younger brother. He didn't quite get it but seemed proud of his effort.

"Mr. Luke, there's a lady on your porch," Robbie said, pointing at Harper.

Harper waved and walked down the steps to the patio. Luke met her with the boys, Robbie at his side and the younger one tossed over his shoulder.

God, he looked good. He was wearing worn jeans, a white fitted T-shirt, and a baseball cap. But nothing was sexier than the grin on his face.

"Hey," he said, dropping the boy at her feet.

"Hey," she laughed when he scrambled to his feet in a fit of giggles.

"Harper, these are my friends Robbie and Henry. They're brothers, and they live two houses down with Mrs. Agosta."

Mrs. Agosta was Dominican and closing in on seventy. Harper was pretty sure she wasn't the boys' mother.

"Guys, this is my friend, Harper."

"Hi," Robbie said, holding out a hand. He had earnest green eyes and a smattering of freckles across his nose.

"Nice to meet you, Robbie." Harper took his hand. "Hi, Henry."

Henry, a miniature version of his brother, waved

cheerfully, and his smile showed that he was missing a front tooth.

"Robbie and Henry are hanging out while Mrs. Agosta takes their sister to the doctor."

"Her snot's green. It's gross," Henry announced, tossing his glove in the air.

"Wow, that is gross," Harper agreed. "Do you guys want to stay for dinner?"

"What are you having?" Robbie asked.

Luke cuffed him on the back of the head.

"What?" Robbie asked. "I don't want to stay if it's, like, liver and garbage."

Luke wrapped him in a headlock. "You're such a little jerk," he said, ruffling Robbie's hair.

"Burgers, tater tots, and salad." Harper ticked off on her fingers. "Is that better than liver and garbage?"

"Well, the burgers and tater tots are," Robbie agreed.

"I love tater tots," Henry squealed. He launched himself at Harper's legs for a quick hug before spinning off to tag his brother. "You're it," he shouted.

The boys tore off in a high-energy game of tag, leaving Harper and Luke alone on the patio.

"Sorry about that. I should have texted you to warn you about the extra testosterone."

"It's a nice surprise. Besides, two extra mouths will go further on the eight-pack of burgers I brought home."

"I'll fire up the grill." He grinned. "Good luck talking them into the salad."

———

Harper did talk them into the salad but had to promise they could each pick an ingredient before they agreed. Harper chose tomatoes. Robbie wanted bacon. Henry decided on Cheetos.

"Can we really do that?" Robbie whispered over the counter with concern.

Harper shrugged. "Maybe they'll taste like croutons?"

She put Henry in charge of putting the tater tots on the baking sheet and Robbie rinsing the lettuce while she fried the bacon and diced tomatoes.

"Do you live here with Mr. Luke?" Henry asked, adjusting the last tater tot.

"I do."

"Are you married?"

"Nope. Are you?"

Henry frowned. "No. Girls are gross."

"Robbie, do you think girls are gross?" Harper asked as he brought the lettuce back to the counter and dumped it in a large bowl.

He shrugged. "Some of them are okay, I guess."

Harper put the tater tots in the oven and set the timer. "So is Mrs. Agosta your grandma?" she asked the boys.

"Huh-uh." Robbie shook his head. "We're not even related."

"We're fosters," Henry piped up, carefully placing Cheetos on the lettuce.

"Me too," Harper said, adding the tomatoes and the bacon to the salad.

"You're a foster kid?" Robbie's interest was piqued.

"Yep."

"Is Mr. Luke your foster dad?" Henry asked.

Robbie rolled his eyes. "No, dummy, they're boyfriend-girlfriend." Harper didn't bother correcting him. The truth would only confuse them…and her.

"Did you get real parents?" Henry wondered.

Harper shook her head. "No, I didn't get adopted. But I got to meet a lot of nice families."

"Mrs. Agosta is nice. She's teaching us Spanish. Do you think we'll get 'dopted?"

Harper paused mid salad toss. Luke, holding a plate of burgers, had come in the back door just in time to hear Henry's question.

The boys were watching her closely, and she knew what they wanted. She had wanted it too. Sometimes still wanted it. Hope.

"Well, you're not overly smelly." She poked Henry in the belly until he giggled. "And you're kind of cute. You seem nice. You haven't destroyed Mr. Luke's house yet. So yeah, you'll have a family. And in the meantime, you get to stay with nice Mrs. Agosta and learn Spanish."

"I can count!" Henry announced. "*Uno, dos, tres...*" He counted out each Cheeto as he placed it on the salad.

"Burgers are done," Luke said, finally venturing past the doorway.

"Awesome," Robbie said, sniffing the air. "I love burgers. Do you have ketchup and mustard? Is there cheese?"

Harper took her time counting out four plates as the boys chattered to Luke. She hoped for their sake that there was a family out there looking for three kids.

———

They ate at the breakfast bar with the boys sitting on stools and Harper and Luke standing. Harper and the kids traded funny stories about foster care. The Cheetos salad turned out to be a hit. Even Robbie cleaned his bowl.

Harper and Luke let themselves be talked into going for ice cream before taking the boys home. Their sister, Ava, a tiny

87

dark-haired version of her brothers, was sound asleep on the couch when they arrived at Mrs. Agosta's house. Diagnosed with a sinus infection, she would be good as new in a few days. Mrs. Agosta thanked them profusely for helping and sent them home with fresh blueberry muffins.

They walked home in silence with the sunset blazing in the western sky. It was nice having the boys over, Harper thought as she mounted the porch steps. Their chatter and energy covered up the low hum of conflict that constantly buzzed between her and Luke.

Something was going to have to change and fast.

"You're really good with them," Luke said, dropping down on the top step.

Harper paused and leaned against the railing. She knew what he was doing, even if he wasn't aware. The pull between them only strengthened behind closed doors. Outside was safer.

"You too. Nice coaching on the curve ball."

Luke smiled. "They're really good kids." He took off his hat and toyed with it. "Did you mean what you said? That you think they'll find a family?"

Harper sat down next to him and sighed. "It's three kids, and none of them are babies. It'll be hard, but yeah. I think there's going to be a family that falls for them hard. How could you not?"

"Why do you think you were never adopted?" He was watching her now, and Harper kept her expression neutral.

"I was seven when I went into foster care. The majority of adoptions are for babies and toddlers. The older kids just can't compete with that. I think some people worry that the older ones are too damaged."

Luke put his arm around her. "You're not damaged."

Harper smiled. "No, I'm not now. But I was then. You have

to be someone really special to want to tackle a project like that. But I, like all kids, was resilient. Someday I'll have my own family, and it'll all be worth it."

Luke squeezed her shoulder.

"Do you ever think about having kids?" Harper asked.

He was silent for a long moment. "I used to."

"Do you ever get lonely?"

Luke sighed. "Yeah."

"Me too."

He leaned over and kissed her on the cheek. "You're going to have everything you want someday."

She dropped her head to his shoulder. "Until then, this isn't so bad."

CHAPTER 11

Harper had an extra spring in her step the next morning. She had slept like a rock, once again ending up in Luke's arms at some point during the night. And Luke's part-time bookkeeper was coming back to work today.

Harper was excited about the prospect of some company around the office and an extra pair of hands to help tackle the work.

Ready for a shower, Harper tugged the T-shirt over her head and dropped it on the floor next to her shorts. Luke was out for a run, his long one. No one was going to witness her mostly naked streak downstairs to grab the new body wash she had left in her bag in the kitchen.

She crooned along to Bruno Mars wailing through her ear buds and busted some serious moves down the stairs. She grabbed the body wash and, since she was in the kitchen, decided she'd pour herself a glass of juice to enjoy after her shower.

She found the juice behind a bag of salad mix and the steaks Luke was going to grill for dinner that night. In her opinion, the fridge's contents had vastly improved since she moved in. Harper stood on tiptoe to reach for a plastic cup out of the cabinet. Damn it. Couldn't quite reach.

She levered herself up onto her knees on the counter and grabbed the cup. Just as she moved to hop back down, someone grabbed her.

She screamed loud enough that she could hear it over the music thundering in her ears and threw an elbow. She flailed and kicked as she was plucked off the countertop. Her heel grazed solid flesh, and together they went down in a heap.

She crawled forward, scrambling frantically. A hand grabbed at her hip and came away with a fistful of the waistband of her underwear. She shrieked before a hand clamped over her mouth.

Her earbuds were yanked out.

"Jesus Christ, Harper! Stop kicking!"

"Luke?" Harper tried to look over her shoulder and found his face looming over her. "Oh my God! You scared the crap out of me! I thought you were some crazy rapist."

"What the hell were you doing? I come in, and you're shaking your ass on the counter." He was shouting.

"I was getting a cup for juice," Harper shouted back. "I thought you were out for a run."

"I was," he gritted out. "I have an early meeting."

"Oh."

"Why don't you have any clothes on?"

Harper realized that her bare breasts were smashed into the kitchen floor and her underwear was halfway down her thighs.

"Oh my God!" Harper tried to wriggle free.

"For the love of God, Harper, stop wiggling."

"Just let me… Oh." He was hard. She felt him through the incredibly thin gym shorts, nestled against the juncture of her thighs. "Luke?"

"Just give me a minute," he muttered.

"You sound mad," she whispered.

"Harper!" He barked her name, and she felt him twitch against her. He sighed. His breath was a warm breeze on her neck. "Okay. Get up."

He pushed himself off the floor and pulled her up by the elbow. Harper set about yanking her underwear back into place with one hand while trying to cover her breasts with the other arm.

"What's the point, Harp? I've already seen it all." He looked annoyed.

"Fine." She dropped her arm and put her hands on her hips. "You're this mad because I climbed up on the counter?"

His gaze flickered up to her face and back down again.

Harper set her jaw. "Eyes up here, buddy."

"Yeah, that's not going to happen."

"Why are you so pissed?"

"Fuck it." He grabbed her—again by the waistband of her underwear—and yanked her against him. They stood that way, mouths a breath apart, for a second and then another one.

Harper moved first. She brought her hands to his shoulders. When he didn't move, she rose on tiptoe and slowly brought her lips to his.

His mouth, like the rest of him, was hard.

His hands moved, splaying across her back and pulling her tighter as his mouth moved in deeper. Harper's head tilted back to accommodate the assault. His tongue forced her mouth open wider. She surrendered to him. He tasted, and she dug her fingers into his shoulders.

He shoved her back against the fridge, his lips never breaking contact. Harper let her hands slide under his tank top. He helped her tug it over his head and moved back in.

Her nipples pebbled against his warm skin. She could feel

his heart pounding under the phoenix tattoo. Hers drummed a matching staccato beat.

She nibbled on his lower lip, and he inhaled sharply. Luke skimmed his hands up her sides to cup the undersides of her breasts. She sighed against him, and his thumbs brushed over her sensitive peaks.

The delicate torture made her ache for him. She slid her hand in the waistband of his mesh shorts and wrapped her fingers around his shaft.

"Harper." It was half groan and half warning.

She stroked his erection down to the thick root and back to the tip. He lowered his forehead to hers, trying to catch his breath. His hands stilled on her breasts.

Boldly, she stroked him again. His fingers tightened around her nipples, tugging and teasing. Harper felt moisture bead at the tip of his penis. She wiped it against her stomach, smearing the wetness on her skin.

Luke abandoned a breast and brought his fingertips to her center, forcing her thighs apart with a knee. He ran two fingers over the damp fabric of her underwear, and Harper felt her world go gray. She ached for those fingers to be deep inside her, driving her need.

He skimmed over the fabric, back and forth in time with Harper's strokes. When his thumb brushed her nipple again, Harper thought she would come apart.

On a growl, Luke tugged the cotton to the side and cupped her. His warm fingers pressed against her wet center. He hitched her leg over his hip to give him better access. Spread open to him, she welcomed the pressure of his rough hand.

He bent his knees, lowering his mouth to her breast.

With the new angle, Harper rubbed the tip of his shaft against her bare core.

He suckled with an intensity that had Harper's knees shaking. Her strokes became shorter and harder, notching him against her sex.

So close. Just an inch lower and—

The doorbell broke through their haze.

Luke's hands froze on her flesh and then disappeared as he hastily stepped back. He swore, readjusting the waistband of his shorts to pin down his hard-on.

"It's Frank. He's riding with me to the meeting." Luke wiped a hand over his face. "Shit."

Harper sagged against the cold metal of the refrigerator, her breasts heaving as she tried to catch her breath.

He grabbed her by the shoulders and lowered his forehead to hers. "I need you to go upstairs. Now."

Harper nodded but didn't move.

He sighed and grabbed his tank top off the floor. "Come on. Let's cover you up." Yanking it over her head, he pulled it down her torso. The deep armholes did little to cover her breasts, but at least her nipples were hidden from view.

Luke tugged her underwear back in place, and Harper shivered when his fingers brushed her sensitive flesh.

He grabbed her by the back of the neck and yanked her to him. He looked like he wanted to say something but instead gave her a hard kiss on the mouth. "Now get upstairs before I let Frank in."

Harper nodded and hurried to the stairs at the front of the house, careful not to look out the sidelights to see if Frank was witnessing her walk of shame.

Luke waited until she made it into the bedroom before opening the door.

She heard Frank snicker. "Am I interrupting, boss?"

What the hell was wrong with him? He had been nothing but clear with her—and himself—and this was how he played it. Ripping her off the kitchen counter and practically banging her against the fridge.

Great, and now he was hard again like he had been most of the day.

He was avoiding the office like the plague because he knew as soon as he saw her, he'd want to do it all over again and more. Frank was yammering on next to him about the job, and he hadn't heard a word of it.

Was he going to get a hard-on every time he went to the kitchen for a beer now?

This was supposed to be a simple, uncomplicated arrangement. He gave her a job and a place to stay, and she played a role. But obviously that role was getting tangled up for both of them. He was going to have to set things straight. Set boundaries.

How was he supposed to sleep next to her tonight without tearing that white T-shirt off her and slamming his cock into her now that he'd tasted her?

"Are you even listening to me?" Frank was staring at him expectantly.

Luke gritted his teeth. "Just handle it, Frank. I have to go."

"Women make you stupid," Frank warned him as he climbed into his truck.

"Ain't that the truth," Luke muttered under his breath as he threw the truck in reverse. Now where the hell was he supposed to go? There was no way he was going to go into the office. One look at her with those soft curves and sweet lips and he was going to bend her over his desk and—

"Goddammit." He punched the steering wheel. Frank was right. Harper was making him stupid. He never should have let her stay. He should have helped her find a nice little apartment on the other side of town where he'd never see her dancing naked on the kitchen counter.

What if Frank hadn't interrupted this morning? What if he had just shredded her underwear and slammed into her tight, hot—

His hands tightened on the wheel as his cock got even harder. His brain was full of reasons why it was a bad idea, but his body wasn't interested in listening to a single one of them.

What if he just stopped thinking about it? Let it happen? The attraction was obviously mutual. He remembered the heat in those deep gray eyes as he touched her. The girl couldn't hide anything if she wanted to. Those eyes would always give her away.

If he gave in, he knew it would be fucking crazy. Just the way she responded to his touch, like she craved it more than oxygen. Could Harper handle it if it were just sex? Would it be just sex?

He shook his head. She deserved better than a quick, casual fuck.

And he knew with a dark certainty that when he was inside her, it would be anything but just sex. It would be a fucking religious experience, and he wasn't ready for that.

Even if it was just temporary. He was leaving and soon. That should be reason enough to keep his dick in his pants. So why in the hell did it feel like a better reason to do it?

He wasn't even stupid enough to pretend that he didn't want it more than he wanted his next breath. If she lived in that house with him, slept in the bed next to him, it was only a matter of time before he lost control.

But for now he needed distance. And the longest, coldest fucking shower in the history of man.

CHAPTER 12

Harper had her suspicions that Sophie was psychic. The woman called her within seconds of her walking into the office to offer up a lunch invitation. "I just wanted to catch up and see how things are going with you…and Luke."

Harper was new to family dynamics but was fairly certain that Luke would be pissed off if she were to share the details of their morning with Sophie. She felt her nipples go hard again at the thought of Luke's mouth on her, his hands roaming her skin.

She let out a slow breath. If she didn't distract herself from the images of this morning that were permanently etched in her brain, she was going to have to skip lunch and go home and change into a new pair of underwear.

The office door opened. Harper bit her lip and sent up a quick prayer that it wasn't Luke. She wasn't ready to see that perfect face yet.

"You must be Harper," a cheerful voice called out.

Harper swiveled in her chair. A curvy redhead with a tiny stud in her nose breezed in holding a giant bundle of flowers.

"Beth?"

"That's me!" She set the vase on Harper's desk and stuck

out her hand. "I want to hug you, but I didn't want my gratitude to come on too strong and scare you off."

Harper laughed as she took Beth's purple-manicured hand. "That bad, huh?"

Beth shook her mass of auburn curls and rolled her eyes. "You have no idea. I've been on Luke's case for a solid year about hiring a full-time manager. He just keeps saying, 'I'll get to it.' And then never does."

"Let me guess, he's been—"

"Busy," Beth finished for her. "Yeah, that's Luke. I'm just so glad you're here, and I can already tell that you're a nice, normal human being, so I'm not even going to worry about how it will be working with you."

"Were you expecting someone with two heads?"

"I wasn't sure what to expect from the woman who finally landed Luke Garrison." Beth dropped her giant purse on the floor next to her desk and flopped down in the chair. "With these long-term bachelors, you can never tell if they'll be bowled over by beautiful and normal like yourself or if they'll just finally go insane from loneliness and grab the first crazy that comes their way."

"I could totally be crazy and just be hiding it to lure you into a sense of complacency," Harper warned.

"That's true," Beth said, booting up her computer. "Maybe I should take those flowers back until you've truly earned them."

"Oh, before I forget. Luke told me you're a caffeine fiend, so I made extra coffee, and there's French vanilla creamer in the fridge."

"You've earned the flowers back," Beth said, springing up and making a beeline for the coffeepot. "I don't care if you're crazy or not. You're thoughtful, and you understand my deep and abiding love for caffeine. This is the beginning of a beautiful friendship."

Harper laughed and turned back to her computer. Beth would be a good distraction from thoughts she didn't need to be thinking right now. Like the feel of Luke's hard cock against her.

Damn it.

———

Harper beat Sophie to the café by a few minutes, so she settled in with the menu and an iced tea. Sophie all but collapsed into the chair opposite her.

"Oh my God, thanks for having lunch with me today. Josh is driving me crazy," she said, wringing her hands around air. "He gave himself a haircut with freaking safety shears. I didn't even notice until I caught him trying to put his hair clippings in the dog dish."

"And here I thought parenthood was all ethereal moments of story time and nap time."

"And scraping dried spaghetti off the legs of the dining room table time and holding your ears because your toddler is practicing for a career in opera time," Sophie added.

Harper smiled into her drink. "Rough day, huh?"

"I should have just had you meet me at the liquor store so we could drink our lunches. But enough about me. How's work? How's living with Luke?"

"It's good. I'm still working through the backlog of paperwork and updates, but I like it."

"Uh-huh. And how's the home life?"

"It's, uh, good too. Luke's pretty easy to live with."

"I hear you both were caught practically naked in the kitchen this morning."

Harper choked on her tea.

"How did you hear that?" she demanded through the paper napkin.

Sophie grinned. "Angry Frank has a bigger mouth than Georgia Rae."

"Oh my God." Harper buried her face in her hands.

"Do you like him?"

"Frank? Not very much right now!"

"No! No one likes Frank. Do you like Luke?"

"Sophie, you're his *sister*. What am I supposed to say?"

Sophie leaned back in her chair and smiled a cat-that-ate-a-whole-nest-of-canaries grin. The server interrupted for their orders, and Harper used the time to try to force the blush from her cheeks.

"You like him," Sophie said simply.

"Of course I like him, Soph. What's not to like? He's smart, he's thoughtful, he's beyond gorgeous, he's good to his family. But liking each other isn't part of the deal. I'm only here for a month. I don't want to complicate anything."

"What's complicated about liking each other?" Sophie asked, accepting the diet soda from the server. She drank deeply. "Oh my God, caffeine, I love you."

"I just don't want to get attached." Harper sighed. "This isn't real. It's for convenience. He's leaving soon, and I'll be moving on."

"Then there's no reason not to enjoy what you have right now," Sophie insisted. "You're both consenting adults."

"I think I'm a little more consenting than Luke is."

Sophie laughed. "My big brother can be very stubborn about staying on course. But I have faith in you. You'll drag him off course, and he'll end up happy about it. Dinner with the family was the most relaxed I've seen him in a long time."

Harper perked up. "Really?"

"You're exactly what he needs."

"And you're the diabolical puppeteer who's making it all happen?"

Sophie waved the words away. "All I did was put two healthy adults alone in a house together in a mutually beneficial arrangement. I had a strong belief that nature would take its course, and judging by Frank's eyeful this morning, nature is winning."

"Hey, I'm all for nature in this case, but I don't think Luke is as receptive. I don't think he wants to…like me. I just can't get a read on him."

The server returned with their meals, and Sophie took a bite of her sandwich. She pointed it at Harper. "You know the reason Luke was at Remo's in the first place that night?"

Harper shook her head. There was nothing about Luke Garrison that said Friday night social butterfly.

"Because the week before, I had some problems with a customer who wouldn't leave and tried to get handsy. Thankfully, Ty was picking me up after my shift and took care of it. But Luke showed up and planted himself on a barstool all night, just to make sure his little sis was okay. That's the kind of guy he is," Sophie said, slapping a hand to her heart. "I love that boy so much it hurts. I want to see him happy again. And I think you're the ticket."

"Why is he unhappy?" Harper asked, stabbing at her salad. She had seen it in those hazel eyes, flashes of sadness, of pain.

"Some things take longer getting over than others, but there comes a point in time when you edge over the line to never recovering. I think Luke's too close to the line."

"Recovering from what?"

"I think it would be better if he told you himself." Sophie bit a french fry in half. "So how did you end up naked in the kitchen?"

———

Harper tried to enjoy the rest of her lunch with Sophie, but she couldn't shake the curiosity. Even when she returned to the office, her head was full of questions. What was Luke's secret? What did he lose? Was that why he lived in an empty house? And what did this morning mean?

She had never *wanted* like that before. Craved. Thinking about Luke's hands on her gave her goose bumps, even under the bright spring sunshine streaming through the office's arched windows.

She tried to focus on what Beth was telling her about accounts receivable when the scuff of work boots on the hardwood floor stole Harper's attention. "Nice to see you in some clothes for a change." Frank snorted and strolled past them into Luke's office.

"Funny, Frank." She shot his departing back a dirty look.

Beth snickered.

"Hey."

Harper spun in her chair. Luke, hands shoved in his pockets, stood behind her.

"Hey." She felt her cheeks flush. The last time she had seen him, her hand had been wrapped around his throbbing, hard—

"Hi, boss," Beth chirped.

"Beth." He nodded without taking his eyes off Harper. "Give us a minute, will you?"

"Sure thing. Gotta call my mother-in-law anyway and make sure the twins haven't destroyed the house yet." She hustled out of the office and down the stairs.

Luke stepped in and leaned against Harper's desk. She felt her nipples tighten and hastily crossed her arms over her chest. *Keep it together, Harper,* she cautioned herself.

"How was your meeting this morning?"

"Not distracting enough," he said, leaning against her desk.

Harper blushed.

"We're probably going to have to talk about this."

Talk about it? She'd rather do something about it.

"You just want to tell me all the reasons this is a bad idea."

"I don't want you to get hurt, Harper. This can't go anywhere. I'm leaving. This is all temporary."

"Haven't you ever made a temporary bad decision before?" she asked lightly.

He shook his head. "I've never been tempted before."

"How about now?"

"Now?" He reached out and ran his thumb over her lower lip. She parted her lips at the touch and tasted him. "I'm very tempted."

He leaned down to her, bracing his hands on the arms of her chair. Her white sundress rode higher on her thighs. Luke's gaze locked with hers, and he ran a calloused palm up the inside of her thigh.

Harper took a shaky breath, her hands in a death grip on the arms of her chair.

"Do you see why this is a bad idea, Harper?" he said quietly. His fingers brushed the edge of her white cotton briefs.

She swore her heart stopped.

"One look at you and all I can think about is being inside you." The pads of his fingers leisurely circled her sensitive folds through the thin layer of fabric. "Of how close I came to making you come today. Of what it would be like to drive you to the edge and feel you come on my cock."

"Any day now, boss," Frank called from Luke's office.

Luke closed Harper's legs and dropped a hard kiss on her mouth. "We'll talk later."

He turned and headed to his office, leaving a boneless Harper trembling behind him.

Harper was still feeling the tremors of what Luke had said to her. She spent a good portion of the rest of the afternoon staring blankly at her screen. When Luke left to hit another job site, the smoldering look he sent left her breathless.

She suddenly wasn't so sure she could survive sex with a man like Luke. If just a glance from him had this effect on her and if the rest of his body was as skilled as his fingers, she might literally die in his arms.

It was a risk she was willing to take.

Beth whistled when Luke closed the door behind him. "Talk about chemistry. I thought he was going to eat you alive with his eyes."

Harper fanned herself to fade the blush on her cheeks. "Is he always like this?"

Beth shook her head. "No way. This is the first time I've seen about-to-erupt-volcano Luke."

That put some hot visions in Harper's head. Luke about to erupt. Oh, God. She was going to get brain damage just thinking about it.

He texted her just as she was packing up her things to go home.

Luke: Working late. Don't wait up.

Harper felt a mix of disappointment and relief. Some time to herself probably wouldn't hurt. She went home and stared at the TV for several minutes before realizing she had forgotten to turn it on.

Shaking herself, she got up and wandered around the house. It was a new experience, having time to spend the way she wanted. What did she want? An image of Luke flexing his jaw as he drove his fingers into her immediately answered that question.

"I need to get a freaking hobby," Harper murmured, trying to ignore the ache between her legs. A hobby that didn't involve getting off just thinking about Luke.

In the end, she made a grocery list and a dinner menu for the rest of the week and hit the store. She unloaded all the groceries, made herself a peanut butter and jelly sandwich, and turned in early with a paperback she picked up at the store. It was a murder mystery. A better choice than the romance novel she had initially picked out.

With any additional stimulation, she'd probably mount Luke in his sleep.

She finally fell asleep clutching the paperback to her chest and dreaming of knife-wielding maniacs.

———

When she woke in the morning, the bed felt empty. Luke's side was undisturbed.

She hurried down the stairs, still in Luke's T-shirt, and stopped abruptly in the living room doorway.

His six-foot-three frame was crammed onto the sofa, an arm thrown over his head and dangling over the wooden arm. He was still in his clothes.

"Luke?"

He woke immediately and tried to sit up. He groaned and stretched the crick in his neck.

"You slept here?"

He had to turn his whole body to look at her because his head wouldn't turn on his neck. "Ouch. Yes."

"Super comfortable, huh?"

"Slept like a rock," he lied.

"I must really scare the hell out of you," Harper snapped over her shoulder as she walked back to the kitchen.

She ignored his grumble from the living room and helped herself to some orange juice.

Luke peeled himself off the couch and staggered down the hall, working the kinks out.

She poured him a cup of coffee and handed it to him.

"Don't give me that face," he said, his voice rough with sleep.

"Oh, you deserve that face. You can't even sleep in bed with me now? I'm not going to ravage you." He sighed heavily, and Harper rolled her eyes. "Just drink your coffee."

"I have to go to the base this weekend for some meetings and training. Will you be okay here by yourself?"

"You're not coming back tonight?"

He shook his head and sipped his coffee. "No. I'll be home tomorrow night. Late."

"Okay." Harper eyed him, waiting.

"Okay." He looked at her, still sexy as hell with sleep creases across his face, and then nodded. "I'm gonna go pack a bag."

Harper watched him leave and sighed.

CHAPTER 13

He was being a huge coward. Luke accelerated onto the highway, his mouth set in a frown. When his CO called yesterday afternoon about the basic combat refresher training, Luke suggested their premobilization team meet on Saturday to prep for Sunday's training. He couldn't face another weekend alone with Harper. He might die from the blood supply being cut off to his brain.

He thought about kissing her goodbye but had regained his wits and casually wished her a good weekend from the safety of the other side of the kitchen island.

He was doing it for her own good, he told himself. She wasn't the kind of girl who would just have a fling and then move on. Harper deserved better than that. So he would just keep his distance from her for the rest of the month, and they would part as friends.

Friends who could have had some serious benefits.

He slapped his hands on the wheel of the truck. "Get it together, man."

Focus on the job, and everything else will be fine.

———

Harper decided to at least pretend to be productive and tackled the laundry first. So she gathered up all the dirty clothes, towels, and sheets she could find and headed downstairs to the basement.

It wasn't as creepy as she had expected. Small windows at ceiling level ringed the perimeter and allowed morning light to filter through. As promised, a washer and dryer sat in the corner next to a dingy laundry sink and a serviceable countertop.

Harper dropped the heaping laundry basket on the floor and started the first load. The modest setup lacked the usual clutter of a well-used laundry area. There were no mate-less socks or shrunken and forgotten T-shirts. Just detergent, bleach, and dryer sheets.

While the washer kicked to life, Harper surveyed the rest of the basement. Like the rest of the house, it was empty except for a few boxes and plastic totes.

There was a small room with a door, probably some kind of storage closet, on the other side of the stairs. She wondered if it was full of Luke's high school yearbooks and childhood memorabilia. Harper tried the doorknob and found it locked.

The knob was new and keyed. Maybe that was where he kept firearms. She hadn't noticed any guns around the house. It was more than likely that he stored them safely under lock and key.

Harper spent the rest of her morning bustling around the house. She opened windows to let in the fresh spring breeze while she swept the hardwood floors and dusted the woodwork. She folded and put away two loads of laundry and remade the bed.

She was sweeping last year's leaves off Luke's front porch, fantasizing about the cold roast beef sandwich she was going to make for lunch, when someone called her name.

A tiny brunette stood on the walkway halfway between the sidewalk and the porch. Her hands were clasped tightly in front of her. A colorful floral scarf was tied around her neck.

"I'm sorry to bother you, but Ty told me where I could find you."

Harper leaned the broom against the railing. "Gloria, right?"

The woman nodded. "I wasn't sure you'd recognize me. We weren't…"

"Formally introduced?" Harper supplied.

Gloria gave her a small smile. "Exactly. I hope you don't mind me stopping by."

"Not at all! You're giving me the perfect excuse to quit cleaning." Harper stepped off the porch. "Do you have time to come inside?"

"Um, sure. If you're sure you don't mind?"

"I would love some company. Especially if you tell me you haven't had lunch yet, because I'm starving."

"Oh, um. I don't know if I should…"

"Please? I'd love to have some company," Harper repeated.

She had seen this before. When a person's right to make decisions had been systematically stripped from them for so long, it was hard to start making choices when the freedom to do so was returned.

She turned and started for the porch. "Come on in." Harper led the way back to the kitchen. She grabbed two plates from the cabinet and put them on the island. "Can you grab the bread for me?" She gestured to the loaf on the counter and busied herself unpacking sandwich ingredients from the refrigerator. She handed Gloria a cutting board and ripe tomato. "Would you mind slicing this?"

While Gloria carefully sliced, Harper started to build the sandwiches.

"Roast beef okay with you?"

"Sure. But you really don't have to go to all this trouble."

Harper coated slices of bread with mayonnaise. "Well, you're helping. So what brings you to Luke's unfurnished abode?"

Gloria's soft laugh floated through the kitchen "It is kind of spartan."

"I don't know if he's a minimalist or what."

"Commitment phobic?"

"Even when it comes to furniture, it seems," Harper agreed. She handed Gloria a plate with a sandwich and pickle spear. "Water or soda?"

"Water, please."

Harper filled two glasses with ice water and joined Gloria at the island. They ate side by side in companionable silence for a few minutes.

"Harper, I just wanted to thank you," Gloria said suddenly.

"You're welcome, but it's just a sandwich."

"Not just for the sandwich, which is really good, by the way. For helping me with Glenn at Remo's. It's been going on for so long, or at least I've let it go on so long that I felt like everyone had stopped seeing me. It took me seeing the situation I helped create hurt someone else to realize that it had to stop. And I'm sorry for that."

Harper traced a finger over the fading bruises on her face. "It was worth it if it helps you build a life you want. How are you?"

"I'm okay." Gloria pushed her pickle around the plate. "I'm staying with my mother for now. And I pressed charges." She picked up her sandwich and took another bite.

"That's very brave of you."

"It would have been braver had I done it years ago."

"Life moves pretty fast. There's not a lot of room for coulda, shoulda, woulda," Harper said, patting her hand.

"Sometimes that's all I can think about. How different my life would be if I had gone to college or never started dating him."

Harper nodded. "Maybe now you have that chance. To see what your life would be without him in it."

"It's hard. I don't really have any friends left. I guess it's not easy to be friends with someone who keeps making the wrong decision over and over again. Eventually everyone has to decide whether it's worth it to keep trying."

"So what are you going to do now?"

"I'm going to get a job, find a place to live, and be worth it."

"Sounds like a good plan to me. Is there anything I can do to help?"

"Wanna be friends? I'll understand if your answer's no, considering I got you punched in the face."

"I got myself punched in the face, and it got me waking up staring into the beautiful eyes of Luke Garrison. I think I owe you a lifetime of friendship."

Gloria laughed. "I went to school with Sophie and Luke. He's a good man."

"Yes, he is." Harper nodded.

After lunch, she walked Gloria to the door.

"It was really nice officially meeting you," Gloria said. "And one more time for the record, thank you, and I'm sorry."

"And again, no thanks or apologies necessary. I fully plan to be BFFs with you, and we should have dinner sometime soon," Harper said, opening the front door.

"Did someone say dinner?" a male voice asked from the porch. A barrel-chested man in shorts and running shoes took the front steps in a single bound. His thick dark hair curled at the ends, and a white-toothed grin split his face.

Harper noticed a pink tinge warm Gloria's cheeks. "Hi, Aldo," she said shyly.

He took off his sunglasses. "Hi, Gloria. How's it going?"

She blushed deeper.

"You must be Aldo because Gloria called you that," Harper said, extending her hand.

"And you must be the famous Harper." He had a strong, warm grip. "I thought I'd stop by while my best friend is out of town to see why he forgot to mention that he has a live-in girlfriend."

"And make sure I'm not some kind of psychopath?"

"You know the saying. Bros don't let other bros date psychos."

"I'm actually not familiar with that one. Is there some kind of test I have to take?"

"Why don't I give you the test at dinner? Monday. Here. I'll grill burgers and dogs."

"Gloria, I feel like I should confirm that this gentleman actually is a friend of Luke's before I agree to let him cook dinner in Luke's house."

Gloria nodded. "He is."

"Since elementary school," Aldo supplied.

"Good enough for me. Seven o'clock here okay for you, Gloria?"

Harper saw the hesitation on Gloria's face.

"Please tell me you'll bring your apple pie. I'll be your slave for life," Aldo pleaded, taking her slim hand in his.

Gloria bit her lip. "I'll bring apple pie." She turned back to Harper. "I'll see you Monday, Harper."

"See you, Gloria," Aldo said, leaning against the doorframe.

She hurried past him, down the walk, but smiled the whole way.

"It's nice to see her smile," he said. "So, Harper, if that is your real name, tell me about yourself."

"Want to come in?"

"Normally, not until I know whether you can be trusted. But I'm four miles into my eight, and I could use some water."

Aldo was indeed Luke's best friend from elementary school, Harper learned. The two ran wild in the summers together, played football together, and in their senior year of high school, they signed up for the guard together.

"So do you know Gloria?"

"I actually just met her officially when she stopped by."

"Rumor has it she moved out and is pressing charges." He toyed with the water bottle Harper gave him.

"Rumor has it," Harper agreed, smiling innocently. "How long have you known Gloria?"

"Since forever. She was a sophomore when we were seniors. Glenn was bad news back then too."

"Yeah, the years don't seem to have mellowed him."

"Heard you had quite the shiner."

"Please. You should have seen the other guy," she snorted.

"Wish I would have been there."

Harper stayed silent and let him sulk.

"So how long have you been into Gloria?"

"Since I heard her sing in the school musical."

Harper grinned as he stared at his water.

"How did handsome football star Aldo not win the girl?"

He shook his head. "I never took the shot."

"Maybe now you can pull the trigger."

Aldo leveled his gaze at her. "I like the way you think, Harper."

"Bring your A game to dinner Monday, sport."

"'Sport'? Are you serious?"

"Let the lousy nickname contest begin."

———

That night, after a dinner for one of canned soup and a BLT followed by pretending to watch TV, Harper curled around Luke's pillow in bed. She picked a shirt Luke had worn, which she purposely didn't wash with the rest of the laundry so she could still catch his scent. She had gone to bed an hour ago and was still staring at the ceiling.

Thinking. About him. The way he could look into her with those eyes that didn't miss a thing. His jaw, usually set in a firm line, was perpetually covered with a five-o'clock shadow. And that body, hard muscle under inked lines begging her hands to—

Her phone signaled a text from the nightstand, jarring her from her fantasy.

Her pulse kicked up a notch when she saw Luke's name on the screen.

Luke: Have a good day?

She'd play it cool, she decided.

Harper: Really good. You?

A few seconds later, he responded.

Luke: Not bad. Getting ready for bed now.
Harper: Hopefully it's more comfortable than your couch.

She included a winky face. That was still playing it cool, right?

Luke: Funny. What are you still doing up?
Harper: Thinking about you.

A minute passed and then two before her phone dinged.

Luke: Same here. For a fake girlfriend, I can't get you out of my head.

Harper did her best version of a horizontal happy dance and then counted to thirty before she responded.

Harper: What do you think that means?

She nibbled on her thumbnail from the time she hit Send until he responded.

Luke: It means I've spent more time regretting my decision to stay away from you than convincing myself to stick to it.
Harper: Then don't stay away. Come over to the dark side.
Luke: Cute. I just don't want you to get hurt.
Harper: We both know there's no future. What's the harm in enjoying the present?

Her screen dimmed and then turned off. A minute ticked by on the bedside clock before, finally, another text came in.

Luke: Get some sleep, baby. I'll see you tomorrow night.

CHAPTER 14

It was a restless night's sleep with dreams of Luke. The next day, she only had to drag her thoughts back to the present—away from all things Luke—every thirty seconds or so while she puttered around the house.

She still hadn't heard from him by the time she dusted every nook and cranny of the banister, cleaned the inside of the first-floor windows, and finished her murder mystery. She was debating on whether she should text him when her phone rang in her hand.

"Tell me you're not busy getting naked with my brother today," Sophie demanded.

"Your brother is currently out of town avoiding me, presumably to protect himself from my incredible magnetism that drops athletic shorts with a single glance. So no."

Sophie snorted. "Perfect! Then you can come with me."

"Where are we going?" Harper asked, opening the back door and stepping onto the porch.

"It's the annual Benevolence Not-So-Polar Plunge at the lake."

"Aren't those things usually in the winter?"

"I'll fill you in on the way. You'll do it, right?"

Some cold water would probably do her hot blood some good, Harper decided.

"Sure."

"Great! Wear your worst bathing suit."

Harper only had one suit, and she hadn't worn it for a few years. She hoped it still fit.

"I'll bring your costume and pick you up in half an hour."

"Costume?" But Sophie had already hung up.

Harper tossed her phone on the counter and dashed upstairs to find her bikini.

———

"Okay, so, forty-five years ago, some high school students decided it would be fun to organize a Christmas cold water plunge to benefit a local cause." Sophie launched into her explanation as she pulled out of the driveway. "I think it was a family whose house had burned down. Anyway, they were all set to do it when the lake froze over. So they decided to postpone it until the water thawed.

"Now, every year, townies get together in April, dress up like it's Christmas, and jump in the lake. This year's cause is a leukemia and lymphoma nonprofit."

"That's kind of awesome," Harper laughed. "So what's our costume?"

Sophie reached behind her into the back seat and dumped a sweater in her lap. Harper held it up and laughed. Garrison Christmas 1987. It had misshapen reindeer flying over lumpy, snow-covered hills.

"These are from Mom's knitting phase. We still do shirts every year, but now we order them online."

"I'm feeling Christmassy already. So how cold is the water?"

Sophie grinned. "Well, it's not December, but it sure as

hell isn't warm! They don't call the lake Arctic Hell for nothing. People don't willingly get in the water until August. I brought a bunch of old towels though, and they hand out shots afterward and have a bonfire. It's pretty fun."

When they pulled into the parking lot, Harper goggled at the number of cars already there. "It looks like the whole town is here."

Sophie nodded. "More or less. James and Ty should be here already. Ty is on duty as a cop slash lifeguard. James will do the plunge with us."

"What about Luke?"

Sophie shook her head. "He's never done it. Even in high school. That boy was born an adult. I don't know if he's ever had a day of frivolous fun in his whole life."

Harper yelped as a face plastered up against her window.

"And then there's my idiot brother James here who's the opposite," Sophie said, pointing at her window.

James yanked Harper's door open. "Let's go, ladies! The lake waits for no one." He was wearing swim trunks and a Garrison Christmas 1993 T-shirt with a mooning Santa on it. Obviously he was much smaller in 1993 because it was more of a belly shirt now. He had plastic light-up reindeer antlers perched on his head.

"You look kind of adorable, James," Harper teased, getting out of the car.

James lowered his sunglasses and winked. "Damn straight." He plopped a Santa hat on her head and tossed one to Sophie. "Suit up, Sis."

Harper and Sophie peeled off their shorts and T-shirts and tossed them into the back seat before pulling on their sweaters.

Harper ignored James's low whistle when he caught a glimpse of her white bikini. But Sophie cuffed him in the back of the head. "No poaching. I don't want to watch Luke pound you into the ground."

"Luke's not here to do any pounding," James grinned.

Harper took in the tailgating madness. It really did look like the whole town of Benevolence had turned out for the event. There were fat Santas and pointy-eared elves mingling with people dressed as stockings and Christmas trees. There was even a group of middle-aged men in red and green Speedos. She also caught a glimpse of Georgia Rae in an "I'm Mrs. Claus" sweatshirt.

James led the way through the crowd toward the lake.

"Excuse me, ladies. You look like you need mouth-to-mouth." Ty, in a lifeguard tank top, red shorts, and yellow-sunscreen-painted nose, stepped up to plant a steamy kiss on Sophie.

"Ma'am, you're looking like you could use some oxygen. Can I be of assistance?" A blond, muscle-bound guy, dressed like Ty and carrying a rescue buoy, sauntered up to Harper.

Ty stopped kissing Sophie long enough to punch him in the arm. "Nice try, Linc. This is Harper, Luke's girlfriend. Harper, this is Lincoln Reed. He's the fire chief and Luke's high school nemesis."

"Girlfriend, huh? Nice to meet you, Harper." Linc extended his large hand, and Harper took it. He pulled her in a step closer. "Luke or no Luke, you let me know if you need assistance."

Harper pulled her hand back and laughed. "Nice to meet you too, Linc. But I'm breathing just fine. You guys look pretty impressive," she said, gesturing at their costumes.

"We take this event very seriously, which is why I'm going to have to insist that you do a shot before getting in the water," Linc said, adopting a serious face.

"It's purely a precautionary measure," Ty agreed solemnly.

"We'd better do what the lifeguards say." Sophie winked at Harper. "Lead the way, boys."

Ty picked Sophie up and tossed her over his shoulder and started weaving his way through the crowd toward a makeshift plywood bar with a Remo's banner hanging above it. "We need shots, stat, bartender!" Ty said, dropping Sophie on her feet in front of the bar.

Linc offered Harper his arm. "Better catch up, sunshine."

Harper rolled her eyes and took his arm. "Lead the way."

The bartender was Sheila from Remo's. "Welcome to Remo's Lakeside, ladies." She plopped a bottle of whiskey and a bottle of tequila on the bar top. "What'll it be?"

"Oh, tequila, my nasty friend," Sophie sighed.

Harper decided on the whiskey, and Sheila poured the shots in plastic cups. "Okay, the rules are each participant gets two warm-up shots. No more. There will be no repeats of Puke Fest 2010. You can have them both now or one now and one later."

"I'd save one for later, sunshine." Linc leaned against the bar next to Harper. "You'll need another to restart your heart from Arctic Hell. Or I could do it for you." He flexed his pecs under his tank top.

Harper snorted. "Does that work on the ladies of Benevolence?"

"Like a charm. I'm thinking about extending my coverage area. Where are you from?"

"You're ridiculous," she laughed.

"I think you like ridiculous." He nudged his fluorescent plastic sunglasses down his nose.

Actually, she had a thing for serious and broody. But a little harmless flirting with ridiculous sure didn't hurt.

"Aren't you gentlemen doing a shot with us?"

"Sorry, sunshine, we're on duty. Gotta make sure no one drowns or gets a charley horse and needs to be carried out and massaged by the fire. How are your calves feeling? Any knots?"

Here was a gorgeous, red-blooded man standing in front of her flirting shamelessly and her pulse had yet to ratchet up a notch. But have Luke walk past her desk into his office without sparing her a glance, and she felt like she had a hammer in her chest. It wasn't fair.

She shook her head. "Sorry, no knots here."

"Bummer. I'm totally great at massage." Linc leaned against the bar and flexed a bicep. Harper eyed the bulging muscle. Yep, not a flutter.

"A toast, Harp," Sophie announced, grabbing her arm. "To your first Benevolence Not-So-Polar Plunge."

"Cheers!"

They clunked plastic cups and knocked back their shots. Harper gasped at the warmth that spread through her chest.

James reappeared and clamped a hand on her shoulder. "Come on. I want to be at the front of the crowd so we can be first in, first out."

Sophie gave Ty a smacking kiss on his cheek. "Keep everyone safe, Deputy Sexy."

"You got it, babe," he said, smacking her on the butt.

"Good luck, sunshine," Linc said with a grin. "I'll be nearby if you need any assistance."

James grabbed them by the hand and led the way through the crowd to the sandy lakefront. A crackling bonfire was already going strong with volunteers from the fire company unpacking massive quantities of s'mores fixings.

A Santa with a snorkel and flippers took his place next to

Harper. He winked at her through his mask. "Get ready for some frigid fun," he said around the snorkel mouthpiece.

"How cold is it?" Harper asked Sophie, reaching her foot toward the water.

"Trust me, you don't want to do that. The key is to run in, turn around, and run back out as fast as you can. Don't stop for anything, or you might actually need Lifeguard Hot Stuff to bring you back to life."

"That cold, huh?"

Sophie's reply was cut off by a shrill whistle. "Ladies and gentlemen! Welcome to the Forty-Fifth Annual Benevolence Not-So-Polar Plunge," Ty announced through a megaphone from his perch on a wooden lifeguard stand in front of the bar. "Linc and I are here to make sure none of you drown or freeze to death."

The crowd cheered.

Linc raised his red buoy from the lifeguard stand by the fire. "Remember the rules," he shouted. "Get in, get out, and don't go under. Try not to trample your neighbors," he shouted. "On your mark, get set, go!"

Linc and Ty blew their whistles, and the crowd surged forward. Harper yelped as daggers of icy water stung her legs, but she kept moving. She rushed in up to her belly and shrieked.

Sophie was next to her, flapping her arms. "Oh my God! Oh my God! Okay, out, out, out!"

They turned and dodged their way through incoming plungers and toward the sandy beach. They were almost out when Snorkel Santa on Harper's left tripped over a flipper. She reached for him to hold him up, but they both went down and under.

The cold stole the breath from her body. Her muscles instantly froze, preventing her from reaching for the surface.

She felt like an ice cube floating in a sea of frigid water. Strong hands grabbed her under the arms and yanked her up. Harper surfaced and swiped a frozen hand over her face. Snorkel Santa was back on his feet and hauling ass out of the water.

Linc appeared at her side, grinning from ear to ear. "Let's move, sunshine, before your feet freeze to the lake bed." He picked her up and carried her out of the water. Harper was too cold to be embarrassed and wrapped her arms around his neck, cuddling into the warmth of his upper body until he deposited her next to the fire.

Harper's shivers started immediately. A blue-lipped Sophie appeared with a giant fluffy towel. "Oh my God, you went under," she said, surveying Harper's wet hair.

"S-s-snorkel Santa took me down," Harper said through chattering teeth.

"She'll be okay, just needs to warm up," Linc announced. "All right, off with your sweater."

Harper hugged her arms to her chest, squishing icy water out of the fabric. "What? No!"

"I'm not trying to get you naked. Yet," Linc laughed. "You're not going to warm up wearing it. So strip." He pointed at the clothesline behind them that was already sagging under the weight of everyone else's wet costumes.

Still not convinced, Harper shook her head until Linc took matters into his own hands and grabbed the hem of her sweater, yanking it over her head.

"Damn, sunshine. Someone kicked the crap out of you." He turned her sideways and ran a hand down the fading bruises on her ribs and back.

"Hands off." The order snapped like a whip, and Harper rooted to the spot.

She didn't need to turn around to know who said it.

Linc took his sweet time removing his hands from her skin. Harper took a guilty step back.

"Garrison," Linc nodded. "Didn't think you were here."

"Obviously." Luke pulled Harper into his side. His heat had her cuddling closer. She shivered against him, and he tightened his grip. "Now get lost, Chief."

Linc smirked. "I would, but I'm here to enforce the rules, and unfortunately, you're breaking one right now. Am I right, Deputy?"

Ty, his arm slung around Sophie, stepped between them. "Unfortunately, Luke, he's right. You know the rule." He lifted the megaphone. "No spectators, only plungers," he announced in Luke's face.

Luke glared at his brother-in-law, but it was too late. James and Sophie grinned as the crowd took up the chant. "In the lake! In the lake!"

Luke looked like he was ready to punch Linc and Ty in the face.

He swore instead and released Harper. "Guess it's better than a cold shower," he muttered just loud enough for Harper to catch the words.

She pressed her frozen lips together to keep from laughing.

———

Luke toed off his work boots, and the crowd cheered.

He dragged his T-shirt off and yanked it over Harper's head to cover her up. Her tits looked like they were ready to pop out of the tiny white triangles of fabric. And if he was thinking these thoughts, then so was that asshole Linc.

He unbuttoned his jeans, and the ladies in the crowd went wild. Harper gaped at him while Sophie and James laughed like a pair of hyenas. He stripped down to his boxer briefs, thankful that he had worn a pair. Since Harper moved in, he spent more time trying to tame his hard cock than he had since the onset of puberty.

He yanked Harper to him by the front of the T-shirt and placed a hard kiss on her mouth. "He doesn't touch you again," he ordered before stalking to the water.

They followed him, cheering and chanting as he marched to the water's edge. He paused long enough to raise his middle finger over his shoulder before diving straight in.

The crowd cheered, and Harper joined them. Luke strode out of the water, icy droplets streaking down his body. He came straight at her and, without slowing his pace, boosted her up, locking her legs around his waist.

"Order has been upheld!" Ty announced in the megaphone. "Now someone make me a s'more."

Harper wrapped her arms around Luke's neck and let him carry her to the crowded bar. He squeezed her ass under the T-shirt, and his cock came to life against her.

"How can you possibly get hard after being in water like that?" she whispered in his ear.

"Baby, it's gonna take more than an icy lake for you to not make me hard." He released her and let her slide down his body before turning her around to face the bar. It was the truth. He had tried the safety of distance, but it only made him want her more. He knew he was fucked. Ready or not, he couldn't stop the reaction that was happening between them.

He signaled Sheila for two shots and pressed himself against Harper. She felt his erection against her and pressed back. He leaned over her until his lips met her ear.

"You're going to have to get me a towel or else the entire town is going to see how hard you make me." He skimmed a hand down over her breast, catching on her pebbled nipple. Harper shivered.

"Are you done avoiding me?" she whispered.

Sheila dropped two shots in front of them and winked at Harper before moving on to dole out more to the crowd.

"Baby, if I thought there was the slightest possibility we could get away with it, I would put my dick in you right here and now." He thrust his hips against her to make his point. "I almost talked myself into keeping my hands off you. And then I see you in that bikini with that asshole's hands all over you." His hand slid to her other breast.

"It didn't mean anything, Luke," Harper whispered.

"When I touch you, it's going to mean something." He squeezed her breast until he felt her nipple harden against his palm. "Now do your shot so I can take you home and untie every string on that bikini."

CHAPTER 15

B y the time they made it home, a spring thunderstorm was brewing. Dark clouds rumbled in the heavens, and a heavy rain hit, soaking them again from the truck to the house.

Luke shoved the door open and pulled Harper inside. She still wore his T-shirt while he wore only jeans. The rest of their wet clothes were balled up in the plastic bag he carried.

She couldn't stop staring at him on the way home. The muscles of his chest, the tattoos. She was minutes away from having free rein to touch every inch of him. Every hard, solid, sculpted inch of him would be hers to touch and taste.

His hand lingered on her hip, his touch scorching her through the thin cotton. "I'm going to go grab us some towels, okay?"

Harper nodded. Maybe a few seconds apart would help her regroup. She had never been this nervous or this excited about being with someone. This was probably a mistake. She made a lot of them. But she had never wanted to make a mistake this badly before.

If she didn't calm the hell down, she would have a heart attack before he touched her. Water. That was what she needed. A nice glass of cold water.

She hurried into the dark kitchen and filled a glass from the tap. Maybe Luke would want a beer. She opened the refrigerator and lost her train of thought when he entered the room.

The only illumination in the room came from the open fridge. Luke kicked it shut and prowled toward her.

Cornered against the L of the cabinets, Harper had nowhere to go. He caged her in, resting his hands on the countertop on either side of her. The rain pattered on the window over the sink. It was the only sound in the house.

He stepped in closer, an inch from her face. She could feel his breath on her hair, her heart pounding unevenly. It was going to happen. There was nothing she had ever wanted more. And that scared her.

The what-ifs flew out of her head as Luke raised his hands to her face. He gently pushed her hair back over her shoulders. He rested his fingertips on the back of her head. His thumbs gently traced her jawline and lifted her face toward his.

"I don't have a condom," he whispered.

"I'm on the pill," Harper said, shifting under his touch.

She was drowning in his hazel eyes. She saw need and want and something deeper, like pain, in them. It went straight to her heart. Harper parted her lips. It was an invitation to fill and be filled.

Gently, reverently, Luke lowered his mouth to hers.

Thunder boomed outside in the darkness, and Harper felt it travel through her.

His lips were warm and soft as they moved against hers. She sighed and opened her mouth to him. He moved his hands to cup her face, changing the angle of the kiss. His tongue met hers, and all gentleness was gone.

He swept into her mouth again and again until Harper lost her breath. Her hands dove into his hair, trying to pull him closer. Luke stroked his hands down to her thighs and back up under the T-shirt to her hips. He lifted her effortlessly and she found herself perched on the edge of the countertop, shirt bunched around her hips. Luke pressed her legs open and stepped between them, never breaking contact with her mouth.

She hitched her legs over his hips and yanked him closer.

"What changed?" She whispered it against his mouth.

"Nothing." His voice was gravel in the still of the kitchen. "I just want you more than I want to stay away from you."

Harper felt the hard length of his shaft through his jeans. His tongue swept into her mouth again as his hands climbed up her sides and under the shirt. She felt herself quiver as his exploration paused under her breasts. She moaned again and moved her hips to rub his hard-on against the damp fabric of her bikini bottoms.

His rough palms slid up to cup both breasts, and Harper drew in a shaky breath. She wanted more. Everything he could give her. "Luke, please." His thumbs brushed over her already aching nipples, and Harper's head fell back against the cabinet, breaking contact with his mouth.

He yanked the shirt up to her shoulders, then over her head. Their gazes held as he tugged on the tie around her neck. The strings tumbled free, but the triangle cups held their position for a moment. The heaving of her breasts was enough to dislodge the fabric, and as the cups peeled their way off her skin, Harper heard something close to a growl rise from Luke's throat. He was trying to be gentle, but she could feel the beast beneath ready to break free.

She wanted him free. Wanted him wild.

She braced herself on one arm and cupped her breast with the other hand. "Take it."

Still controlled, he lowered his head slowly, those eyes

riveted on her face. She knew he was questioning her, knew how important control was to him.

"Take everything." She squeezed him tighter with her thighs and leaned back to give him access.

Those soft, skilled lips closed over her nipple, and Harper felt her breath leave. Delicate little muscles deep inside pulsed, demanding to be stroked. He groaned as he suckled her, strong tugs that gave so much pleasure and a hint of pain. His hand moved to cup her other breast. She could feel his erection against her. He wanted her. He needed her. Harper reached down between them to the waistband of his jeans. Using her heels, she bucked and shoved his pants and underwear down his thighs, freeing his straining cock.

She grasped him firmly, and he groaned against her breast. Eyes closed, he sucked her nipple harder, his tongue lashing it in a fierce rhythm. Harper felt her other breast yearn for his mouth.

She stroked him hard from base to tip and back again. He bit down on her abused nipple. A moan escaped her, and Luke released her breast. Her nipple was rosy, red, and puckered. It strained toward his breath like a flower following the sun. He moved his mouth to her other peak and began the assault over.

His tongue began to lap, hardening her nipple instantly. Luke closed his mouth over her and sucked deeply, feeding. She had never been touched like this before. Never felt so craved.

Harper felt the deep ache between her thighs build. She stroked him again, more violently this time, moving the head of his shaft so it was nestled between her thighs. It was too much, but she couldn't stop. The blunt heat between her legs and the pulls from his mouth were building an orgasm for her that she feared. It was going to tear her apart in his arms.

"Lucas! I can't stop." It was a whisper and a plea. His arm tightened around her waist, and he tugged her nipple with his teeth. The second he started to suck again, she was dimly aware of a streak of lightning through the window, and she shattered over the edge. She pumped forcefully on his cock, riding it against her center as she came and came and came.

He groaned against her breast, still feeding until the pulsing between her legs slowed. Harper felt a tear escape. Devastated. Desperate. There was too much power in this storm. She couldn't survive this.

Luke broke from her breast and returned to her mouth. His hands grasped her hips, and he lifted her off the counter. Harper wrapped her arms around his neck and held on for dear life as his tongue drove into her mouth in swift thrusts. His hands squeezed her butt, pulling her against his cock, creating a wet friction that had them sighing against each other.

He was huge and throbbing, and all Harper wanted was to be filled by him. Her heart was pounding out of her chest, and she fought for air even as she dove into his kiss. She felt herself being lowered and knew they weren't going to make it to the bed. The cold travertine tiles would do.

She opened her thighs wide for him. Luke pulled back from her mouth and knelt between her legs. He untied one side of the bikini bottom, letting his thick penis bob against the lips of her sex. She brought her knees higher, baring herself to him.

Those hazel eyes were staring into her, and she saw him trying to regain control.

When he made no move, she laid a hand over his heart. "Please, Luke."

His chest heaved once under her touch, and his jaw tightened. He gripped her knees, yanked her to him. He drove into her with a force just short of violence. Harper cried out, in pain, in wonder. She was full. Finally full.

Luke grunted and squeezed his eyes shut. He pulled out

and slammed back into her. She felt his heavy sack slap against her. Again and again, he drove into her. The tile seams bit into her back. She felt the throbbing stretch every time he sheathed himself in her, but she didn't care. She wanted more. Every thrust, every inch.

He drove into her again with barely controlled violence. "Am I hurting you?" He ground out the words through gritted teeth, concern warring with want.

She knew what he needed. "Yes. I want more."

His eyes darkened. "I'm not going to be able to stop if I let go."

"Let go." She gave him a greedy little squeeze as she said it. His eyes instantly glazed over, and she knew she won.

He slammed into her again and again, the speed quickening to a frantic pace. Harper felt her breasts tremble with every thrust. He was propelled by need, and she was with him for the ride. The pace was so furious she could only take what he gave her. Could only cling and ride.

Another orgasm was racing up inside her. "Lucas!" she shouted his name. He dove forward onto her, pressing her into the floor with his weight and continued to hammer into her. He grunted with each fierce thrust.

It hit her like lightning. Her entire body electrified as the orgasm exploded around his thick shaft. He drove into her, pacing each wave with a violent rhythm. Harper buried her face against his bare shoulder. She couldn't even scream as the brutal sensations destroyed her.

He grunted again, a primal sound. She felt the first, hot surge of his semen let loose deep inside her. The last waves of her orgasm choked his shaft on the next thrust. He stayed deep inside, thrusting to the hilt as he came over and over again inside her. It was her name on his lips.

CHAPTER 16

They eventually made it upstairs. Luke carried her over his shoulder up the stairs, but sleep was not on either's mind. By the time he had dumped her on the crisp sheets, he was already hard again.

What spell did she have him under? It was breaking the laws of biology that he should want her this fiercely this soon. She was still filled with the proof of the orgasm that had hollowed him out, body and soul, and all he wanted to do was fill her again. And again.

He knew he had hurt her. He'd been too rough with her.

Where was his control? It disgusted him that he had let himself go like that. Harper had no idea that was what lurked beneath the surface. He had no right to take her like that.

"I can feel you glaring at me," she murmured, eyes closed, sprawled across the sheets.

He pinched her hip. "I'm not glaring. I'm just thinking."

Harper opened one of those stormy gray eyes. "You're a lot more fun when you aren't thinking."

"Harper—"

She slapped a hand over his mouth.

"Shut up. Don't ruin this moment for me with your 'We can't do this' lame speech."

He tugged her hand down. "For your information, it's not lame. I've been working on a PowerPoint."

Harper giggled and rolled until she was on top of him. Her breasts pressed against his chest, her thighs cuddling his dick. He instantly got harder.

She cocked her head to the side and traced her fingers lazily over his shoulders and chest. "Before you give me any speech, I'm going to live out the fantasy that I've been having ever since I woke up and saw your face."

Luke's hands slid down and cupped her ass. He told himself he should stop touching her now, but his body wasn't willing to entertain the idea.

"What fantasy is that?"

"I want to taste every inch of your perfect body."

He went hard as stone, and his hands flexed on her flesh.

She silenced any argument he might have had with a kiss. Her tongue glided into his mouth, a gentle tease. He let her take control. She broke free from his mouth and trailed a delicate path of kisses across his jaw and down his throat. She nipped at the skin of his shoulder and trailed lower still.

Her lips paused over his heart.

Harper slid lower, her tongue tasting his stomach, making his taut muscles quiver under her assault.

She rested her face on his thigh and ran her hand up his other leg, pausing just below his heavy sack. He could feel her breath on him, and his cock twitched with need.

He didn't mean for the groan to escape his throat, but it did. And as soon as Harper heard it, she gave him a wicked grin and took him into her mouth. It was heaven and torture. The way her hot mouth wrapped around the head of his dick was enough to send him over the edge.

He fought for control as she took him to the back of her

throat, stroking him with her sweet mouth. He felt he was fighting a losing battle.

"Slow down, baby," he whispered.

She didn't listen. She gripped him firmly and worked his shaft with her mouth and hand, pumping him harder and harder.

He was dangerously close, and when she used her other hand to cup his balls, he almost came in her mouth right there.

"Enough." Yanking her up his body by her hair, he rolled so it was Harper who was pinned. "It's my turn."

He took his time on her breasts, suckling and tasting until Harper was grinding against him. He wanted to slam into her, to fill her and feel that slick heat wrap around his cock.

But first he wanted to taste her.

He slid down her body and pressed her knees apart. "Baby." It was all he could say as she lay beneath him, spread open, ready to give him anything he wanted.

But it was he who would give. She moaned the second his tongue probed her soft folds. He licked into her and felt her body go tight as a bow. He stroked her sensitive nub with his tongue and slid two fingers into her. She was already—or still—wet, and it drove him mad. The way she responded to him was amazing. Like she had been waiting her entire life for his hands on her.

His fingers thrust into her tight channel, faster. He couldn't get enough. He buried his tongue in her sweet, hot flesh and flexed his fingers deep inside her.

"Luke!" It was a gasp.

He could feel her greedy little muscles tighten around his fingers. "That's right, baby," he whispered against her slick folds. "Come on my fingers." His tongue stroked over the most sensitive part of her, and Harper's hips rocked against his mouth. He felt the first tremors of her release clamp down on his fingers. "Beautiful."

She was still coming when he replaced his fingers with his cock. He slammed into her in a desperate bid to feel it all again. She was so tight it took everything he had not to come. He had to slow it down. Get under control.

Harper lifted her knees higher, changing the angle so that she could take every aching inch of him. He filled her with a calculated thrust, and she gave a sexy little whimper.

"Baby, if you keep making noises like that, this is going to be over too soon," he warned her through gritted teeth.

She either didn't hear his warning or paid no attention to it because a sweet little moan escaped her lips, and it made him lose it. He was pounding into her, hitting bottom.

"Harper." Her name was almost a shout as he felt his climax churning in his balls. Her eyes flew open, and they locked gazes.

Her lust-glazed eyes widened just as he felt her tighten around him. "Luke," she whimpered his name.

He drove in to the hilt and came violently in her.

"Are you asleep?" she whispered while tracing the lines on his arm and chest.

"Mmm," Luke answered without opening his eyes.

"Do you feel like I feel?"

"How do you feel, baby?" He rolled over, pulling her back against him and nuzzling her hair.

"I don't know." She sighed happily and snuggled deeper. "Like it's Christmas morning and everything I ever wanted is under the tree."

"Eh, it was okay. Maybe more like an Easter basket or a nice picnic on Labor Day."

Her indignant gasp was followed by a sharp elbow to his gut.

He wrapped his arms around her tighter, his laughter soft against her ear. It warmed her heart to hear him laugh. She didn't hear the sound often.

"There was nothing okay about it! Don't even pretend you didn't feel the earth move, jerk."

He laughed again, a quiet rumble in his chest.

"I want to hear you say it, Luke."

He had her flat on her back, pinned under him in less than a second.

He framed her face in his hands. "Baby, you and I both know that this was something special. But I'm not surprised. I knew from the second I saw you, the moment you opened those beautiful gray eyes and looked up at me, that I needed to be inside you." He tugged her hand up to his mouth and placed a kiss on her palm. "I don't know what's happening here, but you're in my head and my blood. There was no way that this was not going to happen."

"Then why did you fight it?"

He sighed. "You're not part of the plan. You and your perfect body and that sweet smile. Those sexy little moans you make that get me so hard. You are a beautiful, chaotic distraction. I don't like being distracted."

Harper wasn't sure if she should be flattered or offended, but the warmth flooding her chest made up her mind. "You were pretty good too," she said with a satisfied smirk. He pinched her, and she yelped. "So just to be clear, how will we be spending the rest of our month?" she asked.

He lowered himself to her, lips hovering over hers. "Spending as much time as possible exactly like this."

As what seemed to be her new habit, Harper woke wrapped in Luke's embrace. But this time, she made no move to wriggle free. Instead, she snuggled deeper, burying her sleepy smile in the crook of his arm. She could tell from the light filtering through the windows that it was still too early to think about getting up. It was going to take something around a code red to drag her out of Luke's arms.

He stirred, nuzzling her hair. "Morning, sunshine."

"Mmm, morning."

Luke brushed her hair back and placed a soft kiss on her neck.

"This has to be the best way ever invented to wake up," Harper sighed.

His laugh was soft. "I hate to leave this bed, but I've got an early meeting, and I want to get in a run first."

"You're such a grown-up," Harper sighed. "I should probably get up and pay taxes or clean out the gutters or something."

"Stay. I need you rested for later."

"I like the sound of that."

Luke dropped a kiss on her shoulder and slid out of bed. "Get some more sleep, sunshine."

She rolled over and buried her face in his pillow.

Harper didn't know how long she had slept before she was jolted awake by something landing on her butt with a solid thwack.

"Mmph." She rolled over and squinted up at Luke. He dropped a newspaper in front of her.

"Why are you throwing news at me?"

"Because you're in it." He stood, hands on hips, next to the bed.

Harper shoved herself into a seated position and opened the

paper. It was front-page coverage of the Not-So-Polar Plunge. It opened with a very large picture of her being carted out of the water in Linc's arms.

"Oh, crap."

"Yeah. That doesn't happen again."

"Near drowning? Or me being carried around by a buff firefighter?"

Luke didn't laugh. He crossed his arms over his sweaty T-shirt-clad chest.

"You really don't like him, do you?"

"He's an ass. And I don't like any man's hands on you."

"Are you getting territorial? You're not going to pee on me, are you? Because I am not into that."

"When you're sleeping with me, you're sleeping with only me."

Her arm snaked out, and she grabbed a fistful of shirt, yanking him down to her. "It so happens that I have the same rule. So right back at you, Captain."

He tugged the sheet down and palmed her breast. "Just so we're on the same page." His mouth closed over hers, forcing her head back. When she moaned, he swore and pulled back. "Dammit, Harper. You're making it very hard to go to work."

She reached out a hand to cup him through his shorts. "Yes, yes I am."

CHAPTER 17

S he forgot about their dinner guests until Gloria texted her later that morning to see if there was anything besides apple pie she could bring for dinner. Harper slunk into Luke's office to break the news.

"Hey. You want to get some lunch?" he asked, looking up from his monitor.

"Uh, yeah, sure. But I forgot to tell you that we're having Gloria and Aldo over for dinner tonight."

He stared at her for a beat. "When did this happen?" he asked finally.

"Saturday. They both stopped by, and I forgot to mention it because you were all naked and distracting, and I just now remembered. Anyway, it'll be fun, and Aldo said he'd bring hamburgers and hot dogs to grill, and Gloria's bringing pie, so all we have to do is come up with some side dishes—"

Luke sighed and scrubbed his hands over his face.

"Look, I don't know you well enough to know if you're mad or not. So if you're mad and you don't tell me, it's your own damn fault, and I'll probably keep doing it over and over again, secretly pissing you off every day without knowing it," Harper said, wringing her hands.

"I'm not mad. I'm…inconvenienced."

"The way you say that makes me think there's no difference."

"Where are we going to put them? There's no furniture!"

"They've both been to your house before, so I don't think they're expecting any to magically appear."

He swore quietly and shoved out of his chair.

"Get your purse and get in the truck."

"Where are we going?"

"Fucking furniture shopping."

———

His mood hadn't improved much by the time they got to the store. He had planned to coax Harper into leaving work early to spend the whole evening in bed. Instead, he got ambushed with a stupid dinner party. He was trying to be mad at her, but he knew it was his own damn fault. He was the one who agreed to let her move in. He was the one who had nosey friends. And he was the one who had never gotten around to buying a damn couch or table.

He hated shopping. But it was time to pay the piper.

"Hi, Luke!" A chipper redhead dressed in a royal-blue suit crossed the furniture store's glossy tile floor. "You must be Harper," she said, cheerfully waving.

Luke rolled his eyes and tucked his sunglasses in the neck of his T-shirt. Just once, it would be nice to be anonymous.

"Harper, this is Becky. We went to high school together. Becky, this is my girlfriend, Harper." He knew the last few words came out kind of strangled, but it was the lesser of two evils. His mother had tried to set him up with Becky two years ago, and she had good-naturedly accepted his brush-off, but he had felt a little guilty about it. Thankfully, she had since married Bob of Bob's Fine Furnishings.

"What can I show you two today?"

Harper looked at Luke and smiled.

He sighed. "We need a living room suite and a dining table. Today."

"Great! Let's get started." Becky turned and started to wind her way through leather recliners and end tables.

He grabbed Harper's hand and dragged her after Becky.

Before it was all said and done, Luke picked out a couch, a love seat, two accent chairs, a coffee table and matching end tables, an entertainment center, four handmade bookcases that would look pretty great in the second living room that he had planned to turn into his home office, and a dining room table with eight goddamn chairs.

The only enjoyment he got out of the trip was watching Harper get paler and paler every time he told Becky to add something to the bill.

"Luke, are you sure we need all this?" she whispered while Becky discussed the benefits of Scotchgard.

"You're the one who invited people over with no place to sit down. Might as well get it all out of the way now." He draped an arm around her shoulder. "Don't you want furniture?"

"It's a lot of money," she hissed.

"You help with the books. I'm good for it."

"I haven't gotten through your books yet, and this seems like kind of a large investment for one cookout."

"Cookout?" Luke swore. "Now we need a damn picnic table."

While Becky wrote up the sale of her career, Luke rubbed Harper's shoulders. He smiled at the tension he felt there. Maybe it was time to take pity on her.

"I'm not mad at you…anymore," he murmured against her ear.

She leaned back against him and looked up.

"I'm still sorry. It wasn't very thoughtful of me to invite people into your home without asking you."

"Maybe it won't be horrible."

Harper smiled. "There will be beer and hamburgers—and potato salad if we can stop at the grocery store on the way home."

"More shopping? I'll reserve judgment."

"I was thinking. Now that there's a couch in the house, you could have your bed all to yourself if you wanted."

Luke pinched her. "Sweetheart, after last night, you're lucky if I let you leave the bedroom at all for the rest of the month."

He could see her blush creep down her neck.

Harper turned around and put her arms around his neck. "You know, Gloria's bringing homemade apple pie. We could pick up some vanilla ice cream and caramel sauce to go with it…or for later." She grinned wickedly.

Maybe it wouldn't be so horrible after all.

He hid his grin behind a sigh. "You might as well find some kind of breakfast table thing while we're here because we're *never* coming back," he whispered to Harper.

She obligingly scampered off with Becky in tow while Bob himself stepped in to ring up the purchase.

"You ready to head back, son?"

Bob was twenty years his senior and had retired from a thirty-year career with the National Guard before taking on the home furnishings world.

"Yes, sir."

"Word has it you're a strong leader," Bob said, peering over his reading glasses.

"Thank you, sir."

"Thank you for your service, son. Is this her first deployment?" He nodded toward Harper and Becky, who had their heads together over a pub-height table set.

"It is."

"Think she'll hold up?"

"That girl can survive anything." She already had. She would handle him leaving. She would handle starting a new life, yet again.

———

The fire in the cleaned-up fire pit crackled, casting a warm, flickering glow around the backyard. Luke shifted his weight in the new wooden Adirondack chair.

Bob had thrown in four chairs with the purchase of the picnic table and the rest of the furniture. As soon as Luke's credit card had cleared, Bob had loaded everything up on a truck and had it delivered. They had just enough time to get everything set up, the tags cut off, and the potato and pasta salads chucked into bowls before Aldo and Gloria arrived.

Aldo, the smart-ass, accused Luke of nesting now that he had finally convinced a woman to tolerate him. Luke hadn't been amused by the joke, but Harper got a good laugh out of it.

She laughed a lot. It was a sound that warmed him up. A sound that made him realize how quiet his life had become before. A sound that made him wonder why he had valued the silence so much.

He took a sip of beer and watched her through the licks of flames as she and Gloria tried their hands at toasting marshmallows. The firelight danced gold in her hair. She was beautiful to begin with, but add that grin and her bubbly laugh and it pulled at something deep inside, rooting and taking hold.

"Hey, lover boy, if you're done staring dreamily at your girl, I'm empty." Aldo wiggled his beer bottle. "It's your turn to play host."

Luke stood up and took Aldo's bottle before tipping his

friend's chair sideways and depositing Aldo on the ground. "Sure, no problem. Ladies, can I get you anything?"

Harper jumped up. "I'll help you," she said brightly.

"I think I can carry a few beers myself," Luke teased, holding the back door open for her. "Or are you just trying to get me alone?"

Harper brushed up against him as she walked past. "I'm multitasking."

He shut the door a little harder than he meant to in his haste to get his hands on her. Harper ran her finger down his chest to his stomach. He was hard even before she skimmed lower to the top of his jeans. "I'm helping you carry beers, stealing a very private moment with you, and letting Gloria and Aldo talk." She dipped her fingers in his waistband.

"Don't start something you can't finish, baby," he warned.

Harper let him back her up against the refrigerator. He saw the eagerness in her eyes and wondered if it was mirrored in his. His hands slid under her sweatshirt, fingers running over the impossibly soft skin. His mouth hovered over hers.

"The lights are on. They can see us," Harper whispered. Her eyes danced, and he knew she would let him do anything regardless of audience.

Wordlessly he dragged her into the darkened dining room and almost tripped over the table that he forgot he bought. He caged her between his arms against the table.

"I think I've earned a kiss for tonight."

He read hot lust in her gaze. "I think we can start with a kiss," she said in a breathy whisper.

Luke stayed where he was and let her make the move.

She put her arms around his neck and pressed herself against him, her breasts gently rubbing against his chest. She slowly closed the distance between their lips.

He was determined to keep it playful, sweet. But as soon as she bit his bottom lip, all gentleness was forgotten. He growled as she sucked it into her mouth.

Luke grabbed her hand and pressed it against his erection.

"Get rid of them, baby."

She laughed against his mouth, and he almost took her there on the table. The way she responded to him took him closer and closer to the line.

After another scorching kiss, he pried her hands off him and took a step back.

He sighed. "We'd better get back out there."

Harper licked her lip and sighed. "Whose idea was it to have people over tonight?"

He smacked her on the ass and put his hands on her shoulders. She smelled like sunshine and fire. He guided her back to the kitchen. "If you're done attacking me, I'll grab the beers."

"I don't plan to be done attacking you any time soon, Captain." She winked before sneaking a peek out the window. Aldo had taken the chair she vacated and was sitting next to Gloria. Harper smiled.

"Why are you looking so smug?" Luke demanded, coming up behind her.

"Just spying on Aldo to see if he's worked up the courage to tell Gloria how much he likes her."

"Aldo and Gloria?" Luke snorted. "Baby, the day Aldo settles down is the day hell freezes over, pigs fly, and I go vegetarian. Don't get your hopes up."

"I'll take that bet."

Luke dropped a kiss on her neck. "Deal. When Aldo and Gloria get married, I'll go vegetarian."

CHAPTER 18

Their guests left late that evening with Luke practically shoving them out the door. Aldo was on the front porch, offering to give Gloria a ride home, when Luke shut and locked the front door behind them.

It made Harper tingle with the thought that he wanted to have her alone so badly. Luke pushed her back against the door and kissed her with a heat that scorched. "We'll clean up the kitchen tomorrow," he decided.

Harper nodded. "Definitely."

"Shower?"

"Yes, please."

He dragged her, laughing, upstairs to the bathroom and turned on the water.

Luke pulled his shirt over his head while Harper pretended not to watch. When he slid his jeans down his muscular thighs, she wet her lips. His underwear clung to the bulge between his legs.

"What?" he demanded.

"I was just wondering how it's physically possible for a human being to be so perfectly formed." She stepped forward to trail her fingers over his chest.

Luke smirked and stilled her hand on his skin. "I was wondering how it's physically possible for you to still have all your clothes on."

Harper pulled off her sweatshirt and tossed it at him. Her shorts came next. The second her bra hit the floor, Luke was dragging her into the steaming water.

They stroked and played, raining wet kisses on slick skin.

Luke moved behind her and squeezed her shampoo into his hand. Harper let him work his strong fingers through her hair under the spray.

He lifted her wet tresses from her back, lips brushing the nape of her neck. Goose bumps cropped up even under the heat of the water.

She turned in his arms, letting the water cascade down her back. "My turn," she said, nipping his lower lip with her teeth.

He let her lather him with body wash. Harper took her time, smoothing her hands across his chest and across his stomach. His cock twitched the closer her strokes came to it. He dropped his forehead to hers. "Baby, you drive me crazy."

Harper gripped his shaft in her soapy hand. "Right back at you. Put your hands on the wall," she whispered.

He hesitated, and she slid her hands lower to cup his heavy sack. "Please, Luke?"

When he finally did as she asked, she sank to her knees under the spray of the showerhead.

"Harper."

She didn't bother hiding her triumphant smile before she took him into her mouth.

Luke swore, and Harper slid her lips farther down his shaft. Resting her hands on his thighs, she could feel the tension running through his body.

She moaned and felt him get harder instantly. His hips

flexed, forcing him deeper into her mouth, again and again. She eagerly met his short, fast thrusts.

"My God, Harper."

He grabbed her under the arms and pulled her to her feet and out of the shower.

"I don't want to come yet."

Skipping the towel, he pressed her against the vanity and used his knee to spread her legs wider. He took a hand and swiped a path of steam from the mirror. "I want to see you," he said, lips moving against her ear, eyes never breaking from hers in the reflection.

She shivered against him.

"Trust me."

Harper nodded. She did. Something deep inside her recognized him. Knew him.

Luke slid his hand slowly down her spine, following the trail of water from her wet hair to the cleft between her cheeks. His fingers lightly traced the water's path, skimming over her anus. She tensed.

"I've never—"

"Put your hands on the counter." He reached up and squeezed more water from her hair, and she felt it trickle down her back to her behind. Harper shut her eyes as his hand once again followed the water.

"Open your eyes, baby." He said it so softly, so sweetly, Harper couldn't disobey.

Luke's hand snaked around to the front, and he cupped her sex, fingers pressing into her lips. "I can feel how wet you are for me." His fingers spread her open and found her clitoris. He rubbed gently with the pads of his fingers, a smooth, circular motion.

Harper felt the heat pool between her legs, the familiar

heaviness deep in her belly. She had no control around him. She was always wet for him.

Luke's gaze followed the trails of water from her hair as they made a lazy path to her nipple before beading and dripping off.

With his other hand, he took one of hers and brought it to her breast. Harper squeezed, and she heard him exhale behind her. His busy fingers pressed against her in approval. Harper cupped her breast and tried to focus on Luke's eyes in the mirror.

He was fiercely in control but still exploring. She wondered how far he would take it. How far she would let him go.

Watching her, Luke straightened a finger and drove it inside her. Harper felt her knees buckle, and she bumped back against him. His cock rubbed between the cheeks of her behind. He gripped his shaft and slapped it lightly against her back.

Harper moaned and moved her fingers to tug gently at her nipple. Luke withdrew his finger and replaced it with two. He leaned over her, pressing her forward, and she had to bring both hands to the counter to steady them.

Luke reached around to cup her other breast, rubbing his thumb over her straining nipple. Everything he did to her felt like heaven and torture at the same time. Sheathing his fingers in her to the hilt, he curled them inside her.

"I'm going to watch you come." He whispered it darkly against her hair. Like she was under a spell, her body obeyed. He drove his fingers into her again, and she shuddered, already at the edge. He kneaded her breast and pressed his cock against her cleft. She felt herself tighten around his fingers as his other hand tugged at her nipple. Harper fell forward on the vanity and let the sweet waves take her.

Luke's eyes never left hers, and in them was possession.

She felt the last of the orgasm slide through her and braced herself, catching her breath. "Jesus, Luke," she whispered over her pounding pulse. Her body felt like it was designed for his.

He withdrew his fingers and held them up to her. She could see the slick coating and blushed. It was a dark pleasure.

Luke leaned back, still clutching her breast, and moved his hand to the small of her back. She felt his thumb press against the top of her cleft before his wet fingers traveled lower still.

She inhaled sharply when his fingers found her anus. She had never been touched like this before, never been this vulnerable. Luke paused, applying a slight pressure with his finger. Harper felt a need she had never known begin to build. She pressed her back against him, testing the sensation.

He smiled grimly in the mirror and tugged at her nipple again. Rolling it between his finger and thumb, he mimicked the pulls of a mouth on her. Harper's lips parted, and she felt him shift his weight into her. His fingers ever so slowly breached her opening, and she gasped. It felt wrong. It felt good.

She could see the set of his jaw in the mirror and knew he was struggling to hold back. Harper shifted back against him, urging him deeper. Slowly, he fingered her hole, filling her. He reached his hand across to the other breast, rubbing his palm lazily over the nipple.

His fingers withdrew and thrust in again and then again, a slow, consuming rhythm. She felt her herself flex toward him every time he withdrew. She could feel juices gathering between her thighs and mingling with the water on her skin.

This wasn't healthy, to have her body need his like this.

He withdrew his fingers, and she felt him grip his shaft.

Luke slid the rounded head of his cock between her legs, gently probing. She met his gaze in the mirror. Her breathing was shallow. She swallowed, desperate to be filled.

She felt the pressure as his wide crest breached her sex. Felt the gasp escape her lungs as he invaded her. Harper's head spun, but she never took her eyes off his in the mirror. Those hazel orbs bored into her, seeing every corner of her dark soul. She was exposed, possessed.

"Luke," she whispered. She tried to buck against him, to make him move.

He held her hips still with his rough hands. They stayed that way for what felt like an eternity. He pulled out slightly. Harper moaned, and it was all the encouragement he needed to bury himself in her. She cried out in triumph. Luke brought a hand around to tease the lips of her sex apart.

He filled her in a way no man ever had.

She couldn't catch her breath as he started to move. His fingers teased a sweet spot, and his shaft stretched her to capacity. Something was building in her. It was a wall of pleasure so towering, she knew she couldn't survive the break.

Harper could see sweat forming on his brow, his gaze still burning into her. The thrusts were coming faster now, and he gave a quiet grunt with each one. He was going to come like this. Just knowing it put a crack in her wall. Luke reached around her and cupped her breast again. He tugged on her pebbled nipple.

It happened in an instant. The wall broke inside her just as Harper felt Luke's first shudder of release. He let loose deep inside her. She clamped down on his shaft and shattered around it. Luke released her breast and gripped her chin in his hand, watching her as they both came apart.

"Where did you get these?" Luke asked, lazily running his fingers over twin scars high on her hip.

Harper was draped over him, naked on the bed in a

postorgasmic coma. She shrugged and buried her face in his chest. He shifted her to the mattress and sat up.

Harper snuggled facedown into his pillow and ignored him as he studied her skin.

"Harper." He poked her butt cheek.

"Mmm."

"Harper Sue Ellen Wilde."

She rolled to her side. "That is definitely not my middle name."

"I don't know your middle name, so I had to make one up."

"So you went with Sue Ellen?"

"It seemed like a good fit."

"It's Lee actually."

"Parents fans of *To Kill a Mockingbird*?"

"Very good." She arched an eyebrow.

"I'm more than just a pretty face."

Harper's gaze trailed down his naked body. "Oh, I can see that."

"Hey, I'm not a piece of meat, and I asked you a question."

Harper sighed and rose up on her elbow. "Why do you want to know?"

"Because they look like cigarette burns."

"Good eye."

His blood went icy in the span of a heartbeat. "Who did it? Was it that asshole Ted?"

She rolled her eyes. "No, it wasn't Ted. It was a long time ago. It doesn't matter who it was."

"Like hell it doesn't. Someone burned you with a fucking cigarette, and you're telling me it doesn't matter?"

Harper sat up. "I really don't like talking about it."

"I really don't care. Tell me who did this."

He saw the little muscle in her jaw tick and tried to relax.

153

Yelling at her wasn't exactly a smart way to make a woman open up.

He reached out and squeezed her shoulder. "Baby. You can trust me."

"Why does this matter so much?"

Because you matter. He stopped the thought before it became words. Words that couldn't be taken back. *Shit.*

"I don't like feeling like you're hiding something from me." He was such a fucking hypocrite.

"I'm not hiding anything, Luke. It's just, it's something I've never told anyone."

"Tell me what happened."

She sighed, and he knew he had won.

"When I was in foster care, I was living with this really nice family. A mom, a dad, two brothers. I thought they might adopt me. It was great until they got pregnant again and got a job offer on the other side of the country. I was transferred out of their house into another one. That family wasn't as nice."

Luke lay back down on the bed and pulled her in to his side. He stroked the smooth skin of her back as she talked.

"It was an older couple, and there were a lot of kids in the house. Some fosters, some not. They were always yelling, the kids were dirty, there was never enough food."

Luke could feel his heart rate ratcheting up and forced himself to keep his touch gentle.

"After I had been there a week, the mom left, and things got ugly fast. The man had a nasty temper, especially when he drank. Every payday, we'd all do everything we could to stay out of his way. But someone always got noticed. And once or twice, it was me."

Luke felt sick to his stomach. "How old were you?"

"I was twelve. I was the oldest in the house."

"Did he ever do anything…" Luke couldn't get the words out without choking on them.

"Sexual? No, just regular, run-of-the-mill physical abuse."

"What happened to him?"

"Jail."

"Is he still there? Is he any kind of threat to you?"

"He's still there."

He kissed the top of her head and held her close, forcing himself to be gentle when the rage pounding through his veins wanted to destroy something.

"Thank you for telling me, Harper." When she didn't respond, he nudged her chin up. "I'm sorry. I hate that that happened to you."

"Me too. Let's talk about something less depressing. Like maybe another shower?"

CHAPTER 19

Harper worried that her confession to Luke would make him see her as damaged goods or, worse, feel sorry for her. However, nothing slowed down their need for each other. They spent more time in bed than out of it. She kept waiting for the intensity to fade, to not ache to have him inside her. To get used to the sight of his naked body. To not feel that pitter-patter in her chest when he said her name.

Maybe it was the fact that their time together was expiring that fueled the intensity. Whatever it was, it left her breathless.

She watched Luke as he seamlessly folded preparations to leave into his already busy days. At work, Frank and Charlie would be stepping up in Luke's absence. They had done it before, and Luke trusted them with what he had built.

At home, Luke would count on James for property mainte-nance and check-ins. His brother also had access to Luke's accounts and would make sure bills were paid. While Luke double-checked his autopay bills, changed the oil in his truck— and her car—and checked the level in the propane tank, Harper started a list of things she needed to do before leaving.

She and Beth worked long hours trying to get everything around the office caught up and organized.

"Thank God you're here," Beth puffed as she hauled a towering stack of papers to the shredder. "Otherwise, I would have been stuck filing all this crap."

Harper staggered behind her under the weight of her own load. "Scanners." She gasped. "Best invention ever."

Between the two of them, they had managed to scan the last eight months of paperwork and invoices into an online system that was backed up daily. Going forward, all paperwork would be done electronically and stored in the system. But that still left all Garrison's old paper records.

"I think we should get an intern this summer to do all the scanning and shredding." Beth dropped the papers in an unceremonious heap next to the shredder. "And washing our cars and picking up our lunches."

Harper felt a little twinge with the realization that she wouldn't actually be here this summer. Who knew where she was going to end up? But it was probably past time for her to bring up the subject to Luke.

With only two weeks until his unit deployed, she needed to strategize a graceful exit. She had every intention of using this month for résumé polishing and job hunting, but she had spent the majority of her time working or naked.

She didn't feel particularly remorseful about her priorities. However, she was dangerously close to getting carried away with their faux romance. A little shot of reality, however painful, was a healthy reminder of what she needed to focus on.

Guiltily, Harper thought about the handful of emails her friend Hannah had sent her with job postings in Fremont that she hadn't even opened yet.

Thanks to the generous salary Luke gave her and the fact that he refused to let her pay rent or utilities, her savings account was being rebuilt, and she would have plenty for a security deposit and rent on a new apartment. She'd even have a little left over for some furniture.

A little place of her own would be a good thing to focus on when it came to getting over Luke.

Harper sighed and dumped her files on the floor. "Let's go grab some lunch before we tackle the shredding. My treat."

———

When Luke came home that afternoon, he found Harper perched on a barstool squinting at his laptop. Harper lifted her face for a kiss, and he caught a glimpse of the screen.

"Looking for a new job on your boss's computer? Classy."

Harper wrinkled her nose at him and pulled him down for another kiss. "Very funny. And yes." She turned her attention back to the screen. "I'm also trying to figure out how to make being in this position for only a month not sound flaky on my résumé."

Luke went to the sink to pour two glasses of water. "Call it a short-term contract position."

"God. You're a genius. No wonder I want to get in your pants all the time."

He immediately felt himself go hard. Keeping the island between them, he slid a glass to her. "I can write you a reference letter if that would help." Where the hell had that come from?

Those big gray eyes widened with hope. Always a punch in his gut.

"Are you serious? That would be amazing!"

Great. Now he had to do it or look like an asshole. Writing an email was difficult for him. How was he supposed to put a glowing review on paper? Not that Harper didn't deserve it. She had taken his floundering mess of an office and started pushing it down the road to being an efficient operation in just two weeks.

Maybe he could make Sophie write it.

"So where are you looking for jobs?" he asked.

Harper took a sip of water. "I'm focusing on my original plan of Fremont. It's no Benevolence, but I think being close to Hannah again would be nice."

"Have you thought of staying around here?" What the fuck was wrong with him? He hadn't even known he was thinking it before it was shooting out of his mouth.

Harper shifted in her seat and looked away from him toward the cabinets. "Uh, yeah. For about a minute. I don't think it would work."

Now he had to ask. "Why's that?" He pretended to flip through the mail on the counter.

She cleared her throat. "I don't want to say because you'll take it the wrong way and go into panic mode."

Luke decided to just stare her down until she broke. It took her about thirty seconds of squirming before he won.

"I thought about staying until I realized what it would be like to run into you and your future girlfriend and then wife at the grocery store every week. Every time I'd see you, I'd think about what it was like to be with you while knowing that now someone else gets to be with you that way..." She shuddered and shook her head. "That's not the way I want to spend the rest of my life."

His gut churned at the idea. Not of him with someone else. That wasn't going to happen. But Harper would move on. She deserved to move on. He would see her around town with some guy who would ask her to marry him. He'd see her with kids at sporting events. They'd run into each other at the lake in the summer, and it would be some other lucky asshole's hands on those perfect curves.

Luke set his glass down with a bang on the granite. Harper jumped.

"See? I told you you wouldn't like it. I'm not saying I'm in love with you, Luke. I just don't like the idea of you moving on."

Right back at you, baby.

"Good point. Hey, your first mail here." He tossed the envelope with her name written in scrawling handwriting to her.

Harper glanced at it and frowned.

"Just junk mail," she said, shoving it under the laptop. "So since we're on the subject anyway, what are we going to tell your family about me leaving?"

"I hadn't really thought about it yet."

Harper sighed. "Me neither. I let you distract me with that hot, naked body of yours."

"Oh, you mean this hot, naked body?" Luke pulled his shirt off and was dragging hers over her head before she could gasp with laughter.

———

Wednesday evening, Harper headed home without Luke. He was off on a job site somewhere, solving a crisis, reassuring a client. She appreciated his work ethic. No problem was too small for him to tackle when it came to making clients and employees feel valued.

Just that morning, Luke had called their newest employee in for a meeting. John was eighteen, fresh out of high school, and had great promise as a future finish carpenter.

"Listen, John, you need to understand that just because you've got a little money in your pocket, it doesn't mean you get to go out and do a bunch of stupid shit. You don't need to buy a forty-five-thousand-dollar pickup, and you sure as hell don't need a sixty-inch TV for your parents' basement. I want you to be successful, and I'm here to help you get there…"

Harper had grinned to herself as she made copies and eavesdropped outside Luke's office.

He really cared about his people whether they were family, friends, or employees. He was the kind of man you could depend on. Not only to help you out of a jam but to protect you from one if he could.

She carried her purse and lunch bag back to the kitchen and dumped them on the counter. It was such a beautiful spring evening, she decided to open up every window in the house to welcome the breeze. She ran up to the bedroom to change into shorts and a T-shirt and was on the stairs when she heard the knock at the front door.

"Claire! Hi! Come on in." Harper stepped back and waved Luke's mom in.

Claire held up a plastic container of mini cheesecakes. "I was just in the neighborhood with baked goods and thought I'd stop in."

"Oh my God. For those, you can move in," Harper laughed. "Come on back. Can I get you something to drink? Water? Iced tea?"

"Iced tea would be great, thanks." Claire started down the hall behind Harper and made it as far as the dining room.

"Oh, he finally got furniture!"

Harper joined her in the doorway. "I accidentally invited some friends over for dinner without knowing that Luke was terribly sensitive about not having places for people to sit."

"I've been waiting for that boy to turn this house into a home for so long." Claire turned to Harper. "You, my dear, deserve more than half a dozen cheesecakes."

After a quick tour of the rest of the new furniture, they took their iced tea on the back porch to enjoy the spring evening.

Claire pushed off the porch boards and set the swing into

an easy motion. "I have a confession to make. I wasn't just in the neighborhood with baked goods."

"You don't say," Harper said over the rim of her glass.

"Luke calls it meddling. I call it mothering." Claire sighed, running a hand through her short dark hair threaded with silver. It was a standard Luke move that made Harper smile. "He thinks because he's a grown man that his business is his business. But he doesn't understand what it's like to raise someone into an adult. You don't just stop…"

"Caring?"

Claire nodded. "Exactly. He's thirty years old, and I still feel the need to make sure he's okay. I bet your parents are the same way."

Harper cocked her head. "I imagine they would be. They passed away when I was very young, but I like to think that they would have a vested interest in my life if they were still here."

"Oh, I'm so sorry to hear that, Harper. I didn't know! Please excuse me for opening my gigantic mouth."

Harper laughed. "That's all right. It was a long time ago."

"Time doesn't always heal all wounds," Claire said a little sadly. "Some never recover from loss."

"I guess some of us just don't recognize how valuable our time is here. How we shouldn't spend our time mourning our loss but thanking our lucky stars we had someone wonderful in our lives for no matter how long."

"Then Luke's told you—"

Claire was cut off by the screen door swinging open.

Harper felt her pulse flutter at the sight of Luke. His worn jeans were covered in dirt, and the T-shirt molded to his chest had a good deal of sweat mixed in with the dirt. Even his baseball hat had sweat stains. He looked like he had sauntered straight off the pages of a sexy construction worker calendar. The scratch-and-sniff kind.

"Ladies." Luke dropped a kiss on Harper's forehead and crossed to the porch railing where he leaned.

"I was just in the neighborhood and thought I'd stop in," Claire said innocently.

"Sure you were, Ma. You're not interrogating poor Harper, are you?"

"No, but I was shoving my big, fat foot in my mouth since you neglected to tell me her parents passed away. These things wouldn't happen if you'd com-mu-ni-cate." The silvery charms dangling from her ears jingled with each syllable.

"Yes, Ma." Luke rolled his eyes. "So you weren't grilling Harper?"

"I hadn't gotten around to it yet. I'm a polite interrogator. I was easing Harper into it." Claire winked.

"How's work going?" Luke asked. "We got a call today from Della. Says they want to do that addition."

Claire nodded. "The flower business is booming. I'm only supposed to be there two days a week, but I've been called in just about every Friday and a couple of Saturdays to help with wedding orders. Della and Fred are looking to hire someone full-time to eventually take over as manager."

"Do they have any candidates?" Harper asked.

"You're not looking to quit already, are you?" Luke teased.

Harper laughed. "No, but Gloria is looking for something."

"Gloria Parker? Good for her!" Claire nodded briskly. "It's about time she gets a chance to spread her wings. Have her call the store, and I'll hook her up with Della for an interview."

"That would be great! Thank you so much."

"Hey, I owe the girl who inspired my son to get a girlfriend, hire an office manager, and buy furniture more than a few mini cheesecakes."

"Cheesecakes?" Luke perked up.

———

Luke walked his mother to her car, mostly to make sure she didn't corner Harper and try to wrangle any more information out of her.

"I like the new furniture," she told him, digging her keys out of her purse. "It's starting to look like a home."

"Ma." Luke didn't try to keep the exasperation out of his voice.

"Don't you 'Ma' me. I'm allowed to check up on my children. Forty-seven hours of labor gives a mother certain privileges."

"For the love of—"

"I really like her, Luke. You're smiling again." She brought a hand to his face. "It's been a long time."

He grumbled but took his mom's hand and kissed her palm. "She's a good girl, Ma. I like her too. Now can we stop talking about my love life?"

She gave him a peck on the cheek. "Fine. Now go take your girl out to dinner. She deserves it."

Luke waited until his mother had pulled out of the driveway before whipping out his cell phone. His parents liked his girlfriend, and that was a problem.

"I need sneaky, underhanded advice, so I'm coming to you." Luke paced the driveway.

"Is it weird that I'm flattered?" Sophie asked.

"What do I tell Mom and Dad about Harper leaving?"

Josh screamed in the background.

"Is everything okay over there?" Luke asked.

"What? Oh, yeah. That's his happy scream. Hang on. Let me lock him in the basement."

"Sophie!"

"I'm just kidding. I walked into the pantry. I need silence so I can focus on the lies you'll be telling our parents."

"Need I remind you that this whole thing was your idea?"

"Need *I* remind *you* that you're enjoying this whole thing that was my idea?"

"Touché. Now tell me what to do."

"Well, when is she leaving? Before or after you leave?"

"I don't know. After?"

"Do you have a timeline?"

"We haven't really talked about it."

"It would probably make more sense to have her hang around for a little after you leave, plus then you wouldn't need James looking in on the house right away. I'm assuming you don't want either one of you to look like an asshole, right?"

"You assume correctly."

"Well, then it has to be a good news thing that's so good it makes the sad news of her leaving less sad."

"You're losing me."

"You're such a man. Something wonderful happens to Harper, and she has to leave town. Like she gets a part in a movie or she meets the man of her dreams."

"I'm supposed to be the man of her dreams."

"I'm just spitballing here," Sophie said with a sigh. "But since you said it, why not ask her to stay?"

"That's not the plan, Soph. And it's not fair to ask Harper to put her life on hold for six months to see if this might turn into a relationship."

"Okay, okay. Just throwing out options."

CHAPTER 20

The next day, Luke and Aldo were needed on base for the standard predeployment medical exam and some briefings. Before he left, Luke kissed Harper goodbye and got carried away. By the time he pulled up in front of Aldo's house, he was running twenty minutes late, and his friend was waiting on the front porch.

When Aldo chose the tidy Craftsman cottage over one of the new town houses on the edge of town, Luke hadn't batted an eye. A family home over a bachelor-friendly condo? It wasn't what he expected from his play-the-field buddy, but there was a lot of things they never discussed. They didn't have to.

"About time." Aldo climbed into the passenger seat and belted in.

"I'm not that late."

"No explanations needed. I can see from the stupid look on your face why you're late."

"You're full of shit." He wasn't. Luke knew he was walking around with a stupid look on his face these days. He'd just been hoping that no one else noticed it.

"I've known you since I saved your ass from that beatdown in first grade. I know your stupid looks."

"I still maintain that I could have taken those guys on my own." Luke pulled away from the curb.

"There were three of them, and they were in the fourth grade."

"Well, if you did *assist* me in that situation, I saved your ass from drowning in the lake when we were twelve."

"I thought the ice would hold." Aldo shrugged with a white-toothed grin.

"We were grounded for all of January for that one."

"Our moms were so pissed. So what does Claire think of Harper?"

Luke bit back a sigh. He knew his friend wouldn't wait long to pry. Sometimes he had to remind himself not to shut everyone out. "She loves her. Thinks she's just what I need."

"Is she?"

"What I need is peace and quiet. Harper is anything but that."

Aldo laughed. "So why is she here?"

Luke shrugged as he took the on-ramp for the highway. "It started as a favor. The girl had no place to go and no way to get there."

"And then?"

Luke cleared his throat. "Well, you've met her."

"I have. Think she'll stay?"

Luke shook his head. "Nah. She's got things to do, places to go. Six months is a long time to ask someone you just met to wait."

"It's a long time to ask anyone to wait. She would, you know."

"I don't know if I'd want her to."

"Bullshit."

"Kiss your mother with that mouth?"

"Where do you think I learned it?"

It was the truth. Despite the fact that Mrs. Moretta went to church every other Sunday, she had the mouth of a sailor who retired and started a new career trucking. She had never shied away from a healthy four-letter word when the situation called for it.

"Speaking of women, Harper seems to think you have a thing for Gloria."

"She's not wrong."

"You've had a thing for anything with a nice pair of legs and big brown eyes."

"Where do you think I got my type?"

"So if you've been carrying this torch since high school, how is Glenn still alive?"

"I ask myself that every day. The deployments made it easier to think about something else. Gave me something to focus on."

Luke knew exactly what Aldo meant.

His friend shifted in his seat. "I gotta say. I'm thinking about retiring. This is number four, and I want to make it my last."

"Really?"

"We've been doing this since high school. That's twelve years of packing up and moving out and hoping we get to come back after the job's done. I'm ready to stay put. I want to put more time into some engineering projects. And then I want to make a nice girl the next Mrs. Moretta."

"Jesus, Aldo." Just the thought of it made Luke start to sweat. "When the hell did you decide all this?"

"About ten seconds after I found out Gloria moved out. Don't tell me you're not ready to hang it up."

"It's all I've got. The guard and my business."

Aldo snorted. "You've got your family, and you could have Harper too if you wanted. Come home to that sweet face every day and find out what trouble she got herself into? There's something to look forward to."

"She is trouble. I'm concerned about releasing her into the wild."

"She needs you."

"She needs her fucking parents, but they're dead. She's got no family, just scars from all those years in foster care."

Aldo swore quietly. "And you'd do anything to make it better, but you just don't know how to help."

"Exactly." Luke sighed. Of course Aldo got it. "Fact is, I just don't have room in my life for her."

"You've got the room. You're just too chickenshit to make it."

Luke bristled. While Aldo, his family, and everyone else were more than happy to shove their noses into his business, none of them knew what it was like to have everything and then lose it all. He knew. And he had barely survived. There were no second chances.

———

The physicals were fine, the briefings tedious. But they made it home in decent time with a clearer picture of what they'd be doing in Afghanistan. Usually, Luke felt the buzz, a hum of excitement about the next mission, a new project. But this time he just felt *off*.

He had things to do—around the house, at the office. But he was tired. He was used to running on little sleep and too much caffeine or pure adrenaline. But the late nights with Harper under him, over him, wrapped around him, had taken a toll.

Luke wasn't the napping type. Maybe he just needed to

relax with the TV for an hour, and then he could get back to his paperwork and packing.

He woke up an hour later with something warm and heavy in his lap.

A large, gray dog rested its head and a beefy paw on Luke's leg. "Harper!"

She appeared in the doorway in seconds, which meant she had been hovering nearby.

"Before you get mad—"

"Harper, why is there a fucking dog in my lap?"

"We don't have to keep her. She just needs a nice place to stay."

"Harper, why is there a fucking dog in my lap?"

The dog grumbled in its sleep and stretched.

"What the hell kind of dog is this?"

"She's some kind of pit bull, Lab something. She was a neglect case, and just because she has this skin condition and needs heart meds, the shelter was going to put her down."

"That still doesn't answer why there's a dog. In my lap." His voice was loud enough to wake the beast this time. A bloodshot eye opened lazily and stared at him.

"I stopped at the grocery store, and this woman was walking out of the pet store with her. Her name's Lola, by the way."

"The woman?"

"No! The dog."

Hearing her name, the dog turned her massive head toward Harper. Her tail thumped twice.

"Anyway, the rescue in town took her, but they needed a place for her to stay until they can find a foster home—a week tops—and she looked at me with those big sappy eyes. And before I knew it, I was putting her in the car. And I'm so sorry. Please don't hate me. Or Lola."

The dog's tail thumped again.

"Harper, you can't just bring a dog home."

"I know! I think she hypnotized me. I'm so sorry."

Lola swung her head back to Luke. "Why are her eyes funny?"

"It's just a little infection. We put drops in three times a day."

Lola's tongue lolled out of her mouth. "Harper. She's huge. She could swallow you whole."

"She's a sweetheart. There's not a mean bone in her body." Harper was wringing her hands together.

Lola rolled over on Luke's lap, baring her belly.

"A week?"

"Tops."

———

Lola had them trained in a matter of days. She gently reminded them when it was meal time and potty time. Luke's dog-free house soon included a large inventory of squeaky toys and bones that Lola perused hourly. And every night, she snored at the foot of the bed with her huge head resting on Harper's feet.

Harper did her best to make sure she took on the majority of dog care. Walks, meals, medicine—she even tackled the poor dog's overgrown toenails.

She tried to keep Luke's inconvenience to a minimum but still felt the sting of his sighs whenever Lola made her presence known.

Every day, she reminded herself how generous Luke had been to open his home to her and now Lola. Guilt and gratitude had her stocking the refrigerator with all his favorites and bending over backward around the house to be helpful.

She tried to make it home before Luke in the evenings so she could let Lola out, but he was always there first. One night, she came home to find Luke and the boys trying to teach Lola to fetch. Lola wasn't into it, but Henry was a good sport about chasing all the balls that Robbie threw.

Later, when they walked the boys home, Lola didn't even flinch when little Ava toddled over and sat on her. She just yawned and allowed herself to be squished and stroked by sticky fingers.

For the first few mornings post-Lola, Luke asked Harper if she had heard from the rescue on a permanent foster home yet.

When he stopped asking and Lola started disappearing downstairs with Luke in the mornings, Harper got suspicious.

The next morning, she waited in bed until Luke headed downstairs with Lola. When she heard the front door close behind him, Harper threw the covers off and hurried down.

There was food in her bowl but no sign of Lola in the kitchen. Harper snooped through the rest of the first floor and checked the backyard. No Lola.

She grabbed a cup of coffee and sat on the front porch to wait.

Her patience was rewarded ten minutes later by the sight of Luke and Lola bounding around the corner side by side. Lola's muscled legs ate up the sidewalk while her tongue lolled to the side. Luke's mile-wide grin matched his running buddy's. They were happiness in motion.

She saw the slight stutter in his step the second he noticed her. He carefully rearranged his features to an impassive expression by the time they hit the walkway to the house.

Harper tried to hide her grin behind her coffee. "Good morning."

"Morning," Luke said, oozing nonchalance. He handed her Lola's leash. "She, uh, had to go out, so I took her."

"Around the block?" Harper asked innocently, petting Lola's heaving sides. She was rewarded by a huge slurp from Lola's tongue.

"Uh, yeah. The block."

Lola sat next to Harper on the step and leaned into her arm.

"You are such a liar!"

Luke put his hands up. "Hey, we did go around the block. Kind of."

"You've been taking her on your runs, which is why she's totally exhausted when I take her for a walk an hour later!"

She could tell he was weighing his options behind his sunglasses.

He threw up his arms. "For Christ's sake, look at her! She's huge. I was worried she'd drag you around the block and knock everyone over."

"So you took her out first to try her out?"

"Well, yeah. And to tire her out so if she was bad on a leash, she'd at least be *less* bad tired."

"That's oddly sweet and thoughtful of you."

"Hard to be mad at me, isn't it?" The dimple flickered back into existence.

"Well, it would be except for the fact that you've been making me feel so guilty for bringing her into your house when you clearly love having her around!"

"I wouldn't say love—"

"Lucas Norbert Garrison!"

"Charles, actually."

"You love her! Look her in those big dopey eyes and tell her you don't." Harper squished Lola's face in her hands. "Look at Daddy. Make him feel like garbage for playing Mommy. You could have told me, you know. Should have told me."

"I am pleading the fifth. Now if you lovely ladies don't mind, I'm going to finish my run because Lola can only hang for a mile and a half." He leaned in and kissed Harper and moved to drop a peck on Lola's head, but she squirmed free and stuck her tongue in his mouth.

"At this second, I can honestly say I don't love that," he said, wiping his face with the back of his hand.

"Serves you right, Norbert!"

"Can we still have steak tonight?" he asked, backing down the walk.

"You knew I was kissing up to you! You are such an—"

"The neighbors don't need you to finish that sentence," he called as he turned onto the sidewalk.

"Fine, but Lola gets half of yours!" Harper waited until he was out of sight before laughing.

———

Luke avoided the office all day, communicating primarily by text and email, even after Harper called him a chicken.

She beat him home and took Lola for a quick walk before starting dinner. Harper was busy prepping the steaks when she heard the front door. She headed down the hall to greet Luke with Lola ambling after her.

"Look who decided to face the music," Harper teased.

Luke dropped his keys on the table by the door and shifted the strange bundle he was holding.

The bundle barked.

"Not a word. Not one word," Luke muttered.

He was carrying a scruffy terrier under his arm like a football.

Harper bit her lip to keep from laughing.

Luke put the dog down on the floor. It had three legs.

"Wait a second. Shouldn't we introduce them or something first?" Harper started toward Lola.

"Fine. Lola, meet Max. Max, meet Lola."

Max scampered over to Lola and sniffed her. Lola blinked, turned around, and walked down the hall. Max pranced after her on her heels.

"I just went to pick up Lola's meds, and there's this damn dog. Some old lady is trying to surrender him, and they didn't have any foster homes available, and if they took him to the shelter, he'd probably be put down."

"He has three legs."

"And they were going to hold that against him. He can't help it."

Harper covered her mouth so he wouldn't see her grin as he stalked down the hall toward the kitchen.

"It's just temporary," he called over his shoulder. "We're just fostering."

"It's just temporary," she whispered, even as she felt her heart stumble.

CHAPTER 21

They found it was easier to get used to two dogs than the first one. Max scampered seamlessly into their home life. He followed Luke around like a shadow and barked like a dog three times his size. In the mornings, Luke ran with Lola while Harper took Max for a few laps around the block. At night, he slept curled in a tight ball against Lola.

And every time Harper walked in the door, they both greeted her as if it had been decades since they last saw her.

Lola would charge down the hallway with her deep *boof* while Max pranced and yipped around her. The second the front door opened, they lavished Harper—or Luke, or the mail lady—with excited attention. It felt good to be welcomed home by adoring fans.

Just a few weeks ago, she couldn't have imagined her life changing so drastically. She had a man she adored, a comfortable home, great friends, and two dogs who thought she was better than bacon treats. Even though it was all temporary. She tried not to think about what would happen in a matter of days. Luke would be gone from her life, she would be gone from Benevolence, and it would be someone else opening Garrison Construction's massive piles of mail.

Harper opened the envelope with an efficient slash of the letter opener. Only Luke would let office mail go unopened for weeks. She had worked her way down to the bottom of the pile he had carelessly stashed on the shelf in his office. She found a handful of checks from clients buried in the pile. After a lecture from her on the importance of timely response, Luke agreed to let her handle all mail from now on.

As soon as she was done with this stack, she was going to run to the bank and make a deposit.

A check fluttered out of the opened envelope onto her desk. She picked it up and glanced at it. This was one made out directly to Luke in the amount of...

A strangled gasp made its way past her lips. Harper's knees buckled, and she flopped down into her chair.

She had never seen an amount that high on a check before, and there were three more envelopes just like this one. She opened them all and lined up the checks.

Pay to the order of Lucas Garrison.

She knew she was gaping at the surface of her desk but couldn't help it. There was just over half a million dollars sitting on it. What was it for? Was it legal?

Harper glanced into Luke's office where he was on a conference call with a supplier. He was kicked back in his chair, work boots propped up on the desk. Not a care in the world. He wasn't concerned that he had gone and forced her to fall hard for him, only to kick her in the teeth with the reminder that he couldn't even be honest with her about anything.

That withholding, sexy bastard was a millionaire.

She thought of her guilt-laden reaction to his furniture shopping. He could have furnished a dozen houses with the checks in her hand. What the hell was his problem? Why did he expect her to open up about long-buried secrets when he couldn't even say, "By the way, I'm rich."

Riding the wave of anger, she grabbed the checks and stormed over to his closed door. She smacked her palm holding the checks against the glass. "What the hell?" she mouthed.

Luke took his feet off his desk and had the good grace to look embarrassed. He shrugged and held up a finger, signaling her to wait.

But she was done waiting. Harper dropped the checks on the counter outside his office and grabbed her purse. She would take an early, long lunch, and he would just have to deal with it. She didn't owe him an explanation.

———

Luke found her at the diner counter staring into the depths of her coffee mug. He took the stool next to her and swiveled to face her. He figured he could calm her down in a few minutes and maybe even grab a quick lunch. Time was becoming more precious as the days ticked down to deployment.

"Why are you so pissed off about a couple of checks?"

Harper turned to him and shot him a look. "Is that what you think this is about? Did you hit your head today?"

"It sounds like you're questioning my intelligence," he ventured, signaling the waitress for a coffee.

"It sounds like you're trying to play dumb," Harper snapped. "This isn't about the checks. This is about what they represent."

"Money?"

"I will knock your perfect ass off that stool."

She might actually try it. "Me not telling you about money that you found going through my mail?"

"Really? That's how you want to play this? Accusing me of snooping when I opened a stack of mail that you gave me to open? Try again."

She had him there. He sighed. "Harper, there is nothing in our arrangement that says we have to tell each other everything."

"Why are you like that? What is wrong with you? Why can't you just share things? It's not sexy-mysterious anymore. It's hurtful."

"Why is it hurtful? I didn't purposely keep anything from you. The money is from a patent that Aldo and I hold on an engineered joist system. It's not a big deal."

"What's a big deal to me is that I open up to you about all the sordid details of my past and you can't even share good things with me. Why the hell is that?"

"I told you before, I'm not a hearts and flowers kind of guy."

"We're not talking about hearts and flowers. We're talking about intimacy. And you can't just expect me to share things with you when you have no intention of opening up to me."

"That isn't who I am, Harper." Luke shrugged. "Look, I don't know what to tell you. Those checks aren't even on my radar. Not when I have less than two weeks before I leave my home and my family for six months."

"That's another thing you won't talk about."

"What? Deployment? What is there to talk about?" He let some of his frustration seep into his tone. "I'm leaving. End of story."

"That is not 'end of story,' and you know it."

He spun her around sideways on the stool to face him and kept his hands on her thighs. "Look. You want something that I can't give you. I think you're getting in too deep here. You're trying to establish a relationship where there can't be one. I don't share. I don't open up and talk about my feelings or what I'm thinking. And even if I did, I'm leaving. For six months. There isn't going to be an 'us' when I come back. And I'm starting to think that maybe there shouldn't be an us now."

"Do you want me to leave?" She leveled a look at him, daring him to say what he didn't mean.

He sighed. "No, I don't want you to leave." There. How was that for honesty? "I like having you around. I even like having the dogs around. I think our working relationship is great. But maybe it's time we back off the more...intimate area."

"Sex?"

The waitress paused wide-eyed as she put the coffee mug down in front of him.

Luke waited until she wandered down the counter to the next patron. "Yes. Sex," he said quietly. "It's starting to confuse the situation. Let's just go back to the way things were for the rest of the month. Stick with the plan. You're saving money and doing a job search. Thanks to you, I'm getting caught up at the office and getting things organized for when I'm gone. We can make this work, Harper. But not by complicating things."

"So I explain to you that it hurts me when you withhold things from me, and your solution is to further reduce our relationship to boss-employee?"

Why did women always make things so difficult? He was protecting her. Why couldn't she see that?

"Harper, this is in your best interest."

"So you're saying you're protecting me from my own feelings by taking sex off the table."

She didn't sound impressed, but Luke was committed. Maybe it wasn't only her feelings he wanted to protect. There was something about the rawness between them that scared the crap out of him. He didn't want it to go any further, any deeper.

"I'm saying we're complicating a situation that doesn't need to be complicated. Let's just go back to the plan."

"Fine."

He gripped her legs. "Fine?" He had expected more of an argument.

"It's your life. Your decision."

Luke had the distinct feeling he was being played. "You're fine with going back to the plan?"

"Yep." She stared pointedly at his hands on her legs until he removed them. Harper turned her attention back to her menu. "I'll see you back at work."

"How about I buy you lunch?" he offered. The club special looked pretty good.

"No thanks. I'd rather eat by myself." She snapped her menu shut. "But I'll put your coffee on my tab. You can go."

And just like that, Luke was dismissed.

———

He took the moratorium seriously and slept on the couch for two nights, thankful that it was a million times more comfortable than his grandmother's. Yet it still paled in comparison to his bed and Harper.

What he thought was a move to simplify only turned out to be a complication. A rock-hard one. The weekend turned into a two-day erection. Now that her body was off-limits, he wanted it even more. Those sweet curves called to him, demanding his attention, his hands.

He started avoiding her like the drunk uncle no one wants to talk to at a reunion after he found her bent over the kitchen island reading a magazine in freaking boy shorts and a tank top. He turned around so fast he rammed straight into the refrigerator.

And damned if he didn't see the smirk on her face before he hustled out of the room. She had to be playing him. It seemed like her skirts were getting shorter, her shirts tighter, and his dick harder.

He was pissed off all the time. A fact that Frank was currently pointing out.

"What the hell crawled up your ass today?"

"I'm just not in the mood to hear how another client pissed you off."

Frank snorted and tossed the scrap wood in the back of his truck. "I was going to tell you that the doc called today about that addition she's been talking about. She's ready for the expansion. But since you're being a whiny little bitch, I guess I'll have Harper put the consult on the calendar."

Luke slammed the lid of his truck toolbox. When someone like Frank called him out on it, he knew he had to be acting like an ass.

"Sorry, Frank. I'm just…" What was he? Hard, frustrated, agitated, distracted beyond belief by a certain curvy blond who looked through him rather than at him in the kitchen this morning. "Stressed," he finished lamely.

"Stressed? What the hell for? You've done this before. Your dad and I have everything covered."

"It's not work." Luke used some water from his thermos to scrub the drywall dust off his hands.

"Would it have something to do with a certain female office manager who looks like she wants to jump you one minute and strangle you the next?"

"So it's not just my imagination?"

Frank sighed and leaned against the truck. "Son, let me tell you something about women. Don't piss them off under any circumstances. It's not worth it. You're risking life and limb over something that probably doesn't matter in the first place. My advice? If you pissed her off, apologize before she turns your life into a living hell."

It was Luke's turn to sigh. "Should I really be taking advice from a man who's never been married?"

"Don't have to jump off the cliff to know you die at the bottom."

CHAPTER 22

Harper had decided to let Luke have his way and give him some space to be stupid, but the idiot was driving himself out of his own house and making his last days home miserable.

When he texted her to ask if she could come back to work for an hour or so that evening to help with a proposal, Harper decided to put a stop to the madness.

She dressed for war. The tight pencil skirt stopped a few inches short of modest, and she buttoned herself into a tight, short-sleeved blouse in eye-popping red. She decided to forego a bra and shimmied into a simple black thong. Tall, strappy sandals completed the package.

She dried her hair with a little extra volume and painted on smoky eyes and plump lips.

Harper gave her reflection a nod in the mirror and slid on her sunglasses. She would win this.

She made sure to get back to the office before Luke and was already efficiently entering numbers into the accounting system when she heard him return.

She didn't turn when he came in, just kept typing.

He stopped at her desk and dropped a greasy paper bag on it.

"I brought you dinner."

Harper turned in her chair toward him. "Thanks, boss. That was nice of you." He was dressed in his standard uniform of worn jeans and soft T-shirt. She wondered if her heart would always pound over the way the cotton clung to his chest and shoulders.

His eyes immediately tracked to the exposed skin below her neck. She knew the second he realized she wasn't wearing a bra. The muscle in his jaw flexed.

Harper bit back a smile. She turned her chair back to her desk to resume typing.

Luke stayed put, cleared his throat. "You look…nice."

"Oh, thanks," Harper said brightly. "I was going to see if Gloria wanted to go out tonight after I finish up here."

"Out," he repeated flatly.

"Yeah, blow off some steam." Harper hit the Print button on the screen and pushed back from her desk. "Excuse me," she said as she brushed past Luke.

"It might be pretty late," he ventured.

Her back to him, Harper smiled. Who knew torture could be so much fun?

"I don't mind. I'm happy to help you finish up the RFP. Damn, out of paper again." Harper bent at the waist to check under the counter for paper. "Luke? Do you know where the paper is?"

Wordlessly, he appeared at her side. He opened the next cabinet over and knelt down.

Harper moved, deliberately putting her breasts in his direct line of sight. "Oh good, there's another ream." She reached past him, brushing her breast against his arm.

Her nipples hardened instantly, and Luke jumped back as if he had been burned.

Harper bent lower, feeling her skirt ride up in the back, and grabbed the paper. "Thanks," she said, standing back up. "I'll put printer paper on the office supply list."

Luke was running a hand over the back of his head. Harper spotted the familiar bulge between his legs and bit the inside of her cheek.

She strutted back to her desk, enjoying the tease of the fabric over her nipples.

"Um, why don't you email me the draft you have so far, and I'll read it while you eat?" Luke made the suggestion without looking at her.

"Sounds good."

She nibbled at the cheesesteak he brought her, but she was more interested in how his gaze tracked to her through the glass of his office.

She took a minute to check her email and saw that her job interview in Fremont had been confirmed for the following week. The familiar buzz of excitement at a potential new start didn't appear this time. In fact, all she really felt was a ball of ice forming in her stomach. For the first time in her life, the appeal of a fresh start wasn't there.

Harper brought her hands to her face and closed her eyes. There was no way around this one, no way for her current life to continue. Luke was leaving, and even if he wasn't, there was no room in his life for her.

"What's wrong?"

Harper jumped in her seat at Luke's voice. He was standing at her desk staring at her. "You scared me! That's what's wrong. Jeez." She put a hand over her heart, knowing full well the real reason it was pounding. Because he was standing so close to her.

"Liar. What's wrong?"

"I was just wondering if it was going to be hard to find

an apartment that allows dogs." It wasn't. Hannah had already arranged an appointment to see a tiny town house next door to a dog park.

"You're taking the dogs?"

"Well, yeah. I don't think your unit would let you take them. Anyway, did you want something?" She uncrossed and then crossed her legs and smiled when he took a step back.

"Uh." Luke skimmed his hand over the back of his head. "Yeah. Can you come take a look at some wording? Please."

"Sure," she said, hopping up to follow him into his office. She waited until he took a seat behind his desk and then leaned over him to look at the monitor. She heard him stop breathing. "This text here?"

Luke nodded but remained silent.

"You're worried it's not clear enough that the geothermal is included?"

"Yeah. You've really picked up a lot in a very short amount of time."

"It's easy when it's interesting. And there was a lot here I found interesting."

"Harper."

His flat warning tone immediately put her back up.

"Luke."

"We've talked about this—"

She straightened away from him. "Talked about what? First, I was talking about my work here in the office, Captain Conceited. Second, *we* didn't talk. I tried, and you shut down and started sleeping on the couch because you're totally mature."

"And totally mature is playing games with me when I ask for your help. I know you're dressing like this on purpose."

"I never claimed to be mature, and at least I'm honest about what I want."

"You think I'm not being honest with you?"

She leveled him with a look. "You're the one playing games here. You make it sound like you're protecting me when it's you you're trying to protect."

He started to argue and then snapped his mouth shut.

"Can't argue with the truth. You're the one worried about how intense this is. You're the one who's getting scared. Because you feel something, and you think taking sex off the table will make that go away."

"You understand why we can't do this."

"I understand that *you* don't *want* to do this," she corrected.

"Harper." He sounded exasperated. "I want you. I have been hard since the second I walked in here tonight. There is no scenario that involves me not wanting you." He trailed a hand down her arm, his thumb skimming over the soft curve of her breast. "I want you more than I should."

Harper leaned against his desk. "Why does that mean we have to stop? We have a week left. Shouldn't we be making the most of it?"

"It's hard for me to logically explain why when you aren't wearing a fucking bra!" He was yelling now.

She brought her hands to her hips, and the fabric gaped between the top two buttons. "You're overthinking this."

"I don't want either of us to get any more attached. And yes, I'm attached too."

Harper rolled her eyes and pushed away from the desk. "We have ten days, and then you're leaving. I'm leaving. There is no attachment danger. This is all we have left, and you're hell-bent on spending it punishing me."

She turned to stalk out of his office, but he had her by the arm before she had taken a step.

He had her spun around and bent over the desk in the

span of a heartbeat. "You drive me crazy," he growled in her ear.

"And you piss me off," she argued, rocking her hips back into his, trying to get some space.

His stone-hard erection pressed against her, grinding her into the desk. "I can only fight you so long," he warned.

"About damn time," she snipped.

Luke cuffed her hands behind her and shoved her skirt up to her hips. When she heard the sound of his zipper, she was instantly wet. She couldn't help herself.

He forced her thighs farther apart with his knee and yanked her thong down her thighs. Open and ready, she moaned. On the noise, she felt the smooth skin of his penis bob against the back of her thighs. Holding the thick shaft, he guided the crown of it between her legs, rubbing it against her slick folds.

"You're already soaked, baby."

He freed her arms only to grip the opening of her blouse and yank. The first three buttons pinged across the desk and onto the floor. Her breasts tumbled out of the shirt and into his waiting palms.

"Is this what you want?" He squeezed, rubbing calloused palms over the sensitive tips. "Me touching you? Me inside you? Me making you come over and over again?"

Harper's legs trembled. He brought a hand to her hair and fisted it. Pulling her back, he gripped her neck with his other hand.

"That's what I want," he said. "I want you to take all the dark, all the pain, and turn it into something beautiful. I want to fill you, hurt you, please you. Give you everything. I want it so bad I can't think of anything else. The thought of never touching you again—" He trailed a hand down her neck to capture a breast. He tugged her nipple.

Harper gasped for breath, her pulse fluttering under his fingers.

"Is this what you want?" he asked. His fingers pulled her bud like a mouth.

She moaned again. "Yes, Luke. I want you. I want it all." It was a whisper.

His hand left her hair abruptly, and she collapsed onto the desk. "Be careful what you wish for, Harper." The damp fabric of her underwear rent in two with a violent yank and fell to the floor between her legs. With no barriers, she was completely exposed. Luke guided the thick head of his shaft to the juncture of her thighs. "Just remember you asked me for this. I wanted to protect you. Find something to hang on to."

Without further warning, he drove into her with a violence she had never experienced. There was no time to adjust to his size. His thick shaft slammed into her, impaling her. He changed the angle and the last inch of him slid into her, completely sheathing himself inside her.

She felt him in the depths of her belly as he hit bottom.

With blunt force, he began to hammer into her. His hands came around her, gripping her breasts. They worked to milk her, stretching and tugging her nipples, offering intense pleasure with that bit of pain.

Trapped between his driving thrusts and the desk, she could do nothing but take it. Take it all. His heavy balls slapped against her. He was too big, the pace too furious.

He grunted softly with every thrust, and Harper knew he was lost in her. There was no stopping him. She could only submit.

Her tight little muscles squeezed him on every thrust. A yearning so intense it reached her heart clutched at her. She wanted to take it all from him. The shadows, the dark, the pain.

Releasing her breasts, Luke braced his legs. A hand slipped down between Harper's thighs, parting her slick folds to stroke where she needed it. His other hand ran down her back and lower still, just above where his cock ravaged her. He probed and pressed and, with a swift thrust, entered her tight channel.

Full in every way, Harper cried out as she clenched around him, wrenching free the first spurt of hot semen deep in her core. His fingers stroked over her slick bud, and she came apart around him.

She heard him shout her name over the pounding in her ears. He said it again, softer now, as his body went rigid and his cock jerked inside her. She could feel the fluid heat of his orgasm as she continued to climax.

His sweat-slicked body collapsed against hers on the desk. Both of them were gasping for breath. Wrecked, Harper felt wetness on her cheeks. What demons did he have under the surface that hurt so much? She could feel the shadow over his heart, and it broke hers.

————

"Harp, I'm sorry. I'm trying to get up, but my legs don't seem to want to hold me," he murmured against the warm skin of her back.

For once, he was empty. No shadows lurking, no thoughts to push away. Just quiet. And warmth.

He finally pressed himself back up to standing and, stroking Harper's back, pulled out slowly. He watched as a sticky wetness coursed down the insides of her thighs, evidence of how hard he came. Never in his life had it been like this. She chased away the dark and brought him to the light. He felt something loosen in his chest.

She was still silent. He had never known Harper to be this quiet this long. Not even in her sleep.

"Harper." Luke pulled her to standing and slowly turned her around to face him. Her knees buckled, and he caught her. Then he spotted the tears. "Oh, baby. I'm sorry. I'm so fucking sorry. Did I hurt you?" He gathered her in and stroked her.

She shook her head against him.

"I didn't hurt you?"

She shook her head again and curled closer to him.

He lifted her and carried her to the worn leather couch in the corner. "Did I scare you?"

She shook her head and wrapped her arms around him.

He sat down, cradling her in his lap. "Tell me, baby. What's wrong?"

Harper lifted her head and cupped his face in her hands. "I think I love you," she sighed pitifully. "And don't you dare tell me this is why you didn't want to have sex."

His hands stilled on her skin for the briefest of moments before resuming their slow strokes. It was his turn for silence.

"Did I scare you?" she whispered against his neck.

Luke pinched her lightly. "Maybe a little."

Harper sat up in his lap. "This is new for me. I don't know if I like it." She sounded so forlorn, Luke couldn't help but smile.

"I suppose there are worse things."

"Really? Because I can't think of any right at this exact moment. This is really inconvenient." She took a deep breath and sat up again. "Oh my God! What if I spend the rest of my life pining over the guy I met in Benevolence?"

Luke pinched her again. "Look, Harper—" he began.

"I didn't tell you to hear you say it back. I know it's not something that you feel for me, and I don't need to hear the reasons why. I just wanted you to know."

"Harper, we should probably talk. But first, let's find some clothes for you since I destroyed yours."

They ate subs cross-legged on the floor of Luke's office. Luke had scrounged up a Garrison Construction T-shirt and a pair of way-too-big gym shorts for Harper.

She waited until he had taken the last bite of his turkey and cheese. "So let's talk."

Luke took his time crumpling his napkin and tucking the trash back in his paper bag.

He took a deep breath. "A few years ago, I went through a rough patch. I lost some people close to me, and it took me a long time to recover."

"People in your unit?"

He nodded. "And someone at home shortly after."

"Someone you were close to?"

"Yes."

"I'm so sorry, Luke." She put her hand on his knee. "It's never easy to lose someone you care about, and it's even worse when it's more than one."

He thought of a scared little seven-year-old without her parents and squeezed her hand.

"It was a dark time."

"And that's why your family—"

"Tortures me with their well-meaning but overbearing attention?"

"How do you feel about deploying again?"

"I've deployed since. It's never easy. But it's necessary, and that gets you through the hard times."

"Did you feel responsible?"

He answered without hesitation. "Yes. And I still do."

"Even though you know it's not your fault?"

"Fault and responsibility don't have to be related."

"What about the person you lost here?"

"Losing her changed things for me. I won't do it again."

Harper nodded. "Okay."

"Okay?"

"It doesn't make me not probably love you."

"Harper—"

She slapped a hand over his mouth. "I don't need you to drive the point home. You can't love me back. You don't want to be in a relationship. I get it."

"I'm sorry, Harper."

"Don't be. My feelings for you aren't dependent on yours for me. I like you. I probably love you. I think you're an amazing guy. End of story."

"So where does that leave us?"

"Enjoying the rest of the week."

"Why would you want to if there's nothing long-term to be won here?"

"Have you met me? What in my life has ever been long-term? Life is too short not to grab on to the good times while they last."

"You're a pretty amazing woman, Harper Wilde."

CHAPTER 23

Harper was running late. Max had slipped his collar after spotting the beagle from three houses down running loose. She spent half an hour chasing them down, returning the beagle to a very grateful Mr. and Mrs. Scotts and then carrying Max in a viselike grip back to the house.

Luke had called a morning staff meeting, and Harper wanted to get the latest numbers in front of him beforehand. Her hair was still damp from a very hasty shower, and she was pretty sure she had missed a button on her blouse.

It wasn't until she was dashing out the front door digging for her keys that she realized they—and her car—weren't there.

Luke pulled the door closed, wrangling a travel mug and a stack of papers. "You're riding with me today."

"Where's my car?"

Luke started down the front porch steps. "It's at the garage."

"Why the hell is my car at the garage?" She followed on his heels.

He sighed and turned to face her so they were eye to eye. "I asked Shorty to give it a tune-up."

"It runs fine," Harper said with a measured glare.

"Bullshit." He said it so calmly it didn't register for a full second. "I'm not leaving you with a car that barely runs."

"Luke, that's not your concern."

He sighed. "You're my concern, and that extends to any metal container that you strap yourself into and hit highway speeds in."

She was equally touched and annoyed by his gesture. Was it worth fighting over with seventy-two hours left together? She sighed. "When will it be done?"

"Should be done tomorrow end of day."

"Two days? What are they doing to it?"

"Anything it needs." He cut off her outraged reply with a hard kiss on her mouth. "Now get in the truck."

"Fine, but don't even think for a second that you're paying for this," she yelled at his retreating back.

"Truck, Harper," he called over his shoulder.

She climbed in in a huff.

"Listen," Luke said, sliding the key in the ignition. "I want you safe when I'm not here to keep an eye on you. I've gotten kind of attached to you being alive and in one beautiful piece."

"Don't you think you're being just a little overprotective? Especially for someone who is basically breaking up with me in a matter of hours." They backed down the driveway into the street.

"Can we talk about something else for a minute, and then you can go back to complaining?"

She rolled her eyes and sighed. "By all means."

"I saw you started packing last night."

She had. It was just some clothes tucked into a bag and a few boxes of odds and ends. "I didn't want to leave it all until Friday. Too depressing."

"I know you're planning on leaving, and I was thinking maybe you could stay a few more days. After I'm gone."

Harper shot him a look, but his gaze was fixed on the road. "Why?"

"It might be a little hard on my family if we both leave the same day."

"You haven't told them yet?"

He shook his head. "I couldn't think of the right way to do it. Dad's always wanting to tell me about something great you're doing in the office. Mom's always shoving baked goods at me for you."

"That's kind of sweet."

"Yeah, you try crushing their dreams with the truth."

"So what are we going to do? I'm not just supposed to disappear one day, am I?" She watched the tidy neighborhood slide past her window and forced the lump in her throat to release.

"I did something I never do and asked Sophie's advice."

"I'm suddenly intrigued."

"I told her I didn't want either one of us coming across like a jerk."

"Good call."

"So her solution is for us to announce that you've just landed your dream job somewhere else and we're parting as friends."

Harper mulled it over.

"When do we tell them?"

"I was thinking about doing it at the dinner?"

"Before you leave?"

"It's either that or you tell them after I get on the bus."

"That is so not going to happen."

"Dinner it is then."

With her future decided, Harper leaned against the headrest and tried not to think about it.

Harper smoothed the golden waves away from her face and secured them in a clip, leaving the rest hanging loose around her shoulders. She took a deep breath to steady herself before tackling the makeup. She wanted to look perfect.

She even bought a new dress. The white sundress had a fitted bodice with a scoop neckline and a full skirt that floated away from her body. It was too fancy for dinner, but she wanted to be memorable.

"Harper." Luke's voice carried up the stairs. "We gotta go, baby."

"I'm ready," she called back. One last look in the mirror and another deep breath and she told herself she was ready. One last night.

She sailed down the stairs and smacked soundly into Luke as he came around the corner from the living room. He caught her, hands at her waist. "Hey there, beautiful."

His voice was a caress. One she would miss for a very long time.

He was dressed in charcoal slacks and a thin black sweater that fit like it had been poured over him. Perfection. Harper ran her hands across his chest, provoking a growl.

"Baby, if we get started, we're going to be late." He ran a hand up under her dress to gently stroke the barrier of her silky underwear. "Very late."

"I can't believe this is the end," she whispered, tracing her fingers lightly up his chest to his shoulders.

Luke stared into her for a long moment, bringing his thumbs up to trail a gentle path along her jaw and down her neck. "You look beautiful," he said finally.

"I wanted to be memorable."

"Baby, it would take more than all the time in the world for me to forget you."

"I love you, Luke." So much so that she thought it would burst out of her. Love and pride flowed through her veins, feeding her heart. He was the man she had always dreamed of.

He pulled her in tight, resting his chin on top of her head. "I'm going to miss you." There was a fierceness in his voice that had Harper closing her eyes to fight back tears. She took a deep, shuddery breath.

"Okay, Captain. Let's get you to your party," she said brightly, taking a step back.

"We'll take your car." He held up her keys and dangled them in front of her.

"It's back? Yay!" She snatched at the keys, which Luke held just out of her reach.

"It's back," he affirmed. "But you can only have it on one condition."

"I'm not getting naked. We're already late."

He smirked. "Not that condition. You have to promise that you'll take care of her. Change the oil regularly. Don't ignore the check engine light. Check the fluids and the tire pressure."

"Yes, sir." Harper saluted sharply. "Now gimme!"

He handed over the keys and followed her outside. Her squeal of delight had Max charging the front window to bark ferociously.

"It's so clean! And look! They fixed the tear in the roof." The paint job, brought back to life by a professional wax, glowed a glossy blue in the late afternoon sun. Harper slid in behind the wheel and lovingly stroked the dash. "Are these gauges new?"

Luke leaned in the open passenger window. "Why don't you start her up?"

Harper obliged and clapped her hands when the engine caught on the first try. "Oh my God! There's no squealing at all. Shorty is a genius!"

Luke opened the door and slid into the passenger seat. "I'll tell him you said that."

"Thank you so much for getting her all fixed up, Luke! This is going to take a giant chunk out of my apartment and comfy couch fund, but I don't even care. It's the best she's ever looked!"

"Your fund is intact. This is on me. Consider it a going-away gift." Harper opened her mouth to argue, but Luke clamped a hand over it. "Before you start yelling, this past month has been the best I've had in…I don't even know how long. You made my house a home, you took away the chaos at work, and you gave me what I didn't know I needed. You. So this is my very small way of thanking you for bringing me back to life. If I thought for a second you'd let me get away with getting you a new car, I would have. But I know you." He removed his hand from her mouth. "Okay. You can yell now."

"Dammit, Luke. I can't yell now."

"You also can't insist on paying me back without looking like an asshole," he smirked.

Damn that sexy dimple. The perfect picture. Him grinning at her, aviators on, that soft sweater that clung to every muscle. And the sun setting low behind him.

This was how she would always think of him.

Harper sighed. She would go to her grave loving Luke Garrison without regret.

He patted the dashboard. "Now that I've won the gift-giving competition, let's go. I'm hungry."

Harper backed down the driveway and put the car in first gear. "Is this a new engine?"

———

Mr. Romanos himself led them through the restaurant to the small back room reserved for special occasions.

200

Harper paused with Luke in the doorway and took in the chaotic scene. Josh had crawled under a table, and Ty was trying to coax him out. Sophie was topping off wineglasses. Charlie was in deep discussion with Aldo and James while Claire and a short, plump woman with salt-and-pepper curly hair had their heads together.

"That's Aldo's mom, Mrs. Moretta," Luke whispered in her ear, nodding in the woman's direction. She threw her head back in booming laughter. "She's on the feisty side, so try not to get into an argument with her."

Stu and Syl were having a disagreement over the basket of rolls while the frazzled-looking waitress promised to bring a second order out. Frank sat by himself nursing a beer.

"I am going to miss this," Luke sighed, drawing her into his side.

"Me too." Harper nodded. "Well, we might as well make the most of our last night."

He squeezed her waist and winked. "Uncle Stu, put the bread down," he ordered as they entered the room.

Cheers went up and they were surrounded by hugs, handshakes, and slaps on the back. Everyone was talking at once.

Josh poked his head out from under the table. "Unca Luke!" The toddler bolted for his uncle, and Luke picked him up, tossing his nephew in the air. "Unca Luke! Camo!" Josh pointed to the camo T-shirt he was wearing. "Like you?"

"When you come back, he's going to be twice that size," Ty teased. "Kid eats fifteen pounds of mac and cheese a day."

"I don't doubt it," Luke laughed.

Harper skirted around the crowd to Sophie, who handed her a glass of wine.

"Hanging in there?"

Harper nodded. "Yeah." She watched Luke juggle Josh to one side so he could hug Aunt Syl. "Did he tell you what he did to my car?"

Sophie rolled her eyes. "Has my brother ever willingly told anyone anything?"

"Good point." Harper laughed and filled her in.

"The big softie." Sophie sighed and blinked her watery eyes. "He loves you, you know. He protects you like family."

"I know he cares for me, but I don't think he's ready for the L-word. I, on the other hand…" Harper trailed off and sipped her wine.

"I knew you were just what he needed, and now you're leaving too." Sophie sniffled.

"Oh my God, don't you start, or it'll set me off, and then Luke will get pissed at both of us," Harper said, blinking her eyes to fight off the tears that blurred her vision. "Please tell me something funny!"

"Last year, Mom took Josh overnight so Ty and I could have a night out. We stayed in instead and drank an entire bottle of Kraken. Then we ordered a pizza, and I bet him he wouldn't answer the door wearing my pink pajama pants with kitties on them. I lost."

Harper slapped a hand over her mouth, but it was too late. The laughter was already erupting. They both doubled over in hysterics.

"Pink kitty pants?" she gasped.

Sophie, lost in silent laughter, could only nod.

"Ladies, am I gonna have to arrest you for public disturbance?" Ty said, approaching.

It set them off again and had Harper clutching Sophie to stay upright.

"What did you do to my girl, Ty?" Luke appeared at her side, a beer bottle in his hand.

Harper wiped the tears from her cheeks, thankful that she went with waterproof mascara tonight. "Sorry. Sophie was just telling the funniest story."

"If you've recovered your oxygen supply, I'll introduce you to Mrs. Moretta."

Harper nodded and straightened her shoulders. "All recovered. Excuse us, Soph, Mr. Kitty." She clawed the air in front of Ty as she walked past.

Sophie started giggling again.

"Damn it, Soph. Why are you spilling secrets?" Ty sighed behind them.

———

They eventually got everyone seated long enough for the waitress to take the group's order. When everyone's drinks were refilled, Charlie got to his feet, glass in hand. Luke squeezed Harper's thigh under the table.

"It's Garrison family tradition to send our boys off with some words of wisdom. Luke, Aldo"—he nodded at both—"I've witnessed you grow from troublemaking kids to trouble-making teenagers. Now you're grown men, and you still occasionally make trouble."

Harper smiled at the laughter that bubbled around the table.

"But I couldn't be prouder to know you both. You're good men who lead with heart. You believe in loyalty, friendship, family. Thank you for your service, and come home safe." Charlie raised his glass. "Cheers."

"Cheers," everyone echoed, raising their glasses.

Luke squeezed her leg again and stood up. "Thanks, Dad. I'd just like to point out that we learned our troublemaking from you. I don't usually do this toast thing, but I wanted to thank you all for your support. For us, leaving is never easy, but it eases our minds with all of you picking up the slack for us at home. I may not say it often enough, but I appreciate all of you and everything that you do." Luke laid a hand on Harper's shoulder. "A lot of you know that Harper has made predeployment a lot easier for me at work. At home, she got dogs and furniture and generally brought a lot of chaos."

The group chuckled.

"We've talked a lot about what to do with me leaving, and we've decided that it's for the best for us both if we go our separate ways."

Harper stared at her lap and pretended not to hear the gasps.

Sophie, on her left, poked her under the table with her foot.

"Harper was on her way to Fremont when we met. And that's where she's headed in a week or two. She got some opportunities that she's really excited about, and I'm happy for her. She's a great girl." Luke paused awkwardly, and Harper sneaked a peek around the table. Shock, disappointment, confusion.

"Geez, when you got up, I thought you were going to propose to the girl," Mrs. Moretta announced. No one laughed.

CHAPTER 24

"Well, that was horribly painful," Luke said as he shut the driver's door.

The dinner was over. Thankfully, most of the festive feeling had returned by the time dessert was served after Luke's truth bomb, but it had been touch and go for a while.

Harper patted his knee. "You did what needed to be done."

"Did you see my mom's face? I feel like I just kicked my way through a litter of puppies," he groaned.

Harper laughed. "Poor baby. It's fine. It's over, and you'll never have to do it again. Everyone understands that we're both fine with the decision. Sure, maybe they think we're chicken for not trying to stick it out for Max and Lola."

Luke pulled out of the restaurant's lot and headed for home.

"They all thought I was going to propose, and then I had to go and crush their dreams." He sighed, running a hand over his head. "I feel like such an ass."

"If it makes you feel better, I thought you were going to propose too."

"Very funny, brat."

Harper snickered and patted his leg.

"So how do you feel?" Luke asked, changing the subject.

"About all this?"

He nodded.

Harper sighed. "Guilty, sad, worried. You name it, and I feel it. How about you?"

Luke shrugged. "I don't know. I worry about pushing you out the door and leaving you out there on your own."

"I'm a big girl, Luke."

"I know you are, but that doesn't stop me from worrying about you. There's always a mix of excitement and anxiety involved with deploying. I've done it before, so it's not so much the unknowns as it is the knowns."

"Like?" Harper asked.

"Like kids who never have enough to eat. Some of the people there who will never trust us. The sandstorms. The monotony. The danger. But then there are good things too. My unit has a strong bond that comes from a kind of intense shared suffering."

"And you're in charge?"

Luke nodded. "Yeah, I'm the commanding officer of our infantry unit."

"Is that a lot of pressure?"

"Not when we all work together and do what we're supposed to do. I have a great group of men and women who, for the most part, make it all easier."

Harper nodded. "What's it like to come home? Does it feel like you're living two different lives?"

"Sometimes it feels like it's easier to deploy than to come home. You go from getting shot at and facing life-and-death decisions every day to trying to decide which burger to order off the menu. It always takes a little while to remember that just because our families and friends aren't at war, it doesn't mean that how they live their lives is any less important."

"So when you come home and someone is freaking out over getting a speeding ticket…"

"Exactly." He nodded. "Until you've faced extreme situations, it's very easy to take things for granted and get worked up over things that won't matter ever."

"When you come home, how do you spend your first twenty-four hours?"

Luke grinned. "I sleep for most of them."

Harper laughed. "So how would you like to spend your last few hours here?"

Luke's hand on her knee tracked higher, dragging the material of her dress with it.

"Is this a hint?" Willing to play, Harper spread her knees. Her dress hiked up high enough to reveal her white cotton briefs.

"Are you trying to distract me?" Luke teased. His finger trailed lazily over the edge of the material.

He might not love her, but he wanted her with an intensity that scared them both. And that was something.

Harper hooked her legs on either side of the seat. It was an invitation.

"Don't you know it's dangerous to distract the driver?" As he spoke, the pads of his fingers circled her folds through the cotton.

"Mmm," Harper murmured.

Luke tugged the material to one side, baring her to him. This time, his fingers met flesh.

"Jesus, baby, you're already wet." Luke pulled into the driveway, tires squealing. "I want you inside," he ordered.

Harper grabbed her bag and jumped out, hurrying up the walk. When she fumbled with the keys at the front door, he pressed against her. Harper shifted back to grind into him.

Luke pulled the halter tie of her dress loose and let her breasts tumble free into his hands. Harper shoved the front door open and dragged him across the threshold by his belt buckle.

He spun her around to face him and kicked the door shut behind him.

They were interrupted by Lola and Max charging down the hall to greet them.

"I'm putting them in the backyard. Meet me upstairs," he said. "But leave your dress on. I'm going to undress you."

Her pulse skittering out of control, Harper took the stairs two at a time. She had just enough time to pull the clip out of her hair and kick off her sandals before she heard Luke on the stairs.

When he appeared in the doorway, her heart flip-flopped in her chest. Luke approached her, yanking his sweater over his head.

"Damn, you're built," Harper sighed.

"Baby, I was about to say the same thing." His hands were on her now, skimming the sides of her bare breasts. "I've been thinking about taking this dress off you since you came downstairs wearing it."

She shivered under his gentle touch. Her fingers flew over his belt buckle to open it.

Luke stilled her hands with his and tugged the belt loose. He brought his hands to her face. "I'm taking my time with you tonight."

Breathless, Harper nodded.

"You're so beautiful, Harper." His fingers trailed along her jawline to the back of her neck. Luke lowered his mouth to hers, and she gave herself up to the slow burn of the fire, melting into his arms.

His fingers burned blazing paths down her bare skin, igniting nerves with each caress.

He paused at her waist and slowly began to lower the dress over her hips, down her thighs, until it pooled in a frothy puddle at her feet.

Dressed only in her underwear, Harper knelt before him and slid his pants down his muscled legs.

Standing only in boxer briefs, he was her chiseled hero.

She reached into the waistband and took his thick shaft in her hand. The head was already wet. Harper tugged his underwear down to his thighs. Leaning into him, she brought her lips to the broad head of his cock.

His fingers dug into her arm. "Harper." He didn't stop her, but his body tensed.

She opened her lips and slowly took him into her mouth inch by inch.

He made a noise like a groan, and Harper knew she affected him the way he did her. Testing, she ran her tongue around the crest, flicking it over the small slit.

Her reward was a salty bead of moisture.

She licked it off the tip.

"My God, Harper."

It was all the encouragement she needed. She slanted her mouth over him and down, all the way to the back of her throat. His hips flexed, driving him farther into her mouth, and she gasped for breath.

She wrapped a hand around the root of his cock, and with mouth and fingers, she began an aggressive stroke.

Luke levered his hips up and wrapped a hand in her hair.

Harper slicked down over him again and again.

"Baby." She heard the need, the fear in his rasp.

With her free hand, Harper palmed his sack. She tugged and rolled in a rhythm that matched her mouth.

His grip on her hair tightened, and she knew he had no

idea he was hurting her. It made her feel powerful, driving him to the edge like this.

He took a step back, his cock releasing from Harper's mouth. "I'm too close," he whispered. Luke pulled her up to standing and twisted her away from him. While one hand worked at the nipple of her breast, his other hand plunged into the waistband of her underwear.

Harper moaned, rocking her hips into his.

He answered her silent plea by slowly penetrating her with one finger. Harper leaned back against his chest and closed her eyes. The slow shallow thrusts and rough fingers tugging at her nipple unraveled her.

"Put your hands on the bed," he ordered quietly.

Harper bent from the waist and braced herself against the mattress with her hands. Her breasts hung down heavily, nipples brushing the soft quilt.

His hand briefly left her breast to tug her underwear down in the back to expose her. She felt his lips and then teeth grazing her skin high on her cheek. Still stroking her from the front, Luke slid another finger inside her.

His erection was hard against her ass, and she could feel a sticky wetness transferring to her skin.

"Luke," she whispered.

He responded with another thrust of his fingers. Harper cried out as he hit the most sensitive spot.

He withdrew and brought both hands to her breasts. There his fingers rolled and tugged her nipples.

Harper shifted her hips back and up and sighed when his erection nestled between her thighs. "Please, Luke," she begged.

He pushed her forward on the bed and rolled her over onto her back. Harper bent her knees and planted her feet on the edge of the mattress to give him full access.

"You drive me crazy." He knelt on the floor and pulled her hips toward him.

When he pressed his mouth to her underwear, Harper gasped and levered her hips up.

"I love how responsive you are." Luke pulled the cotton to the side and ran a trail of kisses from her knee up the inside of her thigh.

She felt his breath on her and shivered. Using his tongue, Luke gently probed between the lips of her sex.

"Oh my God," she whispered.

His tongue stroked up to her sensitive nub and her legs quivered. Harper's hands fisted at her sides. His magic tongue licked its way to her opening and pressed into her. She arched against his mouth. "Lucas!"

He replaced his tongue with his fingers and drove into her while his mouth moved back to her folds. He teased and probed while his fingers slammed into her again and again. His tongue settled into a steady, driving rhythm that took her to the edge.

Harper fought the build. She tried to wiggle out of his grasp, but his hand forced her hips to be still.

The need hollowed her out. There was nothing left inside her except the craving to be filled. Luke's fingers drove into her again, and she immediately closed around them. His tongue spread her folds and stroked her swollen bud. She shattered against him, tightening on his fingers and arching against his mouth as the orgasm blossomed into a controlled explosion.

Luke groaned against her, his desire ramping higher. He reached down to stroke his cock against her opening. "Baby, I need to be inside you." His voice was rough.

"Let me ride you," she whispered.

He climbed onto the bed and lay on his back, still stroking himself. Harper worked his underwear down his legs and off.

Luke helped her discard her own before lifting her to straddle his straining erection.

She paused with her wet entrance encircling the head of his shaft.

"I love you, Luke," she whispered, watching his eyes go glassy as she slowly lowered herself down onto him. Inch by inch, she welcomed him into her very core. Completely filled, she leaned forward, her breasts dangling just above the hard line of his lips.

He took the peak of one breast in his mouth, and Harper began to ride with slow, deep strokes.

Luke clamped his hands on her hips to control the rhythm. His thick shaft stretched her to a point that was almost pain. His hips levered up and he hit bottom inside her.

Harper moaned against the soft tugs of his mouth on her breast. The pulls were echoed in the muscles that delicately clamped down on his straining cock.

She reared up and rode him, slowly, deliberately. Their gazes locked as Harper set the rhythm for release.

"Yes." He drew out the word on a long exhale. "God, yes."

Every thrust, every stroke was an expression of love.

He thrust with his hips once more, and he erupted on a shout. She followed him into oblivion.

Harper was drowning in the darkness between them but had no desire to save herself. This was a relationship that could wreck a soul. And it was over.

CHAPTER 25

The gray light from the window told Harper she still had time before the alarm, but falling back to sleep was not an option. The day she had dreaded was here. Never again would she wake up to find herself cradled in Luke's arms.

So many things ended today. She wasn't ready to let go, but it wasn't her choice.

She studied him in his sleep as she had their first morning together. She let her fingers trace the phoenix over his heart, silently willing him to be safe while memorizing every plane, every line of his body.

How was she supposed to go back to a regular life after this?

Luke's eyes opened. Sleepy hazel stared back at her.

Harper sighed and cupped her hand to his face.

Luke kissed her palm. "Are you ready?"

"Nope."

"We're still good, right?"

Harper smiled. "Yeah, we're good. I'm just going to miss you for the next ten years or so."

He pulled her in to him and tucked her head under his jaw. Luke pressed a sweet kiss to the top of her head and held her to him until his alarm sounded.

They met Luke's family at the base. The parking lot was packed with family members saying their goodbyes. Harper tried not to stare at the bus in front of them. The bus that would take Luke Garrison forever from her life.

There wasn't time to waste. The schedule had to be kept.

Luke, dressed in fatigues, stowed his pack on the bus and returned to them. Harper watched him walk down the line, hugging and shaking hands. Claire dragged him in for a long hug. "Come home safe," she ordered.

"Don't I always, Ma?"

He shook Charlie's hand and gave James a resounding slap on his back.

"Don't forget to mow my lawn, lackey," he reminded his brother.

"Don't forget to come home to annoy the shit out of me."

"Boys!" Claire censured them.

Luke moved on to Sophie and Josh, wrapping them both in a bear hug. "Take care, Soph," he told his sister.

"You too, Uncle Luke. We'll be missing you." She sniffled, and Josh patted her face.

And then Luke was standing in front of Harper.

He cupped her face in his hands and looked into her eyes.

"Thank you, Harper. For everything."

A single tear slid down her cheek. She shook her head. "I should be thanking you. This was the best month of my life."

"Tell me one more time."

"I love you, Lucas Garrison, and you'd better come home safely to your family, or I'll come back and kick your ass."

He grinned. "That's my girl."

He lowered his lips to hers and held, softly, tenderly. She could taste the salt of her tears on his lips.

Luke pulled back slowly and wiped away her tears with his thumbs. When Harper's lip trembled, he pulled her in tight.

"I'll be thinking about you," he murmured in her ear. "Be good. Be safe."

"Back at you, Captain."

He ran his thumb across her lower lip and smiled.

When he turned, Harper almost grabbed him. She wasn't ready for this. She needed just a little more time.

She watched him stride across the parking lot where the rest of the unit was forming a line at the bus. She was proud and scared and sad all at the same time.

Sophie's arm settled around her shoulder, anchoring Harper to the spot.

"It's going to be okay, Harp." But her voice wavered too.

Claire stepped to Harper's other side and put her arm around her waist. "We're all going to be okay. Together."

Harper nodded, eyes never leaving Luke's retreating form. She knew there was no "together" in her future. She was an outsider, not family.

Luke paused on the lowest step of the bus and turned. He raised an arm in a wave.

Harper blew him a kiss. She saw his fingers close and smiled.

Harper climbed into the driver's seat where Luke had sat barely an hour ago and pulled the door shut. She hid the tears that were starting behind sunglasses and waved to Luke's family as she guided the truck out of the parking lot and back onto the road.

He was gone. The man who had her heart was forever out of her life, and she was expected to carry on as if everything was normal. How did the people in real relationships with children and responsibilities do it? Wave stoically as their partners, their rocks, their hearts, left them to live another life. One that could never be fully shared or understood.

A sob escaped her, and she pulled over to the side of the road, her vision clouded with tears that scalded her eyes. The ache in her chest spread to her throat.

Her heart broke for the men and women separated by war and duty. The fear that clutched at the hearts of those at home, never quite dissipating. At least in their case, the ones left behind could work to build their lives and the lives of their family so the man or woman they loved could come home to it.

Harper's life, as she had so quickly grown accustomed to it, was gone, never to return. Even after Luke came back. He wasn't coming home to her. Benevolence would no longer be her home.

She let silent sobs rack her shoulders until her head sank to the steering wheel. She loved him.

She loved him now, and she knew for certain she would love Luke Garrison for the rest of her life.

From the truck's console, Harper's phone signaled a text.

She wanted to ignore it. She would rather wallow and wail on the side of the road for as long as it took to feel better. There was no room for the outside world right now. But shutting down wasn't an option. It was never an option. She pulled her phone from the console and swiped the screen. It was a text from Luke.

Stay.

CHAPTER 26

Harper shifted the tray to her left hand so she could plug in the order for table seven and close out table twelve.

She sidestepped a pack of giggling thirtysomethings on their way to the ladies' room and nodded at the couple at the pool table who signaled another round. Hustling to the far end of the bar, she started reloading her tray.

It was a busy Friday night. The warm May weather made it too tempting to spend the night at home. It seemed like a large portion of the town's population had decided dinner and drinks were the way to kick off the weekend. Harper didn't mind. The busier the better. If she kept moving, her mind stayed quiet.

But the ache in her chest? Well, that never left her for long.

Not with Luke Garrison seven thousand miles away and one month into his six-month deployment commanding his National Guard unit in Afghanistan.

"Bank's looking good tonight, Harp." Sophie winked from her position behind the taps. "What kind of treasure are we spending our hard-earned tips on?"

Harper tucked the back of her Remo's polo back into her denim skirt before hoisting her tray. It was their favorite game to play at work. "Matching unicorn tattoos."

"Love it!"

Her tray full of beer and her mind full of Luke, Harper spun back into the fray.

A month into it, and she was still getting used to being in a very real, very long-distance relationship. They had planned to go their separate ways, parting as friends. She had been trying to prepare herself to mourn their relationship while forging a new life alone.

But one word had changed everything.

Stay.

His text had arrived just as the full reality of saying goodbye had hit her, sitting in his truck sobbing at the thought of a life without Luke. Her hands shook so hard she could barely reply to the text.

Harper: What??

Luke: I want to come home to you. Stay.

It wasn't an "I love you," but it was enough. His text had found its way through her despair and given her hope. He was offering her a life and a future. With him.

They had talked that night before his flight, and a desperate hope had bloomed in her chest.

"I got on that bus and realized that if you weren't there when I came home, I'd go back to the same existence. And I don't want to just exist anymore. Baby, I know it's a lot to ask. Six months is a long time to wait, but I want you there," he told her.

Her eyes swam in tears as she nodded silently. "Luke, if there's anyone worth waiting six months for, it's you."

"Back at you, baby."

So she stayed. She canceled her interview in Fremont and

unpacked her boxes and bags. And her first night alone in his house, she went stark raving mad.

Knowing that it would be six long months before she felt Luke's hard body raging over her or caught a quick glimpse of that dimple fed her desperation to find a distraction.

But what?

Since moving to Benevolence, her entire focus had been on Luke. Luke's incredible body. Luke's home. Luke's work. Luke's really incredible body.

That first night, she lay awake in the center of the bed wearing one of his T-shirts and stared at the ceiling until dawn. For the first time in her life, she had stability, a future. She just didn't know what to do with it.

She did her best to stay busy.

Harper took up knitting. Until she pierced her knuckle with the knitting needle and bled all over the silky ivory yarn that wasn't looking anything like the pattern anyway. Scrapbooking was next, until she realized she had nothing to scrapbook. There were only so many silly stickers and borders you could stick to a page without any actual photos.

Finally, Sophie took pity on her and offered up a weekly shift at Remo's to get Harper out of the house on Friday nights. Sophie bartended while Harper called on her college experience and waited tables. The tips were good, and it was the perfect way to get to know the residents of Benevolence. Sooner or later, everyone showed up at Remo's for dinner, for drinks, for conversation.

Of course, most of the customers knew her name before they even met her.

Small towns.

Luke was not thrilled when she told him in their first video chat.

"No, Harper. Absolutely not," he said, his tone clipped.

"Are you using your captain voice on me right now?" she asked him in disbelief.

The look he leveled at her through the computer had her grinning. He took a deep breath and tried another tack. "What I meant to say is I really don't like the idea of you closing on a Friday night by yourself. It's too late, and what if there's trouble? Who's going to help you?" She could see the frustration on his face.

"Luke, you don't need to worry about this."

"I hate not being around to protect you."

"It's not your job to protect me."

"Yes, it is. And I take it very seriously. So if something happens to you, I'm going to be fucking pissed."

"I love you. That's the reason I'm doing this. I miss you so much it hurts to breathe. Sometimes I can't fall asleep because all I can do is feel this hole in my heart. This shift will help me keep my mind off missing you."

He sighed. "Baby, I miss you too. Every time I wake up and you're not in my arms, it's like a knife in the gut. But I need you to be safe. Promise me, Harper, that you'll take every precaution."

She crossed her heart. "I promise. Ty got Sophie and I pepper spray, and we carpool to our shift. Besides, Luke, everyone knows who we belong to."

Harper dropped off the beers and a diet soda and raced back to the server station to order for Reece and Dana at the pool table.

She made another lap before circling back to the bar and spotting a familiar face.

Gloria was perched on a barstool sipping a glass of wine.

"Hey, Gloria." Harper waved to her friend. "It's nice to see you out and about!"

A delicate blush tinged Gloria's cheeks. "I'm celebrating my first paycheck from Blooms."

Free from the abuse of her ex-boyfriend Glenn Diller, Gloria landed a job at the local florist and was saving for her own apartment.

"Good for you! Claire says you're doing a great job," Harper told her, reloading her tray. Luke's mom, a plant lover for life, worked at Blooms part-time and had been singing Gloria's praises.

"Thanks. I really like it there." Gloria's blush deepened. "Um, have you heard from Luke?"

Harper couldn't stop the smile that took over her face if she tried. Just the mention of his name gave her a little rush. A fast, electric tingle.

She nodded. "I had an email from him Wednesday, and I talked to him last week."

Gloria turned her gaze to her glass as she twirled the stem between her fingers. "Did he say how Aldo's doing?"

"Ooooooooooh," Sophie cooed behind the bar. "Someone has a crush!"

Gloria turned an even brighter shade of pink.

"Stop picking on her!" Harper rolled her eyes. "Don't mind Sophie," she told Gloria. "She thinks she's Cupid."

"By the way, you're welcome." Sophie winked at Harper.

Harper definitely owed Sophie a debt of gratitude for putting her in Luke's bed that first night. Not that she intended to inflate Luke's sister's head any more than it already was.

"*Anyway.*" Harper looked pointedly at Sophie. "Luke did mention that Aldo's organizing some crazy boot camp workout competition with a bunch of the people from their unit. Tire flipping, rope climbing. He promised to email pictures."

Gloria nodded but remained silent.

"I could give you his email address, you know."

That had Gloria lifting her gaze. "Don't you think it would be…weird?"

Harper shook her head and hefted her tray. "I think you guys waited long enough. Don't you?" She started for the crowd and called over her shoulder. "I'll send you his email address."

That night, Harper collapsed into bed exhausted and alone. On Fridays, James, Luke's younger brother, took Lola and Max overnight so she didn't have to worry about them being alone all day and into the night.

She smiled, imagining the dogs cramming themselves between him and whatever attractive, single girl he had talked into his bed. Just like his brother, he wasn't into commitment. However, in James's case, the girls didn't have to be nearly as persuasive as Harper had been.

Was this Luke settling down? Asking her to stay seemed like a big step. But there were so many things unsaid between the two of them. What was he keeping from her? There were walls between them and not just the ones he had built in the basement.

Harper couldn't help but wonder how things would be when he came home. Would it be the same old cycle of getting too close only to be pushed away? She rolled over and hugged a pillow. Doubts and concerns found their way into her mind in the quiet hours of the night, especially when she hadn't heard from him.

They managed a phone call or a video chat almost every week, and in those precious minutes, everything was better. Just hearing his voice from half a world away made her body come alive.

Hanging up was hell.

Harper instituted a rule for herself. She wasn't allowed to cry on the phone. She wanted to leave him with a warm feeling in his chest that would lift him up, not a sinking guilt or loneliness that would plague him.

After every call, she allowed herself five minutes to cry those unshed tears and embrace the hollow of her heart. And then she carried on.

She curled around his pillow. Tonight, she was wearing a Garrison Construction T-shirt that she found in his office. Wrapped in his familiar scent, she fell into a deep, dreamless sleep.

CHAPTER 27

The next morning, Harper set aside some time to work in her new garden. Charlie helped her till the soil, and Claire had gone on a plant-buying rampage with her. She was determined to make this hobby stick and not just because she liked zucchini and fresh tomatoes. Damn it if she didn't want to add something to this house that was just hers. She wanted to belong here, feel at home. She wanted to provide something tangible to their home together.

Harper brought her gloved hands to her lower back and lifted her face to the sky. The morning sunshine held a hint of humidity, a sure sign that summer was on its way.

Her phone signaled an incoming call from the railing of the porch. It was Luke's ringtone. She sprinted across the backyard like an Olympian and pounced on the phone.

"Harper?" Luke's voice crackled through the connection.

"Luke!"

"Harper, can you call me back?"

"Yes. I have the phone card here. Give me ten seconds, okay?"

"Hurry. Please." He disconnected.

Something was wrong. Harper's heart pounded in her chest

as she dashed inside to grab the phone card out of her purse. She misdialed twice before she was able to calm her fingers enough to get through.

"Luke! Are you okay? Are you hurt?"

"Baby, I'm fine. But Aldo—" Luke's voice cracked on his friend's name.

Harper felt her heart clutch.

"Aldo's hurt pretty bad. It was an IED. They medevaced him to Bagram. I don't know his status."

She heard him take a breath. Heard the catch in his throat.

"Oh my God, Luke. Honey, I'm so sorry."

He cleared his throat, and she knew he was pulling it in, tamping it down.

"Are you okay?" he asked.

"I'm fine." A tear trickled down her cheek at the pain in his voice. "Everything here is fine."

"Please keep talking, Harp. I just want to hear your voice."

"The dogs miss you. I keep coming home and finding your running shoes at the door. Max and Lola go into the closet every morning and carry them down there."

She knew she sounded like she was being strangled, but she pressed on. She told him about Ty's new police cruiser and how they got the bid on the Greek restaurant.

"That's great, Harp. Thanks."

"I love you, Luke."

She heard his sigh, knew he needed the words.

"Can you do me a favor, baby?"

"Anything."

"Go sit with Mrs. Moretta. She'll be getting a call soon. Maybe take my mom?"

"Absolutely. If I hear anything, I'll email you, and you do the same. Okay?"

"Thanks, Harper. I…don't know what I'd do without you."

"Anything for you, Luke. I love you so much."

"I…miss you."

"Miss you too. Call as soon as you can."

"Will do."

———

Luke hung up the phone and dropped it on the pillow next to him. The cot creaked with the motion.

He stared listlessly out the dusty window at the gray mountains looming just beyond base.

He needed that glimpse of home that only Harper could give him. Needed the reminder that there was a life waiting for him beyond the dusty, dry heat of the desert that right now was painted red with his friend's blood.

He reached for his laptop and opened his email.

Luke thought that fixing Harper's car had been a good going-away gift. Harper had him beat. When he opened his email for the first time in Afghanistan, he saw she had sent him close to thirty pictures, many of them ones he hadn't known she took. There were shots of the two of them, the dogs, his family, and his home. She even included a few of his employees. He opened the files almost every day.

Tonight, he took his time clicking through each one. His favorite was one that the newspaper had uploaded online. The paper had run the picture of Harper and Linc coming out of the water on the front page, but in the photographer's album of the event, Harper had found a shot of the two of them at the bar. Luke's arms were wrapped around her from behind, pulling her into his chest. His hand was splayed across her stomach, and she was looking over her shoulder at him. They were both laughing.

He loved her expression. Harper's eyes were bright and her cheeks flushed. Her hair hung in damp waves that framed her face. He could see the excitement between the two of them and felt the corner of his mouth turn up at the fortunate fact that the photographer had failed to capture the raging hard-on he had pressed against her at that exact moment.

It was the night of their first time together. The night he stopped fighting and let go.

He kept the picture open and clicked the next one.

Aldo's cocky grin filled the screen. Harper must have taken it with her phone. It was the night Aldo and Gloria came for dinner. Aldo was manning the grill and arguing with Luke about something. They were both grinning. Brothers without the blood.

Luke shut the lid of the laptop.

He braced his hands against his knees, fingers digging into the dried blood and mud caked to his fatigues.

He closed his eyes and let the plywood walls of his eight-by-eight room close in on him.

CHAPTER 28

Mrs. Moretta lived in a tidy two-story cottage three blocks over from Luke's parents. The front porch was partially obscured by colorful pots overflowing with petunias.

A hummingbird feeder hung from a rafter.

Harper blew out the breath she had been holding. Claire reached across the console and patted her hand on the steering wheel.

"You're a good girl, Harper. Let's go help a friend."

They were only halfway up the walk when Mrs. Moretta burst out of the front door. She was wearing a flopping sunhat and one garden glove. Harper could see tears.

Claire hurried up the steps to her friend. "Oh, Ina."

The two women embraced on the porch. "Thank you so much for being here, Claire. They just called. He's alive."

"Thank God for that," Claire said, holding her tight.

"Harper." Mrs. Moretta released Claire and nodded in her direction. "Let's go inside and get a drink."

They let her lead the way back to a cozy kitchen with a greenhouse window over the sink.

Mrs. Moretta paused, staring off into the yard. "He's in surgery. They think he's going to lose a leg. But he's going to live."

Harper covered her mouth with a hand and closed her eyes. Aldo was alive, and that was what mattered. She excused herself for a moment and fired off an email to Luke from her phone.

To: lucas.c.garrison282@us.army.mil
From: harpwild@netlink.com
Subject: Alive!

Alive and in surgery. May lose leg, but he's expected to survive. We're with Mrs. M now. She's holding up. I'll let you know if I learn anything else. I love you.

H

When she returned to the kitchen, Mrs. Moretta and Claire were talking quietly at the dining room table.

"The base said they'll be sending me to Dover when Aldo gets there, and then I'll go with him to Walter Reed. I'll know more once he's been moved to Germany." She sighed and removed her glove. "What would we ever do without our boys, Claire?"

"We're not going to have to find out, Ina." Claire squeezed her friend's hand. "Aldo's going to come home and be just as big a pain in your ass as he ever was."

"Remember when they were just boys and playing in the creek the entire summer?"

"Remember when they camped out in the backyard in a tent and I found them curled up side by side on the couch the next morning?"

"When did our little boys turn into men?"

"They'd tell you it was a lot earlier than I would."

Mrs. Moretta sniffled.

"Can I get you a drink, Mrs. Moretta?" Harper offered. "Some tea or water?"

"Harper, there is a box of cheap chardonnay in the fridge. How about you grab us three of the biggest glasses you can find, and we'll drink to our boys?"

It was on the third refill trip from the kitchen that Harper returned to Claire whispering to Mrs. Moretta.

"She's just what he needs—"

"Harper, Claire is distracting me with gossip about you and your Luke. She seems to think that you're doing him a world of good."

Harper felt the blush rise to her cheeks. "I think it's more vice versa."

"I wish Aldo would settle down. That boy can't focus on one woman for longer than a month at a time." Mrs. Moretta sighed.

"Maybe they just weren't the one he wanted?" Harper offered.

"You sound like you know something," Claire said, wiggling her eyebrows.

"Spill it," Mrs. Moretta ordered. "The gossip, not the wine."

Harper handed out the glasses, sloshing only a few drops over the rims.

"There seemed to be some sparks between Aldo and Gloria when we had them over for dinner. And Aldo gave her a ride home."

"Hmm," Claire and Mrs. Moretta said in unison.

"Little Gloria Parker," Claire said. "I never would have guessed."

"Aldo also may have confessed to carrying a torch for her since high school. But that I can't confirm without permission from the source," Harper added.

"No wonder he hated that asshole Glenn so much," Mrs. Moretta said, sweeping a hand over her hair and finding the hat. "Why the hell didn't you two tell me I was still wearing this? I was gardening when the base called. I'm such a mess." She yanked the hat off and tossed it over her shoulder where it hit a brass birdcage full of silk flowers.

Claire and Harper snickered.

In the end, the box of wine was empty, the pizza they ordered was mostly gone, and Charlie had to come pick them up.

"I'm so thankful to you two for being here for me," Mrs. Moretta said as she wrapped them both in a bear hug. "It means the world to me."

"You just keep us up-to-date on Aldo's progress and when you'll be leaving. We'll help out in any way we can. Harper will come by tomorrow to get her car—unless you have another box of chardonnay in there, and then we'll just do this again." Claire giggled.

Charlie clapped his hand on Mrs. Moretta's shoulder. "He's a good boy. He'll be home safe and sound before you know it."

"Thanks, Charlie. Harper, maybe you want to let Gloria know?" Mrs. Moretta suggested with a pronounced wink.

"I'll tell her tomorrow after we know more about how the surgery went," Harper promised.

That night, Harper crawled into bed with both dogs and one of Luke's sweatshirts. She buried her face in it and let all the pent-up tears come.

———

The next morning, a slightly hungover Harper woke to news from Luke.

To: harpwild@netlink.com
From: lucas.c.garrison282@us.army.mil
Re: Alive!

Harp, just got word on Aldo. He came through surgery. They had to take his leg below the knee. He's still unconscious, and doctors are worried about infection but think he'll pull through. He just needs to wake up. The medical team was in contact with Mrs. Moretta, so she's up to speed. Are you okay?

Harper breathed a quick sigh of relief. Aldo was alive. And he would wake the fuck up. She couldn't imagine a scenario in which he didn't.

To: lucas.c.garrison282@us.army.mil
From: harpwild@netlink.com
Re: Alive!

There's no way he's not going to wake up. So don't even think about that as a possibility. Aldo's going to wake up, wink at the nurse, and demand a cold beer.

Mrs. Moretta is a rock. A rock with an incredible tolerance for alcohol. She and your mother drank me under the table reminiscing about the good old days until your dad had to come pick us up.

When—and I do mean when—Aldo comes home, the guard is going to take Mrs. Moretta to meet him in Dover and then on to Walter Reed.

Was anyone else hurt? Are you okay? I'm freaking out a little bit, but hearing your voice helped and so did your email. I'm worried about you. So you'd better be taking care of yourself or else I'll do something drastic. Like paint all the original wood trim in the house black. Seriously though, I need to see your face.

I don't suppose you could come home on leave just to wear some clothes so I have something to sleep in that smells like you? No? I'll settle for a video chat. I love you so much it hurts.

H

PS: Here's a picture of Max and Lola enjoying the doggy pool in the yard and one of the garden. Those green things are PLANTS not WEEDS. Success!

Harper clicked Send and took a breath. She needed to tell Gloria about Aldo. And after yesterday, the dogs needed a good long walk. Plus, she wanted to pick up her car and check on Mrs. Moretta.

She whistled for the dogs. Ears perked, Lola barreled down the hallway into the kitchen with Max hot on her heels.

They danced around Harper's barstool, anticipating a bacon snack, attention, or—dare to dream—the W-word.

Harper slid off the stool and patted their heads. "Okay, guys, let's go for a w-a-l-k." She had learned to spell the word after realizing that Max had the tendency to get so excited he peed when he heard "walk."

At the front door, she grabbed her sunglasses and bag. The second she reached for the leashes, puppy pandemonium erupted.

"For the love of God, hold still!" Harper said, chasing Max's wiggly neck with the leash. Lola pranced in place until Harper secured the harness around her.

"Let's go see Auntie Gloria," Harper said. She'd use the six-block walk to Gloria's mother's house to figure out how to break the news to her friend.

Gloria answered the door of the tidy brick ranch with a cheerful smile. "Harper! This is a nice surprise." She leaned down to pet Lola's massive head while Max shoved his tiny body between them. "Yes, I see you too, Max!" Gloria giggled and picked him up. "Can you come in, or are you just passing by?"

Harper pushed her sunglasses up on top of her head. "I actually have some news about Aldo." She took a deep breath and ripped off the bandage. "He's hurt, Gloria. He came through surgery, and the doctors are hopeful. They had to take part of his leg."

She watched the blood drain from Gloria's face. "Aldo?" she repeated.

Harper nodded and grabbed Gloria's arm. "He's going to be okay. Luke emailed me this morning and said the surgery team's only concern right now is infection." She paused, debating. "He hasn't woken up yet."

Gloria cuddled Max closer. "But he will."

"Yeah, he will."

Gloria exhaled a shaky breath. "I emailed him Friday night after you gave me his address."

"Then he'll have something to read when he wakes up." Harper smiled. "So speaking of Aldo, would you mind giving me and my two stinky mutts a ride to Mrs. Moretta's house? I left my car there last night, and I wanted to check in on her."

Gloria glanced down at her denim shorts and pink T-shirt.

Harper grinned. "Are you nervous about meeting his mother?"

"It's Mrs. Moretta! She's terrifying. Who wouldn't be nervous about meeting her?" Gloria said, eyes wide. "Oh, screw it! Just let me brush my hair and bag up some of the cookies I baked this morning."

———————

It went better than expected. Mrs. Moretta opened the door with the announcement that Aldo was awake and, after learning that everyone else in the unit was okay, had demanded a cheeseburger.

Gloria held her own under Mrs. Moretta's inquisition that covered all facets of life, including religious faith, how many children she planned to have, and all the ingredients in her jam thumbprint cookies.

At the end of the question and answer session, Ina Moretta had merely harrumphed and nodded.

"I feel like I just got steamrolled," Gloria said, shell-shocked.

"I think it went well," Harper said, loading the dogs into her car.

"I can't tell. I'm not sure." Gloria sagged against the side of her car.

"She kept the cookies. That's definitely a good sign," Harper offered.

"What was that 'huh' noise there at the end?"

"I think that's her seal of approval. She's recognizing that you're more than good enough for her son."

Gloria shook her head. "I think I'm going to go home and take a nap."

CHAPTER 29

Harper snatched her phone off the coffee table at the first ring of the video chat alert. She fumbled with the icons once but in seconds was treated to the face she had been missing.

"Hi, baby." Luke looked exhausted.

It had been two long weeks since Aldo got hurt, and Luke's reluctance to video chat told Harper that he wasn't dealing well. Seeing his face confirmed her suspicion, and her heart hurt for him.

"Hey there, handsome. How are you?" Harper sat back on the couch, hugging a pillow to her chest.

"I'm okay. How's my girl?"

"I miss you." She fought back the tears that welled up. Seeing him intensified everything. "I'm worried about you."

He sighed under the weight of the world. "Baby, I'm fine. Everything's okay."

"Look, I know you're not much of a talker. But I can't have you stumbling around half a world away fucking things up because you're distracted by a misplaced sense of responsibility and guilt."

He blinked. Luke's mouth opened and then closed.

"I see I have your attention," Harper said primly.

"I would say so."

"Luke, do you think there is any way that Aldo blames you for what happened?"

He sighed. "No."

"In fact, he's probably already told you that you're not to blame."

Luke stared off. "Fine. Yes."

It was like trying to get answers out of a brick wall…or a basement. "Great. So did you place the IED there?"

He rolled his eyes at her. "No."

"Did you tell Aldo to drive over it?"

"No."

"Did you know it was there and not tell him?"

"No. Harper—"

"Not done yet. So logically, you can agree with the *entire rest of the world* that you are not to blame."

He sat stoically without moving for a few seconds. "Was that not rhetorical?"

"Luke, it hurts me to see you hurt like this. I don't know how to help you."

"Harper, baby, you can't make it better. I get what you're saying. I know that I'm not to blame. But I feel responsible for my friend. His life and the lives of everyone in this unit are in my hands. If I don't lead responsibly, people can and do get hurt. People die."

"Aldo didn't die."

"No, but others have."

The men he lost before, Harper remembered.

"I lost good men because we had bad intel. Ultimately that responsibility lies on my shoulders."

"That's bullshit."

"Am I to blame? No. But I'm the leader of this unit, and that makes me responsible for everything that happens within it."

It was Harper's turn for silence.

His sigh was heavy. "All I know is I can't get the blood out of my head. I saw it happen, and we started running toward the truck. He was just lying there in a fucking river of blood." Luke stared down at his hands as if seeing it again.

Harper shuddered.

"I thought he was dead. I thought I lost my best friend right in front of me. And it made me think of everyone else I'd lost. All that I have to lose and how it can just be taken in a heartbeat." He looked up at her.

Harper wiped away the silent tears coursing down her cheeks and wished she could touch him.

"I felt helpless."

"He's going to be okay."

"He got really fucking lucky, Harper. So many times, it doesn't go that way."

"I need to know that you carrying this on your shoulders isn't going to make you do something stupid."

"Like what?"

"I'm new to this military thing, but I assume you have plenty of poor choice options, like going on a rampage, developing a drinking problem, getting careless."

He sighed and smiled a little. "I'm not going to do any of those things."

"I know you won't. I just need some reassurance that you'll take care of yourself. I need you to come home safe and sane."

"I'll do everything in my power to make sure that happens," Luke told her.

"That's all I ask." She swiped a hand under her eyes. "Isn't it the middle of the night there?"

Luke smiled. "It's the only way I can get this place to myself." He turned his laptop around, giving her a view of his tiny room.

It was Harper's turn to smile. Intensely private at home and at war.

"Good, that means you can take your shirt off so I can lick my screen."

That got a real smile out of him and even a hint of dimple. "Baby, if one of us is taking our shirts off, it's going to be you."

"Well, if you insist." Harper tugged her tank top up and flashed him.

She watched those hazel eyes go dark as he set his jaw. She wondered if he had any idea how sexy he was.

"Do you know what torture it is to be able to see you and not touch you?" His voice was raspy, low.

She felt her color rise. "I miss your hands on me. I feel so empty without you touching me. We only had a little time before. But when you were inside me, I felt like all the pieces of me were stuck back together."

He growled. "Baby, you can't talk like that when I'm seven thousand miles away." His hands cruised the back of his head. "God, you get me hard even through a shitty video connection. I miss you so fucking much."

Harper closed her eyes and nodded. "Back at you, Captain."

"Every time I think about fucking you, I go to the gym. I'm going to need to size up in shirts soon. My bench PR is up fifteen pounds already."

"That's hot," Harper teased. "You're gonna give Aldo a run for his money when you both get home."

"Have you heard when he's coming home?"

Harper shook her head. "We've exchanged a handful of emails. He thinks it'll be sooner rather than later. Has he mentioned Gloria to you?"

"I've only heard from him twice. Once to assure me he was alive and that I better not be moping around about it, and the other to show me a picture of his surgeon in Germany who looked like Wolverine from *X-Men*."

"Gloria's emailed him twice now and hasn't heard back. I asked him point-blank if he got them, and he ignored me."

Luke shrugged. "I'm sure he's got a lot on his mind."

Harper was sure he did too. And that was what worried her.

"Show me again," Luke ordered.

"Show you what?"

"Your perfect tits."

She wondered if she'd ever stop blushing when he talked to her like that. "You're sure you're alone?"

"The Wi-Fi signal is strong enough to work in quarters tonight. I'm all alone, baby. Show me."

His voice sounded like gravel but still felt like satin on her skin. Harper bit her lip and pulled her tank top up and over her head, baring her breasts to the screen. "Are we going to—"

"Quiet," he ordered. "I want you to do exactly what I tell you."

Harper nodded breathlessly. Even from thousands of miles away, he could make her wet enough to soak through her underwear. She angled the phone so he could see more of her.

"Good girl. Now take your shorts off."

She leaned her phone against one of the couch pillows and stood, shimmying out of her shorts.

"Fuck, baby," Luke sighed, his gaze glued to the screen. Harper ran a finger over the edge of her light-blue cotton briefs.

"Get on your hands and knees on the couch. Face me."

She slid back onto the cushion, bracing her weight on her hands. Her breasts hung down, and she ached for his mouth on her sensitive peaks.

"Luke, I want to see you." It was a whisper, but it carried across the miles.

He paused for just a moment and then Harper heard the rip of Velcro. A second later, Luke pulled off his shirt and angled the screen down, and she could see what she had been missing for weeks.

Even gripped in Luke's big fist, his cock looked huge. Harper felt the ache deep inside her core start to pulse with need. She wanted to feel his erection drive into her, stretching her walls as it invaded her.

"I'd give anything to be inside you right now, Harper." He stroked his hand down his hard-on. "I want you to touch yourself."

She hesitated.

"Go ahead, baby. Pretend it's my hands on you."

She took a shaky breath and brought her palm to her breast where it hung. The growl from her phone told her Luke liked what he saw. She took her nipple between her thumb and finger and tugged it down in a leisurely pace that matched Luke's strokes.

"Baby—" The audio crackled and went silent, but the video feed remained.

Harper pointed to her ear. "I can't hear you. Can you hear me?"

Luke pointed at his ear and shook his head. But his other hand stayed gripping his erection. Understanding, Harper slid her hand back down to her breast. She rolled and tugged the nipple, pretending it was Luke's mouth teasing her.

She saw him increase the pace ever so slightly, wondering if there was a drop of moisture that so often appeared from the slit in the broad head of his penis. She licked her lips and slid her hand lower into her underwear.

She should have been feeling embarrassed. She wasn't an exhibitionist. But right then, all she wanted to do was see Luke stroke himself to climax across his chiseled abs and chest.

Her lips parted as her fingers found the slick wetness between her folds. Her bud was already straining for contact. Harper shifted her weight back and brought her free hand to her other breast. She squeezed and saw Luke's eyes narrow. His fist slammed down the length of his cock as he pumped himself in his own hand. Harper's fingers circled her clitoris in a frantic pace, a race to the finish.

She felt the need for release blossom inside her. It bloomed as she drove her fingers into her wet channel. She opened her mouth to say his name and saw he was with her. The first rope of cum unleashed across his stomach. It was her name on his lips as a second and a third exploded from him.

She felt herself close around her fingers as they came together.

CHAPTER 30

Aldo Moretta was coming home.

After a few long weeks in hospitals and clinics, he—and his fancy new prosthetic leg—were coming home to Benevolence.

Per his physical therapy team, he was going to stay with his mother for a few weeks before they released him into the wild.

Harper waited an entire day and a half before she went knocking on Mrs. Moretta's front door on her lunch hour. Seeing Aldo in the flesh would put to rest nightmares that had plagued her for the last month. She shifted the bag of goodies into her other hand and knocked on the screen door.

It was drowned out by shouting.

"For the love of God, Ma. I've spent the last two weeks with you. You're driving me fucking nuts."

"That's a fine way to talk to the woman who dropped everything to nurse you back to health because you couldn't swerve around a bomb," Ina Moretta shouted back.

"You played *Candy Crush* and yelled at me if I didn't turn on *The Price Is Right* every day," Aldo roared.

"You aren't driving yourself to PT. I don't care how big and tough you think you are. So you're welcome to walk. Go ahead and hitchhike. See if I care. I didn't raise you to be a grown man who shouts at his own mother."

"That is exactly who you raised me to be!"

Harper gave up on knocking and stepped inside. She dumped the bag on the floor and cupped her hands over her mouth. "Hey!"

Aldo crutched into the foyer from the living room, and Mrs. Moretta poked her head out of the kitchen.

"Come right on in, bursting into my house like that. Didn't your parents teach you any manners?" Mrs. Moretta yelled.

"They must have died too soon, I guess," Harper said in a decibel or two above her usual conversational tone. The shouting was contagious.

Aldo blindsided her with a bear hug, dropping his crutches to the floor. Harper grabbed him and held on for dear life. He was home safe and yelling at his mother. It was another step in the direction of normal.

"Pick up your goddamn crutches! You know the doctors don't want you walking unassisted yet!" Mrs. Moretta continued on in some colorful Italian.

"I'm glad you're home. And alive," Harper said, her face smashed in Aldo's barrel of a chest.

"I will marry you and have your babies if you get me the hell out of this house. I have a PT appointment in thirty," he said, stepping back. Harper looked him up and down. He was dressed in gym shorts and a T-shirt. His gleaming new prosthetic left leg began a few inches below the knee and ended in a sneaker.

"Luke might have a problem with the first, but I'd pay money to see the second, so it's a deal. Besides, I want to see what you can do with that hardware."

"I can do anything. They just won't fucking let me," Aldo muttered.

"If you don't do what the doctors tell you, you'll end up screwing up your stump or breaking that thing," his mother warned, pointing at his prosthetic.

Harper saw red in Aldo's eye and decided to force a truce.

"Mrs. Moretta, I'm going to take Aldo to his appointment today. Is there anything you need while we're out?"

Mrs. Moretta grumbled for a moment. "Well, I suppose I could use another box of chardonnay."

At the car, Aldo tossed his crutches in the back seat and lowered himself into the passenger seat. He dropped his head back against the headrest and sighed. "I love that woman, but I swear to God, one of these days, one of us is going to murder the other."

Harper snickered and shifted into reverse. "That was World War III in there."

"That's what happens when you spend two fucking weeks straight with Ina Moretta. I think it was her goal to drive me crazy."

"I hear that's what moms are for," Harper said, backing down the driveway into the street. "Where are we going?"

Aldo directed her out of town to the north.

"By the way, there's a bag of goodies in the back for you," she told him.

Aldo swiveled in his seat and grabbed at the gift bag. "Where's the candy?" he demanded.

"It's in the bottom. I consulted with Luke on this, so a lot of it you can thank him for."

He pulled out a clear package. "New earbuds"

"For the get-pumped playlists I made you for therapy, and you can also use it to drown out your mom."

"Earplugs," he said pulling out the tiny plastic egg.

"Luke said your mom snores."

"Like a fucking company of lumberjacks at a chainsaw convention. What's this? A bracelet?"

"Yeah, I thought you could start accessorizing," Harper teased. "No, it's one of those step counter heart-rate monitors. It's what normal people who don't run half marathons on the weekends use to measure their fitness. And since, for the next week or two, you probably won't be hitting a 10K, I thought you could use it with your physical therapy. It'll sync with your phone too."

"This is cool, Harpoon. Thanks."

He seemed tired, flat. But he was home.

"Seriously? You're gonna go with Harpoon?"

"We'll see where the day takes us." Aldo unwrapped a mini chocolate bar and popped it in his mouth.

———

The clinic was a twenty-minute drive north of town. Aldo ate candy and stared pensively out the window while Harper called Beth at the office to let her know she'd be back later that afternoon.

"Beth wants me to hug you for her," Harper said, hanging up.

"I have a feeling I'll be getting a lot of that." Aldo didn't seem thrilled with the idea.

"I know there's a certain beautiful brunette who'd be willing to get in line to hug you."

Aldo grunted.

"Have you talked to Gloria?"

"No."

"Care to expand on that? I feel like I'm talking to Luke here," Harper sighed.

"Turn here," Aldo said, pointing at a white stone building on the right.

Harper pulled into the parking lot and eased up to the front of the two-story glass entrance.

"I'll grab your crutches," she told Aldo, pulling the parking brake.

"I'll walk from the parking space," he said, crossing his arms over his chest.

Harper shrugged. "Fine."

Two could play the smart-ass game. She pulled into the very last space at the far end of the lot and turned the car off. She worked the crutches free from the back seat and waited until Aldo pulled himself to a standing position.

"Get your ass in there." She handed him the crutches.

She saw the tic in his jaw and waited.

"You can come in if you want," he said finally before stepping around her and starting toward the front entrance.

Harper grabbed her bag out of the back seat and followed him.

His face didn't show any exertion when they reached the reception area, but there were little beads gathering on his face and neck. His knuckles were white on the padded handgrips.

Angry and pushing himself too hard. Well, he was Mrs. Moretta's son. It was to be expected.

They waited in silence for a few minutes until a nurse in cheery floral scrubs called them back.

"Lieutenant Moretta, welcome to PT." She smiled at him. "I'm Annalise." She extended her hand to him. After shuffling crutches, Aldo shook it.

"Aldo."

Annalise turned her attention to Harper.

"I'm Harper," she said, taking the offered hand.

"Thanks for coming," Annalise said, leading the way through tables and cardio machines. "It's important for family to be involved in recovery."

"We're just friends," Aldo mumbled.

"Well, it always helps to have another pair of eyes and hands," Annalise said, unfazed. She pointed to a pair of chairs next to a set of parallel bars. "Let me get these set to your height, and the doctor will be here shortly."

Aldo glared at the bars while Harper tried not to think of the friendly, funny man who left Benevolence not so long ago.

"Lieutenant." A slim man in a white coat and glasses approached. "I'm Dr. Steers. I've heard a lot about you."

Aldo shook his hand but said nothing.

"Harper," she introduced herself.

"Great to meet you, Harper. Let's get started, shall we? Lieutenant, Walter Reed gave me your file, and you already have our staff impressed. To be where you are right now, barely a month from the injury, is almost superhuman."

Harper saw the corner of Aldo's mouth lift. So he was still in there somewhere.

"He is pretty awesome, isn't he?" She grinned.

Dr. Steers flashed her a grin. "We can understand the lieutenant's frustration with the pace of therapy, and we'll do our best to write a program that challenges him at his level. We just need to make sure we're not asking too much of your body while you're still so early in the recovery process. Okay?"

Aldo nodded.

"So let's get you up. You know the drill." The doctor pointed to the bars.

Aldo stood and handed Annalise his crutches. He gripped the bars and walked, one foot in front of the other, toward Dr. Steers, who paced him backward on a wheeled stool.

"Looks good," the doctor said, making notes. "Go ahead and go back to the top."

They had Aldo walk, holding the bars several more times, pausing briefly to make slight adjustments to the prosthesis.

"Lieutenant, let's try it without the bars."

Aldo dropped his hands to his sides and sauntered toward Annalise.

"That's perfect," Dr. Steers said. "Your gait looks great."

Again, they put Aldo through his paces without walking aids.

His impassive face gave no hint of exertion, but his T-shirt was soaked with sweat.

"Let's take a quick water break, and then we'll move on to some of the balance exercises," Dr. Steers suggested.

Aldo shrugged but dropped into the chair next to Harper.

"Harper, there's some bottles of water in the cooler on the far wall. Do you want to grab a couple for you two?"

"Sure." Happy to be able to do something, Harper hurried to the refrigerator and grabbed two bottles.

"Here," she said, holding one out for Aldo.

"Thanks," he said, twisting the top and downing half of it.

She resisted the urge to rub his shoulder.

"I know the energy expenditure is frustrating. Typically, mobility with a below-knee amputation consumes up to forty percent more energy than what you're used to. That's why you feel like you just finished a marathon. It might only seem like a few steps to you, but to your body, it feels like almost double that."

"I'm fine. I can do more." Aldo shrugged.

"Lieutenant, you live up to the hype," Annalise said, readjusting the bar height. "You're a beast."

"When can I start running?"

Dr. Steers looked at him over his glasses. "I'm going to make a promise that in most cases I don't get to make. Soon. In fact, I think you'd be a great candidate for a carbon fiber running blade."

Aldo's nod was brisk, but Harper saw the spark in his eye. "Let's move on to some balance work."

After another hour of balance and strengthening exercises followed by some electrical stimulation and massage, Aldo was putty on the table.

Annalise handed Harper a stack of papers. "These are at-home exercises that will really keep the momentum high for his therapy. The lieutenant is going to have three outpatient appointments a week here, but if you can help him on off days and work through these, he's going to see more results more quickly."

Harper took the stack. "Absolutely."

"Great! Then we'll see you two Friday."

———

"You don't have to be my new therapy buddy," Aldo said, back in the car.

"I don't mind. But I'll understand if you'd rather have your mom take you."

He smirked. "Very funny. Want to grab some lunch?"

Harper's stomach growled. "More than anything in the world."

They went through a drive-thru and put the top of the VW down in a sunny waterfront park.

Harper chowed down on her burger while Aldo picked at his fries.

"Have you talked to Luke?" she finally asked.

"A couple of times. Not since I came home though."

Harper waited and stewed.

"He sounds like he's doing okay," Aldo said.

"Does he?"

"He won't let me thank him."

"For what?"

Aldo turned to look at her. "He didn't tell you that he dragged my ass out of there under fire while ordering everyone else to pull back?"

Harper dropped the cheeseburger in her lap.

"He *what*?"

Aldo swore. "It's all kind of a red blur to me. One second I'm driving down this stretch of road, the next I'm falling out of the truck. I couldn't hear or feel anything. All I knew was I couldn't move. I thought I was dead." He took a steadying breath. "Then there's Luke hovering over me, looking like he's screaming. He dragged me behind a truck, used my belt as a tourniquet. I passed out, but they tell me he carried me under fire while the rest of the guys laid down cover."

"Why the fuck didn't he tell me?" Harper said, grabbing her soda with unnecessary violence.

"Why the fuck won't he let me say thank you?"

She leveled a look at him, and he shook his head.

"Because he's Luke," they said in unison.

At least Luke was an equal opportunity information withholder. "I'm going to type an email in all caps to him when I get home tonight," Harper announced.

"I'll mail him a thank-you card with all caps."

"So why are you avoiding Gloria?"

"Anyone ever tell you you're tenacious, Harpoon?"

"Oh no, you don't. I live with Luke '*Jeopardy*' Garrison. I will not be put off by you trying to turn Q and A into Q and Q. Aren't you interested in her anymore? Did your feelings change?"

"Harper, look at me." Aldo pointed at his prosthesis. "I can barely fucking walk. How am I supposed to sweep her off her feet like she deserves?"

251

"Okay, I don't even know where to start with your asininity."

"Not a word."

"Totally a word. First of all, you think you're somehow less of a man because you're sporting a new leg? That's the dumbest thing I've ever heard. And I've heard a lot of stupid shit. Your leg has nothing to do with the man you are. Your *attitude*, on the other hand"—she poked him in the chest—"has everything to do with it. This 'woe is me' disabled-cowboy crap act is not doing you any favors. Man up and be the rock star you always have been.

"And second, Gloria isn't some fragile flower. She's funny and smart, and she's clawing out a brand-new life for herself. One you could be a part of. You know what would be amazing for her? Some guy who is willing to be vulnerable in front of her. Someone who needs her. Do you know what that would do for her confidence? Finally being in the position to help someone else?" Harper grabbed a handful of fries out of the box and wielded them at him. "She blushes every time someone says your name, and she survived the Mrs. Moretta inquisition."

"Inquisition? Oh shit."

"By the end of it, your mom was asking her for her jam thumbprint cookie recipe."

Aldo dropped his head back against the seat. "This is too much to take in."

"Eat your burger. You're weak with hunger and stupidity."

He reached into the bag, unwrapped his burger, and took a huge bite.

CHAPTER 31

To: lucas.c.garrison282@us.army.mil
From: harpwild@netlink.com
Subject: ARE YOU FREAKING KIDDING ME?

DEAR LUKE,

YOU'LL NOTICE I'M WRITING IN ALL CAPS TO CONVEY THE FACT THAT I AM SHOUTING AT YOU. HOW COULD YOU POSSIBLY NEGLECT TO TELL ME YOU SAVED ALDO'S LIFE WHILE PUTTING YOUR OWN AT GREAT RISK? YOUR LIFE IS GOING TO NEED SAVING WHEN YOU GET HOME.

RESPECTFULLY IN ANGER,
HARPER

———

To: harpwild@netlink.com
From: lucas.c.garrison282@us.army.mil
Subject: Puppies and fluffy things

Dear Harper,

Please accept the attached pictures of puppies and kittens as my attempt to distract you from your anger. You can't be mad at tiny puppies frolicking. It's against your genetic code.

You're beautiful when you're mad,
Luke

———

To: lucas.c.garrison282@us.army.mil
From: harpwild@netlink.com
Re: Puppies and fluffy things

I've been hypnotized by fluffiness. I'm feeling much less murderous. Perhaps you would like to take this opportunity to explain why you didn't feel that I needed to know the details of "the incident"?

Let me give you some examples of ways you could have broached the subject.

Bragging You: So, babe, I totally rocked life-saving today and dragged Aldo's ass out of a firefight after he was partially blown up. What did you do today?

Subtle You: I'd love to video chat with you tonight, but I'm just really worn out. Worn out from carrying my best friend out of a literal battlefield with guns blazing. It really wasn't a big deal. Tell me more about your crocheting circle.

Normal Human Being You: Aldo was (insert appropriate military terminology here) by an IED. I was able to get to him and get him out under fire, but it was pretty freaking scary. I miss you and think you're the most beautiful, incredible, kind, smart, funny woman in the universe.

Love,
Harper

———

To: harpwild@netlink.com
From: lucas.c.garrison282@us.army.mil
Re: Puppies and fluffy things

Thank goodness for puppies. Stand by for an official apology.

I, Lucas Charles Norbert Garrison, am solemnly sorry for not delivering pertinent facts to one Harper Lee Sue Ellen Wilde, hereafter known as "Hot Girlfriend." The technical and medical term for my mental state was "freaking out," and I had no idea how to put into words what happened to not freak out Hot Girlfriend. The immediacy of the situation required me to put more energy into figuring out whether Aldo Moretta, hereafter known as "Lard Ass When He's Unconscious," was alive and going to stay that way than reporting the fuzzy details of the encounter. However, moving forward, I swear to do a better job of communicating all things, including those of life-and-death importance, as I'd be really pissed too if you didn't tell me something like that.

Miss your smile,
Luke

———

To: lucas.c.garrison282@us.army.mil
From: harpwild@netlink.com
Re: Puppies and fluffy things

Solid apology. I deem this email fight over. Attached please find an olive branch in the form of a picture of my boobs.

CHAPTER 32

Harper huffed and puffed her way up to the third floor under the weight of an ottoman. Making it to the top of the stairs, she took the final steps into Gloria's new one-bedroom and collapsed on top of the ottoman in the middle of the living room.

"You're going to be in amazing shape just from bringing groceries home," Harper gasped. "I can't believe we got the couch up here ourselves."

Gloria laughed from the tiny kitchen where she was unpacking brand-new dinner service for four.

"I can't believe it's mine," she said with a happy sigh. "I can put something on the counter, and it will still be there when I come back. I can watch anything I want on TV. I can lounge around naked all day if I want!"

Harper sat up and surveyed the apartment. Scarred hardwood floors, a handful of cracks in the plaster. But the view of Main Street Benevolence was straight out of a painting. Gloria was three floors over Dawson's Pizza, and the living room's huge bow window overlooked the police station and Common Grounds Café.

She was walking distance to work and the grocery store.

"This is pretty perfect," Harper agreed.

"Want a drink?" Gloria offered.

"For the love of God, yes! Please!" Sophie's voice was muffled by the box of kitchen miscellany she was hefting. She dumped it unceremoniously in the middle of the kitchen floor and collapsed onto a dining chair. "That's literally the last thing. You're all moved in."

Harper jumped up and reached into her bag. "Wait, Gloria! Put the can down. We can't let the first drink in your very own home be diet soda." She pulled out the chilled bottle of champagne she had picked up on the last car trip between Gloria's mom's and the new apartment.

"Nothing happier than the sound of champagne being uncorked," Sophie said, clapping her hands. Harper poured the bubbles into coffee mugs and handed them around.

"I'd like to make a toast," Gloria announced. "Thank you both so much. It means the world to me to be independent, but it's even better to have you two as friends who I can depend on if I need to."

"Aw! Cheers," Harper said, clinking her mug to Gloria's.

Sophie left shortly after to go rescue Ty from Josh, who had decided he was a dog like Bitsy and would only go to the bathroom outside. Harper stuck around to help with some of the unpacking.

"I really appreciate the help," Gloria said, stacking glasses neatly in the cabinet next to the sink.

"I'm happy to help," Harper said, taking another sip of champagne as she untangled cords wrapped around the DVD player. "I'm pretty sure I can figure out how to set this up so you can at least watch movies tonight."

She scooted across the floor to sneak a peek behind the TV. Gloria abandoned the kitchen and sat down on the couch.

"So how's Aldo doing since he came home?" She hugged a cheery yellow pillow to her chest.

Harper's fingers fumbled with an input. "He's, uh, doing okay. I think the therapy is helping mentally. Physically, he's a beast."

"He always was," Gloria said a little sadly.

Harper stopped her fiddling. "Listen, Gloria, I don't know exactly what his problem is, but I hope you know that that's what it is. *His* problem. It has nothing to do with you."

"I think I had got my hopes up a little too high that we could be something together. That I could be something to him."

"Whoa! Let's back that truck up real fast." Harper grabbed her mug and sat down next to Gloria. "You can't put your worth in someone else's hands like that. Whether those hands are stroking you or hurting you. It doesn't matter. Your value comes from inside. Whether you mean something to him or not has nothing to do with how inherently valuable you are."

Gloria sighed and flopped back against the cushion. "I get it. And I think I'm starting to believe it. I know I'll be *okay* without Aldo Moretta, but I'd still like to at least give it a shot."

"Now you're speaking my language."

"Is that how you felt about Luke?"

"That's how I still feel about Luke. I know that I'd be okay without him—after an exceptionally long mourning period, of course. But I want to be great with him."

"So now that I can cross off 'get apartment' from my list, my next goal is to be great no matter who is in my life."

"Bingo." Harper nodded.

"Men," Gloria said into her champagne mug.

"Tell me about it," Harper sighed.

"Let's order some pizza."

"That's the best idea you've ever had in this apartment."

———

For the next three days, Harper ached and pained her way through life. A couple dozen trips up three flights of stairs carrying objects of varying weight had been an eye-opening experience.

She was woefully out of shape.

Harper groaned as she bent to grab a new ream of paper for the printer.

"You want some ibuprofen?" Beth offered.

"Ugh. No. I need to suffer the consequences of my inaction."

"I go to the gym over on Baker Street. It's cheap and clean and has a ton of equipment I don't know how to use."

"I need to do something," Harper sighed, shuffling across the office. "I can practically hear my arteries clogging."

"My granny has a cane you can borrow," Frank said, stomping into the office.

Harper rolled her eyes at Beth's giggle. "Thanks for your concern, Frank."

He shook his head. "Just trying to be hospitable."

"What are you doing here?" Harper grumbled.

"I'm waiting for you to crawl back to your desk so I can go over some of the specs on the doc's reno."

Sinking back into her chair, she groaned and only partly in annoyance.

Frank ran the figures on Dr. Dunnigan's addition to her practice, which included a new imaging suite and expanded kitchen and lounge.

"We went over on the tile." He pointed at a figure on the spreadsheet. "Price jumped up a bit, but it matches what she's already got. So I'm proposing we eat the cost instead of passing it on to her. Everything else is looking on budget or under, so I think we can afford to be a little generous. Besides, she and her partner are thinking about building a house next year, and guess whose name is at the top of the builder's list?"

"Why, Garrison Construction, of course." Harper batted her eyelashes.

Frank nodded and stuffed his hands in his pockets.

"What do you need from me?"

"Yes or no on eating the cost."

Harper blinked. Frank was asking her permission. She cleared her throat and reached for her calculator.

"Yes," she said, looking at the total. "It's a good idea, Frank."

He nodded briskly and gathered up his papers before stomping out without a word.

"What was that all about?" Harper asked, spinning in her chair so she didn't have to turn her head to see Beth.

"I have no idea. I've never seen anything like it," Beth said, shaking her head.

Harper swiveled back to her screen. Maybe she was wearing Frank down with her boatloads of charm. Or maybe Luke told him to deal with her directly. Or maybe she was finally starting to fit in.

If she was starting to fit in, there was no time to slack off. She would continue to show Frank and everyone how seriously she took this job, no matter how she had gotten it. She jumped back into job costing with energy.

A few minutes shy of noon, Charlie walked in.

"I was looking for two lovely ladies to take to lunch." He was dressed in jeans and a Garrison polo, which meant he had just come from a meeting with potential clients on a job.

"I think I can scrounge some up for you," Harper teased. "I just may need to be carried down the stairs. Beth, are you in?"

Beth was already waiting at the door holding her purse. "What?" She shrugged. "I'm starving."

Harper snickered. "I'll drive myself. I'm taking Aldo to PT after lunch."

Charlie took them to the diner where the smell of grilled bread and coffee hung in a delicious cloud.

Harper slid gingerly into the booth next to Beth. "So what's the occasion, Charlie?"

"It's Tuesday," he said, winking at Sandra as she arrived with his soda. "And I'm hungry for a tuna melt."

"Looks like you've got two hot dates," Sandra said. "You must be the infamous Harper. I've been meaning to get over to Remo's to check you out on a Friday. Just haven't made it yet."

Harper laughed. "I should have just called a town meeting to introduce myself."

"Next time, you do that. It'll save us all the trouble of stalking you. Welcome to Benevolence. What can I get you ladies?"

They ordered, and Harper wondered if she'd ever get used to small town expectations.

"You talk to Luke lately?" Charlie asked, taking the straw out of his soda.

"I talked loudly to him about neglecting to tell us about Aldo's rescue. He said he's going to try to call you guys this week."

"My son, the tight-lipped hero."

"I wonder where he gets it." Harper wiggled her eyebrows.

"Probably Claire," Charlie quipped. "But now that we're talking about talking, I wanted to run something by you. I just came from an unofficial meeting with potentials. It's a young couple with a plot of land outside town on the edge of the woods. They're looking for something…unique."

"Like missile silo unique or cookie cutter with a slightly different stone than their fifty neighbors?" Beth asked.

"In the middle. You all ever hear of tiny houses?"

Harper and Beth shared a glance. Both were obsessed with the new lineup of TV shows on the topic. "We're familiar," Harper said casually.

"Well, they're thinking small, not tiny. A cottage around five hundred square feet with geothermal, solar, the whole green design, plus all this built-in storage. I think it would be a real interesting project to get. But I don't want to do it if it's some dumb-looking box on wheels that they're after."

Harper held up a finger and reached for her phone. She opened her Teeny But Adorbs Houses Pinterest board and passed the phone over to Charlie.

"Something like this Craftsman, maybe?" She swiped the screen for him, knowing he could barely work his flip phone. "Or what about something modern like this one? Depending on the land, you could position it so the whole front gets southern exposure. Nice for the heating bill in the winter."

"Huh. Is there any way you could send those pictures to me by email or something?"

Harper smiled. "Sure, no problem, Charlie."

"So you think it's something worth pursuing?"

Harper and Beth both nodded vigorously. "Homes like these are getting more and more popular. They're not for everyone, but a lot of people are really looking for downsized luxury." Harper made a mental note to have Claire record some of the tiny house episodes for Charlie.

He slid her phone back to her. "All right then. I'll take that under advisement and see if I can put together some plans."

CHAPTER 33

I want to learn to run," Harper announced, bouncing on her toes. Aldo squinted up at her midstretch.

"What brought this on?"

"You and Luke run. I've seen him leave the house with his brain full of crap and come back from a run smiling. I want that. Plus, I've been eating a lot of pizza lately, and I helped Gloria move and couldn't walk for three days."

Aldo shrugged. "Okay. So run to that tree over there and back."

"That's not very far. I want to run miles."

"You're not ready for miles yet, smart-ass. I'm going to check out your form and tell you how to do it better. Besides, for someone who sits at a desk and eats pizza all day, that tree is far enough."

Harper snorted. "You're missing part of a leg, and you're already working on slow jogs on the treadmill. I think I can handle running to the tree and back with two regular legs."

Aldo flashed her a grin. "Quit stalling. Run. I'll watch and judge mercilessly."

Harper stuck her tongue out at him and started to run toward the tree on the bank of the lake. The park was one of her favorite places in Benevolence. She and Aldo had been hitting the trails almost every day as extra PT for him and some much needed not-sitting for her.

Watching his steady recovery had made her take stock of her own health. Especially after noticing she was more winded at the top of a hill than Aldo with his freaking bionic leg.

She could totally do this. Be healthy, be strong. There was time now to focus on what her future could be. More salads, some running, maybe even some weight lifting, and when Luke came home, he would find a ripped woman with goals and plans.

The tree was marginally closer now even though she felt like she had been running forever. It must be an optical illusion.

Her breath was coming in shorter bursts now, and her legs felt heavier. Oh my God. She was running downhill. She was going to have to run uphill on the way back.

Finally, the tree loomed in front of her. She stopped a few yards shy of its trunk and bent down, pretending to tie her shoe, while she desperately tried to catch her breath.

"Let's go, Harp!" Aldo's shout carried down the hill to her.

"Please don't throw up. Please don't throw up," she chanted as she headed back up at a much slower pace.

She yelped when a stabbing pain shot through her side.

Clutching at her ribs, she finally stumbled back to the start and collapsed next to Aldo. "That wasn't so bad," she gasped.

He chuckled. "You sound like a pack-a-day smoker, Harp."

"I think I have appendicitis. It hurts like a bitch."

"Welcome to your first side stitch."

"Side stitch?"

"Come on. Help up, and I'll tell you all the things you did wrong."

"Like saying I wanted to learn to run?"

They worked through Aldo's exercises and ended with a leisurely walk to the lakefront.

"So how are you doing?"

"Good enough that I'm moving back to my place this weekend. The doc cleared it."

"Aren't you going to miss your mom?" Harper teased.

"Me moving out is the only way we'll both live."

"Are you sleeping better? Is the pain still keeping you up?"

He shrugged, and the pause was so long Harper thought he wasn't going to answer her.

"Sometimes it's like my mind can't tell the difference between what's happening and what's happened. It's like this blur between past and present, and sometimes the only thing that clears it is pain," Aldo said.

"Maybe that's why you push your therapy so hard?"

"Maybe that's why I push everything so hard."

———

Summer was in full swing in Benevolence. Harper's weekends were filled with cookouts and dog walks and running, which was getting marginally less painful. After she hit her first full mile, Aldo bought her a sleeve for her cell phone and downloaded a 5K training program on it for her.

She still wasn't getting the blissful happy brain from running yet, but the relief she felt when each run was over was enough to keep her lacing up her running shoes almost every day.

Her latest project was sprucing up the outside of Luke's house. She had repainted the banister and railing on the wraparound porch and was slowly adding flowers around the existing greenery.

Today she was going to tackle the overgrown groundcover on the side of the house that was starting to climb up the siding.

She dressed in gym shorts and one of Luke's old paint-splattered T-shirts, grabbed a baseball hat, and went to work.

The groundcover proved a formidable opponent with deep roots and long runners, but Harper enjoyed the physical labor.

The summer sun teased a trickle of sweat down her back, and Harper sat back on her heels to take a water break. She had cleared more than half of the long bed already. If she could keep on pace, she could mulch the next day.

She wondered if Luke would be proud of the care she was taking with his home. She wanted him to come home to a smoothly running office and household.

At work, she had finished converting all their client and jobs data to a new system that integrated with their accounting software, cutting the paperwork down for everyone. She also convinced Frank and Charlie to host a monthly staff meeting where everyone from foremen to high school interns participated in discussing project updates and roadblocks.

At home, the porch was painted and offset by colorful planters overflowing with summer flowers. With Claire and Sophie's help, the vegetable garden in the backyard was really taking shape. Inside, the staircase had shed its skin of dingy age and now shone like new.

Last week, she had cleaned all the windows inside and out. She had nearly given James a heart attack when he came over to mow the lawn and caught her on the extension ladder she found in the garage, busily wiping away the winter's grime from the second-floor glass.

He proceeded to show her that replacement windows hinged open inside for easy, ladder-free cleaning and then buried the ladder in the back of the garage under a canoe and several bags of potting soil.

"You're not a klutz," Luke had once told her. "But you invite trouble." He must have relayed that message to his brother.

The only windows left to clean were the basement level. Harper swiped her fingers through the grime on the glass closest to her. It looked like several years' worth of dirt. On the other side of the glass was a plastic tote at window level that she could just make out.

Harper frowned. She didn't remember any window height shelving on this wall in the basement.

Unless…

She found a window to Luke's secret room.

She hastily wiped away more grime and peered through the glass. The room was empty except for a set of metal shelves with boxes and totes.

Harper sat back on her heels. Whatever Luke had in that room under lock and key was important. Maybe a better woman would have let it go and respected his space and secrets, but a better woman wasn't here. Harper was.

The basement window wouldn't open from the outside, so she hurried inside to examine the lock on the door.

Where would Luke keep the key? Harper paced the floor.

She went back upstairs to the table in the foyer and grabbed both of his key rings from the drawer. There were about a dozen keys between the ring with his truck and house keys and the one for work. None of them were labeled Secret Basement Room.

Back downstairs, she took her time fitting each one into the lock, but none of them opened the door. On tiptoe, she felt along the top of the doorframe but came up empty. She checked his truck in the console and glove box and found nothing.

She returned to the kitchen, spinning the key ring on her finger. Where would he keep a key to something he didn't want easy access to? God, she hoped he hadn't buried it somewhere.

She might need some backup brainpower. Harper grabbed her cell phone and dialed Hannah's number.

"Hey, H! What's up?" Her friend's chirpy voice always made Harper smile.

"I'm about to go all-out crazy person here, and I either need to be talked down or walked through."

"Okay, shoot. What's the sitch?"

Harper quickly filled Hannah in on the situation. "So first of all, am I nuts for desperately needing to know what's inside? And second, how far can I go to get inside without being completely crazy?"

Hannah snickered. "I think it's perfectly reasonable to want to know what's behind door number one. But I wouldn't go clawing through the drywall if I were you. I'd try to find a minimally invasive way to get in there. Depending on what's in those boxes, you might not want him to know you know."

"I'm pretty sure it's not dead bodies or used sex toys."

"Maybe he's just a hoarder, and it's every report card he ever got?" Hannah offered.

"I know it's something big. Something that he doesn't want to deal with. He built literal walls around it and locked it all away."

"So maybe he's not hiding something per se but keeping it separate."

"That's what I'm thinking too," Harper agreed.

"Maybe it's mountains of cash?"

Harper snorted. "He already has mountains of that. So I already tried all the keys on his key rings and didn't hit the jackpot."

"Well, if it's something he doesn't want to deal with, he wouldn't put it on something he uses every day, right?"

"No, he'd put it somewhere he doesn't run across it all the time. Have I told you lately how super smart you are, Hanns?"

"No, but all is forgiven if you tell me what you find!"

"You got it. I'm going to go dig through places Luke doesn't go in the house."

"It's going to be really disappointing if it's just a bunch of old office paperwork."

"No kidding."

They hung up and Harper drummed her fingers on the counter. Where would it be? Someplace close but not visible.

She perked up. On a hunch, she hustled up the stairs to the second floor. A walk-through of the three empty bedrooms revealed nothing new. There wasn't a stitch of furniture in them.

Harper stood in the doorway of the master bedroom and let her eyes roam the room. The dresser was used nearly every day, as was the closet. The table under the window housed Luke's electronics when they weren't in use, and its narrow drawers were practically empty.

She turned and faced the bed. The drawer of her night-stand had slowly filled with books and magazines and a box of tissues. But his? She couldn't remember Luke ever opening his.

Harper slid the drawer open. It appeared to be empty at first, but at the very back, something caught her eye. A single silver key.

She snatched it out of the drawer and held it up. Could this be it?

Harper ran down two flights to the basement and slid the key into the lock. The knob turned easily in her hand, and she pushed it open.

The room was long and skinny with two shelving systems pushed up against the wall. The boxes and totes were all unlabeled and looked as if they had been untouched for years. Her fingers itched to dig in, but where to start? She decided to be methodical and go from left to right, starting with the far shelf.

She pulled the first box off the top shelf and sat down on the floor with it. It held a few photo albums. The first one was labeled "Karen" in a scrawling cursive. Harper flipped through, watching a cherub-faced toddler turn into a gangly softball player who morphed into a pretty teenager. Class pictures from kindergarten through senior year were interspersed.

Was this the girl Luke had lost?

Harper dug out the next one, a skinny worn leather album. This was labeled in a girlish script "Luke & Karen." Harper felt her heart stutter. She took a deep breath and opened it to the first page.

Luke,

This is the story of us. I wanted to give this to you before we head off in different directions so you'd always have a reminder of how much I love you. Someday maybe our grandchildren will page through this album to see where it all began.

Love, Karen

Harper turned the page. It was a photo of a very boyish Luke at what looked like a family picnic. His hair was longer, and the grin on his face made her smile. He was sitting on the grass looking at the same stunning brunette from his homecoming photo. Karen, she guessed.

They were a picture-perfect couple, grinning like there wasn't a care in the world. On the next page was a picture of Luke in his football uniform, his helmet under his arm. A careless grin on his face as he shared a laugh with high school football Aldo.

Harper smiled. The friendship and loyalty there ran deep.

There was a newspaper clipping with a picture of Luke throwing the game-winning touchdown and then a picture of Karen in full cheerleader gear cheering from the sidelines. Her blue eyes were focused on the field.

Another picture of Karen and Luke sharing an embrace after a game. Karen had Luke's jacket draped over her shoulders.

Captain of the football team and head cheerleader.

They must have been like high school royalty. Harper sighed. Luke looked so young and so free. There was a lightness about him in the pictures that was so rarely present in him now. She loved seeing him like this. Energetic. Happy. Ready to take on the world.

There were more pictures. Prom, camping trips, cookouts, senior pictures. Karen with the Garrisons. Luke with Karen and her mother. They all looked so happy.

In the last picture, Luke and Karen stood front and center in their caps and gowns at graduation. They had eyes only for each other. Bright smiles at the future ahead of them.

Harper closed the album and held it to her chest. What she would have given to grow up like that. To be young and in love and excited about the future.

What happened to them? Where did it go wrong?

The next album was a heavy ivory book with gold lettering.

The Garrisons

CHAPTER 34

Harper opened the heavy ivory album to a breathtaking picture of Karen in a confection of a gown. Off-the-shoulder sleeves in lace reached her forearms with sheer material covering the gown's modest scoop neck. Her dark russet hair was pinned back in a classic twist with a long veil tucked under it. She carried lilies.

Harper brought a hand to her mouth.

Luke grinned at Claire as she pinned his boutonniere in place.

Another of Karen with Sophie and three other women in deep purple gowns, laughing as a flower girl twirled.

Luke at the altar, with Aldo by his side, his eyes focused calm and steadfast at the back of the church. Karen walking down the aisle, escorted by her mother. The ceremony. The kiss. The happy exit.

Harper put the album down gently. They were married. He had never mentioned it.

She wanted to rest. To process. But there was so much more. Another album. A honeymoon, a first home. Luke in his National Guard uniform. His first deployment. His homecoming. Job sites, parties, holidays. Luke's second deployment. And then nothing.

At the very bottom of the box were two wedding rings and a small diamond engagement ring. She gently ran her fingers over the gold before tucking them back in the box. Harper carefully replaced the albums and returned the box to its spot on the shelf.

She continued on. The totes were full of women's clothing. An entire wardrobe, neatly boxed away.

One box was entirely filled with papers. A marriage certificate. Newspaper clippings of their engagement and wedding announcements. Clips of articles written about Luke's unit. Letters. Cards. An entire relationship fit neatly in a box.

Harper looked up from the floor and rolled her shoulders. It was dark now. Hours had passed since Harper opened this world of boxes.

She should stop, but she still didn't have answers. What had happened to Karen? There was only one box left.

At the very top of the box was an opened letter from Karen to Luke while he was stationed in Germany.

Well, my dear,

You're going to be coming home to a very different life next month. Thanks to your leave two months ago, it looks like we'll be a family of three! I wanted to call and tell you, to hear your reaction. But this is how my mother told my father she was expecting me, so I thought it was a worthy family tradition to continue. You, my dear Lucas Garrison, will be a daddy in October. I guess we'd better start working on emptying out the guest-storage-catch-all room to make room for our little boy or girl. I haven't told anyone yet. It'll be our little secret until you're home

and we can tell the families together. You're going to
be an amazing father.

Love,
Karen

Harper clutched the letter to her chest. Luke was a father? How could that be? There were no pictures. He never mentioned a son or a daughter.

She slipped the letter back into the envelope and continued digging.

She found two tiny onesies neatly tucked away in flattened gift bags. One proudly proclaimed "The Spoiling Begins," the other "I Have the World's Best Grandma." It must have been how Karen planned to tell the families.

They were new, the tags still on them. Never gifted, never worn.

Harper's heart started to thud. At the bottom of the box, she found a series of newspaper clippings from a few years ago.

Local woman killed in accident on way to meet soldier husband

Her hands shook as she read.

BENEVOLENCE, MD—Local resident Karen Garrison was killed when her vehicle crossed the centerline and was struck head-on. Garrison was on her way to meet her soldier husband, Lucas Garrison, whose guard unit was returning from a yearlong deployment to Germany.

Harper felt sick to her stomach. No wonder.

No wonder.

She scanned the rest of the article. Karen was killed on impact on her way to meet the rest of the Garrisons to welcome Luke home.

Hot tears streaked their way down her cheeks.

Luke felt responsible, she was sure of it. Karen was going to meet him.

The police weren't sure why her car crossed the centerline. There was a picture taken by the newspaper of the crash site. A welcome home banner lay crumpled just beyond the wreckage.

She pulled the rest of the articles and read them all, including Karen's obituary.

But through it all, there was no mention of the baby.

Had Luke kept that from everyone? To protect them from further loss? Had he held it close, holding the guilt, the agonizing loss to his heart? Locked up?

Gently, Harper replaced all the items in the box and put it back on the shelf.

She stood, aching from hours of sitting on the concrete floor. She stepped out and closed the door but didn't lock it.

She was sharing her home, her life, with another woman. One who didn't deserve to be locked away anymore.

Harper climbed the stairs to the first floor, mechanically turning on lights as she made her way back to the kitchen. The dogs, who had been napping in the dining room, thundered after her, hungry and restless. She let them out first and then fed them their dinner. While they ate, Harper stared out into the darkness.

She reached for her cell phone and, ignoring the handful of texts and voicemails, dialed Sophie's number.

"Hey, can you come over? I want to talk about Karen."

Sophie wrapped her hands around the glass of iced tea that Harper set in front of her. The condensation worked its way down to form a ring on the picnic table's surface.

Harper stirred the fire in the fire pit before sitting down on the opposite bench. She watched the dogs take turns chasing each other in the dark with a stick.

"So," she said.

"So," Sophie echoed.

Lola gave up the game of chase and rolled onto her back in the grass next to the patio.

"He told you?"

"Nope."

Sophie swore. "My brother, the idiot. He should have told you."

"Agreed. So why didn't he?" Harper pulled a leg up on the bench and rested her chin on her knee.

"You've met Luke. He doesn't talk. He's always been that way—private, quiet—to some extent. But after the accident, he shut down. I've never heard him say her name since then. It's almost like he wants to pretend she never existed, but maybe he just wants to be alone with his pain."

"Were you and Karen close?"

Sophie nodded. "We weren't best friends or anything, more like family. Our personalities were different. She was very pragmatic and calm. Kind of stoic. But she was warm and solid. We got along well. She and Luke were together for so long, she was family before she was officially family."

Harper nodded.

"I saw the wedding pictures."

"He kept them?" Sophie straightened. "I wondered. After the funeral, I left Luke alone for a few days. When I went to see him, the whole place was packed up. He moved in here shortly after. But I never saw a hint of Karen or their life together."

"It's all in the basement. He boxed it up, built walls around it, and locked the door."

Sophie put her chin in her hands and peered down at her tea. "Have anything stronger?"

Harper went inside and returned with a bottle of Jack Daniel's and two cans of Coke. "How's this?"

"Perfect." Leaving the ice, Sophie drained the tea out of her glass onto the ground. She repeated the process with Harper's glass before cracking open the bottle.

"So how do you feel about all this?"

"I think I'm feeling every feeling in the world right now. I don't even know what makes sense to feel at this point. I'm devastated for him. I can't imagine a loss of that magnitude, especially in that situation." She sighed heavily. "But I'm also mad or disappointed or maybe scared that he tried to keep this all to himself. I mean, it wasn't just him who lost her. It was all of you. And then to top off everything else with some self-centeredness, I feel selfishly sad that Luke is the love of my life but he's already had that with someone else. Someone who is so sacred to him he can't talk about her." Harper took a deep gulp of her drink and choked. "Did you forget to add the Coke?"

Sophie laughed. "This is a Jack and Jack with a teeny layer of Coke."

"So I know what 'happened,'" Harper said, using air quotes, "but could you tell me what happened? Is that okay?"

Sophie nodded. "I think you need to know. It's well past time that Luke should be allowed to carry around secrets and hide from us all. I'm sorry you're hearing it from me and not him." She stared off into the night sky. "The plan was Karen was going to meet me, my parents, and Joni—her mom—at the drop-off about half an hour before Luke's bus came in. Ty was working, and at the time, we were broken up. Karen was bringing the welcome home sign. I had a bunch of helium balloons in the back seat of my car. She was a stickler for being early, so when she didn't show, I got nervous. I heard the sirens and knew something was wrong. Just this sick feeling in the pit of my stomach.

"The bus was pulling into the lot, and my phone starts ringing. It's Ty. He was on the scene. He told me she was dead. I just kind of collapsed onto the pavement. Ty is talking in my ear, but all I hear is blood rushing to my head. Mom is trying to pull me up. Thinks I'm having some kind of seizure or something.

"And then Luke gets off the bus. He's got a mile-wide grin on his face until he locks eyes with me." Sophie took a steadying breath as tears welled up. "I swear to God, he just looked at me and knew. He started shaking his head and running. I was just hysterical and crying. He grabbed me by the shoulders. Ty was still on the phone. And all I could say to Luke was 'Karen,' and I handed him the phone."

Harper reached a hand across the table and laid it on Sophie's. "I'm so, so sorry, Soph."

"I will never forget his eyes when he heard the words. The light died right out of them, and I just kept thinking he would never be the same after this. I think that's why we let him get away with locking himself up and keeping us at arm's length. His life was destroyed in front of us, and we're just so grateful we still have him. I think they were thinking about starting a family. They kept it pretty hush-hush, but I had a feeling that they'd start 'trying' when he was home again."

"Were you afraid he would…" Harper trailed off. She couldn't even finish the thought, let alone the sentence.

"I don't know. I honestly don't know. He didn't answer his phone for days. Wouldn't answer his door. He took care of all the funeral plans himself and just told us when and where to be."

"What about Joni?"

"That went about as bad as it could have. Karen was Joni's only child, and they were so close. Karen's father had skipped out on them when she was a kid. Luke shut her out with the rest of us, and at the graveside, Joni lost it. She told Luke it was his fault that Karen wasn't here. That he chose his country over his wife and that's why her family was gone."

Harper brought her hands to her mouth. "He believed her, didn't he?"

"I can't say for sure because he never spoke about it, but yeah. I think he thought he was to blame. She was sobbing and yelling 'You took my family from me.' He just stood there and took it. Like it was penance. Dad got her away and calmed down, and that was the end of it. She never spoke to any of us again. She lives just outside town, and I still see her occasionally. She just kind of shrinks up and goes in the opposite direction when she sees me. Like I'm just too painful a reminder."

"How did you cope with it?" Harper asked, braving another sip of Jack.

"I married Ty. We had been off and on in typical high school sweetheart fashion. We were off again at that point. I was worried that I was missing out on what else was out there. But when he called me that day...he came to the house after his shift that night, and we stayed up all night talking on the porch. It was like we had both realized how short life was and how we were just wasting time doing what we were doing. He proposed a month later, and we got married six months after that." She shifted on the bench. "Part of me had hoped that

280

a big, splashy wedding full of love and happiness would help bring Luke back to life. He was a groomsman, and he did his part. But you looked at him, and all you saw was a hole where his heart should have been.

"Sometimes I look at Ty and wonder if that's how I would be if something happened to him. I love that man so much. He is such a good, solid, kindhearted soul. And he's not afraid to get in my way and tell me when I'm being an idiot. He's an amazing father, and sometimes I just send up a little thank-you to Karen because, if it weren't for her, I might have stayed stupid and stubborn and wanting to see what else was out there instead of hanging on to what was in front of me."

Harper smiled. "I've never heard you get so mushy before."

Sophie laughed and swiped at a stray tear. "I'll deny it if you ever share a word of this!"

"You've got a good heart, Sophie Garrison Adler."

"It's nothing compared to Ty's. Or Luke's. Every once in a while, you can still see a glimpse of it."

Harper nodded and thought of her first look at him. Those warm hazel eyes filled with concern as he hovered over her in the parking lot. Yeah, he still had a big heart in there. It was just behind a locked door.

"I see it sometimes in the way he looks at you," Sophie said suddenly.

"Really?"

"I don't think he knows what he feels for you or how deep he feels it. But there's a reason he asked you to stay. And it wasn't to take care of his house or run the office. He looks at you with this…softness. He needs you."

Harper poured more soda in her glass. She wanted it to be true. But craving the security of being loved made her so vulnerable.

"It breaks my heart to know that he believes he's responsible for Karen's death," she said, changing the subject.

Sophie nodded and drank deeply. "It was an accident. Karen didn't cross the centerline on purpose. The other driver didn't hit her on purpose. It was just a horrible accident. You can't take ownership of it. You can't place blame for it."

"But Luke did. Joni did."

"Some people just handle loss like that. How about you? How do you handle not having parents?"

Harper shrugged. "That's different. I was seven. And after a long time of not understanding, you're just kind of forced to accept and move forward."

"I'd think a seven-year-old learning to cope is harder than an adult. An adult has reason and logic. They can understand the concept of never seeing someone again."

"There's no logic behind death and loss," Harper argued. "Trying to reason it out can take you to some pretty dark places. Guilt. Blame. Hiding from your pain by distracting yourself with work, booze, sex, shopping."

"You're right. Being an adult sucks."

"I'll drink to that." Harper raised her glass to Sophie.

CHAPTER 35

She was just curious, Harper told herself. That was why she was detouring to the cemetery instead of going straight home. Her talk with Sophie still hung heavy in her heart.

She glanced down at the tiny bouquet of wildflowers she had picked up at the farmers' market. They were a summery impulse buy while she waited in line to pay for her strawberries. After all, you couldn't go empty-handed to meet the woman who still had Luke's heart.

The cemetery was a grassy stretch of park a few blocks back from the center of town. She thought back to all the times she and Luke must have driven past and wondered if she had missed him gazing out the window for his wife.

His wife. The mother of his child.

To be starting a new life, a family, only to have it all taken from you. Harper's heart ached.

She put the car in park and climbed out. She knew the general direction of the grave thanks to a morbid but helpful website dedicated to mapping cemeteries. While summer had blanketed Benevolence in a dry heat, the grass here stayed vibrantly green.

Harper wandered down the skinny asphalt path that wound

its way through the park. She hung a left at the winged angel statue and found a pocket of graves on a gentle slope.

The headstone caught her eye immediately. She recognized the carving before she saw the name. It was Luke's tattoo. The phoenix he had over his heart.

She heard the far-off sounds of a lawn mower and an airplane in flight, but all she saw was the phoenix.

Holding her breath, she approached the glossy black stone.

Karen Garrison
Loving wife and daughter

There was no mention of the loving mother she would have been. In a tragic way, she had taken their secret to the grave.

Harper let her breath out and knelt down gingerly on the grass. She sat back on her heels. It was a beautiful spot. The tree line at her back cast its shade over the dozen graves decorating the copse.

There was already a pretty arrangement of colorful blooms that was starting to dry out tucked in the metal urn behind the stone.

It didn't feel sad. It felt…peaceful.

Harper toyed with the twine around the wildflowers and cleared her throat.

"I'm not really sure how to introduce myself or if I even should," she started. "I'm in love with your husband, so I'm pretty sure that wouldn't make us friends if you were still here. But maybe, given the circumstances, you'd be okay with it?

"I think you must have been a pretty amazing person. I think Luke is too. You must have been so happy together.

"I don't really know why I'm here. He shouldn't be trying to keep you locked away. I can't tell if he's trying to protect everyone else or himself.

"I fell in love with a man who can't be honest with me, and I don't know what this is going to mean for us when he comes home."

Harper sat in silence for a few moments. She leaned forward and ran a finger across the phoenix. She missed him. Missed him with a hard edge that rubbed everything raw. She didn't know what the future would hold, but right now she knew that she wanted him home.

———

The work week was passing in a blur. Harper found if she kept herself busy, she didn't have as much time to focus on the keen edge of need just below the surface. It was only at night that she couldn't block out the ache. She found herself getting up earlier and earlier in the mornings to head out for a quiet run.

Like today.

It was still hours away from the full heat of a summer day when she laced up her shoes. Hours away from work, from words, from people. Now there was only time for thoughts and dreams.

She chose a different route today, one that wound through the still-silent streets of town. Harper had finally found that space between the beats of her foot strike where peace reigned.

Aldo was impressed with her progress and she with his. The last round of modifications made to his prosthesis really seemed to help. His gait was smooth, and he was steadily increasing the intensity of his physical therapy. She was surprised she hadn't seen similar progress between him and Gloria.

"Not everyone is a love story waiting to happen," Luke had teased her last night from seven thousand miles away.

He was smiling on the screen, and Harper knew it was a good sign. After Aldo, she had seen the gray, the shadows, and she knew that he was fighting battles not just on the ground. As strong as he was, he took sustenance from the good news at home. They discussed work in brief broad strokes, but Harper saw his expression come to life most when she talked about home. Aldo's latest stunt at physical therapy or Josh's new saying or what new tofu recipe Claire had tried on Charlie.

She didn't mention Karen or her trip to the cemetery. They would talk eventually. Face-to-face.

It was Karen on her mind that had Harper choosing this route. She stopped to catch her breath in front of a tidy two-story duplex. 417 Meadow View. Their home together. Luke and Karen. Behind those walls, they had cooked breakfast together, made love, argued, and planned a family.

She didn't know what she expected to feel being here. What was someone supposed to feel when they stalked ghosts?

Hands on her hips, she paced the sidewalk, glancing every now and then at the house. Did Luke ever do this? Did he come back to the place where there was life? Did he visit the cemetery where there was only death?

Harper felt something. A presence. A ghost?

But it was a woman. Flesh and blood. Haunting the sidewalk. They studied each other from several paces away. The trim figure was dressed casually in shorts and a T-shirt. She had her brown hair with its silver strands pulled back in a short curly stub.

Harper felt like she had been caught in the act. She gave an awkward wave. "Morning," she called.

The woman simply stared. There was something familiar about her face. It reminded her of Karen.

Harper felt her heart skip a beat. "Joni?"

The woman's face transformed into an impassive mask.

"So you're her," she said, her tone soft but laced with pain.

286

"I'm who?"

"Luke's replacement for my daughter."

Harper froze where she was.

"Joni, I can guarantee there's no replacement for Karen."

"That's not how it looks to me. What it looks like to me is he tried to pretend she never existed until he found someone new to help him forget."

Harper started toward her. "Now hang on a minute—"

"I've been hanging on for five years." Joni's voice broke. "I lost my family because of him. He never loved her enough. His country came first, and my daughter came a distant second. He'll do it to you too."

Harper could see the tears now. She shook her head. "I think we need to talk."

———

It took some coaxing and some strong-arming, but Harper got Joni to come home with her. They walked back, the summer humidity teasing a line of sweat down Harper's back.

"What was Karen like?"

Joni sighed. "She was everything to me. Her father left us when she was very young. He just up and walked out one day. Said he didn't want to be a husband and a father anymore. So it was just the two of us from then on."

The abandonment had stung and still did. Harper could hear it in her tone.

"Karen was this driven, ambitious girl. Even when she was eight, she had her entire life mapped out. She was going to go to college to be a scientist and marry a man who would 'be a good daddy.' It was amazing to watch her set her sights on a goal and then march toward it until she captured it." Joni took a breath. "And now she's gone. And he pretends she never

287

existed. Did he ever love her? If he did, how could he have walked away from her, from us, so easily?"

Another abandonment.

They arrived home, and Joni stopped to take it in. "Karen would have loved this house. That town house was just a waypoint. They were going to have a home, a family. They were going to have it all."

Harper led her up onto the porch. "Are you okay with dogs?"

Joni sighed. "Of course you have a dog."

Harper pushed the front door open, and Lola and Max rushed to greet them.

"Oh my, hello there," Joni said, crouching to greet the mass of tongues and paws and wiggling rear ends.

"Let me give them some t-r-e-a-t-s, and we can head down to the basement."

Harper hurried down the hallway to the kitchen and grabbed a bag of bacon treats. She shook the bag and the dogs hurtled down the hall toward her.

"Good puppies. Okay, sit. Good job. Here's one for you and one for you."

She found Joni peering into the dining room. "This is all new. Luke was in such a hurry to get out of that town house. He sold it for less than they paid and sold or gave away every stick of furniture. He got rid of everything they owned, everything that was hers."

"And you think he did that because he wanted to move on?"

"There's no other explanation."

"I think there might be. I think you're wrong about Luke. Let me show you something." Harper opened the basement door.

"You're not taking me down there to chop me into pieces to feed to the dogs, are you? I'm not ready to be one of those 'missing and never heard from again' people," Joni said.

"Very funny. Now let me just go get my rusty axe."

"Ha-ha." But she followed Harper down the stairs.

Harper paused outside the door. "Luke is still in love with your daughter. He never stopped."

"What did he tell you?"

"It's not what he told me. It's what I found." She twisted the knob and pushed the door open. "Go ahead. You can look through it all. I'm going to go make us some coffee."

Joni nodded, but her attention was on the contents of the room.

Harper gave Joni her privacy and went back upstairs. She took the dogs out in the backyard while coffee brewed.

She didn't know if she was doing the right thing. But spending years believing your daughter's husband had cast aside her memory and moved on without a second thought? A mother deserved to know the truth.

She gave it another half an hour before venturing back into the basement with a tray of coffee, sugar, creamer, and tissues.

"Joni?"

She found her sitting cross-legged on the floor holding a photo album. "He kept everything," she whispered tearfully.

Harper saw the box with the onesies was open. She set the tray down on the floor and sat next to Joni.

"Everything. Every article of clothing, every picture, every newspaper clipping."

"They were going to have a baby." Joni ran a finger over one of the onesies. Her eyes welled up again. "I was going to be a grandma."

Harper handed her a tissue.

"It wasn't his fault," Joni said, tears falling freely now. "I always knew it wasn't, but when I thought he had just moved on… I blamed him for that. It was easy to point the finger." She took a moment to dab at her eyes with the tissue. "At the funeral—Oh, God. The things I said to him. And he kept my secret. He knew and never told a soul."

"Your secret?"

"It was my fault," Joni said, crumpling the tissue in her hand. "Karen died because of me."

CHAPTER 36

"I t was an accident," Harper started.

Joni shook her head. "I was the reason she was in the accident. I texted her to tell her I was running late. She was reading the text when…when it happened. The police told me. Luke knows."

"Joni." Harper laid a hand on her arm. "It wasn't your fault."

"If I had just waited. I knew she always checked her phone while driving. I should have known not to text her."

Harper shook her head. "Karen was running late too. You couldn't have known that. You didn't make her pick up her phone. You didn't make her car drift into the other lane. You're not responsible."

"Two little words. 'Running late.' They seemed so important at the time."

"Between you and Luke and your misplaced sense of responsibility…" Harper shook her head. "Neither one of you is to blame. Neither one of you is responsible. It was a terrible accident. Nothing you did or didn't do caused it. You have to understand that. And blaming yourselves isn't helping anyone. Is that what Karen would have wanted? The two people who loved her most in this world wasting the rest of their lives blaming themselves for her death?"

Joni shook her head, brushing an imaginary speck of dust off the album in her lap.

"Blame doesn't heal anything," Harper said. "Acceptance and gratitude do."

"How can I be grateful that my daughter is dead?"

"You can be grateful that she lived."

Joni nodded slowly. "It makes sense, but how? How do you stop thinking about the loss?"

"It's not easy, but what's the alternative?"

Joni glanced around the room. "Point taken."

"Joni, there's no amount of grief and guilt in the world that will change the past. What matters is what you do now," Harper said, stirring sugar into her coffee.

"So what does 'now' mean for you two?" Joni asked. "Does Luke know you know?"

Harper shook her head. "It's not a conversation we can have while he's gone. I don't know what it means for him, for us, for me. He tells me he can't love me. I didn't understand why before. Now that I have a name for it, for her, I don't know if I can live in her shadow," Harper said.

"Is that what we've been doing?"

"Maybe you've been living in the shadow of her death."

"It's amazing how much can change in a morning." Joni sighed and picked up a coffee mug. "I just don't know how to let go of the guilt."

"Well, maybe you can start by letting the Garrisons back in?"

————

They started with breakfast at the diner with Charlie and Claire. And it gave Harper hope to see slates wiped clean and what was once a strong friendship begin to rebuild.

She wondered what Luke would think if he could see his

parents talking about chickens with his mother-in-law and for once was glad he wasn't present.

Joni might be ready for a fresh start, but there was no telling what Luke would be ready for.

She decided to put it out of her mind. There was no point in worrying about what she couldn't control. She was relieved to head back to the office on Monday and distract herself with work rather than all the reasons she shouldn't panic about what Karen and Joni meant to her future with Luke.

She was plowing her way through her to-do list when her desk phone rang.

"You'd better send another crew over here 'cause I'm about to walk off the job," Frank bellowed through the phone.

"What's your problem now, Frank?" Harper asked, rolling her eyes.

"My problem? My problem is this idiot lackey didn't bother showing up to work today, and now I'm down a pair of hands for drywall."

"Does you calling him an 'idiot lackey' have anything to do with him not showing up?" she asked mildly.

"Just get an extra pair of hands down here now," he growled and disconnected.

Harper sighed and hung up. She brought up the week's schedule on her computer. Every crew was swamped. They had managed to hit critical points in several projects at once, and while that was good for the bottom line, it made the logistics tricky. She dialed a few of the foremen and got the answer she knew they would give. "Can't spare anyone until next week."

She scrubbed her hands over her face. Well, hopefully Frank wasn't going to be too picky about what pair of hands showed up.

She hopped out of the car at the job site. Frank was oversee-ing the addition of an in-law suite on the back of a cute little bungalow for the Delanos. Garrison had built the home ten years earlier, and now that Mr. Delano's mother was getting a little lonely, they wanted her closer.

Harper had looked up the plans before she left the office. The addition was going to be a large bedroom with a sunny sitting area and bathroom and good-sized walk-in closet. There was even a private back porch accessed through a set of French doors.

She tugged her ponytail through the back of a Garrison baseball hat and grimly set her shoulders. Time to deal with Frank.

"What the hell are you doing here?" he demanded from where he was wielding a pencil over a sheet of drywall on sawhorses.

"Nice to see you too, Frank. I'm your extra hands. And before you start complaining"—she held up said hands as a warning—"I'm literally all you've got. None of the other crews can spare anyone."

Frank swore colorfully and rolled his eyes heavenward. "Why me?"

Harper ignored him and looked around the framed-out addition. The insulation was in, and the cathedral ceiling was, thankfully, already drywalled. New windows had been installed, making the whole space feel bright and airy.

"This is really good work, Frank," Harper said, poking her head into the bathroom.

"Of course it's good work. I did it. Why does everyone always act so surprised?" he grumbled.

Harper hid her smile.

"Well, if you're the best I'm going to get, we might as well get started," he sighed. "How much can you lift?"

It turned out it wasn't much, but it was enough to help Frank tackle the walls. Harper was sweating in minutes.

"Bet you're missing your desk now, huh?" he snickered as Harper huffed and puffed trying to hold an eight-foot sheet in place.

"Can you screw a little faster?" she gasped.

"That's what she said," Frank said, nimbly moving the screw gun around the sheet.

"I'm sorry. Was that a joke you just made?"

"Oh, now don't go getting your undies in a bunch over a 'that's what she said' joke. If you can't take a joke, you shouldn't be on a job site."

Harper snorted and stepped back from the wall. "I'm not offended. I've just never heard you do anything but whine and complain. A 'that's what she said' joke is pretty impressive."

The rest of the morning passed in a blur of insults and heavy lifting. Frank showed Harper how to cut drywall using a T square, her foot, and a utility knife. "Not bad," he said, rubbing his grizzled red beard as Harper triumphantly snapped a sheet in half. "Let's put this up, and then you can take me to lunch."

They finished up that afternoon. Harper dumped the dustpan in the garbage bag. "If you're good to go, I'm going to head out. I have some stuff to catch up on at the office."

Frank nodded. "I guess you did okay today."

"I'll take that as the glowing compliment you meant it to be."

"I heard you talked to Joni Whitwood this weekend."

"Did you also hear what I had for breakfast?" Harper rolled her eyes. "Yes. I ran into Joni, and we talked."

"How is she?"

Harper tried to gauge from his expression what his interest in the topic was but came up empty.

"She's doing okay." She slung her bag over her shoulder.

"She's had a rough time. Her and Luke."

Harper nodded.

"It looks like Luke's starting to do better what with you and all. It'd be nice if the same could be said for Joni."

"Do you know her?"

He looked at the toes of his boots. "I used to. A long time ago."

She waited for him to continue, but he went back to checking the lid of the drywall mud.

"Will you need help tomorrow?" Harper finally asked, digging her keys out of her bag.

"I've got the mudding covered. You can go back to sitting on your ass behind a desk." The rudeness was there, but it sounded softer somehow.

"You're welcome, Frank. I'm happy I could help too," she quipped on her way out the door.

CHAPTER 37

The Fourth of July was an even bigger deal in Benevolence than the Not-So-Polar Plunge.

The town festivities kicked off in the morning with the Red, White, and Blue 5K. Aldo had surprised her the day before with an American flag tank top and a racing bib.

"A 5K? I can't do a 5K!"

"Like hell you can't. If I'm doing it on this stupid hand cycle, you're running with me." He had flopped down on her couch.

Aldo's therapists had put the kibosh on him walking the race on his new leg and instead wrangled a hand cycle for him.

"If you're flailing around like an idiot beside me, no one will notice ol' Peg Leg Aldo on the freaking circus bike."

"Don't even pretend you're embarrassed. You're going to eat up all the attention." Harper poked him in the shoulder.

"It's kind of hard to impress a girl when you're acting like you're handicapped."

"Just take your shirt off, and no one will care if you're doing the race on a miniature pony. Is there any girl in particular you're trying to impress?"

He took a swig of water. "Maybe."

Now they were lined up next to each other at the start. There had been a flurry of people coming up to shake Aldo's hand, hug him, and thank him for his service. He handled the attention gracefully. She thought about the reclusive Luke on the receiving end of attention like this. The well-meaning attention after Karen's death must have smothered him.

More racers filled in around them at the start line, and the clock ticked toward nine. Harper put a hand over her fluttering heart. "I'm so nervous! Is it normal to be nervous?" she hissed at Aldo.

"It's not nerves. It's excitement."

The race's announcer cut in on their conversation. "Ladies and gentlemen, please rise for our national anthem, sung by Peggy Ann Marsico."

Aldo climbed off the bike to stand at attention in a military salute. Harper felt tears well up watching a man who gave so much for his country salute the flag.

What would Luke and his unit do today to celebrate? Was it just another day? Or did they celebrate with the rest of America?

Peggy Ann shocked Harper back to present with an amazing soprano. An entire crop of goose bumps shot up on every inch of her skin.

She stood in the sunshine of a beautiful Fourth of July morning and basked in her pride of the man she loved and his best friend.

———

"Oh my God. I'm dying. Aldo, I'm dying," Harper gasped.

"If you couldn't talk, I'd be concerned."

"You're not even out of breath," she muttered.

He flashed her a grin. "You're fine. You've got a great pace."

He waved from his bike at a group of kids cheering from the end of their driveway. Almost the entire course had been lined with Benevolence residents. Harper could see Mrs. Moretta's house coming up on the left, but she wasn't outside.

"Where's your mom?"

"Finish line probably."

"How much farther? I don't think I'm going to make it. Maybe I'll just wait here. You can come back and pick me up."

"Don't be so dramatic. Do you hear the yelling?"

"I can barely hear anything over the wheezing of my lungs."

"That's the finish line."

"Are you kidding? We're almost done?"

"Half mile to go."

"Seriously?" Harper perked up. "I think I can run that."

"I know you can. And so can I." He pulled the cycle into his mother's driveway.

She stopped and bent at the waist to catch her breath. "Aldo—"

He carefully stood, reaching down to adjust his leg. "Before you even start, I cleared it with Steers. A half mile at a slow jog. Are you up for that? We're not stopping until the finish line."

"Let's do it!"

They left the driveway at an easy jog and rejoined the race. Aldo's gait was smooth.

"You make this look so easy," Harper puffed.

"Believe me, it's anything but easy. But it's necessary."

They rounded the next corner together, and the noise level exploded. The finish line was two blocks away, a straight shot down Main Street Benevolence. The sight of Aldo running was enough to create a good-natured pandemonium.

"They must think you're some kind of hero around here," Harper teased.

Aldo merely grinned, and she knew that he was finally home. Elated, she let the cheers of the crowd carry her to the finish line. As they crossed, Aldo grabbed her wrist and raised their joined hands high overhead.

The momentum carried Harper almost into the arms of two older veterans in dress uniforms who were handing out medals.

The two men snapped to attention and saluted Aldo.

"Thank you for your service, Lieutenant."

Aldo saluted and then accepted a medal.

"And here's one for you, young lady." The shorter man with thick glasses and an even thicker head of white hair placed a medal around her neck.

Tickled, Harper couldn't resist. She leaned over and kissed him on the cheek. "Thank you!"

"Luke is going to kick my ass if he sees I let you cast him aside for another soldier," Aldo laughed, dragging her toward the water.

They were intercepted by Mrs. Moretta and the entire Garrison clan.

"You did it!" Sophie leaned in to hug her. "Ugh, you're sweaty and disgusting, but I'm still proud of you!"

Harper laughed. "I can't believe I did it! I don't think I'm going to be able to move for the rest of the day, but it was worth it!"

"Did you know Aldo was going to ditch his bike?"

"No clue. That was pretty awesome!"

"Aunt Hawpa!" Josh, in a little baseball hat and sunglasses, threw himself at her legs. "Up!"

She picked him up and settled him on her hip. "Hey there, handsome. Are you having fun?"

"We're going to the pawade," he announced cheerfully. Josh patted her shoulder. "Sweaty. Ewh!"

She laughed and gave him a hug before putting him back on the ground. "Go tell Aldo he did a good job."

Josh darted over to him and launched himself into Aldo's arms. "You sweaty too!"

Claire approached, banana in hand. "Here you go, kiddo. You're going to need this after a finish like that! You two had the whole town on its feet."

Grateful, Harper immediately inhaled the banana. "Did anyone get a picture of Aldo finishing? I think Luke would love to see that."

Sophie held up her phone. "Only about seven hundred or so shots. I'll pick out a few good ones and send them to you."

"Thanks, Soph." Harper sat down on the curb and took the rest of her congratulations from a seated position.

"Hey, Harper! That was some finish." Gloria appeared out of the crowd. She was dressed in white shorts and a navy-blue tank with a cute red headband tied in her dark hair.

"You look gorgeous," Harper said. "I'd hug you, but I'd ruin your cute outfit."

Gloria laughed. "You can hug me after you shower. I wanted to see if everyone wanted to sit with me at the parade? You can't beat the seats." She pointed to her front steps. "The parade goes right past."

"That would be great, thanks! What time does it start?"

"It starts after the last finisher of the 5K. They call it leading the parade." She grinned.

"Do you have room for one more? Maybe two? My mom's a sucker for parade candy."

Gloria jumped at the sound of Aldo's voice, and Harper saw her square her shoulders before turning around.

He had taken off his T-shirt and stood in all his ripped, sweaty glory.

Harper was pretty sure Gloria's jaw hit the cement before she recovered with a polite "Hi, Aldo."

"Hi, Gloria. You look beautiful and festive."

The tips of her ears turned pink. "Thank you. You look… good."

He grinned. "Do you mind if I join you for the parade?"

"Sure. I mean, not at all. The more the merrier."

"Great. See you soon." He walked off, and Gloria fanned herself.

"Oh my. What just happened? Did I pass out?" she asked.

Harper giggled. "I think this is Aldo coming around and pulling out all the stops. Prepare to be swept off your feet."

"I don't think I'm ready for that. Can't he just say hello to me once a week for a year or so until I get used to looking at him?"

"I don't think that's how he works. You'll be married in no time."

Gloria playfully swatted Harper's arm.

"Miss Harper!"

She turned at the sound of her name and saw Robbie and Henry waving at her as they crossed the street to her. Mrs. Agosta, carrying Ava, was hot on their heels.

"Miss Harper! You did it!" Robbie high-fived her.

"Way to go, Miss Harper." Henry fist-bumped her and then made an exploding noise with a tiny bit of spit.

"Thanks, guys. Are you here for the parade?"

"Yeah, we're scopin' out seats so we can see the fire trucks and get lots of candy," Henry said.

"Congratulations, Harper," Mrs. Agosta said. "I see you running past the house a couple times a week, and every day you get faster."

"Yeah, you don't look like you're going to die anymore," Robbie added helpfully.

"Oh, good. I'm glad," Harper laughed.

"Would you like to join us? We've got prime parade seats right here," Gloria offered.

"Oh, boy! Can we?" Henry dropped his kid-size folding camp chair on the sidewalk next to Harper. "This is perfect."

"Are you sure you don't mind some very loud, energetic company?" Mrs. Agosta asked Gloria.

"The more the merrier," Gloria insisted and winked at Harper. "Since we've got a good crowd and some fine seat savers here, do you want to help me make some lemonade and iced tea?"

"Can I have my own gallon, and can you carry me up the steps?"

"Sure, why not?"

———

The parade was a huge hit. The very last 5L finisher was a seventy-six-year-old veteran carrying the American flag, followed by the high school marching band playing "Stars and Stripes Forever."

The action paused long enough at the finish line for Aldo to place the 5K medal around the man's neck and salute him. The gentleman saluted back and then hugged Aldo, slapping him on the back, and the crowd was on its feet cheering.

Harper saw Gloria swipe away a stray tear as she applauded.

The kids kept Josh entertained, freeing Sophie to run out onto the road to give Ty a kiss when he drove by in the squad car with lights blazing.

"Miss Sophie just kissed that policeman!" Henry shouted with glee.

Charlie, Claire, Mrs. Agosta, Mrs. Moretta, and Gloria's mom, Sara, set up chairs on the top step of Gloria's building and enjoyed their iced teas and lemonades.

Harper snapped picture after picture and emailed them all to Luke. She missed him fiercely.

Her phone signaled a new email.

To: harpwild@netlink.com
From: lucas.c.garrison282@us.army.mil
Re: Parade

Keep the pictures coming, baby. I'm looking at every one of them. I miss your beautiful smile.

Love,
Luke

Harper hugged her phone to her chest and sniffled.

"Aw." Sophie spotted her watery eyes. "Missing him?" she asked, draping an arm around Harper's shoulders.

Harper nodded. "Yeah. A lot."

"What's wrong with Miss Harper?" Henry asked.

"She misses Mr. Luke," Sophie told him.

Henry patted her arm. "It's okay, Miss Harper. We'll take care of you. We'll take you to the carnival tonight to see the fireworks. That'll make you feel better!"

"Thanks, buddy. That's really nice of you," Harper said, surprising him with a hug. He grinned, showing off a missing front tooth, and hurried back to his prime candy catching spot.

Mrs. Agosta sighed from her perch on the stoop. "I don't think I can survive a carnival and fireworks after all the excitement today."

"How about if I took the kids over to the park tonight?" Harper asked. "I'd love to have some extra company for the fireworks."

"Oh, dear, I couldn't ask you to do that."

"I would love to do it. And think how well they'll sleep."

"There's car seats to worry about, and Robbie is allergic to bees…"

Harper could sense she was wavering. "I'll have them home fifteen minutes after the fireworks, and I won't let them have any soda after seven."

"If you're sure…"

———

Harper knew it would take some creative maneuvering to cram three kids plus a stroller into her Volkswagen, so she invited Claire, Joni, and Gloria to join her. Between two vehicles and four adults, Harper felt reasonably confident they could manage the evening.

"Fireworks!" Henry shouted as he sprinted toward the park.

"Slow down, crazy," Harper laughed after him.

"Fwoks!" Ava, in her hot-pink sunglasses, chirped from the stroller.

Robbie retrieved his brother and gave him a piggyback ride back to the group. "You're a good big brother, Robbie," Claire said, playfully adjusting his baseball hat.

His freckled nose wrinkled. "They're okay, I guess. When they're not annoying me all the time."

"Obbie piggyback!" Ava held out her arms to her brother.

Robbie rolled his eyes. "Everyone always wants something," he sighed.

"Wise beyond his years, that one is," Joni laughed.

They took a poll of the kids and prioritized the route through the carnival to hit the highlights before claiming their spot for the fireworks display.

Gloria and Harper shared a funnel cake while Robbie and Henry did the goldfish toss.

"Mrs. Agosta is going to kill me if the kids come home with fish," Harper moaned.

Robbie hooted in victory as his ping-pong ball landed in a fishbowl.

"Crap. Looks like Max and Lola have a new sister."

Henry whooped and did a victory dance.

"For the love of—Claire! Stop giving them money! Joni! Don't think I don't see you slipping him that dollar!"

"Guess you're going aquarium shopping tomorrow," Gloria teased.

"Laugh all you want because here comes trouble for you," Harper nodded.

Aldo was striding toward them. Clean-shaven now, he was sporting cargo shorts and boat shoes. His aviators were tucked into the neck of his fitted navy T-shirt.

"Why do I have this reaction to him?" Gloria whispered in a panic. She brought her hands to cool her flushed cheeks.

"Just enjoy it," Harper hissed. "Ask him if he wants to watch the fireworks with us." She gave Gloria a little shove forward and hurried back to the goldfish stand to give them some privacy...and stop the diabolical Claire and Joni from feeding the kids more fish cash.

———

As dusk fell, Aldo sprang for a round of lemonade for the fireworks. They let the kids choose a spot in the open field by the lake where they spread out blankets and set up chairs. Harper, snuggling sleepy Ava, smiled when Aldo made himself comfortable on the blanket next to Gloria.

Robbie and Henry took turns asking Aldo questions about his new leg while Joni and Claire caught up on any tidbits of town gossip that had spread since the parade. Harper noticed them sneaking peeks at Aldo and Gloria—who were covertly holding hands—and knew they were probably the topic of speculation.

There were no secrets that could be kept in Benevolence. Sooner or later, everything was brought to light.

The first volley of fireworks lit up the sky, and the crowd oohed as the colors sparkled and shimmered before winking out.

Ava squirmed to sit higher, and Harper was worried she might cry, but the toddler pointed to the sky in awe.

"Boom," she whispered.

"Boom." Harper nodded.

CHAPTER 38

To: harpwild@netlink.com
From:lucas.c.garrison282@us.army.mil
Subject: Again?

What does a guy have to do to keep you away from other men?

Attached was a picture of Harper kissing the man handing out medals at the 5K.

To:lucas.c.garrison282@us.army.mil
From: harpwild@netlink.com
Re: Again?

I wasn't kissing him. I needed oxygen after rocking my first 5K. I'd rather be kissing this guy.

She attached a picture of Luke making a fish face at Josh.

To: harpwild@netlink.com
From:lucas.c.garrison282@us.army.mil

Re: Again?

He looks awesome. You should definitely make out with him.

When Harper checked her email later that day, she got unexpected good news.

To: harpwild@netlink.com
From: hannahnanner@mail.pro
Subject: Miss your face

I've gone Harper-free for too long. I'm starting to forget what your face looks like. So if you're free this weekend, I'm heading your way! Break out the facial masks and pizza because we're having a sleepover!

Xoxo,
Hannah

To: hannahnanner@mail.pro
From: harpwild@netlink.com
Re: Miss your face

Are you serious?? You wouldn't tease me about this, would you? This isn't some cruel joke?

Don't destroy my fragile heart,
Harper

To: harpwild@netlink.com
From: hannahnanner@mail.pro

Re: Miss your face

My bag is already packed! Finn's heading to the cabin with some friends, and it's the perfect opportunity for me to come meet your new friends, check out your house, and hug your dogs. Finn promises to have bail money ready if we need it. It's going to be awesome!

It was guaranteed.

———

Friday night, Harper's friends, new and old, crowded into the kitchen in their comfiest summer pajamas to launch the festivities with a drink.

Gloria was perusing takeout menus while Sophie mixed margaritas in the blender. Hannah was busy digging through the stack of movies on the counter that hit all the high notes that a girls' night needed—romantic comedies, tearjerkers, and a few full-frontal man-part movies.

Harper let the dogs out the back door to romp around in the warm night air. "So what fat-free, calorie-free deliciousness are we ordering tonight?"

"We were thinking pizza and chicken bites from Dawson's," Sophie called over the whir of the blender.

"What about dessert?"

"I brought cookie dough," Gloria chirped. "We can either make cookies or eat it raw."

"Best. Night. Ever." Harper sighed with contentment. She tried to remember the last time she did something like this, the last time she had a pack of girlfriends. In high school, she hadn't been in one school long enough for lasting friendships. But now? With the roots she was planting, she had friends, family, and a future.

Sophie brought the blender pitcher over to the island and expertly sloshed margarita into four pink plastic cups. Gloria added a lime wedge, and Hannah plunked a straw into each cup.

"A toast, ladies," Sophie said, raising her drink. "To the lovely Harper. May she know how lucky we all are to know her."

"To Harper," they said in unison.

"You guys! My turn. To all of you. Thank you for being my family. I love each one of you so much."

They aww-ed as one and sipped.

"I approve you as a bartender," Hannah said, nodding to Sophie. "Well, let's get this party started." She dialed Dawson's.

With the order placed, Hannah held up a movie in each hand. "So what do we want? Full frontal or rom-com?"

Harper groaned. "You guys have full frontal at your beck and call. Let's not torture me with it when mine is on the other side of the world."

"Oooh, let's talk about boys," Sophie said, clapping her hands.

"My 'boy' is your brother. Isn't that gross?" Harper asked, wrinkling her nose.

"For tonight, I'll pretend he's someone else's brother."

"Actually, there is a relationship I'm curious about." Harper grinned. "Gloria, what's the scoop on you and Aldo?"

Gloria choked on a gulp of margarita.

"What makes you think there's anything to tell?" she asked innocently.

"I have eyes and a brain," Harper teased. "I saw some patty-cake during the Fourth of July fireworks in the park."

"Hmm, Gloria Moretta. It's got a nice ring to it." Sophie nodded.

Gloria blushed to her roots.

"You liiiike him!" Harper laughed.

"Who is this Aldo, and is he Gloria-worthy?" Hannah demanded.

"Aldo is a muscly Italian stud who's had the hots for Gloria since high school," Harper supplied.

"Luke's best friend, right? That's a long time to be carrying a torch," Hannah said. "You must be pretty great."

"She really is," Harper agreed.

"You guys." Gloria laughed. "I'm still just getting used to the idea."

"The idea of what?" Sophie demanded.

"Of Aldo…and me…dating."

Harper whooped. "So it's official?"

Gloria smiled and nodded. "Official. I'm trying to take things slow, but boy is he intense." She fanned herself with the Dawson's menu.

"I can't believe our little Aldo is finally all grown up," Sophie sighed.

"Do you have any pictures of this Italian stud?" Hannah asked.

Gloria blushed again and nodded. "I have some on my phone."

They stuck their heads together over the screen, and Harper winked at Sophie while Hannah whistled her appreciation for the male form.

Sophie's hot-pink phone rang from the table. "Speaking of hot studs, it's the hubby." She took it into the dining room to answer.

Harper hugged herself. Happiness all around. The only thing that would make it better was if Luke was home safe.

He would be in a few months, and they would talk. And then she would know exactly where she stood. She knew what she wanted. The honest, mutual love that she saw Sophie and

Hannah shared with their husbands. The kind she saw blooming between Aldo and Gloria. Would she really be willing to settle for less than that?

Sophie came back into the kitchen holding her phone out to Harper. She looked worried. "It's Ty. He wants to talk to you. Sounds like he's in full-on cop mode."

Harper raised her eyebrows and took the phone. "Hey, Ty, what's up? I thought you had the night off."

"Harper, listen to me. Glenn posted bail and was released today. He was supposed to go straight to his mother's house but hasn't showed."

Her stomach flip-flopped. "Do you think he'd come here?"

"It's more likely that he would go to Gloria's place, but you could still be a target."

Shit. Shit. Shit.

"Gloria's here with me and Soph and Hannah. We were just waiting on pizza, which has no bearing on the situation at all. I'm just nervous, and I'm going to shut up now."

"Listen, I'm going to swing by Gloria's and then her mom's and check things out. I'll let you know if we find him. Just do me a favor and keep your doors locked."

Harper gulped and hung up. Her three friends were watching her expectantly.

"What the hell is going on?" Sophie demanded.

"Glenn's out. Ty thinks he might be heading to Gloria's."

"Oh my God," Gloria whispered, bringing her fingertips to her mouth.

"It's going to be fine. Ty is heading to your place now to check things out. The police know he's missing. They're looking for him. He's not going to get to you. No one is going to let that happen."

Gloria took a steadying breath and nodded. "I think I'm going to text Aldo and let him know."

"Good idea," Sophie said, patting her hand.

They watched her as she took her phone into the dining room. Sophie's eyes met Harper's. Her voice was low. "So what's going to happen if Glenn doesn't find her at home?"

"He's going to come here."

"Crap," Hannah sighed.

"Ty doesn't think we need to be worried, but maybe that's his way of trying not to worry us. He told me to lock the doors. Just in case."

Gloria's voice sounded softly from the dining room. "Aldo must have called her," Sophie whispered.

Harper nodded. "It wouldn't be the worst thing in the world if Aldo stopped by. Sophie, will you let the dogs in the back and lock the door? I'll get the front door. Hannah, can you check the windows on the first floor. I'm sure it's just a precaution. But I think we should be prepared just in case."

She picked up her phone and dialed Mrs. Agosta just in case the kids were out late catching lightning bugs and made her promise to keep everyone inside and lock up tight.

"It's probably nothing. We're just taking precautions," she told her.

It was probably nothing, Harper told herself when she hung up. They were probably just overreacting. The odds were that Glenn had just gotten good and drunk and was passed out somewhere far away from here.

Her fingers shook as she twisted the dead bolt on the front door. Lola trotted down the hallway toward her, a rumbly growl in her throat. "It's okay, sweetie." Harper bent down to pat Lola's silver body. "We're safe."

The dark outside the windows made her nervous, so she reached over to flick on the porch lights.

And there he was.

CHAPTER 39

Glenn Diller peered at her through the cut glass of the sidelight window. The night shadows made his face look even more sinister. Harper's heart jumped into her throat.

Before she could shout a warning to her friends, he hefted the fern in the terra-cotta pot and heaved it through the dining room window.

"Everybody out! Go to Mrs. Agosta's." Harper screamed as his thick leg swung over the sill. Glass crunched under his boots.

Lola growled low at her side, her fur bristling into a mohawk down her back.

"Well, look who's home." His eyes were unusually bright.

Harper backed up a step and prayed that the girls made it out through the backyard.

"Gloria's gone. She's safe and calling the cops right now."

"I'm not here for her." He reached behind him and pulled out a hunting knife. The light from the kitchen glinted off the four-inch blade. Glenn took another step toward her, and Lola's growl became a snarl. "Aren't you gonna run?" He licked his lips, and Harper's stomach churned.

"If I run, my dog is going to rip your face off, and I really like this rug."

As if in slow motion, Harper watched Glenn lunge forward. He grabbed her arm in his meaty fist as Lola coiled and sprang, closing her jaws around the forearm of his knife-wielding hand.

He shrieked, and the knife clattered to the floor. Glenn flung Lola off him into the wall. She landed with a sick thud and a yelp. Harper screamed and launched herself at him. Her fingernails raked his face.

He grabbed for her again, catching her by the ponytail, and they crashed to the floor. Harper scrambled forward on her hands and knees, reaching for the knife, but he caught her by the ankle and yanked her back. His body ranged over hers, crushing her to the floor, and she saw his hand close around the handle of the knife.

She heard more screams and barely recognized that they were coming from her own throat. She wasn't scared. She was enraged.

Harper threw an elbow over her shoulder that connected with his face, but he didn't drop the knife.

Suddenly it seemed as if every light in the house came on, and Sophie and Hannah barreled in from the hallway. Sophie was wielding a baseball bat. Harper couldn't see where the first blow landed, but the satisfying crunch told her it was somewhere crucial.

Glenn howled like a feral animal and brought the knife to Harper's face. She froze. The tip of the blade trailed down her cheek. It scratched a shallow path in her jaw before coming to rest against the delicate skin of her throat.

She felt her blood pumping through her system. Saw Lola try to right herself. Heard Glenn's snarl in her ear. Felt the blade prick her skin. This couldn't be how it ended.

Then bare feet were sailing over the hardwood past her, and there was a clanging crunch. Glenn's weight went limp on top of her.

Everyone was screaming at once.

"Get him off me!" Harper groaned. "He's crushing me." Lola crawled over to Harper and licked her nose. "My sweet girl," Harper whispered. Lola's rear end wiggled.

Gloria and Hannah shoved Glenn's deadweight off her, and Harper could breathe again. She rolled over onto her back and stared up at the ceiling as Lola nuzzled her ear.

"Tape him up!" Sophie ordered. Hannah straddled Glenn and wrapped camo duct tape around his wrists.

"Get it up higher into his arm hair," Gloria suggested, her breath coming in short gasps.

Harper rolled to face her. Gloria was leaning against the staircase in her plaid pajama shorts, clutching Luke's cast iron skillet.

The first giggle slipped out, and there was no stopping it.

It was contagious. Her friends slid to the floor in a loose pile, shaking with laughter and adrenaline.

Lola limped over, pausing to lick each one, reassuring herself that they were all okay.

The front door exploded off its hinges and crashed to the floor, narrowly missing Sophie. Ty and Aldo tumbled through the opening. Ty's gun was drawn, and Aldo looked like he was breathing fire.

"You could have come in through the window," Harper said.

It was silent for exactly two seconds before the girls exploded in peals of hysterics again.

———

The pizza arrived at the same time the cops did. Harper took the food and sent the delivery guy back for four more pizzas to feed all the extra company.

Between the cops, the pizza, and the neighbors, Harper knew the news was all over town by now.

Glenn was once again cuffed and carted off to the hospital for what held the promise of a massive concussion.

No one wanted to leave Harper alone for the night, so Aldo and Ty decided to join the sleepover, and an hour later, Hannah's husband, Finn, arrived with his sleeping bag and fishing gear.

"I can't leave you girls alone for an hour without someone getting arrested," he teased, wrapping them both in a bear hug.

Ty called an emergency vet from the next town over, and one of the veterinarians made a house call in her pajamas to check on Lola, who was deemed the hero of the night.

"She's going to be sore for a couple of days, but there's no breaks. She's a tough little girl, aren't you, sweetie?"

Lola ate it up and rolled onto her back to bare her belly while Max danced in circles around them. The vet gave Harper a bottle of pain meds and told her to keep Lola away from any strenuous activity for a few days.

As the police were wrapping up their interviews, Frank and a full crew of Garrison guys showed up with plywood to cover the door and broken window.

"We'll be back in the morning to get measurements and order new glass," Frank said, wiping his hands on a napkin. "Thanks for the pizza. Try not to let any more maniacs in the house."

Everyone made the necessary calls to the appropriate relatives letting them know they were all safe. Harper could imagine the story spreading like wildfire through Benevolence. Tomorrow there would probably be paparazzi from the high school paper on the lawn.

They traded versions of the break-in.

When Harper had hung up with Ty, he had sped over to Gloria's apartment. Finding nothing, he sent an officer to Gloria's mother's house and headed straight to Harper's. He and Aldo had pulled in the driveway at the same time and bolted for the door when they heard the screams.

When Harper yelled for everyone to get out, Hannah had ushered little Max into the basement while Sophie and Gloria ran for weapons.

They converged in the hallway for the ultimate beatdown. Gloria had hit Glenn once in the face, knocking him out instantaneously.

"It was so weird. It was like he didn't even see me," she said. "He was so intent on you and that knife, Harper." Gloria shivered, and Aldo pulled her into his chest.

"I hate to say it, but, Harper, you know what you have to do," Ty said.

"I don't want to." She shook her head. "He's going to think it's my fault and be very upset."

"I don't want to hear it. Dial. Now." Ty handed Harper her cell phone.

"It's two a.m. here," she tried again.

"Nice try. They're eight hours ahead of us. Do it, or I will, and you know that'll piss him off even more."

Grumbling, she took the phone and opened her video chat app. He'd want to see everything rather than just take her word for it. So she might as well get it over with.

Luke answered immediately.

"Baby, what's wrong?"

"How do you know something's wrong."

"It's two a.m."

Ty crossed his arms, and Harper frowned at him. She stalked out of the living room and into the dining room.

"Harper, why are there people in the house at two a.m., and what the hell happened to our window? Are you okay? Why do you have a bandage on your chin?"

Harper brought her fingers to her jaw. "Okay, so everyone is fine. No one got hurt. But there was a little incident here. Glenn got out of jail and broke in here tonight and smashed some stuff up until Lola bit him and then Gloria coldcocked him with your cast iron pan."

Luke's face went white, and she saw him take a deep, steadying breath.

"Everyone's okay. Lola was checked out by a vet, and none of the rest of us have more than a scratch."

He was holding the laptop with both hands, and Harper was worried he was about to snap the monitor off.

"Ty," she yelled over her shoulder. "I think you need to talk him down."

Ty, cop face on, took the phone from her.

"Everyone's fine—" he started.

"What the *fuck* happened there?"

Harper ducked into the hallway and let Ty deal with it.

Once Luke stopped yelling, she only caught snippets of the conversation, including "knife" and "duct tape."

Their conversation lasted several minutes, and when Harper saw Ty panning over the damage to the window and front door, she hoped Luke was calm enough to talk.

She poked her head back in the dining room. "Is he okay to talk to me?" she whispered.

Ty nodded. "I'm gonna turn you back to Harper now. Please don't freak out on her. She's had a rough enough night."

Harper took the phone back.

Luke took a deep breath. "Hi."

"Hi. I'm really sorry, Luke."

"Baby, you didn't do anything to be sorry about. You did everything right. I'm just having a hard time with all the what-ifs right now."

"Lola and Gloria were incredible."

"Ty said that fucker put a knife to your throat." His voice was controlled rage.

"It's kind of a blur."

"I could have lost you." Pain and helplessness made his throat tight, his tone harsh.

"It wasn't that close. I think he was just trying to scare me."

Luke scrubbed his hands over his face. "Okay, here's what we're going to do. You're going to go upstairs and take every piece of clothing off so I can see for myself if you're hurt. Then we're going to talk about how many armed guards I'm posting in the house until I come home."

Harper laughed. "God, I miss you."

"Yeah, you think I'm joking. Get your ass upstairs."

———

The next morning, Harper couldn't feel her legs when she woke up. Briefly fearing paralysis, she opened her eyes and discovered the culprit was two sleeping dogs draped across her lower body. The crick in her neck told her it had been a really bad idea to sleep on the floor.

She sat up and surveyed the room. Aldo and Gloria were sound asleep spooning on the couch. Ty and Sophie were jammed onto the love seat, recliners extended. On her right, Hannah and Finn snuggled under Finn's sleeping bag. James was sprawled at her feet, half on Lola's dog bed.

He had arrived at 3:00 a.m., presumably after his mother called him to tell him about the break-in.

Everyone was safe. The danger of the night was behind

them. Harper shivered as she remembered the glint on the blade against her skin.

She was safe now. With her extended, hand-picked family.

Harper wriggled out from under Max and Lola, who grumbled in their sleep, and tiptoed into the kitchen.

It was 8:00 a.m., the perfect time to start a gigantic breakfast.

She pulled the packs of bacon from the freezer and tossed them in the microwave for a quick defrost. Thanks to Claire's chickens, she had two dozen eggs in the fridge.

She started a full pot of coffee.

She was glad Ty had made her call Luke. Just seeing his face, hearing that familiar voice, made her feel safer. Luke had surveyed her bruises and scrapes and—satisfied she wasn't hiding a life-threatening injury—made her swear she wouldn't get so much as a hangnail for the rest of the summer. Harper was happy to promise.

By the time the first stirrings came from the living room, the bacon was crisping—in a pan that had *not* been used to brain a criminal—and the coffee was ready.

It was a new day.

CHAPTER 40

I'm impressed, Harpsichord." Aldo whistled through his teeth as they rounded a corner on the path. "A few months ago, you couldn't run the length of a football field, and now look at you."

Harper rolled her eyes at the nickname and tossed a smug look over her shoulder. "I could say the same about you," she teased, enjoying the pace he set.

"Yeah, but I'm a perfect physical specimen. I'm designed to run no matter how many legs I have. You were a late-sleeping desk potato."

She gasped, her breath forming a cloud in the brisk morning air. "Desk potato?"

"Someone who doesn't watch a lot of TV but spends all their time sitting at a desk."

"Where do you come up with this stuff?"

He tapped his finger to his temple. "It's all up here. All the secrets of the universe."

"Let's see if those secrets of the universe help you move a little faster." She picked up the pace. Aldo was right. A few months ago, the thought of a five-mile run before 7:00 a.m. would have had her pulling pillows over her head. And now, here she was, feeling her legs come to life beneath her as her feet skimmed the surface of the jogging path.

She and Aldo hit the park once a week together for a longer run. The man was a freaking machine. His physical therapists were thrilled with his progress, and her heart warmed at the fact that she no longer saw frustration lining his handsome face. Love was the ultimate motivator.

Gloria and her genuine sweetness had worked wonders on the depression that had threatened to envelop him. The woman had probably single-handedly saved him from murdering or being murdered by Mrs. Moretta.

"Now you're just showing off," Harper laughed as Aldo sped by. "Don't let your leg fall off," she called after him.

"Gotta get there before sunrise!"

Harper lengthened her stride and caught him on the down slope. In a mile, the wooded path opened to the lake and the perfect view of the sunrise. It was her favorite part of the day, when she got to see those colors bleeding across the sky into the waters of the lake. She felt like the sunrise was a gift from her parents, telling her everything was going to be okay. That life was beautiful and it would be crazy to waste a moment of it.

"So you ready for Luke to come home? Next week, right?" Aldo asked conversationally. The sprint had taken nothing out of him.

"I'm trying not to think about it too much, so only every half second or so," she said. "We didn't have much time before he left, but I still feel like I've been missing a limb—no offense—for the last six months. I'm excited and terrified and everything in between."

"Terrified?"

"Our relationship has lasted seven months. Six of those, he was on the other side of the world. What if he doesn't like me anymore? What if everything is different? What if I can't handle the reason he didn't tell me about Karen?"

Aldo stopped and put a hand on her arm.

"What's wrong? You need a break?"

He smirked. "Do I look like I need a break?"

His olive complexion glowed with healthy exertion. His hooded National Guard sweatshirt and track pants covered all the hard planes of his body, every inch earned with hard work and dedication.

"No. You look like you could breeze through a half marathon if you wanted to."

"Damn right. And stop worrying. You two have what it takes to make it."

"I love you, Aldo."

Surprise lit his eyes.

"Not like *that*." Harper rolled her eyes. "You're the closest thing to a brother that I've ever had, and I love you."

"Well, shit. I love you too, Harpsichord," he said gruffly.

"Don't say it because I said it!" She punched him in the arm.

Aldo put her in a headlock and ruffled her hair. "I didn't, dummy. You're the little sister I never wanted."

They started forward, slowly working their way back up to speed. "So you planning to surprise Luke when he comes home?"

Harper snorted. "Can you think of anything he'd hate more? No. In fact, he told me he doesn't even want me to meet the bus. He wants to meet me at the house."

"You know why he wants it that way."

Harper sighed. "I do. But it still hurts my heart to think of him coming home with no one there to greet him. It's been so long. I don't want to waste the time it would take him to

325

drive home. Ever since he told me that he's coming home, every second feels like half an hour. I just want him here. I want to look into his eyes and…"

They broke through the woods just as the sun began its climb over the trees. A lone figure in fatigues stood facing them, his back to the spectacular sunrise.

"No," Harper whispered, shaking her head. Shock flooded her system. "I…"

He opened his arms, and Harper was in motion, sprinting to him.

He was running too now, and they collided in midair. Luke boosted her up, clutching her to him. Harper wrapped her legs around his waist and cupped his face in her hands.

"Is it really you? Are you really here?"

She drank in the hazel eyes, the long lashes, the strong cheekbones, the growth of stubble on his perfect jaw.

"I'm home, baby." His voice was rough and raspy.

A sob escaped her, and then Luke was pulling her in. His mouth found hers in a kiss laced with a frantic need and possession. The lick of flame swept through her as Luke's tongue met hers. Alive. That was how she felt with his hands on her.

She couldn't breathe anything but his air. Didn't want anything else. She had everything she needed in this moment.

Harper tasted salt and realized it was her own tears.

A whimper worked its way free from the back of her throat, and Luke groaned, slowly retreating from the kiss with her lower lip between his teeth. Her hands fisted in his collar to keep him close. His grip on her ass tightened.

Harper moved to kiss him again, but the clearing of a throat stalled her.

"You guys are ruining my view of a perfect sunrise," Aldo teased.

Luke let Harper slide down his body, but he kept her anchored to his side.

"You knew, and you didn't say a freaking word!" Harper smacked Aldo on the arm.

He grinned. "Surprise!"

"Thanks, man," Luke said, wrapping his friend in a one-armed man hug.

Aldo clapped him on the back, a blow that would have brought Harper to her knees.

Her throat tight, Harper stepped back and gave them a moment. The one-armed hug moved into a crushing embrace of brothers. "You look good, Moretta." Luke pulled back to ruffle Aldo's dark curls.

"I feel good. Check out the hardware." Aldo pulled up his pant leg to show off his prosthesis.

Harper saw Luke's Adam's apple work and knew that he struggled with the raw memory of his childhood friend in a pool of his own blood. He nodded, but no sound came out.

"Hey," Aldo said, clapping Luke on the shoulder. "I'm good. I'm better than good."

Luke's jaw clenched, and he brought his friend in for another hard hug. "I'm sorry, man."

Aldo smacked him on the back of the head. "Shut up. There's nothing to be sorry for. Asshole."

Luke gave him a playful shove. "Dick."

Aldo wobbled, flailing his arms. Luke reached to steady him, concern in his eyes.

"Psych!" Aldo grinned, bouncing on the balls of his feet. "Solid as a rock. Thanks to your girl there."

Luke reached his arm out to Harper, pulling her back in. His hand skimmed under her jacket and tank to stroke the skin of her lower back. "She took good care of you?"

"She even got me a woman."

Harper rolled her eyes. "Don't make Gloria sound like a prostitute!"

Aldo checked his watch. "Love to stay and chat, but speaking of my woman, she's waiting for me. That gives you two about forty-five minutes before you have to be at the diner."

"The diner?" Luke looked at Harper.

Aldo's plan hit Harper. "Oh, you're good! Does anyone else know?"

He winked. "Nope." He tossed Luke a set of keys. "Your truck is in the lot on the other side of the trees."

"How did you get his truck here?"

"Gloria and I stole it from the garage last night. You're one sound sleeper."

"You riding back with us?" Luke asked Aldo, but his eyes were on Harper.

"Nope, Gloria's waiting with my truck. I'll see you soon. Glad to have you home, Luke. Later, Harpsichord!" And with that, he loped off toward the parking lot.

————

Luke didn't waste time watching his friend leave. He only had eyes for Harper. He pulled her into his arms. Her blond locks were pulled back in a high ponytail. She was covered from the neck down in spandex and Under Armour to block the early morning chill, and it was the sexiest thing he'd ever seen.

He hadn't thought of anything but seeing those hungry gray eyes since he got his orders. Somehow she was more beautiful than when he had left. It had been a long time since he was this eager to come home.

Harper wrapped her arms around his neck and stared into his eyes.

"I can't believe you're here," she said finally.

"Miss me, baby?" He tugged her off the path through trees and brush.

"Only every second of the last one hundred and eighty-nine days." She brought her hands to his face and ran her thumbs over the stubble. "How is it possible to love you even more right this second than before you left?"

Luke let out the breath he didn't know he had been holding. Was that relief? Deployment could and did change people on both sides. The thought that she wouldn't wait or wouldn't want him the way he wanted her when he came home had crossed his mind a few times in the long, dark hours of the night.

There had been too many nights that stood between him and those words.

He crushed his mouth to hers until he felt her knees give out.

"I need you." The words sounded harsh to his ears, but he couldn't soften them. He was rock-hard for her. His hands cruised over her body, unzipping her thin jacket and tugging up her long-sleeve shirt so they could roam over her skin. Her breasts were bound by a sports bra. "How do you get this off," he growled against her mouth.

Harper's husky laugh had him forgetting to be gentle.

"I need my hands on you, Harper. Do you trust me?"

She drew back a fraction of an inch, wide-eyed but nodding.

Luke pulled the pocketknife from his pocket and yanked the fabric away from her skin. "I'll buy you a new one," he breathed, slicing the fabric cleanly in two. He tossed the knife to the ground as her breasts tumbled into his palms. He hefted her soft flesh and said, "Baby, we're not going to make it to the truck."

"I was hoping you'd say that," she said, spreading hungry kisses down his throat and tugging at his belt.

He needed to be inside her, to feel her close around him. He wanted to watch her eyes go dreamy as she slowly came down from the high.

Luke stayed her busy hands and dragged her back into the trees. He yanked off his shirt and dropped it on the mossy ground. In a single fluid motion, he swept Harper's feet out from under her and took her to the ground. She gasped into his mouth, and he got impossibly harder.

It would be a miracle if he could last beyond the first thrust. Luke tore his mouth away from Harper's and moved lower. He pressed a kiss to her sternum before turning his attention to one perfect breast.

"I've dreamed about this," he whispered against her straining nipple before taking it into his mouth. She arched against him, and he could feel her heat through the layers that separated them. "Are you wet for me?" He already knew the answer, could almost feel it as he pressed his hard-on against her. He moved to her other breast and licked and sucked until her nipple stood at attention. She was so responsive to him. One touch, one taste, was all it took. He captured the taut peak into his mouth and worked it with his tongue until she moaned his name.

He had waited so long to hear his name on her lips like this again.

"Once I start, I won't be able to stop, baby," he warned.

"Please, Luke. I just want you inside me. Please." Her breathless plea had him ripping open his nylon belt and thanking God for the Velcro fly of his pants. Freed, his thick cock strained toward Harper's heat.

She wriggled under him, trying to free herself from her running tights. With his help, they wrestled them down to her ankles before peeling off a shoe.

Unable to wait any longer, Luke pushed her back against

the forest floor and positioned his erection at her wet entrance. He paused for just a second. He wanted to memorize her face. The devastating need. The desire she had for him to fill her, to take her over the edge. She belonged to him.

Luke drove into her in one fierce stroke. Harper buried her cry in his shoulder.

He was finally home.

He didn't give her a chance to get used to him.

"Jesus, baby, you are so fucking tight," he grunted as he thrust into her again. All the way to the hilt, every inch of him was surrounded by her. Again and again, he drove into her, his heavy sack slapping against her. Already he could feel the flutter of her muscles around him. She was so close to coming apart.

He leaned down and took her nipple in his mouth, suckling hard enough that he knew she felt both pleasure and pain. His thrusts became shorter, faster. Harper hitched her legs up higher on his hips.

He heard the snap of twigs, the rustle of leaves, but it didn't matter. Harper's eyes widened, and she turned her head toward the direction of the trail just feet away, but Luke clamped a hand over her mouth and turned her gaze back to him.

He shook his head and continued his assault, looming over her, driving into her, changing the angle at the last second. Harper's eyes glazed over as he slammed into her again, grazing the sensitive ache in her deepest center.

It was a small group of joggers that thundered by on the path, but all Harper saw was Luke mouthing the word, "Come," as he drove into her again. Her quivering muscles obeyed, clamping down on him as he let loose inside her. He let those beautiful squeezes milk him dry before collapsing on top of her, her bare breasts crushing into his chest.

She locked her legs around him to keep him inside her. "Don't leave me," she whispered.

"Never again, baby."

He rolled over so she was on top of him and stroked whatever bare skin his hands could find.

"I don't know if I like you running with other men dressed like that. Remind me to get you some really baggy sweats."

"I run with Aldo. Not every man wants to drag me behind a tree and ravage me," she teased.

"Any man with a dick and half a brain would have those thoughts." He pinched her hip as he helped her work her running tights back up. "Let's go home so we can do this for the rest of the day." His voice was husky as he placed a kiss to the flat of her stomach.

"We will, but first we have to make a pit stop." She grinned at the thought of the surprise Luke's family was about to get.

CHAPTER 41

They pushed the glass door of the diner open, and Harper spotted their group. A weekly breakfast had taken shape after Luke left. The participants varied depending on schedules, but today, they had to lay claim to a table plus a booth to accommodate the breakfast crowd.

"Sorry I'm late! Do we have room for another?" Harper said as she pulled Luke with her. She watched with pleasure as Claire looked up to greet her and froze. A shriek exploded from Sophie's lips as she frantically climbed out of the booth over a stupefied Ty holding Josh. Claire shoved her chair back, almost tripping Sophie as they fought to get to Luke first.

Harper let go of Luke's hand and stepped back as the women rushed him.

"For Pete's sake, you just saw the girl two days ago. What's all the—" Charlie turned in his seat to see what all the commotion was.

Spotting his wife and daughter wrapped around Luke, he stood slowly. James jumped into the fray hugging his brother, and the diner patrons broke into applause.

Charlie put his arm around Harper's shoulders. "Good surprise, kiddo."

She wrapped an arm around his waist. "I had no idea. He surprised me in the park on my run with Aldo the Sneak over there." She jerked a thumb in Aldo's direction.

Aldo winked from his seat with Gloria grinning next to him.

Charlie cleared his throat and leaned in. "You got twigs and leaves in your hair." He winked and made his way over to Luke, leaving Harper frantically combing through her ponytail.

Wiping away tears, Claire and Sophie stepped back and let Luke and Charlie have their moment.

"Dad." Luke extended his hand.

"Son." Charlie took his hand and yanked Luke in for a hug. "Welcome home."

Charlie released Luke, and Harper saw shock register when Luke realized who the next person in line to greet him was.

"Joni," Luke said quietly. His gaze flew to Harper's face, and she saw a war of emotions wash over him.

"Hi, Luke," Joni said quietly. "Welcome home." She took a deep breath and opened her arms to embrace him.

Harper sniffled, and Claire put a steadying hand on her shoulder as they watched Luke stiffen at Joni's touch and then carefully put his arms around her.

Luke's gaze never left Harper's face.

"I'm so sorry," Joni whispered into his shoulder.

Harper squeezed Claire's hand. "Why don't you two take a minute to talk, and I'll order you a coffee, okay, Luke?"

Luke stepped back from Joni's embrace and into Harper's space, cupping her face gently in his hands. "I'm so sorry," he whispered so that only she could hear.

Harper pressed her lips together and gave him a teary nod. "Go talk. I'll be here when you get back."

He leaned in as if he was going to kiss her and at the last

second changed his mind. He dropped a chaste peck on her cheek instead and turned to hold the door open for Joni.

Harper sat down with the rest of the group and tried to ignore the sinking feeling in her stomach. This was what needed to happen for both of them. Regardless of what it meant for her, Joni and Luke needed this to move on.

Claire claimed her attention, demanding to know why she had leaves in her hair.

Luke hunched his shoulders against the chill on the steps of the diner and shoved his hands in his pockets. He was the one who was supposed to do the surprising, yet here he was talking to his dead wife's mother. How had his past and present collided while he was gone? And what the hell did it mean for all of them?

"I had no idea you were home," Joni started. "Otherwise I would have given you and your family space."

"You are always welcome, Joni," Luke said, skating a hand over the back of his head.

"You're probably wondering what I'm doing here with your family." She cracked a smile. "At least, I would be if I were in your shoes."

"The thought had crossed my mind." He felt his mouth lift slightly.

Joni took a deep breath, her brown curls dancing in the chilly wind. "It all started a few months ago when I ran into Harper. When I found out who she was, I laid into her something fierce." Luke tensed, and Joni held up her hands. "Don't worry. She set me straight. Told me I was being stupid but that sometimes grief makes people do stupid things. And she was right. When I lost Karen—when *we* lost Karen—I felt like I died that day too. You had your family and your business and the guard, but she was my life. I was scared that you were going to move on and forget about her. That her life—and mine—meant nothing in the grand scheme of things. I blamed you." She choked out the last words, and Luke crossed his arms but said nothing. "I wanted it to be your fault, but the truth is it was mine."

"Joni, you were right to blame me. If I hadn't asked her to meet me—"

Joni was shaking her head, tears threatening to escape. "I texted her. Told her I was running late. She was reading my text when she crossed the center line. It was me. It was my fault."

Luke's breath rushed out of him. He shook his head. "It's not your fault. It was an accident."

"How many people have said that to you over the years? And how many times has it made you stop feeling guilty?"

"A lot. And zero." He leaned back against the railing. "I don't blame you, Joni."

"I don't blame you either, Luke. I don't think I ever really did. I'm so sorry for what I said at the funeral. I'm sorry for shutting out your family when all they tried to do was help. And I'm sorry for saying what I said to Harper, even though she told me if I apologized one more time, she was going to smack me."

Luke cracked a smile at that.

"Anyway, after Harper and I hashed it out, she invited me to Sunday dinner at your family's and…well, here we are. I'll understand if you don't want me…around."

"You're family." He said it and meant it.

They glanced through the glass of the diner window to their little group passing plates of pancakes and eggs.

"I know coming from me and our situation, this might be awkward, but I like Harper. A lot," Joni said.

Luke nodded. Yeah, that was awkward.

She put her hand on his arm. "There's one more thing."

"I'm not sure if I can take anything else right now." Luke was only half kidding.

"I knew about the baby. Karen told me and swore me to secrecy. I just wanted you to know that I know all that you lost that day."

———

Harper watched anxiously through the window. At least there wasn't any screaming or storming off. That had to be a good sign.

She took a deep breath. When she crawled out of bed this morning, she had no idea what an emotional day she would be facing.

Joni and Luke returned. Joni was smiling, but Luke's expression was unreadable. His gaze locked on Harper's face. He took the seat next to her, but instead of hauling her up against his side, he maintained a careful distance. She wished they were alone and turned her attention back to her eggs.

He was home, and that was what mattered. They would figure everything else out.

The happy breakfast crowd lingered over coffee and stories. Everyone was eager to fill Luke in on the last six months, and he was happy to listen. Harper listened with half an ear and tried not to worry about all the things she and Luke would have to catch up on.

Joni left first to tackle a list of errands.

Luke's hand snaked under the table and gripped Harper's knee. She put her hand on his and squeezed. His touch made her entire body hum.

"Let's get out of here," he whispered in her ear, lips brushing her sensitive flesh.

CHAPTER 42

Home. Luke had thought of this house and what it held more times than he could count in the last six months. The bones were the same, but the passing of time was evident in the small details.

A lot had happened in six months. And he wasn't sure how he felt about some of it. He wasn't sure how a lot of people felt about it. Harper had been unusually quiet during the ride home. He didn't know how Joni had come into the picture, but he did know what it meant. Harper knew about Karen.

The tickle of panic he felt when he saw Joni and Harper together hadn't subsided yet. His worlds had collided, and he wasn't sure what the ramifications would be. Seeing Joni at breakfast with his family, with Harper, had knocked him back. He never expected that relationship to resurface. Being around Joni was like being catapulted into the past. The words she'd said at Karen's funeral still cut at him. Her words were his thoughts. And now an apology? Joni owed him nothing. He was the one who owed the apology—to Joni and to Harper.

He had been an ass, thinking he could keep his past separate. Didn't Harper deserve to know why he could never offer her more? It had been selfish and stupid to think that he could keep her in the dark. And now there was a distance between them.

He had tried to set up his apology on the drive home. "So. Joni?"

But Harper wasn't biting. "Yeah." She nodded. And that was it.

At least home was still intact.

The flower beds were neatly trimmed and hidden under a fresh layer of mulch for the winter. Harper had dotted colorful annuals among the greenery this summer, sending him a picture a week of her efforts. The pumpkins and mums that she put out for Halloween still flanked the front door. The new front door, Luke noticed, clenching his jaw.

It was a near perfect replica of the original. Frank had done a good job of finding the right one. But it was a reminder to Luke of the danger he hadn't been able to protect Harper from.

Harper turned her key in the lock and glanced over her shoulder. "I can't wait to see this reunion." She grinned.

He tugged her blond ponytail, bringing her back to face him. "Kiss me first."

She took her time, stepping into him and winding her arms around his neck.

His grip on her hair tightened, tilting her head back. His mouth found hers already parting. His lips fused to hers, binding them together with breath and taste until he couldn't tell where he stopped and she started. He invaded her mouth, taking what he wanted most—her surrender. He would never get enough of her flavor—sweet with a belt that knocked him back every time.

The second his mouth closed over hers, he felt the current course through them. Need matched need, and he knew, no matter what, their bodies still craved each other. There was no hiding it. No denying it.

He needed Harper Wilde like he needed his next breath.

"God, I missed you." His lips moved over hers.

She was silent, but her fingers dug into his collar and held.

He tasted again, and when he felt her tremble against him, he forced himself to pull back before he shredded her pants there on the front porch. He groaned. "Inside, baby."

She sighed and nodded. "Dogs first. Then upstairs." She turned back to the door. "Are you ready for a slobbery reunion?"

Harper was smiling, but there was a coolness back in her eyes.

It was a challenge. He would take down that wall brick by damn brick until there was nothing separating them.

Maybe he couldn't love her the way she deserved, but he could give her everything else.

Harper opened the door to seven legs of chaos. The second Lola realized he was there, her excited woofs turned to whimpers and wriggles. Her tail whipped so hard Luke was afraid it would strip the wainscoting from the wall. He dropped to his knees, and Lola jumped, putting her front paws on his shoulders so she could nibble his nose.

Max pawed at his back, yips shaking his tiny body. Luke grabbed the little dog and held him to his chest. He thumped Lola in the chest. "I heard you saved Mommy's life, pretty girl."

Lola dissolved into shivers of joy. She launched herself at his shoulders again, bowling him over onto his back.

"I think they missed you," Harper said, laughing softly.

"I missed them. Almost as much as I missed you." He climbed out from under the pile of dogs. "I need a shower after that welcome." He pulled her to him. "Will you go to bed with me?"

She cuddled into him. "Of course."

Luke let the water wash away six months of desert, worry, and exhaustion.

He was home, and it was time to start living life again. At the diner, he couldn't touch Harper the way he needed to. Not with Joni there.

The guilt tugged at him. How could he be with Harper after Karen? He pushed it aside. No one could take Karen's place. He wouldn't let that happen. But he was still here, still living. Didn't that count for something?

He shut off the faucet and reached for a towel. It was new too. The giant fluffy kind that could dry a car, not just the human body.

He wrapped it around his waist and headed into the bedroom.

He was rock-hard in the half second it took to register that Harper was waiting for him on the bed. She had discarded her running clothes and was wearing a dark, sheer corset with satin and lace panels that barely covered her full breasts.

"Come here," she said, rising to her knees.

His body obeyed as if under a spell. He stripped off the towel and crawled across the mattress to her.

"You are so fucking beautiful, Harper," he whispered as his mouth met hers. "This is new." He trailed his fingers over the lacy edge.

"I bought a few things for when you came home."

He couldn't give her the words she wanted to hear the most, but he could give her all the others she deserved to hear. "I thought of you every second, baby. I couldn't get home fast enough." His mouth moved over her lips, her jaw, down to her neck. "I missed you so much."

Harper trembled. Her fingers dug into his shoulders. "I love you, Luke."

"Baby, don't cry." His thumbs brushed away the tears that trailed down her smooth cheeks.

She blinked them back. "Do you still want me?"

His hands stilled on her skin. "Harper." He breathed her name. "There is nothing I want more."

She pushed him backward until he landed against the pillows at the head of the bed.

Harper slid her body over his, the silky barrier teasing his skin. She started at his jaw, running her soft lips down to his throat. She kissed, nibbled, and licked her way down his chest, across his abdomen. And then lower.

The first brush of her lips across the head of his cock nearly brought him off the bed. His hips flexed into her as her sweet mouth closed over him.

She pulled him into the back of her throat, and he groaned. "God, baby."

Harper gripped the base of his thick shaft and worked his length with her hand as her mouth slicked over him again and again.

She moaned, and the vibration nearly sent him over the edge.

Luke fisted his hand in her hair. "Baby, I need this to last. I need to be inside you."

Harper let him drag her up his body until she found his mouth. He made a move to roll with her, but she braced her hands on his shoulders. "Stay," she whispered, straddling him.

She reached between their bodies and positioned the broad head of his erection against her wet center. His hands found her hips and guided her down his length. Inch by glorious inch, she took him into her core until he was fully sheathed in her.

Luke fought the urge to take over the rhythm and hammer himself home.

"Make it last, baby," he whispered.

She cupped a hand to his face. Harper rose up, her golden waves framing her face. Her eyes closed tight as she set a slow, sensual pace. Her body was leaner, stronger than before. She looked like a goddess riding into battle.

"Open your eyes, Harper."

Those lust-glazed gray eyes opened almost lazily. She smiled as he flexed into her. He let her ride him, losing herself in the rhythm. Time stood still as the magic of what she made him feel bled through him.

He reared up and yanked the fabric from her breasts. Her nipples were already pebbled and straining for him. He took one into his mouth, drawing on it with long, deep pulls.

Her sharp inhale went straight to his dick. He sucked again, harder this time, and felt her tighten around him. His own need for release churned deep in his balls.

"Luke."

"Let it happen, baby." He gripped her hips harder and yanked her down on his cock, thrusting deep. Her thighs tightened around him as he felt the first flutter of her release around his shaft. Her hungry squeezes wrenched his own orgasm from him, and he came deep inside her, branding her from within.

Trembling, Harper collapsed on top of him. No matter what words did or didn't pass between them, this connection was undeniable.

She loved him body and broken soul.

"We should talk," he murmured against her shoulder.

"Sleep first. Talk later."

He stroked her back while her silent tears fell on his neck and shoulder.

———

When Harper woke a few hours later, she was still sprawled over Luke. He was still inside her. And hard. She squeezed him reflexively as she tried to ease off him, but the movement woke him.

Without pulling out, he rolled them over. He kept his face buried in her neck as he partially withdrew and then thrust into her.

Instantly wet, Harper bent her knees to take more of him.

He clutched a hand to her bare breast, kneading, as his thrusts came faster and harder. Luke set a frantic pace, a race for release.

"Squeeze me, baby," Luke groaned.

Harper flexed around him as he slammed into her. He grunted with every thrust, and Harper could feel her orgasm building violently.

Luke thrust into her to the hilt, and she felt the first jet of his release. It tore her over the edge, sending her spiraling after him. Her orgasm milked every drop from him.

"Mine," he whispered against her neck. "Mine."

———

It took her another hour to extricate herself from the bed and Luke's arms. He reached for her in his sleep, and she pressed a kiss to his forehead before tugging the quilt over him. She patted the bed, giving Lola and Max the all-clear signal. Lola curled into Luke's side while Max settled on his chest.

Harper padded into the bathroom and turned on the water in the shower. She peeled off the midnight corset and stepped under the stream.

Her body was sore from unexpected use, and it made her smile.

Luke was home. It was a new beginning.

Back in the bedroom, Harper quietly opened drawers and grabbed comfy clothes before tiptoeing downstairs. The house was chilly, but rather than bumping the heat up, she turned on the gas fireplace in the living room. While the room warmed, she headed into the kitchen and started a pot of coffee.

It was a little early for dinner, but since they had missed lunch, Harper reached for the Dawson's menu and called in an order.

When Luke woke, they would eat, and they would talk.

————

The doorbell woke him. Luke trudged downstairs in pajama pants and a T-shirt. He followed the scent of pizza into the kitchen.

Harper, in leggings covered by thigh-high wool socks, shot him her golden grin. Her soft sweater, the color of ripe blueberries, hung off one shoulder. Her blond hair was tied up in a knot on top of her head, leaving the graceful curve of her neck exposed.

"Hey there, handsome. Want some coffee?"

"Like I want my next breath."

She reached for a mug, and he stepped in to nuzzle that delicate skin behind her ear.

"Are you hungry?" Her voice was breathy.

He nibbled on her neck. "Yes."

"Lucas Garrison, if you give me a hickey—"

He pulled back and smacked her on the ass. Her very firm ass.

"Jesus, baby. You got ripped while I was gone."

Harper laughed and handed him the mug. "I joined a gym. Had to do something besides think about you all day."

"Aldo says you're a beast on the trails."

She smiled. "I learned from the beastiest," she said, pulling plates out of the cabinet.

"How's he doing?"

She handed the plates over and pointed to the pizza box on the island. "He's doing great. I was a little worried when he came home. He seemed like he was in a pretty dark place. But you know Aldo. The bigger the challenge, the harder he's gonna knock it out of the park."

Harper poured herself a cup of coffee and topped it with creamer.

Luke opened the pizza box and breathed in the smell of sausage and green pepper. "I had dreams about this pizza," he sighed. He tossed two slices on each plate.

She grabbed the coffees and led the way into the living room.

"Is this new?" Luke asked, dropping the plates on the surface of the glossy low table angled in front of the fireplace he had never used.

Harper sat cross-legged on a floor pillow and reached for her plate. "Found it at a yard sale. Twenty bucks."

"Nice." Luke glanced around the living room. Again, the bones were the same, but now there were colorful throw pillows and books on shelves. A few pillar candles dotted flat surfaces around the room.

It was the first time in a long time that he came home to "different." Usually the only difference in the house was the thick layer of dust over everything that took him the better part of a week to exorcise.

It was going to take a lot longer than a week for him to discover all the subtle differences this time.

He sipped his coffee and dragged a slice of pizza from his plate.

"So, Joni." Harper left his mother-in-law's name hanging in the air between them.

"I feel like I owe you an apology so big I'm not sure where to start." He sighed. Guilt and that too-familiar pain made the pizza clog his throat.

"Let's start with how you felt seeing her this morning."

"Panicked." Luke shook his head. "She's the last person I ever expected to see having breakfast with my family. I didn't know what it meant. To me. To you. To her. I still don't know."

"I didn't mean to spring her on you like that. I was so surprised to have you home, I forgot everything else."

He shook his head. "It's my fault for keeping all this from you."

"Why did you?"

Luke stared into the fire. How could he ever put it into words? Why he had to keep it all in. How just her name could still tear him apart.

"I was doing everything right. Married my high school sweetheart. Joined the military. Started my own business. I had a plan. I knew where I was going.

"We were talking about buying a house. Starting a family." He swallowed hard on the word. The baby he never got to meet. "When she died…the way she died…"

Harper laid a hand on his arm. Her eyes welled.

"I lost everything that day. My past, my future. My plan." He cleared his throat, hoping to dislodge the lump. "I didn't know how I'd get through a day without her, let alone years. So I just focused on getting through the day. Work hard. Keep it locked down. Get through another day."

"Why don't you talk about her?" Harper's pizza sat forgotten in front of her.

He shook his head. "I don't know how to do that without

feeling this incredible hole. I shouldn't be here. I was the one who was prepared to die. You don't deploy without making peace with that possibility. I wasn't prepared to lose my wife."

He paused. It felt wrong that he was talking about his wife to his girlfriend. He couldn't reconcile his past and his present.

Harper crawled into his lap, straddling him. She pressed her face into his neck.

"I'm so sorry, Luke."

His hands slid under her shirt to stroke her back. If he was touching her, if she was in his arms, the darkness wasn't so dark.

"I'm sorry, baby. I wish I could give you more. You deserve everything, but I just can't…"

Harper wrapped her arms around his shoulders and held tight. "I don't want more. I want this. I want you."

"Baby. I'm so fucking selfish. You deserve someone who's going to fall head over heels in love with you. Marry you and spend the rest of his life giving you everything you've ever wanted. I can't love you. I can't love anyone again. But I want you. I want you so bad that it feels like any moment without you is empty."

She sighed against his neck. "I love you, Luke. What does this means for us?"

"If you're up for it, we take it one day at a time."

CHAPTER 43

Harper decided not to let the fact that Luke hadn't opened up to her about the baby bother her. Joni had been a big enough surprise to ambush him with, and that had sparked their first and only conversation about Karen. She considered that a great deal of progress, and there was no need to rush him if he wasn't ready to tell the entire story.

He was quiet at times, especially around Joni. Harper noticed he kept a distance between them when Joni was around. But she hoped he would be able to move past it.

She started to relax as they worked to establish a new normal. Some of the old routines remained. Luke still ran with Lola in the mornings, and Harper's pulse rate continued to ratchet up every time she saw Luke in any state of undress…or dress.

But with a new sense of permanency came new circumstances.

Harper kept her Friday shift at Remo's, and Luke became a regular. The weekly Garrison diner breakfast continued, now with all family members in the same time zone.

During the days, they worked as a team at the office. And at night, they made love with an urgency that never seemed to lessen.

She had given him the grand tour of the life he was

returning to. He admired the drywall work she and Frank had done in the walk-in closet. But the bunk beds in the spare room gave him pause.

"Harper, do we have children...and fish?"

"Surprise!" she teased. "No, I take the kids overnight every two weeks or so to give Mrs. Agosta a break. I got tired of blowing up air mattresses, so I got these from Bob's. The kids won the damn fish at the Fourth of July carnival, and I kept them here rather than give Mrs. Agosta one more thing to worry about. Ava sleeps in the double bed in the other room. She calls it her big girl bed."

Luke poked his head into the third bedroom and took in the purple throw pillows and floppy stuffed unicorn.

"You've been busy. Any surprises on the third floor?"

There weren't any on the third floor, but there were some in other areas of life. With the success of Garrison Construction's first tiny house, his dad insisted on continuing his weekly lunch dates with Harper and Beth. And who could forget the expression on Luke's face when he showed up on a job site to find Harper drywalling with Angry Frank?

On any given day, he'd come home to find his mother or Aunt Syl having coffee in the kitchen with Harper.

It was Claire who suggested that Harper and Luke host Thanksgiving to celebrate Luke's homecoming. Harper threw herself into the planning. She had an entire Pinterest board dedicated to sweet potato side dishes and bought new place settings for twelve.

Luke just smiled and nodded every time she launched into another one-sided debate of the merits of oven-roasted brussels sprouts or dried cranberries in stuffing. It would be her first big family Thanksgiving, and she was determined to make it everything she'd ever dreamed of.

Finally, the day arrived. Harper dragged herself from bed at 4:00 a.m. and started her prep. She would make this the best Thanksgiving Luke had had in a long time.

———

He was lost in a dream. Dressed in his fatigues, Luke was on the bus coming home. Buoyed by the excitement of his men, he was counting the miles to Benevolence. To Karen.

They would share their news with the family today. A new Garrison baby.

And Luke had made a decision. He would be leaving the guard. His business was growing fast enough that it demanded more of his attention. And he wanted to be the kind of father Charlie had been to him. Present. Involved.

The bus rounded a turn, and Luke could see the lot. He could pick out the spot where his family would be waiting.

But someone was missing.

The bus braked hard. The impact was unavoidable. They pitched violently to one side, and Luke felt the sickening crunch of grinding metal and shattering glass deep in his bones.

In the seconds that followed the crash, a tainted silence hung in the air. Luke dragged himself through the wreckage over shards of glass and twisted metal.

There was no movement from inside the bus, just him and his driving desire to get out.

He kicked through a window and crawled out onto the asphalt. Acrid smoke clouded his senses. Still, he was drawn forward.

Karen's car—the car they planned to trade in on an SUV for their growing family—was almost unrecognizable. The front end was smashed into the cabin. Smoke rose from the wreck. The windshield was shattered. The deployed airbag was slowly turning scarlet under the blond head that rested on it.

Wait. That wasn't right. It should have been Karen's chestnut waves on the steering wheel. Not the blond locks of…

Luke raced to the car. His shaking hands reached through the broken window and touched her. The still form shifted, and he saw her face.

Her beautiful face marred by a gash across her forehead.

Harper.

He knew with a sick certainty that he'd never again see the light in those gray eyes.

He heard screams and sirens but saw only her lifeless face.

Luke woke with his heart racing, breaking. Instinctively, he reached for Harper. He felt raw with the dredges of the dream still clinging to him. He needed Harper's touch to chase away the dark. But the bed was empty.

He pushed into a seated position, pressing his fingers into the phoenix over his aching heart. When did he start needing her touch to steady him?

It was the problem he dreaded from the beginning. He didn't have room in his heart for anyone. His memories of Karen took up all the space he had.

He shouldn't be distracting himself from his loss with someone else. How had he stumbled so far down this road?

Luke shoved out of bed and turned the water in the shower to scalding, hoping to melt the ice in his veins.

By the time he made it downstairs, the kitchen was fully involved. Food prep was happening on every flat surface. Lola and Max were happily slurping up a gravy spill near the stove.

Harper, with the light of life in her eyes, breezed past him and brushed a kiss to his cheek. "Morning, handsome." She handed him a cup of coffee and turned back to the stovetop. "I know what you're thinking, but I swear I'll clean it all up. I just want everything to be perfect."

"How many people are coming? This looks like enough food to feed a military base."

"Twelve for lunch and then Mrs. Agosta's bringing the kids by for dessert."

He did the math. "Mrs. Moretta, Aldo, Gloria. Who's number twelve?"

Harper ducked her head over the steaming pot on the stove. "I invited Joni. Her sister and brother-in-law usually host, but this year they're in North Carolina with their son."

Of course she invited Joni. The one woman whose presence reminded him of his loss and his role in it. "I don't suppose you thought to ask me first," he snapped.

He saw her wince under his words. The timer buzzed, and she sidestepped Max to pull two pies out of the oven. She set them on cooling racks on the counter and dropped the hot pads. "I'm sorry. I should have asked you first."

She looked contrite, but it wasn't enough.

"This is still my house, isn't it?"

Harper crossed her arms and leaned against the counter. She didn't fight back, and that was what he wanted. A good fight, but she wouldn't even give him that.

"I'm sorry. Sometimes I'm not sure when I'm overstepping my bounds."

"Here's a hint. When it's my family and my house or my business, it's my decision." The words were sharp enough they could have drawn blood.

Harper narrowed her gaze at him. "Understood. Thanks for clearing that up."

"I don't think you want to mess with me right now." He slammed his mug down on the counter, sending coffee sloshing over the rim.

"No, I don't. I'd rather give you a great holiday with your

family in your house." She turned her back on him and picked up the cutting board of neatly diced potatoes.

"I'm going for a run," Luke announced and stormed out.

———

He let the pounding of his feet on pavement quiet his brain. It was just a dream, but he couldn't convince himself that it was meaningless. Harper wasn't Karen. And that was the problem.

He chose his route at random, pushing himself. He focused on the speed, his breath. Houses with full driveways passed in a blur and gave way to the closed storefronts of Main Street. He turned down a street and then another until the buildings were replaced with trees and headstones.

The cemetery. Of course his subconscious had brought him to Karen. Luke slowed his pace and let the skinny ribbon of asphalt carry him to her.

There was a small, festive pumpkin resting against the black granite of her stone. Probably Joni's work.

Joni.

Try as he might, he couldn't keep his past in the past. She was a constant reminder of the life he once had. The life he would never get back. He didn't understand her blossoming relationship with Harper. Was she trying to replace the daughter she lost?

Didn't she know that Karen was irreplaceable?

He laid a hand on the stone, warm from the morning sun. "Happy Thanksgiving, Kare."

———

Harper allowed herself ten minutes between timers to run upstairs to change. The Garrisons kept it casual to the point of pajama pants and elastic waistbands for the holiday. It was a tradition she could get behind. She dragged on yoga pants and a soft, stretchy V-neck sweater the color of cranberries.

If only Luke would come around. She was more worried than she cared to admit. The anger in his tone, in his eyes, scared her and pissed her off. If he wasn't willing to talk about it, how could she help?

The doorbell rang at the same time as the oven timer buzzed. Harper wiped a stray tear from her face with a tea towel. She would not give in to the strong desire she had to kick Luke's ass today. Maybe tomorrow.

She couldn't ignore the periodic silences and the gulfs of distance that cropped up between them anymore. Something was wrong, and it needed to be addressed. She only hoped it was something fixable. She loved that man so much it shook her to the core. And when he hurt, she hurt.

Harper turned off the timer, squared her shoulders, and welcomed Luke's family into his home.

They entered en masse—Claire, Charlie, James, Ty, Sophie, and Josh. They made themselves at home in the kitchen and living room, carting in food, sneaking tastes. Charlie turned the game on the TV while Josh and the dogs took turns chasing each other through the kitchen and dining room.

She told everyone Luke was out for a run to make up for the thirty pounds of food he planned to eat. Everyone seemed to buy it.

When Luke returned, sweaty and exhausted, Harper painted a bright smile on her face and avoided him in the kitchen. She wanted to be supportive, and stabbing him with a meat fork in front of his family would not be supportive.

She was thankful that his greetings to everyone seemed genuine. He hoisted Josh up on his shoulders and gave his mother a peck on the cheek. He hip checked Sophie on his way to the refrigerator where he grabbed beers for himself and Charlie and James. Ty was on call.

Luke avoided eye contact with her, which was fine with Harper. She breathed a sigh of relief when he headed upstairs to shower again.

Joni arrived at the same time as Gloria, Aldo, and Mrs. Moretta. Thankful for the chaos of a full house, Harper stayed in the kitchen and directed her new team of helpers. Luke mainly stayed in the living room with everyone else.

She couldn't tell if he was avoiding her or Joni. Or, more likely, both.

She caught him watching her once. Joni handed over her green bean casserole and a handwritten recipe card. "It was my mother's," Joni said with a sentimental smile. "I'd like another generation to continue the tradition."

Overcome, Harper hugged her. Her first family recipe during her first family holiday. She saw Claire smiling at them across the island and felt another gaze leveled in her direction. Luke stood in the doorway, a look of shock on his face.

Their eyes met and held. Harper released Joni from the hug, and Luke grabbed another beer out of the fridge before hightailing it down the hallway.

No one else seemed to notice the tension. Not even during lunch when Harper chose a seat at the opposite end of the table from Luke.

While everyone went back for seconds—and, in James's and Ty's cases, thirds—Harper pushed turkey and mashed potatoes around her plate. It all tasted like gravy-covered packing peanuts to her.

Luke didn't touch much on his plate either, preferring to refill his wineglass instead.

Conversation flew around them.

Gloria and Aldo teased each other with forkfuls of stuffing while Mrs. Moretta and Sophie argued good-naturedly about organic vegetables.

"When Aldo was growing up, he ate all the pesticide-laden broccoli I put in front of him and turned out just fine." Mrs. Moretta, in her best turkey sweater, snickered.

Charlie and James took turns sneaking into the living room to check the score of the game.

As the action around the table died down, Joni, on Claire's left, cleared her throat. "I just wanted to thank Harper and Luke for inviting me today. It's been a hard few years, and it means so much that you still treat me like family. It's good to be reminded of what's really important in life, and you all have done that for me. So thank you for that. And Happy Thanksgiving!" She raised her wineglass.

Everyone raised their wineglasses. "To family," Charlie said, winking at Harper.

"To family," everyone echoed.

Aldo patted Harper on the back and winked at her. "Nice job, Harp," he whispered.

She snuck a glance at Luke, who was frowning into his empty glass.

CHAPTER 44

They decided to leave the dishes for later and run off some of the food with a friendly football game. As with all Garrison games, the friendly pickup fun quickly turned into a skirmish.

Harper, Luke, Aldo, and Gloria squared off in the backyard against Ty, Sophie, and James while everyone else hunkered down in front of the TV to watch football or fall asleep.

After a few leisurely jogs down the "field," Harper felt her spirits lift.

Safely out of Claire's earshot, the siblings trash-talked playfully. James scored an early touchdown, and Luke criticized Harper's defense, so on the next long bomb Ty threw, Harper was ready. She jumped on James's back and hung on for dear life as he caught the ball.

With his free hand, James spun her around to his front and tossed her over his shoulder. He took off, unhindered by the extra weight, and didn't stop until he was in the end zone next to Harper's garden.

He spun her around in circles as she laughed.

"Oh my God, put me down or I'm going to barf on you," she gasped.

Her feet no sooner hit the ground before Luke slammed into James like a runaway school bus. He shoved his younger brother back a pace.

"What the hell, man?" James shoved back. In the span of a second, they were on the ground wrestling.

"Luke!" Harper's sharp tone did nothing to break it up.

Sophie smacked Ty in the chest. "What are you waiting for, Mr. Law and Order? Get in there and break it up."

"Soph, I just ate three plates of turkey. I can't bend over."

"For the love of—" Aldo charged into the fray and dragged Luke off James. "Knock it off," he ordered, pushing Luke over to the patio. "Cool off before you make a bigger ass of yourself."

"What's your problem?" James looked more confused than pissed off.

Harper crossed her arms against the November chill. "He's been drinking. A lot," she said. "I don't know what's going on with him."

Sophie shook her head. "You better find out before Mom catches wind of this. She'll want to hook him up with a therapist next."

"That's way worse than a spanking," Aldo said.

Harper sighed and crossed the yard to Luke. He was sitting on the picnic table examining a cut on the back of his right hand. He stared as a trickle of blood rolled off his hand onto the brick of the patio.

"Come on inside. I'll clean that up for you," she said, reaching for him.

He pulled back. "I can take care of it."

Harper leaned in. "Don't be an asshole. You've got two choices. You either go upstairs with me now to get this cleaned up, or I let Sophie tell your mom you just tried to tear your brother's head off at Thanksgiving because his team was beating yours."

"He had his hands all over you."

"That's bullshit, and it's not going to go over any better with Claire. Let's go."

The muscle in his jaw ticked, but he got up and followed her inside.

In their bathroom upstairs, she gently cleaned the cut with soap and water. "I can do this myself," he grumbled.

Harper ignored him and taped a piece of gauze over the wound.

"What? So now you're pissed at me?"

"Now? More like still," she said coolly.

"What the hell do you have to be pissed about? You got everything you wanted."

He stood up, towering over her. Hands on hips, Harper went toe-to-toe with him.

"I don't know what is going on in that head of yours, but I'm guessing the beer and wine didn't help. I'm pissed because once again, you can't be bothered to talk to me. What is going on with you? Is it coming home? Joni? Me? I'm not a freaking mind reader." She poked him in the chest. "You're upset about something, and it's probably valid. But instead of talking to me about it, you just want to wallow in it and lash out. *That's* what I'm pissed off about." She wiped her hands on the towel and threw it back on the counter. "So either go find someone to talk to or find some way to deal with it. Don't take it out on everyone else."

Harper made a move to brush past him but found herself caged against the vanity and between Luke's arms.

She lifted her chin and stared him in the eye. For a second, she caught a glimpse of something beyond sadness. And then it was gone, and he was crushing his mouth to hers with a need so intense it stole her breath.

"Goddammit. Why do you do this to me?" Luke asked as his lips roamed her face. His hands streaked under her sweater. Busy fingers cruised to the front closure of her bra and flicked it open.

He filled his hands with her breasts and brought his mouth to hers.

They moaned together.

He slid a hand into the waistband of her yoga pants, fingers sliding over her slick folds and into her heat.

"I hate how much I want you." His fingers drove into her tight center, and she gasped at the invasion. His erection begged to be released.

He drove into her again and again, spreading her thighs farther apart with his knee. She wanted to stay angry, but her body didn't care. When Luke's hands were on her, nothing else mattered.

"Luke!" Her breathy moan brought him back, and he pulled his fingers out of her. Dropping his forehead to hers, he tried to catch his breath.

"Why do you let me use you like this?"

And with that, he pushed back and left the room.

Harper's knees shook, and she leaned against the sink for support. Use her? Was that what he thought he was doing?

———

It was hours before everyone left, but not before every plate, dish, and bowl were spotless and put back in their rightful places. Lola and Max took care of any floor cleanup and helped themselves to the secret plate of turkey that Charlie put under the dining room table for them.

Night had fallen, and Harper sat down with a cup of coffee in the kitchen to fight the exhaustion of an early rising

361

and a full day of chaos. She was physically and mentally exhausted.

Luke had stopped drinking after their encounter upstairs. He had withdrawn to the living room where he remained, watching TV.

How long could he live like this before he broke down and talked to her about what was going on in his head?

A stack of envelopes shoved against the backsplash caught her eye. Judging from the height of the pile, it was several days' worth of mail. Luke's disinterest in opening it was one thing that hadn't changed during his deployment or since his return.

She flipped through the stack, sorting as she went.

Harper's fingers paused on the envelope with handwriting as familiar as her own. She held the letter gingerly between her fingers. Was it her imagination, or could she actually feel the hate through the paper?

She had read each and every one of the letters in the past few years. Sometimes she boosted her bravery with a large glass of wine. Sometimes she waited until she was good and mad about something else before opening one. Sometimes, if things were good, she put it away for a few weeks before opening.

Anything to help build a wall between her and the violence simmering within the ink. However, the luxury of waiting days or weeks to read had passed. Now there was an urgency as time ticked down. Someday, she promised herself, she would feel nothing but pity when she opened these letters. And someday they would stop.

Taking a deep breath, she tore open the envelope. It was the usual single piece of lined notebook paper. The handwriting was a scrawling script that slanted and slashed across the page.

My dear Harper,

It's been too many years since our time together. Why haven't you come to see me? Are you afraid? I think of you often. There is never a shortage of time here to think and to plan. I have so many plans for you and me. How will I ever choose where to begin? How will I impress upon you the price for these last twelve years? Because there will be a price to pay for taking so much of a man's life. What have you done with these years? Whatever it is, it won't be enough to cover the cost of what you took from me. I suppose we will both find out soon enough. Until December.

Daddy

December. The years had finally ticked down to a handful of weeks and days. She went upstairs and pulled the box out of the back of the closet. She kicked the lid off and tucked the letter into the folder with the rest.

She would copy it and send it on its way tomorrow. Melissa would add it to her own file, but there was nothing either of them could do now. No more stays. Not this time.

She needed to tell Luke. It wasn't just her anymore. Her past would now affect others. There was no way to keep this from him without putting him in danger. She wanted him to know. It was time to stop running, hiding.

Harper put the lid on the box and slid it back into its spot on the closet floor. She went downstairs and hovered just inside the living room door.

CHAPTER 45

Luke pretended not to see her standing in the doorway and stared blankly at the screen. He just wanted this day to be over.

"Luke, can I talk to you about something? It's kind of important."

He glanced in her direction, and she took it as an okay.

"Something happened, and I'm a little worried—"

He flicked a button on the remote, muting the TV. "I need to talk to you about something too."

"Okay. You go first." She waited where she was.

"This isn't working," he said, his tone short.

"What isn't?"

"You being here. Us."

She stayed silent, eyes wide.

He stood up, pressed on.

"'It's just a night. It's just a month. We're just fostering.' You came here and just took over. You keep thinking if you tell me everything is just temporary that I'll let it slide. And maybe you were right. But it's not going to work anymore."

Harper flinched. "Luke, I'm so sorry. I never intended—"

"You built an entire life around a relationship that doesn't exist."

He saw the shock, the hurt.

"You know it exists. This isn't something I made up in my head. I love you."

"I don't love you."

She took a step back as if the words physically hurt her.

"We're done here." He turned to stalk out of the room, but Harper grabbed his arm.

"Is this because of Karen? I know you blame yourself. But it's not your fault."

"We're not discussing this. You don't know." He tried to shrug her off.

"Luke, I know about the baby."

He froze under her grip before he rounded on her.

"I let you into my home, into my life, and this is how you repay me? Invading my privacy?" It was boiling over. There was no keeping the lid on it now.

"I'm so sorry, Luke. I'm so sorry that you lost your family. I'm sorry that you feel responsible." Her gray eyes welled with tears, and he hated himself for it.

"I don't *feel* responsible. I *am* responsible."

"You can't live the rest of your life blaming yourself for an accident that had nothing to do with you."

"She was coming to bring me home." He turned and paced. "We were going to tell everyone about the baby. Do you know how that feels? To anticipate the happiest moment of your life, to live for it for weeks only to have it destroyed in front of you. I got off that bus, and she was dying in mangled metal. Our baby died while I walked across that asphalt to where my family should have been. They died because I wasn't there. They died because I came back."

The tears were coursing down her cheeks now. He looked at her with her sunny golden hair, her angel face.

She wasn't for him. No one was. He had had his chance and blew it.

"You're only here because she's gone." He whispered the words, which somehow made them sharper. "And you can't take her place. Not with Joni and not with me."

She nodded slowly. "I know that. I'm not trying to do that."

"You shouldn't be here. I don't want to do this anymore. I can't do this, Harper. I need you to go."

She stood there, watching him, hope and hurt in her eyes.

"I can't look at you without wishing she was here."

The hope died.

She dropped her gaze to her feet. "I'll pack a bag and come back for the rest of my things later."

He didn't say a word as she left the living room, just held on to the doorframe for dear life.

"I'm the one who shouldn't be here," he whispered to the dark.

———

Upstairs, Harper did what she had done dozens of times before. She packed a bag.

Numbness had swallowed her, and she was grateful. She knew when the pain broke through it would be too much to bear. Keep moving. Don't think. Just get it done. Get somewhere safe and then…and then.

She tucked some toiletries and makeup into a small zippered bag and hastily packed a few outfits and her running shoes. She grabbed her phone charger from the nightstand.

Lola and Max followed her every move. Lola watched with those soulful sad eyes while Max scampered and whimpered. They knew something was wrong.

She knelt down to bury her face in Lola's short fur. "I love you guys so much. Thank you for being my family. I have to go, but I need you to take care of Daddy. He needs you right now. So take care of him the way you took care of me when he wasn't around. Okay? I promise I'll figure something out. I'll come back and see you."

Lola sighed, and Max put his front paws on her leg and yipped.

Harper did her best to swallow the lump in her throat.

He watched her with the dogs from the doorway, and his stomach twisted. He was throwing her out, ending things. While he was taking back his life, she was still worried about taking care of him.

He wasn't good for her, and she had to learn that.

Harper Wilde had to learn to take care of herself. He swiped a hand over his face. God, who was going to be there to keep her safe, to remind her to charge her phone or get gas or lock the doors at night?

She was a smart, sweet, beautiful girl. She wouldn't be alone for long.

For just a second, he let himself think about her with another man. His hands fisted at his sides. She would be loved. She would be taken care of. It was what she deserved.

Harper glanced up from her packing, and noticing him in the doorway, she swiped away the tears. She didn't make eye contact, just zipped her bag closed and slung it over her shoulder.

She gave the dogs a last scratch. He saw the tremble in her jaw and watched with admiration as she pulled it back in, tamped it down. His free-spirited girl had a spine of steel.

"Here," he said, holding out her phone. "I didn't want you to forget it."

Wordlessly, she took it and slid it in her back pocket.

She still hadn't raised her gaze to meet his. He was almost grateful. Looking into those storm-cloud-gray eyes might undo him.

"I want you to take this too." He held out a roll of cash.

She ignored him and pushed past him into the hallway.

He followed her down the stairs. "Harper, take the money. I don't want to worry about you sleeping in your car or—"

She rounded on him at the foot of the stairs. Their eyes met, and in that second, he realized for the first time that he had no idea what was going on in her head. She had shut it down, cut him off.

It cut him to the quick.

But this was the right thing to do. He chanted it in his head. Just get through it. Like ripping off a bandage. A little pain now instead of the years of suffering he would cause her by not being the man she deserved.

"Please. Take it." He tried to tuck it into her hand, but she let the bills fall to the floor.

"I'm no longer your concern," she said flatly. She looked him in the eye, into his very heart, and turned and walked out the front door, closing it softly behind her.

Luke watched her toss her bag in her back seat and climb behind the wheel. She never looked back at the house. Just backed out and drove away.

He walked into the living room and sat down on the couch, expecting to feel relief. But there was only a gnawing emptiness.

Where was she going to go?

Why hadn't he waited until morning? He could have helped her find a place, taken her somewhere. Now, thanks to him, she was roaming around at night.

He stood up and started pacing.

Everything that his gaze rested on was connected to her.

The furniture. The glossy magazines and paperbacks under the coffee table. The raspberry pink fleece hanging next to the front door. Had she even taken a coat with her?

He pulled the fleece off the hook and brought it to his face. It smelled like her. Sunshine and lemons.

He didn't feel relief. He felt sick.

Maybe he should pack her things for her. So every damn thing in his house didn't remind him of her.

———

Luke woke up on the couch to the early gray dawn. Both dogs were snuggled against him. He was still clutching Harper's fleece to his chest.

He had finally dozed off barely two hours earlier after carefully packing her things into the boxes neatly stacked in the dining room, each one labeled "Harper" and a description of the contents in permanent marker.

After months here, she still hadn't managed to accumulate more than a dozen boxes of things. He would give her the furniture when she settled wherever she was going and most of the kitchen stuff that had appeared in drawers and cabinets while she was here.

He glanced down at the coffee table and saw the picture. Harper and her parents. She had left it behind, tucked in a box in the closet. He'd keep it safe for her until she was somewhere she could call home.

Luke rubbed a hand across his chest. The hollow was still there. His life was once again his own. He was free to focus on his plan, his goal. Didn't have to worry about anyone else.

So why did he feel like he was suffocating?

He went into the kitchen to grab some coffee, but the pot was empty.

The quiet was too much. He whistled for the dogs and let them out the back door.

The ache would go away, he told himself as he watched Max chase Lola around the garden that hadn't been there when he left.

CHAPTER 46

He arrived at the office early enough that no one else was there. His gaze immediately scanned to Harper's desk. When had that happened? How was that the first place he looked every time he came up the stairs?

Shit. He was going to have to tell everyone that they were down an office manager. There would be questions that he wouldn't answer. And more paperwork that he wouldn't file. But this space was his again. It was what he wanted.

Wasn't it?

Luke mashed the buttons on the coffee maker until it started to brew. He took his first mug into his office and kicked the door shut behind him.

He was in the middle of listening to a voicemail for the third time, because he kept spacing out, when Frank burst in without knocking.

"Why the hell is your door closed?"

"Because I wanted it closed."

Frank shrugged. "Okay. Next question. Why is your woman calling in sick to me?"

Luke stood up before he thought better of it. "Did she say where she is?"

Frank crossed his arms. "No. Don't you know where she is?"

Luke ignored the question and sank back into his chair. "She said she was sick?" Well, at least she was alive. Somewhere.

"Said she wasn't coming in today because she wasn't feeling well. Why are you hearing this for the first time? Why didn't she just roll over and tell you herself?"

"Harper's not going to be around anymore," Luke said briskly. "Let me make this call and then we'll go out to the Adams site." He turned back to the phone and started dialing, dismissing Frank and his dumbfounded expression.

———

Harper woke curled in a ball in a sunny bedroom. She was still dressed in last night's clothes. There were no strong arms wrapped around her. No dogs at her feet.

She was alone.

She wrapped her fingers around the edge of the quilt and pulled it over her head. She wanted to block it all out. The sun. The hurt. The loneliness.

———

"What?" Luke didn't mean to snap at Sophie, but he already knew why she was calling. It would figure that Sophie would be the first person Harper would go to.

"That's a fine greeting for your favorite sister."

He shifted the phone to his other ear. "Sorry. What do you need?"

"Just some reassurance. I was supposed to meet Harper for lunch, and she didn't show. She's not answering her cell. And I tried the office, and they said she didn't come in today. I know I'm just being silly, but…" Sophie trailed off.

Luke remembered another time when Sophie had tried to

reach someone and couldn't find her. All their lives had changed that day. It wasn't just his.

"I guess Harper didn't tell you?"

"Tell me what? Did you send her to the spa for the day? Is she adopting another dog?"

"We broke up."

He was ready to yank the phone away from his ear in the event of a deafening screech. But there was only silence.

"Soph? Are you there?"

More silence. And then finally a whispered response.

"I…I don't understand. You guys are so…"

"It just wasn't working out. We wanted different things." The words clogged his throat.

"You just…broke up? Where is she?"

"I don't know. She left last night."

"Is she okay? I mean… Jesus, Luke. I feel like I got sucker punched. I didn't see this coming. I can't imagine how she feels."

"It's Harper. Of course she's okay. She's been through worse than a breakup. She always lands on her feet."

Sophie was quiet for a moment. "Luke, she loved you with everything she had. She waited six months for you. She's not just going to land on her feet. And if you're not going to try to find her, then I will."

He wasn't about to admit that he spent the forty-five minutes he had allotted for lunch driving around town looking for her car. He just wanted to know that she was safe. That was all.

"I don't think we have anything to worry about."

"You're worried. I can hear it in your tone."

"I don't have a tone."

"What if something happened to her? We both know shit happens to good people. And we sure as hell know she's a trouble magnet. What if she got kidnapped trying to check into a hotel?"

Luke would have laughed if he hadn't already thought of that exact scenario. He'd called both motels in town that morning to see if Harper was registered.

"She called Frank this morning and told him she wouldn't be in."

"And that's good enough for you? 'She called Frank, so now I don't have to worry.'" He could hear Sophie getting angry.

"No, it's not good enough for me, Soph. She's not answering her phone, she hasn't been on Facebook, Aldo and Gloria haven't seen her. I thought she would have gone to your house last night. Short of calling the cops, I don't know what else to do."

"Why did you do it?"

"How do you know it wasn't Harper breaking things off with me?"

"Because Harper isn't a chickenshit who runs when the going gets scary."

"I'm not a chickenshit. It wasn't working. She built this whole life around me without me having a say, and then everyone's so fucking surprised when it turns out that wasn't what I wanted." He was yelling now but couldn't seem to stop.

Unintimidated, Sophie yelled back. "Yeah, I can't think of any man who would want a woman who thought he hung the stars in the goddamn sky. Who worked her ass off making his house a home, not to mention organizing his work life so he could concentrate on something other than chaos."

Luke swore. "You don't understand."

"Oh, I do understand. I just keep waiting for *you* to wake up and understand. You just threw away something that most people only dream about having. I can't even talk to you right now."

He could picture his sister pacing in exasperation. "Are you going to look for her?"

"What do you care?"

"Just— If you find her, let me know that she's safe." Luke hung up the phone and tossed it on the passenger seat.

He stared at the front of his house. Harper's planters from the summer had been stowed in the garage and replaced with ropes of heavy green garland. She had asked about Christmas lights. She had never had Christmas lights before.

He had been parked in the driveway for a full ten minutes before Sophie called. He couldn't concentrate on work, so he came home. But the thought of setting foot in the house and facing the stack of boxes, all the evidence of Harper in his life, boxed up and put away as if she had never been there, was enough to keep him in the truck.

When would his life be his own again?

He'd go for a run, he decided. A long, cold run to clear his mind.

———

Harper stirred at the knock on her door.

When it opened, she pulled the covers down and directed a watery smile at the tray-bearing woman.

"I made you some tea and toast," Joni said, putting the tray down on the nightstand.

"You don't have to go to any trouble, Joni. I'm just so grateful that you let me stay here."

She patted Harper's hand. "It's nice having someone else in the house."

"Even if they don't leave the bed?" Harper tried to laugh, but it came out as a hiccup.

Joni handed her the sturdy mug of tea.

Harper took a sip, and her eyes widened as the hot honeyed liquid slid down her raw throat.

"I hope you don't mind that I put a little whiskey in it. It always made me feel better."

Harper wrapped her hands around the mug and sighed. There would be no feeling better. There was only now and the ache. "This is a nice room," she said softly. The walls were a dusky blue green accented with ocean prints. A large window seat overlooked the backyard of the comfortable two-story.

"Thank you. It used to be Karen's. She helped me repaint it when she moved out."

"When she and...when she got married?" Luke's name hurt too much to say.

Joni nodded. She sat down on the edge of the bed. "You're a sweet girl, Harper. Everything is going to work out in the end."

Harper bit her lip to fight back the impending flood of tears. She sniffled weakly instead and squeezed Joni's hand.

Joni glanced around the room. "You're not the only girl who's cried over Luke Garrison in this room." A ghost of a smile played at her lips.

"Karen cried over him? But they were so perfect for each other."

"Honey, no one is perfect for anyone at eighteen."

"Did they fight?"

"They broke up." Joni nodded at Harper's wide eyes. "Luke broke up with Karen a few weeks before graduation. He was joining the guard, and he wanted Karen to go to college, but she wanted to get married. He thought she was throwing her future away and ended things."

"How did they get back together?"

"Karen enrolled in school and went out on a date with

Lincoln Reed. She and Luke were back together by the next afternoon."

"Is that why he doesn't like Linc?"

"Oh, there's always been a rivalry there."

Harper remembered Luke's reaction to Linc hauling her out of the lake and what happened later that night. Would she ever feel like that again? Desired? Craved?

Now she only felt discarded.

"So your phone has been 'blowing up,' as you young people would say, out there since this morning."

Harper's eyes widened. "I'm sorry. I should have turned it off."

"It's no trouble. But there may be some people worried about you."

Harper shook her head and cleared her throat. "I just can't. Not yet."

"Is there anyone you want me to contact? Just to tell them you're all right?"

Harper started to shake her head. "I don't know. I feel like everyone here belongs to him, and I don't want to complicate that for him. I don't want him to think that I'm trying to…"

"Turn everyone against him for being an idiot?" Joni supplied helpfully.

"Yeah, that. Pretty much exactly that." Harper managed a shaky laugh. "I don't want anyone to feel obligated to choose because this is his home, and I'm just…passing through." She couldn't stop the tears this time.

Joni took the tea from her and handed her a fresh box of tissues. "Don't ever think of the relationships you've built here as just 'passing through.' Benevolence belongs to you just as much as anyone else, and we're all lucky to have you here."

"I just love him so much." Harper sniffled.

"I know you do, sweetie."

"And I'm so sorry for bringing all this into your house. It can't be easy on you dealing with me when it's Karen who loved him first. And the only reason I'm here is because she isn't." She buried her face in her crumpled tissue.

Joni's eyebrows shot up. "Harper Wilde. I'm surprised at you. Don't you see it? Karen brought you here for Luke. You are exactly what he needs to get him to start living life again." She fingered the fine stitches on a bright blue quilt patch. "If there's anything that would infuriate my daughter, it would be watching the people she loved refusing to live and love again. I was doing the same thing. Hiding behind blame and guilt, just trying to hold on to what was. And in doing so, I missed too many years of what is. But that's all changing now. I'm not going to hide anymore. And eventually, neither will Luke."

Harper nodded, but she knew she would be long gone before then. She would be in another job in another town far away. She would have another casual circle of friends who could never quite fill the hole in her heart where family should be.

Maybe it was her destiny to always be a little bit lonely. To always be hungry for love.

"You're exhausted, you poor thing. You just rest and sleep, and we'll talk again in the morning."

Harper nodded, her shoulders slumped.

"How about I let Gloria know you're here? Then no one will worry, okay?"

She reached for the tea and cupped it in her cold hands. "Okay. Please tell her that I'll talk to her later when I'm...ready."

"You take all the time you need. You're welcome here for as long as you want to stay."

Harper's eyes welled with tears. "Thank you, Joni," she whispered.

CHAPTER 47

After almost three full days, Harper vowed that she was done crying. She wasn't done hurting, but her body had wrung out every drop of water through her eyes and was now barely functioning on dehydration.

It was time to get up.

She dragged herself out of the sunny cocoon of Karen's bedroom and into the bathroom where she did her best to shower off the grief.

She wiped a hand through the steam in the mirror and stared into hollow gray eyes. "Just keep moving," she whispered.

Back in the room, she rummaged through her bag and pulled on a pair of jeans and a sweatshirt before padding barefoot downstairs. Sophie and Gloria had visited her the day before and brought her more clothes. Harper didn't even want to imagine how Sophie's conversation with Luke went.

Her head ached, as did her heart. But she was on her feet. She would survive this. Somehow.

She found a note from Joni on the counter.

Running errands. If you're reading this, please eat!
Sandwich fixings in fridge. Ice cream in freezer.

She ignored the suggestion of food and instead grabbed a glass of water before sitting down at the dining table with her phone. Time to rejoin the world.

Her voicemail was full, and a scan of the numbers in her call log indicated that Sophie had done most of the blowing up.

Another handful from Gloria, several from work, and a few from Aldo, Beth, James, Claire, and Hannah, who likely had no idea what was happening. There were even two from Angry Frank.

She added a layer of guilt to everything else she was feeling. It had been selfish of her to shut down and shut out. She had worried her friends needlessly and owed them better than that.

She would make up for it.

Starting with the night she left, there were two messages a day from *him*. She wasn't ready to hear his voice or his "I'm sorry, but this is the way it has to be" reasoning, so she archived them and listened to the rest.

Next, she tackled the texts and then moved on to emails. There was a lot of work to catch up on, and handling it from Joni's house on her phone wasn't going to cut it.

Harper checked the time: 5:00 p.m. on a Sunday. The office should be empty. She'd go in and see what kind of progress she could make. Alone. She didn't owe it to him. She owed it to the rest of the team there. She'd get them back on track before moving on.

Joni's house was farther from the office than she was used to, and she made the trip unnecessarily longer by taking a less direct route that didn't pass his house. She may be ready to crawl out of her bed cocoon, but that didn't mean she was interested in pouring salt in fresh wounds.

She breathed a sigh of relief when she found the office dark and locked. Safe.

She locked herself inside and leaned against the door. Refusing to look into his office, Harper immediately decided to shift the position of her desk. There would be a new focus for her remaining days here.

Satisfied with her new view through the window—her back to the empty office—she got to work.

There were a few new invoices to enter and payroll to review for next week's checks. She was working her way through staff and client emails when her phone signaled a text.

Luke: Frank says you emailed. Are you at the office? Can we talk?

Her stomach churned, and she shoved her phone in a drawer. How would she ever be able to look at him when she could barely read the words he wrote?

She had to leave Benevolence. There was no way around it. There couldn't be any running into him at Remo's or on the jogging trails. She wouldn't survive it.

She knew what she had to do.

To: luke@garrisoncon.com
From: harper@garrisoncon.com
Subject: Two weeks' notice

Please accept this email as my two weeks' notice. I will be leaving Garrison Construction on December 15. Until that time, I plan to start my workdays at 6:00 p.m.
Please don't be in the office when I'm here.

She hit Send and closed her eyes and covered her face with her hands. "Just keep moving," she whispered to herself.

Her phone started ringing from the drawer. She slid it open a crack and saw his name on the screen. Harper snapped the drawer shut and got up to pace. Part of her wanted nothing more than to hear his voice saying her name, but she knew the only way to get through this was without contact.

Her desk phone rang, and she rolled her eyes. The only thing he could possibly want to say to her was that he didn't want her working her two weeks. *Well, tough crap, Garrison. This isn't about you.* She had a job to do and people depending on her.

Harper's cell phone dinged. A new text message from Sophie.

Sophie: Did you just email Luke? He got up from the table so fast he knocked over his water. Now he's pacing Mom's front yard swearing and dialing like a madman.

Harper felt her lips curve just a little.

On cue, her cell phone rang again. It was him. She hit Ignore and texted Sophie back.

Harper: Just emailed my two weeks' notice. Had a feeling he wouldn't be happy about two more weeks with me. I'll be working nights until the 15th.

Sophie responded immediately.

Sophie: Almost feel sorry for the idiot. Looks like a shaggy insomniac. I think I see some gray hairs. Mom had to ask him to pass the beets three times before it registered.

Harper sighed and tucked her phone back in the drawer. She didn't want to think of him at all, let alone the entire Garrison family gathered around the dinner table. It was the closest thing to family she ever had, and the circle had closed without her.

Maybe this was all there was for her.

She turned her attention back to her computer and saw a reply from Luke.

To: harper@garrisoncon.com
From: luke@garrisoncon.com
Re: Two weeks' notice

If you don't answer your phone, I'm coming over there now.

And another one.

To: harper@garrisoncon.com
From: luke@garrisoncon.com
Re: Two weeks' notice

And if you leave, I'm showing up at Joni's.

Harper set her jaw. He was the one who wanted it this way.

To: luke@garrisoncon.com
From: harper@garrisoncon.com
Re: Two weeks' notice

I respected your wishes. I expect you to respect mine. I don't want to talk. I'm only staying on until the 15th so you can find a replacement. And as much as you would prefer to not have me here at all, you don't know how to use the new payroll system or the database. I won't be in your way as long as you stay out of the office when I'm here at night.

He replied within a few minutes.

To: harper@garrisoncon.com
From: luke@garrisoncon.com
Re: Two weeks' notice

Fine. Let me, or Frank if you prefer, know what you need. Are you okay?

Harper decided not to respond and went back to work.

From his truck, Luke stared at the lone light in the window, willing a shadow to appear. He didn't know what he was doing here. He'd bolted from his parents' table and, without so much as a goodbye, driven the five minutes to the office where he knew she was.

He hadn't seen her in three days.

She had responded to him. After he threatened her, of course, but at least she responded. She was alive and safe. And that was enough. Wasn't it?

He looked around the deserted parking lot. Why was he here? He ended it because he couldn't stand to see Harper throw her life away on a relationship that would never be what she deserved.

And yet here he was, hoping for just a glimpse of her through the window.

He just wanted to make sure she was all right, he decided. Maybe then he could sleep.

He scrubbed his hands over his face. The woman was out of his life and still driving him crazy.

It was time to regain some semblance of control. He started up the truck and headed home.

———

Harper woke with a start just a few hours after tumbling into bed. She hadn't left the office until after midnight. She was surprised at how much work she could get done without being interrupted by phone calls and visitors.

And Luke's presence.

It was a dim, gray morning. The clouds looked like they held the promise of snow.

There was no use lying in bed thinking or pretending that she could go back to sleep. Harper got up and pulled on running tights and a fleece. She laced up her sneakers and quietly left the house. She grabbed a fuzzy headband and gloves in Day-Glo yellow from her car and hit the pavement.

Benevolence was still asleep at this predawn hour. There was something peaceful about being utterly alone.

She hit her stride and changed her course to head into the park where streetlights dimly lit the path around the lake in the frosty dawn.

Aldo had called a few times to see if she wanted to go running, but she knew it would just complicate things between him and Luke. Luke needed his life back, and that included his friends too.

She shook her head. Focus on the breath. Forget thinking. Forget him.

Her breath puffed out in white clouds in a rhythm that matched her footfalls.

It was just her and the cold morning air. Nothing else.

CHAPTER 48

He spotted her as if his thoughts had conjured her in front of him. A flash of blond hair and cherry-red sweatshirt as she crossed the path a hundred yards in front of him.

Luke stumbled in his stride and stopped. Maybe his sleep-deprived mind was playing tricks on him. Harper would never willingly be out of bed at this hour. Especially not after leaving the office so late.

Maybe he wasn't the only one who couldn't sleep.

He thought about turning around, running home. And then of catching up to her and just running next to her. She shouldn't be out alone at this hour. Why didn't she worry about these things?

He didn't bother asking himself why he did. He just returned to his run and turned right where he planned to go straight.

He caught sight of her at the lake and tried not to notice that it was the same spot where he came home to her just a few weeks earlier. She stood with her shoulders hunched against the cold, watching the slow rise of the sun. It was just beginning to crest the trees, turning the grayed-out clouds a rosy pink.

He stopped just within the tree line. She didn't want to

see him. And he was half afraid if he talked to her, he'd end up asking her to come home.

So he stayed where he was. Even from this distance, he could tell she was crying. Her shoulders shook, and she kept swiping her sleeves over her face.

He knew he was an asshole for putting her through this. He couldn't help it, but he could feel good and guilty about it.

The sun broke through the trees, warming the lake's icy waters with its pink glow. Luke watched her straighten her shoulders and take a deep breath and then another before she returned to the path and resumed her run, her blond ponytail swinging rhythmically behind her.

He watched until she was out of view before turning around and running home.

———

His mood did not improve when he arrived at the office and found newly drafted ad copy for an office manager job listing on his desk and instructions on how to use Craigslist.

Luke slammed down his coffee mug and barely resisted the urge to crumple the paper and throw it in the trash.

She was just doing her job. A job that she clearly excelled at, judging by the updated bookkeeping entries and the completed payroll awaiting his approval.

He shuffled the help wanted ad to the bottom of the pile and picked up a folder labeled Bonuses/Raises. Inside, he found a neat spreadsheet detailing the projected profit for the year and two breakdowns of potential bonus amounts and hourly rate raises.

She had remembered when he said in passing he wanted to look at the year-end books and see what he could give the crew. He stared out the bank of windows behind him, watching as the first flakes of snow began to fall.

Goddamn it. What was he going to do without her?

———

That night when Harper arrived at work, a familiar woof greeted her. Lola jogged to her with Max skittering behind her. She dropped to her knees and let the dogs wiggle and lick their greetings. Lola had a note on her collar.

> Thought you might be missing them as much as they miss you. You can drop them off at the house or text me when you leave, and I'll come pick them up.
>
> Luke
>
> PS: Are you up for shared custody? Let's talk.

Harper spotted two new dog beds under her desk. There was a basket of toys that had already been tipped over and dug through.

She handed the note to Lola, who promptly carried it to her bed and shredded it. Shared custody? She hadn't thought that far ahead. She had just assumed that when she left, the dogs would come with her.

Would they be like those long-distance co-parents who met in a fast food parking lot to switch the kids from one car to another, barely a civil word spoken? Ugh. No. She couldn't do that. There had to be a better way.

She shot off a quick text to Luke.

> **Harper:** Thanks for leaving the dogs. I'll be done here at midnight.

He responded immediately.

Luke: They miss you. I'll pick them up after you leave.

Harper: Thank you.

She shoved her phone in the desk drawer and went back to work.

It was their new normal.

———

Harper pushed her cart into the vestibule of the grocery store, enjoying the puff of heat from above. The snow had brought with it an early winter, and she couldn't seem to get warm enough. But that was most likely due to the giant block of ice that had once been her heart and the fact that her winter coat was still at Luke's.

She was clawing her way through the pain, but what lay beyond that didn't seem worth the fight yet. Maybe someday she wouldn't feel as if her smile was painted on. Maybe someday she would remember what it was like to laugh. Maybe someday the hole wouldn't be so big.

For now, she had shopping to do. She had volunteered to pick up Joni's groceries and even made a show of adding a few things to the list for herself. Fake it 'til you make it was her motto. Well, fake it until you can pass out exhausted in bed. She'd worry about making it later.

Harper navigated through the produce section, half-heartedly perusing the bananas and turnips. She was approaching the scale when Georgia Rae intercepted her.

"Well, hello there, sweetie! It's good to see you out and about since...well, you know."

She did know. Thank you very much, Georgia Rae. "Thanks, Georgia Rae. How are you doing? Ready for Christmas?"

Harper felt like a robot mechanically spitting out pleasantries. She walked alongside Georgia Rae as the woman chattered on, nodding and making um-hmm noises. They rounded the aisle to find Linc in conversation with Sheila from Remo's and Luke's neighbor, Mr. Scotts, by the beverage cooler.

They all called out greetings. This was why grocery shopping took forever in Benevolence. You knew literally every single person in the store and were obliged to talk to each of them.

Why hadn't she gone shopping out of town?

Linc winked at her. "Hey there, sunshine. How's it going?"

"It's going," Harper said, trying for positive and landing somewhere around morose.

She was saved from further interaction by Peggy Ann. The curvy cashier hustled down the aisle, frantically waving her hands. "I'm sorry to interrupt," she said in the loudest whisper possible. "But, Harper, you're going to want to avoid who just came in."

Harper felt her stomach flip-flop.

Georgia Rae peeked around the corner into produce and gasped. "He's here!"

Panic careened through her system. Not here. Not him. She couldn't see him.

While Harper froze to the spot, Georgia Rae took control of the situation. "Mr. Scotts, you and I will run interference. Linc, you take Harper here and stash her somewhere until it's safe. Sheila, you run distraction if he gets too close. Everybody move!" She clapped her hands, and they dispersed.

Harper watched as Peggy Ann hurried back toward her register and Mr. Scotts steered his cart of frozen shrimp and canned dog food toward produce with Georgia Rae.

She remained rooted through the blur of activity until Linc took her by the arm and dragged her into the beverage cooler.

"Wait! My cart," she hissed.

"Leave it," he said, shutting the door behind him.

Harper put her hands over her face and bent at the waist, trying to catch her breath.

"Are you okay?" Linc asked, laying a broad hand on her back.

"If you offer me mouth-to-mouth right now, I'll kill you."

His laugh had her straightening.

"I'm sorry," he said. "I don't mean to laugh, but I believe you. You look like you've been put through the wringer and are ready to come out swinging."

"That's actually kind of nice," Harper said with suspicion.

"I'm a nice guy," Linc insisted.

She shivered. Between the snow, the cooler, and the danger of coming face-to-face with the man who broke her heart, Harper didn't think she could get any colder.

"Come here before you turn into an ice pop." Linc wrapped his arms around her and pulled her in to him.

She resisted for a second, but the heat coming off him was too comforting. Harper tried to hold herself stiffly against him, but when he shoved her head against his chest, she gave up the struggle and let herself be held.

"You're not going to start crying, are you?" Linc asked.

Harper sighed. "No, I think I can control myself."

"Good. It's going to be okay, you know?"

"Really? Do you have some magic fireman crystal ball?"

"It's more like one of those magic eight balls."

This time, she laughed a little. It sounded foreign to her ears.

"What does your magic eight ball say?"

"That you're going to be just fine. You're strong and smart and look really, really good in a bikini. You're not meant for a life of misery and hiding in beer coolers."

"That's an oddly specific magic eight ball you have."

Linc gripped her shoulders and made her look at him.

"You're going to be good. You're a fighter. That counts, especially when life sucks."

"Thanks, Linc." The small smile felt good.

"And if that asshole out there doesn't figure out what an amazing catch you are, you just come by the fire station and—"

Harper clapped her hand over his mouth. "Don't ruin this touching moment by being gross."

"I was just going to tell you I'll let you slide down my pole," he said through her fingers.

This time, the laugh was real. "And the moment is over."

Linc grinned.

They froze when the door swung open. "That's great, Georgia Rae. I'm just going to grab—"

Luke stopped midsentence in the door of the cooler. His eyes went from confused to fury in the span of a heartbeat. Harper struggled to free herself from Linc's grip, but he only pushed her behind him.

"Garrison," Linc said, his tone cooler than the chilled air.

"Well, you don't waste any time, do you?" Harper saw Luke's jaw twitch when she peeked around Linc's back.

"I don't know what you're talking about," Linc said evenly.

"I wasn't talking to you."

Harper felt the sick change to fury in her gut. She made a move to sidestep Linc, but he was already halfway across the cooler. Luke met him in the middle, and Harper shrieked when the first blow landed.

Georgia Rae, Mr. Scotts, Sheila, and Peggy Ann stood in the doorway, mouths agape.

"Call Ty," Harper yelled, grabbing at a thrashing arm and a jacket. "Stop it! Both of you."

She wedged herself between them, Luke at her front and Linc at her back.

"You ever touch her again, and I'll—"

Harper slapped her hands against Luke's chest. "Shut up! Just shut up!" She shoved him back with all her strength. "You have no say anymore in who does and doesn't touch me. I don't belong to you anymore." Her voice broke, and she hated herself for it.

Luke gripped her wrists and brought his gaze to her face. Tears threatened to spill onto her cheeks, and time stopped.

His lip was cut, his eyes wild. He hadn't shaved in days. She could see the hurt, the anger. But he wasn't hers to love or heal. He was the man who discarded her.

She wrenched her hands free.

"Harp." It was hurt now in his tone.

"No," she whispered, staring at his chest.

He made a move toward her, and she stepped back, holding up her hands.

"She said no," Linc said, pulling her back.

"Stay the fuck out of this, Reed." Luke shoved Linc, and they tangled again, crashing into a rack of six-packs.

Two tumbled to the floor and shattered as Harper jumped out of the way. Linc shoved Luke up against the rack. "Why do you have to be such an asshole?"

Luke's fist caught him on the jaw, and Harper yelped. "Someone help!"

A crowd had gathered in front of the cooler. Every door was wide open so the spectators could get a better look.

"Damn, that was the lager they just broke," someone sighed as another six-pack fell to its frothy death.

Harper flinched as Linc's fist plowed into Luke's middle. They were going to pound each other into oblivion. Harper grabbed Linc's arm as he pulled it back to hit Luke again. Her body felt weightless as she was carried through the air by the momentum of Linc's blow.

Luke threw another punch, and Harper felt the breeze of it brush her face. He was too angry. She wasn't going to be able to stop him.

An arm nipped her around the waist, dragging her out of the fray.

Ty, in uniform, deposited her in the doorway of the cooler.

"Ty! Make them stop!"

"On it. Stay here."

Ty threw himself into the brawl with the practiced form of law enforcement. In seconds, he was able to disengage Linc. It took a little longer with Luke, who took an angry swing at his brother-in-law. Ty shrugged it off and punched Luke square in the jaw, knocking him back a step.

"Don't make me tase the shit out of you. I'll do it and probably enjoy it," he warned.

Luke held up a hand in surrender. "Just keep that asshole away from her." He shot a look at Harper. A bruise bloomed on his chin, and blood trickled from his mouth. "Are you okay?" Those hazel eyes held so much.

She could only shake her head and turn away.

"Harper," he called after her.

Insulting her one second and then looking at her like he just wanted to pull her into his arms the next. Making love to her like he couldn't survive without her and then discarding her like yesterday's trash. She couldn't survive the wait for him to figure out what he really wanted. He might never know.

"Can I trust you to not kill each other for a few seconds?" Ty asked before stepping out of the cooler. "Georgia Rae, you mind keeping an eye on those two for me?"

Ty drew Harper over to the cereal aisle.

"Are you sure they won't fight?" Harper worried.

"They wouldn't dare fight with Georgia Rae in the middle of them. She'll have their hides. So what the hell happened?"

Harper filled him in. "I was just trying to get Joni's groceries. You know, do something nice for her since she's been so great to me. And I can't even do that…" She stopped herself before she screamed in frustration. "This is the first time I've seen him since he asked me to leave, and this is what happens."

"The guy is stupid in love with you, Harper."

"I don't think so, Ty." She shook her head.

"Honey, I know stupid in love when I see it. He's just stupider than most."

"How much trouble are they going to be in?" she asked, changing the subject.

"Gotta talk to the owner and see if she wants to press charges. Do me a favor and stay put while I figure this out."

When Ty brought them out of the cooler, Linc, sporting the beginnings of an excellent black eye, winked at her. Luke started toward her, but Ty slapped a hand on his chest. "Not gonna let you do that, Luke."

"You can't stop me from talking to her." Anger crackled off him like electricity.

"That's exactly what I'm doing until she says different. Now stand over there and try not to hit anyone else."

"Do I need to remind you that when my sister broke up with you, I was the one who told her she was being an idiot?"

"The difference is I wasn't busting up a grocery store and some guy's face at the time, and now you're the one being the idiot. Now stand there, shut up, and we'll get this worked out." He said it so amicably that Harper just blinked.

Luke stayed where he was but didn't take his eyes off her. He shoved his hands in his pockets and ignored the crowd that had grown to over a dozen people. Tangles of abandoned carts blocked aisles while customers and store staff mingled around sale displays of boxed stuffing and canned pumpkin. Linc leaned against a cooler door and chatted up a pretty stock girl.

Harper did her best to look everywhere but Luke's face. It felt like an eternity before Ty came back.

"Okay, here's the deal. Ms. Valencio won't press charges if you agree to the following terms. One, you split the cost of the nine six-packs that died unnecessary deaths and clean up the mess."

Linc shrugged at Luke. Luke rolled his eyes and nodded.

"And two, you finish Harper's shopping and pay for her stuff."

"Give me your list," Luke said, holding out his hand to her.

"Oh no. Ty, they don't have to do that." She had tampons on the list.

"It's Ms. Valencio's call. She doesn't want you to leave empty-handed because these two 'yahoos got their testosterone in a bunch.'"

"Give me your list."

She was being lured to her doom but couldn't see a way out of it. Harper approached slowly. She pulled the list out of her back pocket and held it out between two fingers, eyes on her hand. Luke's hand closed over hers and pulled her closer.

"Harper."

He waited until she looked up at him.

"I'm sorry for what I said. Are you okay?"

She nodded slowly, not trusting her voice. His touch sent a heat spreading through her.

With his free hand, he reached up and gently brushed her hair back from her face. "I'm sorry I scared you."

"Christ, Garrison, keep your hands to yourself," Ty said,

stepping between them. He took the list from Harper and handed it over. "Peggy Ann is bringing a broom and a mop. Harper, why don't you go next door and get yourself a coffee. We'll be done here in an hour."

CHAPTER 49

I was literally just trying to keep her warm in here, you know," Linc said conversationally as he held the industrial-sized dustpan.

Luke glared at him as he swept and stayed silent.

"I'm just telling you that it wasn't like we were making out or having sex. We were just talking, and she was cold."

"Yeah. Right. Just having a conversation in a walk-in refrigerator in December."

"Don't get me wrong," Linc continued. "I'd be happy to get to know her better. I mean, look at her."

Luke tightened his grip on the broom and pretended it was Linc's neck. "You don't owe me an explanation," he growled.

Linc emptied the broken glass into the trash can. "We were only in here because of you anyway. Harper doesn't even want to see you. Don't know how she's still working with you."

"She's working nights so she doesn't have to see me."

"You let her do that?"

"Harper's not the kind of woman you 'let' do anything."

"She's tough." Linc chuckled. "And I was just reminding her of that when you stuck your head in the cooler and threw a hissy fit."

"I didn't throw a hissy fit."

"I clearly remember you stomping your foot."

"If I did, it was because I was trying to break yours." Luke went back to sweeping.

"It just seems to me that's an overreaction from the man who let her go. What's with you and always trying to set your women free? What do you expect them to do? Be alone forever?"

"For the love of God, can we please just finish this in silence? Ty'll be pissed if I smash your face in with this broom."

———

Harper took the hour and, following Ty's advice, grabbed a latte at the café next door.

She clutched the mug in her hands and tried to think of the bright side. She hadn't burst into tears, which was a plus. She hadn't begged him to touch her one more time, huge plus. Unfortunately, she had gone to the store sans makeup with her hair in a crappy knot. If she had her choice, Luke wouldn't have spotted her looking so sad-sacky. She would have been dressed to kill, and he would have spotted her from a safe distance, not up close and personal in a beer cooler. She couldn't even begin to understand Luke's reaction to seeing her with Linc.

Harper snuck into the tiny bathroom with chalkboard walls to slick on lip gloss and take her hair down from its messy knot. She fashioned it into a braid that hung over one shoulder.

On her way back to the store, she thought about just getting in her car and driving away. She'd make an excuse to Joni about the groceries and lie down in the fetal position for, like, ten hours.

But she was too proud. *Don't let him see you break*, she reminded herself.

Harper found them arguing about how to bag her groceries

at the self-scan checkout. She cringed when she saw Luke hand Linc a box of tampons.

She should have just gone for the fetal position.

———

Luke spotted her first in the midst of his argument with Linc on how to bag chicken breasts.

"Hey, sunshine. We got you reusable bags," Linc announced, grinning at Harper.

Luke wanted to punch him again. He settled for elbowing him in the gut instead and then shoved his hands in his pockets. It was the only way he could be sure he wouldn't reach out and grab her…or break Linc's nose.

Looking at her was still a punch in the gut. Those damn eyes—stormy now—were shadowed with dark circles. The light was missing from them. She was thinner too, noticeable even with her wearing a fleece. He could see the hollows in her cheeks.

Tired. Empty. And all he wanted to do was fill her. But he had made his choice. His bed was empty, his house quiet. And that was the way it needed to be.

When he opened that cooler door to escape Georgia Rae's small talk, just seeing Harper in Linc's arms, smiling up at him… His gut still churned.

The reaction, that blind, burning fury, took him by surprise. He lost control as quickly as if a leash had snapped inside. Luke didn't like that that was coiled within him, ready to strike.

And strike he had. Not just with his fists. He had cut Harper to the quick with his accusation. He saw the sting of his words register on her face just before Linc came at him. He was nothing without his control. But she had taken him past his limits before.

It wasn't her fault. The blame fell on his shoulders.

He owed her an apology. Ty too. And while he was at it, he could throw one in for Linc but probably not. Even if the man did have a point. He let Harper go. What did he expect?

Didn't she deserve to be happy, to be loved, to have someone remind her to wear a damn coat when it snowed?

"Where's your coat?" He regretted the harshness in his tone, but not being able to control himself was par for the course with Harper.

She shrugged. "Your house."

Along with everything else she owned. Waiting.

"I'll drop it off. I can bring the rest of your stuff."

Harper was already shaking her head. "Joni doesn't need—"

The song "Bad Boys" shrilled from her phone. Luke saw the flash of pure panic and watched as her fingers fumbled on the screen in her haste to answer.

"Hi. Hey," she said, spinning away, clutching her phone to her ear. "No, I didn't get it. I moved." Her eyes darted to Luke and away again. She lowered her voice. "I know. I'm sorry. It was kind of sudden."

She listened in silence for a moment, and he swore every ounce of color drained from her face.

"He's getting out? When?" She sank down on a narrow bench next to the window.

She bit her lip and looked his way again, her gaze darting away when she saw him watching.

Linc shoved a bag of lettuce at him. "Keep up, bro."

"Give me a minute…and don't call me bro."

"Fine. Keep up, dick."

Luke stepped closer to Harper but couldn't catch much. She was arguing quietly now.

"You don't need to come here to play bodyguard—I can protect myself…"

After another minute of whispering, she hung up and, without a word, hurried out of the store.

"Where's she going?" Linc demanded, coming up next to Luke. "She forgot her stuff."

Of course she wasn't answering his texts. Frustrated, Luke tossed his cell phone on the passenger seat. His debt to Val's Groceries paid, he volunteered to haul Harper's items with him so he could personally deliver them.

He'd swing by the house first to get her damn coat.

He couldn't get her reaction to the mystery phone call out of his head. Harper wasn't one to be afraid of anything. Luke worried what would have caused a reaction like that.

Leaving the groceries in his truck, he went inside and dug through the boxes until he found a belted black wool coat. He held it to his face and breathed in her scent.

Feeling pathetic, he folded the coat and put it on the dining room table. He would pack a few sweaters for her so she didn't freeze her ass off. She should have some kind of ski jacket too, he thought. Maryland winters weren't exactly balmy. Maybe he could find a decent one at the outlet—

Christ, what had this woman done to him? They weren't even together anymore, and here he was planning a fucking shopping trip. He was losing his damn mind. Any progress he'd made toward shutting thoughts of her out was lost after today. One look at her, and he was back to the beginning.

He threw two sweaters on top of the coat on the table. Enough was enough. After he found out what was going on with her, he'd take her stuff to the office to store until she left.

He remembered the growing stack of mail that he'd ignored in the kitchen all week. He'd check it for anything for her and then head over to Joni's. One last time to see her, make sure she was okay, and then leave her alone forever.

Luke flipped through the pile, tossing junk mail in the recycling can as he went. There were two envelopes addressed to Harper.

A red stamp on the first caught his eye. Victim Services. He felt his heart start to pound. The second envelope was hand addressed to Harper and had a small ink stamp in the corner.

Mailed from a state correctional institution.

There was something familiar about that second envelope, something that he couldn't quite pull to the surface. There was no name in the return address. Luke pulled out his phone and looked up the address online. Sussex Correctional Institution.

He dialed Harper. When her voicemail answered, he swore and hung up.

Drumming his fingers on the counter, he weighed his options. There was no way she was going to tell him what was going on. But if she was in danger, he needed to know.

"Fuck it." Luke shredded the envelope and yanked out the piece of notebook paper inside. A cold fury washed over him and made his hands shake. There was no name. Just "Daddy."

He slammed the letter onto the counter and started to pace. This couldn't be the first letter. There must be others...

Her boxes. Back in the dining room, Luke tore the lid off the innocuous "Paperwork" box. In the very front was a folder labeled SCI Letters. Dozens of letters opened, filed chronologically starting when Harper was eighteen. Luke resisted the urge to heave the entire box through the window.

That fucker. Every letter was signed "Daddy." He had caught up with her every move since she had aged out of the foster system. Blaming her for his sentence. It had to be the cigarette burns. This man had physically hurt Harper until he was caught and then spent years trying to torture her psychologically.

There were five other letters in the box sent to his address. Three while he was deployed. But the other most recent one was just days before Thanksgiving. She had never said a word.

Except…she had tried.

"Luke, can I talk to you about something? It's kind of important."

He had been sitting on the couch, pissed off at himself, pretending it was her, and had shrugged at her. Just shrugged because he was angry and scared.

She had faltered but tried to press on. "Something happened, and I'm a little worried—"

He had cut her off and cold-bloodedly proceeded to cut her out of his life. In the exact moment when she was reaching out to him for help, he pushed her away.

She had trusted him, and he had betrayed that trust on so many levels. And now she was alone.

He swiped a hand over his face and cursed himself. What had he done?

He needed a name and thought of the Victim Services letter. Well, he had already opened one of her letters. Why stop now?

It was a form letter stating that as a victim of Clive Perry, Harper was entitled to be aware that he was due to be released from prison on December 18 after having served his full prison sentence.

Luke pulled his phone out of his pocket and dialed.

"Hey, we have a situation."

CHAPTER 50

"You know, when I saw it was you, I was expecting you were calling to apologize," Ty drawled, kicking back in his desk chair. "Then when you said you had a situation, I thought you were calling to tell me that you were driving around with Linc's body in the back of your truck."

Luke shifted in Ty's visitors' chair. The station smelled like stale coffee and old books. "I do owe you an apology, and I haven't killed anyone. Yet." He dropped Harper's folder on Ty's desk. "Harper's in trouble."

"What kind of trouble?"

Luke filled him in on the details he knew.

Ty gave a low whistle when he'd finished. "Sounds like our girl's in a bad spot."

"How can we keep this asshole from getting out?"

"I'm gonna look into it. But, Luke, in the eyes of the law, this Perry guy has served his time." He skimmed the letter on top of the file. "How about you give me some time to run Harper and this son of a bitch through the system? I want to read these letters too. Why don't you go get us a couple of coffees and meet me back here in half an hour?"

"Just so you know, this guy never gets near her. No matter what."

"I understand what you're saying, and we'll cross that bridge when we have to. Now go get some coffee. Two sugars in mine."

Luke got coffee and, because it was almost time for dinner, a pizza. The late afternoon sun glinted off the small mounds of snow on Main Street. You couldn't get more quintessential than Main Street in Benevolence at Christmas. Sunday, the caroling would start in the park near the Christmas tree and wind its way through the neighborhoods before ending at the fire station for hot chocolate and a toy and clothing drive. Balancing the cup carrier on top of the pizza box, Luke nodded a greeting to his high school math teacher and his wife on their way to the second-run theater. He waved hello to Sheila from Remo's when she whistled at him from across the street.

No one was a stranger here, no matter how often he wished he could be. Walking down the idyllic street under the snowflake lights and garland strung over anything that would hold still gave residents the feeling that nothing bad could ever happen here.

But bad things did happen, even in Benevolence. Luke just hoped he could prevent this one.

When he pushed back into the station, he was greeted with a blast of warm air and silence. Alma, the sheriff's wife and station office manager, had headed home for the day, so Luke let himself in and walked back to Ty's office.

Ty was just hanging up the phone when Luke walked in.

"Pizza, coffee, and I got to punch you in the face? This must be my lucky day."

Luke dumped the pie on the desk and rubbed his jaw. "Yeah, about that."

"What about that?"

Luke plucked his coffee from the carrier and sank into the chair. "I guess I owe you an apology for acting like an asshole."

"Apology accepted."

"Well, that was easy."

"We all do stupid things for the women we love." Ty didn't give him a chance to argue. He just plowed right on with his drawl. "And speaking of the woman you love, I got some information, and I don't think you're going to like it."

"What is it?"

"I found the case file on this Clive Perry. It was pretty bad. Perry had a houseful of kids who were all beaten, malnourished, and suffering from neglect. Harper lived with him for about eight weeks. According to the report, one night he came home drunk and started wailing on one of the younger ones, and Harper got the others out of the house to a neighbor's and went back for the little one."

Luke braced his hands against his knees.

"Anyway, there was a confrontation, and she put herself between him and the kid and held steady until the neighbor's husband busted in with a shotgun and got Perry cornered in the kitchen. Police showed up, and Harper was pretty beat up. Broken arm, cuts, and bruises. Took her to the hospital and found she had broken ribs from an earlier beating. She told them everything. Got him put away for twelve years."

"She was just a kid." Luke stood up to pace Ty's miniscule office.

"I put in a call to the investigating officer. He's retired now, but I got him at home. He gave me the name of a rookie cop who was on the scene. Seems she bonded with Harper, and the two of them have testified at every one of his parole hearings."

"Did you talk to her yet? Does she know Harper's a target?"

"I have not. I was about to when you showed up with Dawson's." Ty eyed up the pizza box.

"Call first, eat later."

"On it." Ty nodded, picking up his desk phone. "While I'm dialing, here's a little something to brighten your day." He slid a printout across the desk.

Luke picked it up. It was a news story, from a year and a half previous, about a building fire in the city. The lead picture was Harper, covered in ash and soot, half carrying an elderly woman in her nightgown out of the flames.

Luke pinched the bridge of his nose as what felt like a stroke pounded behind his eyes. "Christ. She just told me she was home when the fire started. She didn't say anything about dragging people out of the building."

"Two people and one cat," Ty said, covering the receiver.

Luke skimmed the story while Ty talked his way through a police station switchboard.

His brave, wild girl. Ready for any challenge. He wondered how she felt about Perry. Was she scared? She was probably planning something stupid like meeting him face-to-face.

Like hell she would. He'd make sure she never had to face that monster again.

"Detective Rameson? This is Deputy Adler out of Benevolence... No, she's just fine, but she is the reason I'm calling. I'm here with a...colleague." He darted a look at Luke. "Do you mind if I put you on speakerphone? Great." He stabbed a button on the phone and hung up the receiver. "You there, Detective?"

"I'm here." Her voice was clipped with a touch of Jersey. "What's happening down in Benevolence?"

"Clive Perry. What kind of a threat is he going to be to Harper?"

Luke heard her sigh. "Thank freakin' God she finally decided to tell someone. I've been on her for a year. 'Ya gotta have a plan,' I keep telling her."

Luke snorted. Harper with a plan.

"I can tell by that response that you know her pretty well then. You're not the asshole who dumped her, are you? God, she's got shitty taste in men."

Ty cleared his throat. "I'm not, but my colleague is. He's not so much an asshole as a dumbass."

"You ask me, pretty often they're one and the same," Rameson said.

"Look, we just need to know if this Perry guy is going to come after her when he gets out," Luke cut in.

"You read the letters?" she asked.

"I read them all. Ty here read enough to call you."

"Here's the deal. This Perry moron writes to her every couple of months since she hits eighteen. Everywhere she goes, he finds her, and the letters start again. Always the same shit: 'You owe me, you'll pay, blah blah blah.' Good thing is, the letters didn't play well for him in his parole hearings. Bad thing is, he never directly threatens her. No one's gonna take him as a serious threat unless he gets more specific, know what I mean?"

"What's your take on him?" Ty asked.

"I don't know too much. I've kept tabs on him, and the locals keep me up-to-date occasionally. Professional courtesy. Guy's in his sixties and not the strapping, healthy, TV-commercial sixties. More like the 'my liver's failing, and I smoke two packs a day' sixties. But there's something dark about this guy. My gut tells me he's trouble, only I don't got the proof. I need something on him that'll get the key thrown away. I'm concerned we won't have that something until he's out and pulls some shit on Harper."

"That's not an option," Luke growled.

"In this case, I agree with the dumbass. But I got nothing on the creep right now."

Something shimmered at the edge of Luke's consciousness and slowly started to take shape. "He's in Sussex, right?" Luke asked.

"Yeah, been there his whole sentence."

"Ty, where was Glenn serving time?"

"Son of a bitch." Ty's fingers flew over his keyboard. "Overcrowding in County and a repeat offender? Yeah."

"You got something?"

"A few months back, a local guy awaiting trial in Sussex— assault and battery, domestic—gets out on bail and shows up at Harper's house with a very large sharp knife and tries to tear the place apart. Harper and the girls took him down. We thought he was there for the girlfriend and the rest of them were just collateral."

"Goddamn that girl. She never mentioned a B and E. You thinking he knew Perry?"

"I'm thinking we should have a talk with Glenn."

"Mind if I tag along?" Rameson asked.

"Counting on it, Detective."

———

Harper pulled the car over next to the curb and dropped her head against her seat. She closed her eyes and willed her heart rate to slow. The phone call from Melissa had rattled her when she was already feeling vulnerable.

When they met, Melissa was a rookie beat cop, and Harper was a scared twelve-year-old. Academy-fresh Officer Rameson, with her immaculate uniform and scary perfect bun, had sealed their friendship with a hot chocolate and her straight-out-of-Jersey accent.

Things were a little different now. Melissa had made detective in Baltimore a few years back, and Harper was anything but a scared kid. But their dynamic hadn't changed much. Melissa still looked out for her no matter how much the adult Harper protested. Together, they attended every parole hearing and testified, facing the monster. Clive Perry had never made parole.

In twelve years, he had laid nothing but his gaze on Harper. He witnessed her growing stronger while she watched his slow descent into frailty. He wasn't a physical threat to her anymore, she felt sure of that. But that didn't mean he couldn't still do harm.

Would he target her or someone she loved? Or was it all a game? Maybe he would decide to make the best of his freedom and...

What? He was a bitter, warped old man. There was no remorse, no hope for the future. He would die having lived his entire life in hate and pain.

A life wasted.

Well, she wouldn't waste hers. And she wouldn't bring danger to the people she cared about. She would pick up and move on. Fremont wasn't an option at this point. He could find her there and, with her, Hannah.

Maybe she would head east. Find a cozy beach town and stay for a few months. It wasn't much, but it was a plan. She wasn't ready to go back to Joni's yet. Harper eyed her gym bag on the passenger seat. She could hop on a treadmill at the gym until she was ready to laugh at everything.

CHAPTER 51

A run on the treadmill led to half an hour of circuit work and then a quick shower. By the time she got back to Joni's, it was already dark, and she was exhausted. Lights glowed through the frosted windows, beckoning her tired body.

Harper let herself in the front door and sniffed the air and followed her nose back to the kitchen. "What is that amazing smell?"

Joni looked up from the pot she was tending on the stove and grinned. "Oh, just my grandma's chicken corn soup with fresh biscuits. Grab a bowl," she said, pointing at the kitchen island where two soup bowls waited to be filled.

"If it tastes half as good as it smells, I might just cry."

"That's all right, and then you can tell me how it was Luke delivering your groceries here and then moping around when he found out you weren't here."

"Oh my God, the groceries!" Harper clapped a hand to her forehead. "I walked right out without them!"

"Not to worry. They were delivered personally by Luke, who also dropped off your coat and some sweaters. He kept muttering about it being winter and you running around with no clothes."

Harper sighed. "I just don't understand him. How can he say he doesn't love me and doesn't want me around and then do all this?"

"He's scared, Harper. I think you bring out feelings in him that are bigger than what he can handle."

"I don't know if that makes me feel better or worse."

"You can imagine how many different versions of the story I've already heard, so I'm pretty anxious to hear yours. Luke was sporting a pretty nice bruise on his jaw."

Harper covered her face with her hands. "I went to the gym and tried to run until it was funny, but I got too tired. So I'm still in the pissed off and embarrassed phase."

"Well, why don't you grab the bottle of wine in the fridge, and we'll drink until it's all funny."

Harper obliged and grabbed two wineglasses out of the cabinet. She filled them both and handed one to Joni before hugging her. "You're the best, Joni. I really, really, really appreciate everything that you've done for me."

Joni hugged her back, hard. "Oh, honey, right back at ya. Now come on. Let's eat, drink, and be merry."

They took their soup into the living room where a fire crackled in the fireplace and Harper filled Joni in on the grocery store incident. She left out the mention of Melissa's phone call.

"They were throwing punches and slamming each other all over the cooler. There was glass and beer everywhere, and they kept going. Thank goodness for Ty. He broke it up fast. Linc stopped right away, but Luke kept coming, so Ty punched him right in the face. And then we all had to do the walk of shame out of the cooler and face half the town." Harper pulled her feet up under her and spooned up more soup. "It was the first time I'd seen him since…since."

"And he finds you in Linc's arms, smiling up at him. Oh, that's too good." Joni snickered.

"He thought we were making out!"

"Honey, it's better that he sees you in the arms of a drop-dead gorgeous fireman than moping around in your sweats with 'I'll shower next week' hair."

"Excellent point."

"He got to see exactly what he was pushing you into. A life without him."

"It was so hard to see him. I just can't look at him and not love him. Why can't I just accept it and move on gracefully? You know, like an actual adult?"

Joni laughed into her wine. "Harper, I think you proved today that you're handling it more maturely than he is. You didn't throw a hissy fit that involved the police."

"That's true. Do you think he and Ty will make up? I feel like I caused a lot of trouble in the family today."

Joni patted her leg. "They're men. I'm sure they've already made up with beer and meat."

"You are so wise when it comes to men. Do you think you'll ever dip your toes back into that pool again?"

"It just so happens that I have a dinner date tomorrow night."

"What?" Harper sat up so fast she almost bobbled her soup. "Who?"

"A gentleman named Frank Barry. I believe you may have met him." She wiggled her eyebrows.

"You and Angry Frank? How did that happen?"

"Well, a long time ago, Frank was my high school sweetheart. We only dated a short time, but it was memorable."

"Are you the reason he never got married?" Harper gasped.

Joni waved it away. "I doubt that very much. But I am

looking forward to dinner with him. I asked him, by the way. I ran into him at the diner when I was picking up lunch today."

"Good for you! What are you going to wear?"

"Probably something warm since it's so damn cold."

"Good thinking. See, running into old flames is what you do in Benevolence. I can't stay here. Luke can't even look at me without going all Hulk smash in front of Georgia Rae of all people. And I can't look at him without wanting to kiss him and slap him until he realizes what an idiot he's being."

"Don't let one bad trip to the grocery store scare you away from Benevolence, Harper."

Harper picked up her glass of wine and sipped. "I keep thinking that if this is how he reacts when he sees me with another man, how am I going to feel when I see him with someone else? I don't think I could take it. It's for the best. Distance will heal us both." She hoped.

"I wish you'd stay."

"I wish I could too. Do you think you'd be willing to come visit me when I'm settled?"

"I would love to. I promise I will. Especially if you move someplace warmer."

"I'll see what I can do. I'm leaving Saturday."

Joni sighed and laid a hand on her shoulder. "I'm really going to miss you, Harper."

"I'm going to miss you too. And not just for your cooking and your wine. I think we should go sweater shopping for your date. Maybe something with a little scoop neck that you can cover with a scarf. Then if things are going well, you can take the scarf off."

Joni laughed and poured them both more wine.

———

Luke leaned against Ty's cruiser. His anger and frustration at being kept out of the interview with Glenn kept him warm against the frosty morning air and the subzero look Detective Rameson had tossed his way.

He kicked at the cracked asphalt.

He should be in there, not waiting in the fucking parking lot. He felt useless, and that was new for him. It wasn't easy to step back and let someone else take care of a situation. One that he wanted to handle himself, in his own way. Let that fucker take one step in Harper's direction. That was all it would take.

He was in charge, in control. At work, in the guard. That was how he liked it. The responsibility was heavy, but the alternative was this. Standing and waiting for someone else to get the job done.

He had tried calling Harper again after he left the police station last night. But all he got in return was a text thanking him for dropping off the groceries and coat. She didn't respond to him after that, and he had to talk himself out of driving over to Joni's house and dragging her out of there to talk to him. In the end, he decided it would be better to take care of the problem without her knowing.

He spotted Ty and Rameson as they exited the building, and he pushed away from the car.

"Well?"

"We got him," Ty said, tapping the hood.

"What did he say? Did Perry send him?"

"You guys wanna grab some breakfast and talk strategy?" Rameson asked, zipping her coat.

Luke grilled Ty on the way to the restaurant.

"Don't even think of making me wait until we get there."

"Yeah, yeah. If it were Soph, I'd have my undies in a wad too." Ty sighed. "Glenn sang like a damn soprano as soon as

Rameson told him he'd die in prison like his pal Clive Perry. He told us he met Perry his first week in, and as soon as Perry found out that he knew Harper, well, they got nice and chummy. Says Perry was the one who got his mom the cash for his bail and promised him more than that after the deed was done. All he had to do was slit Harper's throat and whisper that fucker's name in her ear as she died."

The image flashed into Luke's mind before he could guard against it. He took a second to push it back, catch his breath.

"Glenn swears he wasn't actually gonna kill her, but he felt like he at least owed it to Perry to rough her up some." Ty pulled into the parking lot of a long, squat building that promised "Homemade Everything." Then he asked, "You okay?"

Luke wanted to put his fist through the window of the cruiser and pretend it was Clive Perry's face. He wanted to bolt out the door and run the twenty miles home to find Harper and wrap her in his arms and promise nothing bad would ever happen to her. She had come within inches of her life, and he hadn't been there to save her.

This time, he would.

"I'm fine. Let's go," Luke said, trying to keep his tone neutral.

They got out of the car and met Rameson at the door. "Well, I can see from your cheerful expression that Adler here told you what we got."

"Perry doesn't walk," Luke snapped out.

"Yeah, yeah, tough guy. Get inside already. I'm hungry." Rameson pushed past him and into the restaurant.

They ordered coffee and eggs from a waitress who looked like she was twelve, and they talked strategy.

"We got a good start with Glenn rolling on him. He'll testify to save his own ass."

"Case would be airtight with a confession from Perry," Rameson said, stirring an endless stream of sugar into her coffee.

"He's not going to talk to you," Luke said.

"No shit, he's not," she said, eyeing him. "However, a pissed-off boyfriend who tries to tell him that he's never gonna get near her?"

Luke smiled grimly. "Because he's a weak, pathetic old man."

"Exactly." She grinned. "Maybe you'll be useful after all, dumbass."

CHAPTER 52

Luke pulled open the heavy metal door of the prison's visitor entrance and stepped into the cramped vestibule. A guard behind glass pointed to the speaker on Luke's side.

He leaned forward. "Here to see Clive Perry." He felt like he was ordering movie tickets.

"Any weapons or other contraband?" The guard pointed at a poster listing, among other things, cell phones and drugs and slid a clipboard through the opening above the skinny counter.

"No."

"Sign in." The guard's tone was as bored as a seventh grader conjugating verbs.

Luke scrawled his signature on a blank line and wrote Perry's name next to it. He was surprised the pen didn't snap in his grip.

"Go on through that door through the metal detector. Visitors' desk is on the right," the guard said, buzzing him through.

The next door opened, and Luke walked into a large waiting room. The block walls were painted a pale, industrial gray. A handful of people waited in plastic chairs facing the desk.

After answering the contraband question again, Luke

tossed his sunglasses, keys, and wallet in the tray and passed through the metal detector.

The woman behind the visitors' desk looked more like a cheerful grandmother than a prison guard.

Her graying strawberry-blond hair was pulled back in a bun that tight, frizzy curls were exploding out of. Her round face had a dusting of freckles across her cheeks and nose.

"What can I do for you, sugar?" Her drawl echoed West Virginia mountains.

"I'm here to see Clive Perry."

"Okay, I'm gonna need your driver's license, please."

He handed it over, and she copied it before returning it to him.

"All right, sugar, you go ahead and have a seat, and I'll send someone to find Mr. Perry. We'll set you up in an empty room."

Luke thanked her and took a seat facing the desk. His fingers drummed a silent beat on his jeans.

No matter what, it ended today. Perry's stalking and manipulations, any threat he posed to Harper, ended today. No matter what.

"Mr. Garrison?"

Luke approached the desk.

"We've got you in room B. Just follow Bill here, and Mr. Perry will be in shortly.

"Thanks." He followed Bill, a guard with a shock of white hair, who topped the scales at maybe one hundred pounds.

The room was a dingy ten-foot-by-ten-foot space with a scarred table, an ashtray that hadn't been emptied for at least a week, and two plastic chairs. The walls were covered with wood paneling from the seventies.

Luke ignored the chairs and stood in the corner, facing the door, to wait.

A few minutes passed before the door opened again. It was Bill again, and behind him was Perry.

Clive Perry might once have been intimidating, but a lifetime of poor choices left him stooped and hollow. He was five foot eleven, but his stooped shoulders made him look shorter. His gray hair was combed and neatly trimmed.

The lines on his face were deep, making him look older than his sixty-two years.

There was nothing remarkable about the man. Nothing that screamed "unstable psychopath." Except maybe the eyes. A pale, watery blue. There was an emptiness in his gaze. Luke had seen it before. In the enemy's eyes. And once in his own reflection.

Perry thanked Bill and took a seat at the table. Long gnarled fingers, stained yellow, reached for a cigarette.

He lit it and exhaled a cloud of blue smoke.

"What can I do for you, Mr. Garrison?"

Play it cocky, Luke reminded himself. The cocky, overprotective boyfriend.

He took the chair opposite Perry and tucked his sunglasses into the open collar of his button-down.

"Do you know who I am?" Luke asked.

"I haven't the faintest." Perry's small, mean smile showed teeth stained with age.

"Let's cut the bullshit. You are done harassing Harper."

"I'm sure I don't know what you're talking about."

Luke pulled the letter out of his pocket and slid it across the table. "I think you do."

The smile broadened. "Ah, my letter."

"Letters," Luke corrected him.

"So she's read them. I wasn't sure. We're something like pen pals," Perry said.

"No. You're something like a stalker."

"I pose no threat to her."

Luke smirked. "I can see that." He kicked back in the chair.

"I've served my time, Mr. Garrison. I've been a model prisoner," Perry said, steepling his fingers. "And I've made no specific threats to your girlfriend."

"You don't have the balls to make a direct threat, much less carry it out."

"There, you see? Nothing to concern yourself with. My history with Harper is just that, history."

"Then why do you still write?"

Perry opened his hands and shrugged. "Maybe it's as simple as I don't want to be forgotten. We played important roles in each other's lives. It would be a shame to forget that."

"You abused children under your care." Luke didn't have to add the revulsion to his tone. It was already there.

"Like I said. I've served my time. In the eyes of the law, I'm rehabilitated." Perry fingered the edges of the envelope. "Tell me, what did she say when she opened my letter? How did she take my news?"

And there it was. The hunger. Feed him just enough.

"She assures me that you're no threat. You're just a crazy, frail old man who blames her for your own crimes."

"She took twelve years from me," Perry said, slamming his palm down.

Luke gripped the table. "You raised your hands to those kids. You beat them, neglected them. No one made you abuse them. You deserve to be in jail for the rest of your life, and if you think for one second that I'll let you near Harper when you're released, you're even more senile than she thinks."

"You're confident you can protect her."

"Just try and get through me. You'll learn what fear feels

like," Luke said quietly. "I won't rest until you're dead or behind bars for life."

"You're awfully cocky in your ability to protect. Tell me, where were you when that man broke into your home? Where were you when he held that blade to her throat? Were you there to protect her then?" Perry licked his thin lips.

"How did you know about that?"

"I could have read about it in the paper," Perry said, stubbing out his cigarette. He raised his gaze to Luke's. "Or I could have sent him."

Luke stood so quickly his chair flipped over. He put his hands on the table. "You're fucking lying."

"Oh. You didn't know that Glenn and I are old friends? That I was able to get him released in exchange for a small favor? It's dangerous to underestimate your enemies, Captain."

"That's not true."

"All he needed was the motivation of freedom. I secured the money for his bail and had it delivered to his mother."

"You have nothing. You made jack shit before prison. Where did you come up with the money for Glenn's bail?"

"Prison is an excellent marketplace for an entrepreneur. I merely find a need and fill it. Some want drugs. Others need higher priced items that feed their, shall we say, singular interests."

"Kiddie porn?" Luke's gut churned.

Perry shrugged. "Whatever the customer requires. I can get it and distribute it. For a fee."

"You expect me to believe that you spent twenty grand to send someone into my home to scare my girlfriend?"

"Of course not. I sent someone into your home to kill her."

Luke lunged across the table and grabbed Perry by the jumpsuit, yanking him out of his chair. "You failed, asshole. Talk about the dangers of underestimating someone. You or your lackeys will never lay a finger on Harper again. Because if you get lucky enough to get through me, she will take you down just like she did when she was twelve." He released Perry and straightened.

"You have no control. No patience." Perry sighed with disdain. "No finesse. Just brute force."

"Oh, is finesse what you call burning a twelve-year-old with a cigarette? Or is it hiring a fucking drunk to do a job that you're too weak to perform?"

"Hiring Glenn was a mistake. But at least I got the pleasure of imagining him holding the blade to her throat."

Luke slammed his fist on the table.

"Patience is what I call biding my time until she feels safe. Finesse will be me taking away everything she values, one by one. I'll start with the dogs. And then when she's all alone, when she has nothing left, then I'll take her life."

Luke growled and fought for control. The manic light in those sick blue eyes made him want to snap. To crush the man's face.

"You'll never get through me, asshole. You'll never get out of here alive." Luke kept his voice low.

"You have no say in that. I'm being released." Perry smiled through thin lips. "And when I am, I will end her life. And there's nothing you can do about it."

Luke's fist plowed into Perry's face. Cartilage crunched, and the man crumpled to his knees.

The door flew open, and Detective Rameson strolled in. "Christ, Garrison, I thought you'd never get around to doing that." She nodded to the man in a suit on her right. "We got enough, DA Willis?"

The man shoved his glasses up his nose and nodded, "Oh yeah. There's no way he'll see the outside with this."

"You have no evidence!" Perry scrambled to his feet, still clutching his nose. "These rooms aren't bugged!"

Rameson stalked to the table and grabbed the sunglasses out of Luke's shirt. "You've been stuck in here too long, asshole. Technology's advancing. These pretty little things record audio and video."

"You can't do that! You can't record me without a warrant!" He was shrieking now.

Rameson shrugged. "Oh, you mean this little piece of paper here? Know what else we have? We've got a full confession from your buddy Glenn Diller. Conspiracy to commit murder carries a max of twenty-five years. Welcome to the rest of your life." She turned on her heel and stalked out of the room.

Luke followed her and paused in the door. "You know what she really feels when she reads your letters? Pity."

He slammed the door behind him on the feral wails and walked out into the light.

CHAPTER 53

Luke shrugged off Rameson and Ty's offer of a celebratory lunch. He couldn't face the office either and instead went home. He needed to be alone. Sort through what happened.

He flopped down on the couch and was immediately covered in dogs. "Oh my God, guys. Give me a break. I had a hard day keeping sick psychopaths away from Mommy."

Lola wiggled her entire back end, and Max licked his face.

A knock on the front door interrupted the mauling. "Hey, you home?" Aldo said, letting himself in.

"In here," Luke answered.

The dogs jumped off Luke to dance around Aldo.

He stooped to pet them. "What are you doing home in the middle of the day?"

Luke stood up. "What are you doing in my house in the middle of the day? And do you want a beer?"

Aldo shrugged. "Sure. Why not?" He followed Luke into the kitchen.

"So to what do I owe the pleasure?" Luke opened the refrigerator and pulled out two beers.

Aldo popped the top and took a sip. "You're probably gonna want to open yours before I say what I have to say."

Luke sighed. "We're doing this now?"

Aldo shook his head. "Yeah. So what the hell is your problem?"

"I don't have a problem," Luke said.

"You have a huge problem." Aldo jerked his thumb at the boxes of Harper's stuff stacked in the dining room. "Is this what you think Karen wants?"

"What the fuck are you talking about?"

"Do you think Karen would have wanted you to spend your life miserable and alone?"

Luke felt his jaw clench.

"I don't care that we're not supposed to mention her name around poor, delicate Luke. You're being a dumbass, and as your friend, it's my job to knock you on your ass when you're being a dumbass."

Why did everyone keep calling him a dumbass?

"You don't know what you're talking about." Luke drilled a finger into Aldo's chest.

Aldo shoved his hand out of the way. "Let's say you died. You're dead. Karen's still alive. What kind of life would you want her to have without you? Would your stupid fucking ghost be happy to see her locking herself away from everyone who loves her? Burying herself in work. Coming home to an empty house every night to relive her misery?"

Luke turned away and put his hands on his head. "Of course not."

"Then why the hell would you do that to Harper?"

"I didn't do that to Harper! She was the one who built this whole pretend life—"

"Pretend? So she didn't love you? She didn't love us? She didn't love this whole fucking town?"

"Of course she did."

"Then why did you take that away from her? For Karen? For you?"

Luke put his hands on his hips.

"It's a completely different story if you didn't love her, Luke. But if you love her and threw away that life that she built for both of you, you're a fucking idiot."

Luke stared at his feet. He felt his throat tighten. "Of course I love her. How could I not? I just don't know how to be with someone who isn't Karen."

Aldo grabbed him in a bear hug and slapped him on the back. "You're such a stupid asshole."

"Learned it from watching you."

Aldo released him but kept a hand on Luke's shoulder. "It doesn't have to be one or the other. Do you know that Harp puts flowers on Karen's grave every week?"

"That's Harper doing that?"

Aldo nodded. "You aren't choosing between them or replacing Karen with Harp. You're allowed to love them both. How do you think parents have more than one kid? They don't just love the first one."

"I just assumed that's what my parents did," Luke joked.

"No, if they would have stopped at one perfect child like mine did, then you'd be right. The human heart can love more than one person. You love your parents, don't you?"

Luke nodded.

"Soph? Josh? James? Obviously you love me. Otherwise, you wouldn't idolize the shit out of me. You have room, and just because you love someone else doesn't mean you're wiping the slate clean."

"Thanks, Moretta. Sometimes you're not a complete idiot."

"No need to be a dick when I've been holding back my comments on how fucking creepy it is that you have the lives of two women boxed up in your house. I didn't want to crush your fragile feelings."

Luke's gaze tracked to the boxes. Shit. That was creepy.

———

Luke stopped the truck at the tree-lined curb. The cemetery rolled on to his right. He always parked here. The slow walk to and from Karen's grave was as much a part of the ritual as him standing quietly over her headstone. He usually came at night when the chances of running into anyone else were slim.

He could see her plot from here. She had a visitor.

Luke felt his heart stutter at the familiar flash of blond hair. She was wrapped up in a cheery red scarf but no coat. Probably forgot it in the car or at the office.

He watched as Harper carefully laid something on the grave. She was kneeling next to it, shoulders hunched to the cold.

The vulnerability burned in his gut. He had hurt her, purposely out of fear, and now they were both paying the price. Luke reached for the door handle. But a movement from Harper caught his eye and stalled him.

He watched her straighten her shoulders, kiss her fingertips and lay them lightly on the stone. Luke felt his heart shatter into a million pieces.

Harper stood briskly and brushed off her knees before disappearing.

Luke waited a beat before approaching the grave.

There was a small arrangement of evergreen sprigs and holly wrapped in a checkered ribbon resting against the cold granite. He ran his fingers over the K.

"I've made a mess of things, haven't I?" He sighed and squinted up at the thick December clouds. "I'm just not good at life without you. I don't know what to do. Things were so much…easier when you were here. Harper is not easy. She's a walking disaster." Luke sighed. "I worry about her. She's the kind of person who would offer a ride to a serial killer or open the door to a homicidal clown. She's flighty and stubborn. When I was gone this summer, I had James mow the lawn because I was afraid she would chop off her foot with the riding mower.

"I don't understand why I feel this pull to her. Why I want to be near her. Why I can't wait to hear what she's going to say next. She's not you. And I love you. But I love her too. And I don't know if that's okay. I don't even know if it's okay to talk to you about this. But you're the smartest person I know, and if anyone has the answer, it's going to be you." Luke scrubbed his hands over his face. "Tell me what to do, Karen."

"She would probably tell you to get your head out of your ass."

Luke jumped at the voice and turned around.

Joni stood with her hands tucked into the pockets of her charcoal-gray barn coat. Her cheeks flushed from the wind and the chill.

For years, it had been his fear that he would run into Joni at Karen's grave. Confrontation on hallowed ground. There would be nothing to say to defend himself because he was guilty of everything she accused him of.

What would she say now with two women between them? The living and the dead.

"Oh, Luke," she sighed, moving to stand next to him so they faced the stone together. "We've failed our girl in so many ways."

"I didn't mean to love Harper. I tried not to."

"That's not what I meant, dummy. Do you really think

Karen would want you to live alone for the rest of your life? What are the odds, Luke, that Harper would end up here in Benevolence? There is no way this was a coincidence. She was meant for you. She needs you. To love her, to protect her, to be her family. And you need her."

"I feel like I'm turning my back on Karen."

"By being happy without her?"

Luke nodded and swallowed hard.

"That's the greatest gift you could give her. It's the only thing she would want from you, from me. Us living lives full of love and happiness and remembering how lucky we are to have known her. And I don't know about you, but I'm tired of letting her down."

"Do you think Karen would like Harper?"

"Who do you think sent her to you, Luke? Harper was picked out for you and delivered straight to you."

He looked at his feet and blinked back the blur. "I miss her so much."

Joni wrapped an arm around his waist. "Honey, Karen was once in a lifetime. We both know that. But guess what? So is Harper. Don't turn your back on this gift."

Luke wrapped her in a bear hug, and they stood in silence for long minutes before Joni finally patted him on the back.

"I'll let you talk things over with our girl. But don't wait too long. Harper's leaving town Saturday."

His heart stuttered. Benevolence without Harper?

He nodded and wiped at his face. "Thanks, Joni. For everything."

She smiled. "You're a good man, Luke. You'll make the right choice."

He hoped so. He watched her get in her car and drive off before kneeling down in the grass.

"Well, you heard your mom. So I'm depending on you to help me. Tell me what to do, Karen."

The late afternoon sun broke through the heavy clouds. Its light warmed Luke's face and chest.

He almost missed it. It was only there for a second, but a beam of sunlight fell and held exactly on the phoenix carving on the headstone.

Luke kissed his fingertips and dropped them to the phoenix. "Thank you," he whispered.

CHAPTER 54

Harper took a deep breath and knocked on the apartment door. She pulled her gloves off and shoved them in her pocket.

The door opened on a giggle.

Gloria's already bright eyes lit up. She was wearing Aldo's National Guard sweatshirt and leggings. Her dark hair was a tousled mess. "Harper! What a nice surprise! Come on in."

"Am I interrupting?"

Gloria laughed and stepped aside, waving Harper in. "No, Aldo's in the kitchen making grilled cheese sandwiches and trying not to burn the place down."

"Are you sure I'm not interrupting?"

Gloria laughed again. "Ten minutes earlier, and you would have been." She winked.

Instead of laughing, Harper wrapped her friend in a tight hug. "I'm so happy for you, Gloria. I really am."

Gloria returned the hug. "Me too. I owe it all to you, you know."

Harper released her. "Don't be silly. You got yourself here, in a real home with a sexy man making you grilled cheese. You deserve every bit of it."

"I'm so happy, Harper. I never imagined life could be like this." She hugged Aldo's sweatshirt closer. "Enough gushing. Can I interest you in a half-burnt grilled cheese?"

"Is that my old pal Harpoon out there?" Aldo poked his shirtless torso out of the kitchen.

Harper laughed. "Hey, sport. I haven't seen you in a while."

"When are we hitting the trails again? Got a new blade that'll leave you in my dust."

"Nice. I actually wanted to let you both know that I'm, uh…" She swallowed hard. "Leaving."

"Vacation leaving?" Gloria asked, her brow furrowed.

"Happy trails leaving?" Aldo offered.

"Happy trails. Or just reasonably okay trails at this point," Harper said, keeping her tone light.

"It's not because of Luke and Linc's fight to the death in the grocery store, is it?" Gloria asked.

"I heard they were both banned for life after they destroyed the bread aisle," Aldo interjected. "Buns and loaves everywhere."

Harper rolled her eyes. "Well, the small town rumors are one thing I won't miss."

"Are you giving up on him?" Gloria asked, her brown eyes pools of compassion.

"I have to. For my sake. For his. I can't change him. And I can't stay here either." *It's not safe for any of you if I do*, she added silently.

"You have friends here," Gloria reminded her.

"And I'm so grateful to have you all in my life. But Benevolence is Luke's home, and me staying here is just going to be a painful reminder to both of us of what was."

"I disagree with you, but as your friend, I will support your decision. As long as you promise to let us come visit you."

"Of course," Harper said with a teary smile.

"So where exactly will we be visiting you?" Aldo asked, hands on hips, still clutching a spatula.

"I'm not really sure yet. I'm leaving Saturday, so obviously I have to have a plan then. I'll let you know." She bit her lip. "Listen, when I do tell you where I am, do you promise not to let anyone know?"

"Anyone meaning Luke?" Aldo crossed his arms.

Harper shook her head. "No. Just anyone who doesn't need to know. Like if a stranger asks you…or something." She was fumbling this, making a mess.

"Are you in trouble?" Gloria asked, concern showing.

"Everything's fine. I just wanted to tell you both personally. You've been such good friends to me. I'm really going to miss you." Harper's voice cracked, but she battled through it. "I love you guys so much."

Gloria wrapped Harper into a hug again. "I wish I could talk you into staying."

"Is there room for me in there?" Aldo grabbed them both and squeezed.

"One joke about a threesome, and I'll smack you with that spatula," Harper threatened.

Gloria giggled. "Promise me you won't give up on love."

"I promise." Harper nodded. It may have been the first lie she had ever told her friend.

———

If telling Gloria and Aldo goodbye was hard, telling Sophie was proving to be impossible. Harper couldn't get the woman to slow down long enough to give her a chance to spit the words out.

"I don't know, Sophie. Karaoke?" Harper listlessly stirred her coffee in Joni's kitchen. She hadn't been to Remo's since she had given up her Friday shifts. She had said it was because she was working nights at the office, but really she didn't want to face the town.

"Oh please, Harp. You don't think Luke would voluntarily show up on karaoke night, do you? I'm worried about you. You need to get out, have a little fun. Forget about things for a while."

As if she could forget, Harper thought wryly. *Things* were never out of her mind or what was left of her heart.

"How did you even get the night off?"

Sophie shrugged. "I get one Friday off a month. This was it. Are you in?"

Harper rubbed a hand over the ache that never left her chest. Well, maybe it would serve as a kind of goodbye to her adopted town. One last night in the first place that ever felt like home. She would tell Sophie then.

"What time are you picking me up?" she sighed.

Sophie whooped and threw her arms around Harper. "You won't regret it! I promise! It's going to be a night to remember."

"Every night with you is a night to remember."

"That's what Ty says." Sophie wiggled her eyebrows.

"Please don't joke about sex to the woman who is facing an epic dry spell after—" How could she even label what she shared with Luke?

"Honey, the way you two have always looked at each other—the intensity. That doesn't just go away. Especially not with a temporary breakup."

Why did it feel like everyone else was having a harder time letting go than she was? "Soph, we're done."

"Never."

"For the love of God, can we please talk about something else?"

"How about it was reported that Frank came to work this morning whistling a happy little tune and didn't yell at anyone?"

Harper grinned. "You don't say? Joni certainly seemed like she was in a chipper mood when she left for work this morning."

"A well-placed source spotted them at Remo's for after-dinner drinks last night, where they stayed until almost closing."

Harper clapped her hands. "It's about damn time! I asked her how it went this morning, and she actually blushed."

Sophie squealed. "I love love. I feel like the whole town caught the bug this year. Gloria and Aldo, Joni and Frank, you and—"

"Give it a rest, Sophie, or I'll tell Ty what really happened to his favorite coffee mug."

"Traitor."

"What are you going to do when Josh is old enough to realize he's been Mommy's scapegoat?"

Sophie shrugged. "Probably have another baby and blame everything on that one."

"Good plan."

———

Harper let Sophie talk her into the tight navy scoop-neck sweater and skinny gray pants. "Why are we getting decked out for a night at Remo's?"

Sophie rolled her eyes. "I haven't gotten dressed up since Easter. It's time to show this town a thing…or two." She adjusted her boobs. Sophie turned away from the mirror and eyed Harper's chest. "If you get any skinnier, you're going to start losing those."

Harper crossed her arms in front of her. "Hands to yourself, lady. I've been eating just fine."

Sophie snorted. "Yeah, right. We're getting nachos *and* cheese sticks tonight, just so you know."

"Whatever you say, Soph," Harper sighed.

Remo's was packed by the time they got there, but they found an empty table in front of the stage. It was a pretty kind of symmetry to have the beginning and end of her story happen right here. A kind of closure.

"Are you sure we should sit this close?" Harper questioned over the music. "How good can karaoke in Benevolence be?"

"Don't judge, Big City. We've got some talent in this town," Sophie teased.

"How much talent can you have since this is the first karaoke night since I moved here?"

"Shut up."

Sophie signaled Hazel the server and ordered two beers and the nachos and cheese sticks as promised.

"Listen, Soph, tonight's on me."

Sophie waved the offer away. "Don't be ridiculous. We're here to cheer you up, and how can we do that if you're paying?"

"I'm serious," Harper insisted. She sighed. "I'm actually leaving tomorrow. Shaking off the dust of this little town." The joke stuck in her throat.

"What are you talking about?" Sophie choked the words out. "You can't leave! You have a life here. You're family!"

Harper shook her head. "Not anymore, Soph. It hurts too much to be here. And I'm sure it's not comfortable for your brother to have me here." She still stumbled over his name.

Hazel returned and mercifully dropped off two beers.

"Harper. You can't go!" Sophie slammed a hand down on the table.

Harper reached across to steady the bottles.

Sophie kicked back in her chair, shaking her head. "No. Nope. You're not fucking going."

Harper smiled. "I'm really going to miss you, you stubborn freak."

Sophie set her jaw in a painful reminder of her brother. Harper had seen the look often enough. It was the "no discussion, decision made" look.

"I'm *not* going to miss you because you're *not* going anywhere. And you're a stupid jerk for even considering it."

Harper rolled her eyes. "If you pout, it's just going to ruin the 'best night ever.' Why is it so packed in here anyway?" Glancing around, she noted that Remo's was standing room only. "I can't believe karaoke pulls in this kind of crowd."

Hazel interrupted again with two baskets of food. "You two want plates?"

"No thanks, Hazel," Sophie said with a wave. "We're just going to pick out of the baskets like classy folks." She shoved the nachos at Harper. "Eat before you waste away."

Harper rolled her eyes and sampled a nacho. Her stomach just wasn't into it. Sometimes she was scared that, even if she moved on, the hole, the ache, would never go away.

"I gotta pee," Sophie announced, jumping from her seat. "Save me some nachos."

Harper watched her friend weave through the crowd. She was going to miss that woman like a limb. Sophie's boundless energy and fierce loyalty would never be forgotten. Harper hoped they could still be friends, even from a distance.

Harper nibbled on a cheese stick and tried not to mope until Fred took the skinny stage.

"Ladies and gentlemen, welcome to karaoke. Tonight we've got a very special theme for you. Let's see if you can figure it out."

He exited the stage to the hoots and applause from the crowd. Harper settled back in her seat to watch the show.

The house lights dimmed, and as the first group took the stage, Harper's eyes widened. "Is that Frank?" she hissed to no one.

Sporting a fresh haircut and his cleanest Garrison button-down, Frank was accompanied by Beth, Aunt Syl, and Georgia Rae. They were all in sunglasses.

He grabbed the mic. "Yeah, okay. This one goes out to a very dear friend of ours, Miss Harper Wilde."

The crowd cheered. Stunned, Harper looked from side to side. What was going on?

There was no one to ask because the crowd erupted when Frank belted out the first few bars of "With a Little Help from My Friends."

She knew she was gaping but couldn't help it. Frank's gravelly voice was certainly a departure from the Beatles, but he wasn't bad. And when the ladies joined in as the chorus, her heart lifted for the first time in weeks.

Frank moved back so the ladies could croon in unison.

Harper put her hand over her heart. They were telling her they loved her.

The feeling was mutual.

She joined the rest of the crowd with thunderous applause when they exited the stage. One by one, the ladies stopped at her table to plant a kiss on her cheek.

Frank was last in line. "I'm glad you're my friend, kiddo," he said gruffly.

"Frank—" She just couldn't get the words out. So she hugged him, hard. He patted her on the back awkwardly and disappeared as soon as she released him.

Fred was back on the stage, calling for quiet. "It's gonna be an old-school night, folks. Put your hands together for our next act, Sonny and Cher."

Harper gasped and clapped a hand over her mouth as Aldo and Gloria took the stage in matching tie-dye T-shirts.

Hand in hand, they approached the mic. "Thank you, ladies

and gentlemen. Gloria and I would like to dedicate this song to the woman we owe everything to. This one's for you, Harper."

"We love you," Gloria said, blowing Harper a kiss.

The music started, and Aldo and Gloria swayed together. Gloria broke into "I've Got You Babe" in a crystal clear voice.

"Oh my God," Harper laughed.

Aldo warbled, Gloria tossed her hair Cher style, and the entire bar hummed and swayed along.

Harper felt like her smile would split her face.

As Aldo crooned about wearing his ring, he held up Gloria's hand, and a distinct sparkle caught the light. Harper's heart exploded along with the crowd.

She was blinded by happiness as Aldo and Gloria grinned at each other.

She could imagine them standing at the altar beaming at each other and hoped that she could be there to witness such happiness.

Gloria hopped off the stage, and Harper grabbed for her hand. The diamond sparkled like its owner's eyes. She wrapped the tiny brunette in a fierce hug. "I am so happy for you two."

"We wouldn't be here without you, Harp," Aldo said, moving in for his hug.

"So we're hoping you'll agree to be our maid of honor," Gloria said, clasping her hands together.

"Are you serious?" Harper yelped. "Oh, you guys! I would be honored!"

Gloria hugged her again. "Mind if we join you?"

"Please! Sophie disappeared. I can't believe she's missing this."

A third chair was magically produced, and Gloria and Aldo crowded around the tiny table.

"This is a pretty incredible send-off," she whispered to Gloria.

Her friend smiled but said nothing.

Aldo dug into the nachos. "I was too nervous to eat dinner tonight."

"You guys were great."

"Wait until you see the next act." Gloria winked.

She didn't have long to wait. They were already taking the stage.

The Garrisons. And Joni.

Sophie was front and center with Claire and Joni flanking her. Charlie, James, Uncle Stu, and Ty crowded in behind them. They were all wearing ugly Christmas sweaters that said Garrison Xmas.

The funky '70s beat of Sister Sledge's "We Are Family" filled the bar. The women moved toward the mic in unison.

They pointed to Harper and sang to her about family. Tears pricked at her eyes and quickly changed to laughter when the men stepped forward for their off-key chorus.

From the stage, Sophie tossed her something soft. Harper unfolded it to reveal a matching sweater. She hugged it to her chest and mouthed, "Thank you."

The Garrisons took their bows to wild applause, and the people at the front tables scrambled to make room for them.

Charlie stopped next to Harper and put his hand on her shoulder. "You're family, kid."

Claire swooped in for a hug, giving Harper a few precious seconds to compose herself.

"Thank you," Harper said, squeezing Claire tighter.

"Oh, sweetheart, we're thanking you."

"Me? Why? You've given me so much."

"And this is what you gave us," Claire said, pointing to the stage.

Harper's heart clutched. Luke stood alone in front of the mic, hands in his pockets.

CHAPTER 55

It hurt to look at him. The perfect face, the body that had been so familiar. Now he was someone that she used to know. It broke her heart all over again.

He was watching her, oblivious to everyone else in the bar.

"I'd like to dedicate this song to one of the women I've been lucky enough to love in this lifetime. I don't deserve you, Harper, but I hope you won't hold that against me because I love you with every piece of me."

The crowd whistled and whooped, but Harper didn't notice. There was only Luke standing there, telling her he loved her.

She could barely see him through the tears.

He cleared his throat as the first bars of "Angel Eyes" played. The women in the crowd aww-ed. Harper brought her hands to her face. He was her dream come true.

She watched Luke as he sang the words she had longed to hear. Her heart filled until it felt like it would burst. As the last guitar note faded, Luke held out his hand to her. Harper stood, but the crowd was so big, there was no way to get to him. Ty and James solved the problem. They lifted her onto the table, and Luke met her on the other side, plucking her off and holding her against him, her feet dangling.

"I love you, Harper, and I'm done hiding. Can you forgive me?"

Words failed her, but she could nod, which she did until she felt like her head would snap off.

Luke grinned up at her, his dimple winking into existence. He let her slide a little lower so his lips could find hers in a salty, sweet promise.

Neither of them noticed the crowd erupting, the lack of dry eyes, or the way that the couples in the audience scooted a little closer to each other. They only had eyes for each other.

———

Luke said he wasn't ready to let her go, so they left her car at Remo's, and —just like the night they met—he drove her home.

When they pulled into the driveway, Harper grabbed his arm in a death grip. "Christmas lights!"

The entire front of the house was covered with white lights. Candles burned in the windows. A cheery wreath adorned the front door. Harper's green garland on the porch's railing was threaded with more lights. There was a giant inflatable Santa waving at the street from the front yard.

"You put up lights." Harper couldn't drag her eyes away from the perfect spectacle.

"I wanted you to have the perfect Christmas. I figured more is definitely more."

"It's perfect." She turned back to him and started to reach for him but stopped.

He shook his head and pulled her closer. "You don't have to be scared, Harper. You can touch me. I'm not going to go away again." His grip tightened on her arms. "And I'm not letting you leave either. I owe you so much, and the biggest apology in the world is just part of it. Come on."

They got out of the truck and walked up the front porch.

"Before we go in, I need to say some things," Luke said.

Harper crossed her arms against the cold and nodded. "Okay."

Luke took a deep breath. "I'm sorry for pushing you away. I'm sorry for hurting you on purpose. I was scared. Down to the bones. I felt things for you that I never thought would be possible to feel again and some things that were completely new. I thought that by loving you, I was being unfaithful to Karen. When I lost her, I thought it was my fault that she died. I vowed that I would never forget her and the price she paid for my decisions."

Harper reached out to him and put her hand over his heart.

He covered her hand with his own. "I thought that meant living my life alone. Never loving again. But it was so easy to love you. I don't even remember ever not loving you. I think I loved you the second I saw you launch yourself at Glenn. Something in me said 'she's finally here.' You're what I've been waiting for. You're the light that got me through the dark, and I'm not willing to go back to a life without you." He let out a shaky breath. "I know that you don't owe me anything and that even though I'm going to spend the rest of my life trying to make this up to you, it still won't be close to enough. I know all that, but I'm still asking you to please forgive me. I love you. I want you. I need you. And I'm so sorry for hurting you, baby."

Harper launched herself at him. She pressed her tear-streaked face against his chest and just let herself breathe him in.

He stroked her hair and kissed her forehead. "I'm so sorry, Harper. I'm an asshole. But I'm an asshole who loves you more than anything in this world."

"I love you, Luke."

"Do you forgive me?"

"I did that ages ago."

He shook his head. "How the hell did I ever get so lucky?"

"You might not think that when I tell you this," Harper said, pulling back.

"You can tell me anything."

"I can't stay here."

"Why the hell not?" He gripped her shoulders.

"It's not safe. There are things you don't know—" she started.

"Baby, do you really think a sixty-two-year-old with a failing liver can get through me to get to you?"

Harper took a step back. "How did you... I don't understand."

"Clive Perry will never be a threat to you again." Luke gently brushed her hair back from her face. "He's never getting near you. We made sure of it."

"We?"

"Melissa says to call her tomorrow."

"Oh crap. Are you kidding me? You met Melissa?"

"Oh yeah. She wasn't impressed with the 'asshole' who dumped her friend at first, but we're good now. He's never getting out, baby. And if you're okay with it, tomorrow we'll file a PFA with Ty so he can't send you any more letters. We can do it after we pick out a Christmas tree."

"How—"

"I'll tell you later, okay?" He hugged her closer and buried his face in her hair. "I meant it when I said I wouldn't leave you again. Aldo and I officially retired."

"Oh my God, I don't think I can physically handle any more surprises."

"Let's go inside."

"Why? Is there a marching band and the Publishers Clearing House guy in there?"

"God I missed your smart mouth." He laid his lips on hers. "Let's go in. You'll freeze to death if I start taking your clothes off out here." Luke kept a tight hold on her hand until they crossed the threshold. He closed the door behind them and pulled her in to his arms. "This is where you belong."

He kissed her on the top of the head and slowly turned her around.

She spotted the framed pictures on the wall next to the door.

One was Karen, laughing in the sunshine. The other, Harper and her parents.

"You framed them." Her breath caught in her throat. The picture that had followed her from place to place carefully tucked in an envelope was framed and hanging on a wall.

"You're home, Harper."

"Luke." Tears clouded her vision, and she turned back to him.

But he wasn't standing behind her anymore.

He was down on one knee.

"Harper Wilde, I don't want to spend another day of my life without you. I want to wake up with you wrapped around me every morning. I want you pushing me to do things I'm scared to do. I want to grow our family. I want to spend the rest of my life protecting you from yourself and thanking my lucky stars that you drove east instead of west. Be my wife. Grow old with me." He opened the velvet box to reveal a stunning ring. "It's an eternity band because that's how long I want to spend with you. And you have to say yes because I bought it in town, and everyone knows by now."

The tears flowed freely down her cheeks. For the second time that night, she could only nod her answer.

"I really need you to say it, Harper," he teased.

Harper sank down to her knees and fell into his arms. "Yes to everything with you, Luke."

EPILOGUE

Harper cheered with the rest of the crowd at the crack of the bat and then laughed when she realized the toddler in her arms was still sound asleep.

"I can't believe she can sleep through this," Harper said to Claire.

"She feels safe." Her mother-in-law smiled. "And why wouldn't she? Look what you two have done for her and her brothers." Claire nodded toward home plate where Luke leaned over, giving a serious pep talk to eleven-year-old Robbie.

Harper dropped her nose to Ava's wispy dark hair. "I think it's more what they've done for us."

"Mom!" Henry, in untied sneakers and a grass-stained T-shirt, rushed up to them, stopping just short of barreling into Harper's folding chair.

"Henry!" Harper answered with as much enthusiasm.

"Mom, can I spend the night at Brady's? Can I, huh? Can I?"

"Let me check with his parents, and if it's okay with them, it's fine with me."

"Wooo!" Henry zoomed off again.

"What in the world are you and Luke going to do with four of them?" Claire laughed.

Harper patted a hand to her slightly rounded belly. "We'll find out in five months."

"You'd better get all the rest you can now."

Harper laughed. "Joni and Frank are taking all three of the kids tomorrow so we can have a quiet night in."

"Well, if it's a quiet night in, at least you won't have to be picking leaves out of your hair," Claire teased.

Harper blushed scarlet.

"Oh, don't be embarrassed," Claire laughed. "Garrison men aren't known for being tentative in bed."

"Or woods…" Harper supplied.

"Or the back parking lot of the hardware store."

"Claire!" Harper hissed, pretending to cover the sleeping Ava's ears.

They fell silent as Robbie stepped up to the plate with a swagger that was all Luke. He brushed off the first pitch, a wide ball. But Harper could tell from the set of his thin shoulders that he had the swing away signal from Luke. The pitch rocketed toward Robbie, and he swung for it, connecting with a satisfying clink. The ball arched high over the outfield, and he was sprinting for first.

Harper and Claire cheered as the Garrison jersey rounded the bases, Robbie streaking home to vault into Luke's arms.

The adoption was finalized two weeks after they found out they were pregnant, but Harper still had to pinch herself sometimes. She had the life she had always dreamed of. Luke had seen to that.

There were no more shadows between them. A fact illustrated by the rising sun Luke had tattooed on his chest around the phoenix. She felt his gaze on her now and lifted hers.

He strode toward her, a grin splitting his face. He jerked a thumb over his shoulder where Robbie was celebrating his home run with the team.

"Nice coaching," Harper called to him. She rose and handed Ava over to Claire and met her husband on the slope of the hill.

He brought his hands to her waist and placed a hard kiss on her mouth.

"Hi, beautiful. Let's go home."

**Want more from Benevolence?
Check out the first chapters of Aldo
and Gloria's story in *Finally Mine*.**

CHAPTER 1

This was the second stupidest thing she had ever done in her entire life. But since *this* stupid thing was going to remedy the first, Gloria Parker cut herself a tiny sliver of slack.

This was necessary, she reminded herself, running her hands down the front of her white T-shirt, wincing when she brushed bruises. Life and death. Hers.

Her rusty little car was packed with her meager belongings. She wouldn't be going "home" tonight.

"It's going to be fine," she assured herself, stepping onto the skinny front porch of the bar. Remo's was the favorite—and only—bar in the town of Benevolence. Built like a log cabin, the cedar-shingled exterior invited thirsty patrons inside with its hand-painted sign and cozy patio off the right-hand side. Its only view was the gravel parking lot, but if you were visiting Remo's, you weren't worried about ambiance. You were there to catch up with your neighbors. Enjoy a pitcher. Sample a plate of hot wings. Or, in *his* case, drink until you couldn't see straight.

She was twenty-seven years old and had never once stepped foot in Remo's. There were a lot of things she hadn't done. Yet. And one reason for all of it. Today, it all ended, and her life could finally begin.

It was spring, early enough that she could still feel a few curling tendrils of winter in the air. Spring meant new beginnings. As the sun went down over the town she'd been born and raised in, so would the curtain on ten years of stupid. Ten years of pain. Ten years of a history that she was ashamed of.

Gloria swallowed hard. "You can do this," she whispered. With a shaking hand, she pulled the thick wood door open, ignoring the purple welts around her wrist. She'd gotten good at that. Ignoring. Pretending.

She stepped through the doorway and into her future.

Cozy, not seedy, she thought. Wood-paneled walls showcased beer signs and pictures of Benevolence over the decades. There was a skinny strip of stage against the back wall. A crowd of mostly empty tables and chairs clustered around the pine floor. The glass door on the right led to a patio for warm weather socializing. But her attention was on the big man hunched over the bar.

Glenn Diller.

Judging from the slump in his shoulders, he'd either left work early, or he'd been laid off again from the factory and neglected to tell her. Either way, he'd been drinking for hours.

She took a shaky breath and let it out. It was now or never. And she wouldn't survive never.

The bartender, Titus, was an older man she recognized as the father of one of her classmates. His son had just finished law school in Washington, DC. And here was Gloria, still frozen in time. Titus spotted her, and his gaze slid uneasily to Glenn.

He knows. Everyone knows. It was part of the shame Gloria feared she would never shed. But she had to try.

Sophie Adler, crackling with energy, danced behind the bar, tying her raven hair in a tail. "Sorry I'm late, Titus. Josh hid my car keys in the toilet again."

Titus grunted and reached for the tip jar without taking his eyes off Glenn. He was expecting trouble.

Gloria prayed to God the man was wrong.

She cleared her throat. "Glenn." His name came out clear as a bell with a confidence Gloria didn't know she still possessed.

He turned slowly on his stool, an empty shot glass and a beer in front of him. His eyes were bloodshot already.

He focused in on her and lurched to his feet. "The fuck you doing here?"

That guttural growl, the threat of violence it carried, had cowed her for years. But not today. Today she was immune.

She wanted this, she reminded herself. She *needed* this.

She watched the man she'd fallen for at seventeen, the man she'd let systematically strip her of everything right down to her dignity, approach. Alcohol and a feeling that life owed him more had made his high school muscle bulky and bloated. It had dulled his eyes, sallowed his skin. He looked a decade older than his thirty years.

Glenn listed to the right as he shuffled toward her. Drunk but still capable of inflicting so much damage. That was why they were here. Not in the shabby trailer they shared where no one paid any attention to the sounds of fists and screams.

Here, there were witnesses. Here, there were people who might help.

She put an empty table between them, the hair prickling on the back of her neck.

"What the fuck are you doing here?" he demanded again. His bark drew the eyes of everyone in the bar.

"I'm leaving," she said quietly. "I'm leaving, and I'm not coming back, and if you ever touch me again, I'm going to the police." The words poured out like water rushing over the falls. They'd been lodged in her throat for so long they'd strangled her.

His once handsome face twisted into a gruesome grimace. His cheeks flushed red. The veins in his neck corded into a topographical map. But they weren't within the walls of his trailer. They had an audience.

It was a thin veneer of protection, and Gloria clung to it.

He laughed, a slow, dangerous wheeze. "You're going to be very, very sorry."

A chill ran through her body, lodging itself like an iceberg in her heart. She'd made a miscalculation. Her eyes flicked to Sophie behind the bar. The woman was watching her. She nodded toward the phone. A subtle signal.

Gloria gave a small shake of her head.

No. She needed to do this on her own. Make the break.

"Glenn. I'm serious. We're done. You're done hurting me. It's never happening again. If you try it, I'll take out a restraining order against you."

He'd been a king on the basketball court in high school. Big, mean, aggressive. He'd fought his way to win after win. She'd thought winning fueled him, that hero's adoration. But instead, it was the attention, the recognition that he was someone not to be messed with. A man. Respect through fear. Just like his father. His father drank and beat his wife…until his untimely death of a heart attack at forty-five. So Glenn drank and beat his girlfriend. Because that was what men did.

He reached across the table quick as a snake, his meaty hand settling on her arm in a painful grip. "Let's go have ourselves a little talk," he said pleasantly. But there was menace behind the words, laced like poison ivy around the trunk of a tree.

Gloria fought against his hold. It always started the same, that hand wrapping its way around her upper arm and choking the blood out of it. The last three months had been so bad she'd never healed. Just bruises on top of bruises.

"Stop it," she gritted out, desperate to yank her arm free. But it was a comedy, her small frame trying to deny his hulking strength.

He towed her toward the door like a man with a dog.

"Gonna settle up?" Titus called nervously after them.

Glenn didn't deign to answer, just shoved the front door open so hard it bounced off the wooden, shingled exterior.

She fought in earnest now as he dragged her toward his pickup at the back of the lot. Her sneakers slipped and stumbled over the gravel.

"Let go of me!"

He tossed her against the side of his truck. Her spine jarred at the impact. "You belong to me, Gloria Parker. You don't get to leave. Ever."

"You don't even love me," she shouted the truth in his face. He didn't know what love was. She wasn't sure if she did either.

"I don't have to love you. I own you," he hissed.

Every warning bell she'd developed to alert her to his changes in moods, to danger, clanged to life in her head.

"You don't," she told him. "You don't own me. You have to let me go."

"I don't have to do shit," he slurred.

The backhand caught her by surprise, stunning her. She shook it off as she had so many others and pushed him back. She had to fight now like never before. Her life was at stake.

"You stupid fucking bitch. Ungrateful slut," he breathed, shoving a hand into her hair and pulling it until she yelped. He liked when she cried. Liked when she was terrified. He wanted her to know that he had the power to end her life.

"I'm leaving you," she said through chattering teeth. He'd never hurt her in public before. But then again, she'd never tried leaving him before.

"I warned you!" It was a shout of rage that carried across the parking lot.

Benevolence was a town of good people who worked hard and cared about their neighbors. He was a stain on them all and proud of it. But there was no one here to help her. It was her against him. Until the police that Sophie probably—dear God, please—called. She just needed to hang in there for a few minutes.

Gloria shoved against his chest with all her strength, but his meaty fists closed around her arms, shaking her until the back of her head hit the truck window. With a bleak realization, she knew she didn't have minutes.

"Hey!" She heard a voice snap through the air. A woman. Blond hair.

But Glenn was obstructing her view. "Mind your own business, nosy whore."

"Glenn—" Gloria gasped.

"I'm sick of hearing it!" he said. His face was fire-engine-red with rage. He gripped her by the throat, lifting her off her feet.

Her air was cut off. She felt the pressure build in her head, watched the black creep in on the edges of her vision. Her feet swung uselessly, inches from the ground. It couldn't end this way. Her life couldn't stop at his brutish hands. She wouldn't be just another sad statistic.

Weakly, she reached for the hand around her throat. Everything was starting to go gray as her lungs screamed for oxygen.

With the last of her strength, she lashed her foot out and connected with his bad knee. At the same time, she saw a flash of blond, and Glenn was dropping her to the ground. She landed in a crumpled heap. The gravel bit into her legs, her side, but she was too busy sucking in broken breaths to notice.

There was a commotion behind her—shouts and curses—but it sounded so far away. She rolled over onto her back and stared up at the spring sunset coating the sky in pinks and oranges.

Never again.

CHAPTER 2

The stiff paper covering the exam table crinkled under her legs. She was cold in the anonymous gown designed to make examining bodies easy, impersonal. The curtain dividing the bed from the door was made out of the same threadbare blue material. There was a poster of a basket of golden retriever puppies on the wall, innocent and happy, tongues lolling.

In that moment, Gloria felt as though she were a stranger to innocence and happiness.

She thought about her alter ego, the Gloria who left Glenn after the first time. At this very minute, that girl would be meeting friends for beers—no, martinis—in some swanky bar that no one had ever heard of in a city that everyone wanted to live in. She'd proudly walk inside in shoes that would make other women whisper, "I don't know how she does it." Pay for a round of drinks with her own money. Spend the rest of the night laughing and dancing.

But this Gloria? Was someplace else entirely.

Her body ached, but the pain felt dull, far away, as if it belonged to someone else. She was empty, cold. There was no sense of the victory, the pride she'd expected to feel. She'd done it. Almost died in the process. But she'd left Glenn Diller. And others had paid the price. The blond woman from the parking lot had been knocked unconscious. Luke Garrison had stepped into the fight. And now the town doctor had kindly canceled her evening plans to examine Gloria's bruised and battered body, saving her an expensive trip to the emergency room. She wondered if her freedom was already a bigger inconvenience than her abuse had ever been.

Why couldn't she feel anything?

The door to the little room opened, and Dr. Dunnigan poked her head around the curtain, her frizzy, strawberry-blond curls rioting above her ivory skin.

"I hope this means you finally left the bastard."

Sturdy and brisk, Trish Dunnigan suffered no fools except for the perennially foolish Gloria Parker. The woman had given Gloria her booster shots in elementary school and for the past few years had met her in the grocery store parking lot—one of the only places Gloria was allowed to go—to examine and treat her injuries.

Dr. Dunnigan had been the voice of judgment-free reason when everyone else had given up or been chased off.

He will kill you. He's escalating. It's a textbook abuse cycle. He's going to kill you, Gloria. Soon.

She'd told Gloria that a week ago while fixing her dislocated shoulder. Still she'd stayed. It hurt too much to think about leaving. About doing anything different.

And then last night, it had all changed.

It was just a kid and his friends playing music a little too loud in his first car two trailers down. But to Glenn, it was a reason to posture. He'd ripped him out of his car, thrown him on the ground, and screamed in his face about trying to sleep and peace and quiet and respect.

Humiliation. He dealt in it. Gloria. His coworkers. His mother. Strangers who served him food or expected to be paid for services. There were people in this world who couldn't feel big unless they were making someone else feel small.

He'd dehumanized her, made her so small she'd all but disappeared. And when she'd tried to stop him last night, he'd thrown her to the ground next to the boy and spat on them both. Stripping them both of their power, their humanity, their worth.

He'd waited until she'd followed him back to the trailer before he slapped her and pushed her down, kicking her once. But he'd spent most of his anger on the boy and, deeming her of no consequence, sat back down to finish watching TV.

And then today, she'd packed her things, retrieved her small stash of cash she'd hidden behind the trailer's broken skirting, and left the bastard.

"It's over," Gloria returned numbly.

All business, Dr. Dunnigan checked her pulse, the dilation of her pupils. She pulled out her stethoscope, cool green eyes skimming what Gloria knew was a necklace of bruises forming around her throat.

The door flew open and bounced off the wall, temporarily obscuring the basket of puppies. Sara Parker, still in her hairstylist apron, burst into the room. For a woman never prone to dramatics, it was quite the entrance.

"Oh, God. Gloria. *Mija*!"

Gloria didn't want to see the pity in her mother's eyes. Didn't want to acknowledge that her pain hurt her mother as viciously as if it were her own.

"When I got that phone call, I thought he'd killed you."

The words broke down the walls of her shock, and hot tears spilled over onto her cold, pale cheeks. "I'm sorry," Gloria whispered as the thin, strong bands of her mother's arms welcomed her.

"My sweet girl. Are you done? Is this the end?" Sara asked. Gloria nodded. "It's over. He's in jail."

"Good." Sara swore colorfully in Spanish and then promptly closed the book on her anger. "You'll stay with me. I'll make chicken noodle soup."

"My bags are already at your house," Gloria confessed with a ghost of a smile. Even after all these years of estrangement, Gloria had known she could go home. With Glenn gone, her mother would be safe.

"Mm-hmm," Dr. Dunnigan harrumphed. "Now, if you don't mind, Mrs. Parker, I'd like to continue examining my patient."

Sara cupped Gloria's face in her hands. "Welcome home, *mjia*. I'll wait for you outside."

"Thank you, Mama."

A little of the cold in her soul faded. The sliver of fear dulled just a bit.

"Ooof," the doctor tut-tutted when she looked at Gloria's side where the gravel had abraded her skin. "It hurts now. But you'll heal," she predicted.

Gloria hoped the woman meant inside and out. Because right now, she wasn't sure if she'd ever feel normal again. Hell, she didn't even remember what normal was. What did her future look like? A girl who had barely graduated high school, never worked, and handed over any sense of self-respect to a monster. What kind of a place was there for her in this world?

In silence, she bore the humiliation of the exam, so familiar, somehow again dehumanizing—being reduced to injuries that she wished she'd been strong enough to prevent.

Dr. Dunnigan's fingers clicked away officially on her laptop, updating her records. "Pictures," she said, peering over her reading glasses.

Gloria had always refused the doctor's offer to document her injuries before. She'd never told Dr. Dunnigan that she had her own documentation, hidden away. Every bruise, every sprain, every broken bone. There had been days when she thought she'd never use it, never leave.

But she had.

"What am I going to do?" Her voice was hoarse as much from emotion as Glenn's brutish hands.

"You're not going to worry about making decisions today and for a while," Dr. Dunnigan said briskly. She shut her laptop and opened a drawer to pull out a small digital camera. "You made the hardest decision today. Now it's time to heal, rest, remember who you are without him."

Was she anyone without him? Was poor little Gloria Parker anybody without the stigma of abuse? Did she even exist in this world anymore?

"I feel like a ghost," she confessed softly.

Dr. Dunnigan helped her to her feet. "Feel real enough to me. Give yourself some time to heal, kiddo. Inside takes a lot longer than outside."

Gloria lifted her chin so the doctor could record the garish handprints around her neck and closed her eyes when the motion made her dizzy.

The camera shutter clicked quietly.

"Today you're not a victim. Today you're a survivor."

Author's Note

Dear Reader,

Hi! I wrote this book as something special just for me after binge-watching military homecoming videos for a week straight. I didn't think anyone else would get the feels that I did from Harper and Luke's story, but I'm so happy I was so wrong!

This is the book that allowed me to go from a nights-and-weekends writer to a full-time romance novelist. For that, I'll always be grateful to Luke and Harper.

If you've already finished the rest of the Benevolence series and you're looking for more steamy small-town vibes, check out my Knockemout series next, starting with *Things We Never Got Over*!

Thank you again for reading and for making my dreams come true! I wouldn't be typing this in my pajamas at noon without your support. If you thought this book was awesome and that I must be awesome too, please sign up for my newsletter at lucyscore.com. I'm super nice and funny. I swear!

Xoxo,
Lucy

About the Author

Lucy Score is a *New York Times* and *USA Today* bestselling author. She grew up in a literary family who insisted that the dinner table was for reading and earned a degree in journalism. She writes full-time from the Pennsylvania home she and Mr. Lucy share with their obnoxious cat, Cleo. When not spending hours crafting heartbreaker heroes and kick-ass heroines, Lucy can be found on the couch, in the kitchen, or at the gym. She hopes to someday write from a sailboat, oceanfront condo, or tropical island with reliable Wi-Fi.

Sign up for her newsletter by scanning the QR code below and stay up on all the latest Lucy book news. You can also follow her here:

Website: lucyscore.net
Facebook: lucyscorewrites
Instagram: scorelucy
TikTok: @lucyferscore
Binge Books: bingebooks.com/author/lucy-score
Readers Group: facebook.com/groups/
BingeReadersAnonymous
Newsletter signup: